Praise for
The Other Half of the Sky

It is a great pleasure to see such a strong collection of stories about women and men in space, focusing on women who are dealing with problems in reality-based ways. The stories are not only fun, but interesting. This is what science fiction should be!

—Kim Stanley Robinson,
author of the *Mars* trilogy and *Galileo's Dream*,
winner of the Hugo, Nebula, Locus, World Fantasy and Campbell awards

In *The Other Half of the Sky,* editor Athena Andreadis has brought together a splendid assembly of writers, both rising stars and established names, and a fascinating collection of new stories, promising serious entertainment for SF fans of all genders. I loved Vandana Singh's thoughtful and lyrical "Sailing The Antarsa"; Kelly Jennings's, crisp, wisecracking cyberpunk tale, "Velocity's Ghost"; Christine Lucas's richly layered Martian encounter with the unconscious past, "Ouroboros"; and Aliette de Bodard's painful revisioning of an old story about a "ship who sang". Every entry here, bar none, engaged me emotionally, entertained me and made me think. If there's a theme, maybe it's in a refreshing approach to the SF short story that's about opening doors, and not closing them; about scenes and episodes that tell the reader a great deal about some strange world, some frantic [illegible] r few neat solutions and no finalities. [illegible] -
ited continue, out of our sight, as un[illegible]
We've been here before, but it never [illegible]

show the world again, that women can and do write excellent, challenging and satisfying science fiction.

—Gwyneth Jones,
author of the *Aleutian* trilogy and the *Bold as Love* cycle,
winner of the World Fantasy, Tiptree, Clarke and Dick awards

Treacherous, colorful, heartbreaking. Work, play, symbiosis. Survive, evolve, transcend. These stories deserve your time, your attention, your appreciation.

—Vonda McIntyre,
author of *Dreamsnake* and *The Sun and the Moon*,
winner of the Hugo and Nebula awards

Sure, science fiction moved out of its boys-only clubhouse years ago, but that was just a first step. If we're really going to have a grownup literature of the future, then we don't just need women writers; we must cast more women as vital characters in our stories. The editors of *The Other Half of the Sky* have assembled here sixteen hard science adventures for your enjoyment. All feature capable professional women—engineers, scientists and yes, starship captains among them—with love interests, if any, very much on the side. While this anthology definitely has a modern feminist sensibility, the emphasis here is most often on good old-fashioned interplanetary fun. Check your preconceptions at the air lock and strap in for a wild ride because space sisters kick ass!

—James Patrick Kelly,
winner of the Hugo, Nebula and Locus Awards

The Other Side of the Sky grew out of an obvious question, but one that we apparently have to rediscover and ask yet again: What if there were many more female characters in science fiction who weren't restricted by gender and inhabited a wide variety of cultures unlike the Western male-centered model that has predominated? The writers in this anthology have answered the question with stories that provoke thought, offer original speculation, and provide great entertainment. What a treat this book is—I'm only sorry I'm not here with a story myself.

—Pamela Sargent,
author of *Earthseed* and *The Shore of Women* and editor of *Women of Wonder*

A constellation of dazzling stories forms *The Other Half of the Sky*. It is an important anthology, original and bold. Not to be missed.

—Lavie Tidhar,
World Fantasy Award-winning author of *Osama*

Melissa Scott's "Finders" is as rock-ribbed as the hard SF from any so-called master, but without the baggage associated with the genre. Sue Lange's "Mission of Greed" is as evocative as it is provocative. What else can one say about this anthology but this: Finally.

—Nick Mamatas,
Hugo-nominated editor

An excellent science fiction anthology whose many fine stories feature strong women from all walks of life, a diverse range of culture and background, and an essential blend of gripping story, real science, and a serious look at how competent people function in the world. My particular favorite, Vandana Singh's "Sailing the Antarsa," to me represents the epitome of what a science fiction short story can unfold in its brilliant weave of speculative cosmology and compassionate insights into human emotion and culture. There is plenty of sense of wonder within the pages of this anthology: Highly recommended.

—Kate Elliott,
author of the *Spiritwalker* Trilogy, the *Crossroads* Trilogy,
the *Crown of Stars* series, and the Novels of the Jaran

Good science fiction stands on its own, notwithstanding the politics of its editors or the gender of its protagonists. Readers expecting a jolt of didactic feminism will not find it in *The Other Side of the Sky*, which focuses instead on the human experience of distant worlds and the even stranger territories of the spirit. Biology, sociology and poetry take precedence over physics in stories that at their best display an elegance of conception and execution that enriches the genre. From doors that mysteriously open to other places and minds running starships who have forgotten who they are, to giant trees with orbit-reaching seeds, the tales in *The Other Half of the Sky* impart a new spin to classic science fiction tropes and, as the field is prone to do, conjure them afresh.

—Paul Gilster,
founder of the Centauri Dreams website
and co-founder of Tau Zero Foundation

Bold, brave, struggling, erring, redeeming, failing, overcoming, dying, transcending—the female characters in *The Other Half of the Sky* explore the full, rich spectrum of human nature, and at the same time, they take readers on moving and memorable adventures.

—Jeanne Cavelos,
bestselling author of *The Passing of the Techno-Mages*

In *The Other Half of the Sky*, space travel is seen, experienced, and driven by women. And while it certainly does not avoid politics, power games, conflicts, and controversies (rather the contrary), it also rekindles a kinder sense of wonder, where people—and other creatures—are part of a nature that stretches across the whole universe. The stories in this anthology are stand-alone but also—like the women in its pages—part of a larger whole: a series in each author's universe. So if you want more, there is plenty to explore. Therefore, *The Other Half of the Sky* not only shows you how SF can be done differently, but is also a portal to more diversity: I highly recommend it.

—Jetse de Vries,
editor of the *Shine* anthology and ex-editor of *Interzone*

The stories gathered together in this collection, varied and entertaining as they are, share a simple idea that in many places, for many people, is radical—that women are people. For those who have always known this and lived accordingly, these stories show us as well that women are remarkable people, that they are heroes (and villains), human (and alien), special (and ordinary), and contain the full measure of all that we are.

—Mark Tiedemann,
author of the *Secantis Sequence*,
Tiptree and Dick award shortlist nominee

Delightful and thought provoking reads, ever single one of them. Your head will say let's think about that as you fingers demand you turn the page and read more!

—Mike Shepherd,
author of the nationally best-selling *Kris Longknife Saga*

Athena Andreadis and Kay Holt have teamed to achieve an amazing feat with *The Other Half of the Sky.* They have snagged exciting, mind-boggling tales of space exploration and interstellar drama by women heroes from an array of talented science fiction writers, and the result is a storytelling repast. I have been delighting in these stories. Some of my favorite writers are here. There is Melissa Scott's Cassilde Sam on the Burntover Plain and Terry Boren's Alakie on a planet somewhere in post-singularity space; there are stories from Martha Wells and Alliette de Bodard, Joan Slonczewski, Ken Liu, Jack McDevitt and others—I can't resist saying it: this anthology achieves orbital velocity with the first story and it just gets better from there. When I was a kid, a lover of science fiction hungry for stories of women heroes, I would have crawled over broken Denebian glass to get my hands on an anthology like this. In fact, heck, I still would. Run, do not walk, to get a copy for yourself.

—Laura Mixon (Morgan J. Locke),
author of *Burning the Ice* and *Up Against It*

The Other Half of the Sky

edited by Athena Andreadis

co-edited by Kay Holt

First edition published 2013.

For information, address
Candlemark & Gleam LLC,
104 Morgan Street, Bennington, VT 05201
info@candlemarkandgleam.com

Library of Congress Cataloging-in-Publication Data
In Progress

ISBN: 978-1-936460-44-1
eISBN: 978-1-936460-43-4

Cover art and design by Eleni Tsami

Book design and composition by Kate Sullivan
Typefaces: Pyke's Peak and Calisto MT

www.candlemarkandgleam.com

To Peter,
who was unshakably convinced I could.

Wings I have woven for you
a wind-driven ship to lift you up
from your citadel to take you
from your masters to free you.

—Victoría Theodhórou, from ***The Lute***

Contents

Dreaming the Dark

Athena Andreadis

"There was a time when you were not a slave, remember that.
You walked alone, full of laughter, you bathed bare-bellied.
You say you have lost all recollection of it, remember...
You say there are no words to describe this time,
you say it does not exist. But remember.
Make an effort to remember.
Or, failing that, invent."
– Monique Wittig, *Les Guerillères*

Being a voracious bookworm, I came to science fiction very young. My first well-remembered book was the unexpurgated *Twenty Thousand Leagues Under the Sea*. By cultural background and temperament, I didn't like the Leaden... er, Golden SF Era. I preferred the Silver Age and the New Wave, with their explicit charters to push boundaries and write worlds and characters with more depth and flavor than cardboard. And since my mythology and history haunt my dreams and steps, it's also not surprising that one SF mode I like is space opera.

Most people conflate opera with Wagner. Likewise, most SF aficionados conflate space opera with galactic empires, messianic anti/heroes (invariably white men) and gizmos up the wazoo, from death stars to individually customized viruses. And herein lies a tale of an immense, systemic failure of imagination.

Science fiction wishes to be the genre of imaginative extrapolation. So it has come to pass that SF writers have conjured all kinds of planetary systems, ecologies, lifeforms and societies; FTL, stable wormholes, time travel, teleporters, ansibles; clones, uploading, downloading, genetic tinkering, nanotechnology; virtual reality, remote sensing, telepathy, telekinesis, precognition.

Yet the same universe-spanning visionaries seem to have difficulty envisioning women (or other "non-defaults," for that matter) as full humans—that is, not defined by their helpmate/mother role but as rounded people fully engaged in their vocations and wider network of relationships and, furthermore, people who can be heroes, not merely heroines. Linked to this is an equally odd inability to envision societies and kinship systems that aren't based on pyramidal dominance, alpha males (of whom more anon) and the equation of capable women—especially older, non-nubile ones—with evil. This blinkering is exacerbated by two persistent tendencies in SF.

One is what I call neoteny: the focus on coming-of-age or finding-one's-self stories, linked to the Campbel/lite quest that makes much of SF fit for the emotionally immature and genre-locked of all ages regardless of its purported target audience. This is abetted by the false dichotomy between inspiration and craft, which resulted in the "novel of ideas" that is supposed to make SF superior to mainstream fiction no matter how lousy its execution (this stance also conveniently ignores the fact that the "work of ideas" concept existed in general literature several aeons before SF became a distinct genre).

The other, interlinked with the first, is the parochialism imposed by the monoculture dominance of the US mindset (and its Blair-like UK satellite), which ever since the eighties has been regressing to a siege mentality and to "Kinder, Küche, Kirche" politics—partly a response to the waning of the US as the undisputed global leader, partly a resurgence of fundamentalisms, partly just a continuation of the Anglo-Saxon puritanism that has always been suspicious of both intellectual and aesthetic depth, including the pleasures of the body. Among other things, this has led to much SF looking like US fifties white suburbia despite the efforts to move the defaults even slightly by such writers as Tiptree, Le Guin, Russ, Vinge, Mukherjee, McIntyre, Butler, van Scyoc, Friedman and Cherryh—to name just a few from my broad age bracket.

This may sound like moaning in an esoteric quasi-vacuum, but these stances reflect and amplify real life—from decisions over science curriculum and funding to the starting of preemptive wars and everything in between, with civil rights and social infrastructure prominent targets. The "new" SF modes (cyberpunk, steampunk and their successors) mirror this malaise by depicting dystopias in which the laissez-faire fungus has overrun everything and women have become mostly sexbots, though they occasionally also serve as wombs, distractions from worthwhile goals or focal points of evil. Too, there's still a widespread dogma in the publishing/reviewing industry that women can't write space opera (or "mind-altering" SF, for that matter), forcing those who do to hide behind fig leaves of initials or "ambiguous" pseudonyms.

So this is what I found myself facing at this junction in my life—a sad state of affairs for a non-feminine woman who is a practicing scientist and an unapologetic feminist; an avid reader of literature across genres in several languages; and a native of a culture that's very different from the dominant. My choices were unpalatable. I could abandon SF and concentrate on fantasy, where women are less rare as both authors and protagonists. However, fantasy is even more childish than SF, if possible, and most magic systems and secondary worlds are an instant cure for insomnia (to say nothing of the Hero's Journey obligatory team assembly and literal floods of Chosen Ones). I could abandon the genre altogether and fall back on good biography and history books which repeatedly demonstrate that truth can be stranger and more complex than fiction. But I have an incurable yearning for starry lanes. Or I could re-read the old collections—Sargent's *Women of Wonder* and its sisters—fall out of touch and become a relic myself.

So I decided to do some conjuring of my own: I'd produce a collection in which women stand as protagonists, rangers, and agents of destiny in unimagined universes that treat them as fully human—and at the same time, maybe strike a blow for SF as quality literature in its own right.

First I pondered: "What do I want in a story?" My needs are actually middlebrow. I want swashbuckling but also nuancing, people who act well despite fears and doubts, protagonists who lodge in my cortex and under my breastbone. I want layers, the frisson of depth that comes from a world that's fully realized by a sensibility whose boundaries extend beyond the borders of US sub/urbia. I want configurations that are neither pyramidal nor male-dominant: cat, elephant, bonobo, orca societies, not the baboon and dog ones that over/underwhelm SF. I want humans who are aware of limitations and consequences, who do not "conquer" new planets and act as neo-colonialists of the Manifest Destiny stripe. I want women to be nexuses, pivots, movers, shapers, creators and destroyers—loved, feared, admired (or all three, I'm not picky). And I want these women and their worlds to be brought to life by language that's not the Hemingway-wannabe workshop-101 hackery that passes for writing craft in much of SF.

I knew SF authors who could and would write such stories if I asked. Some are long-burning suns, others rising stars. Some I knew personally, some through their writing. Several have created worlds and cultures I wanted to see more of: Aliette de Bodard's Xuyan, Alex Dally MacFarlane's Tuvicen, Nisi Shawl's Amenders, Alexander Jablokov's Martians (in particular, the half-glimpsed figure of Miriam Kostal), Kelly Jennings's Combines and their Pirian nemeses, Martha Wells's Raksura (especially their court queens). Others have wide ranges and pyrotechnic imaginations: Cat Rambo, Ken Liu, Vandana Singh, Terry Boren, C. W. Johnson, Sue Lange.

I asked Melissa Scott, whose *Shadow Man* was way before its time and who was writing exquisite cyberpunk before it became fashionable (and smug). I asked Jack McDevitt, whose *Talent for War* is one of my lodestars: not only is the novel a retelling of the Hellenic-Persian wars, but its off-stage protagonist is hauntingly similar to a key figure in the World War II resistance against the Germans. I asked Joan Slonczewski, whose *A Door into Ocean* is another of my lodestars—a complex, densely interwoven narrative replete with solid biology, possibly the best depiction of an alien ecosystem in SF. And I asked Christine Lucas, whose stories are seamless fusions of SF and myths that murmur in my bone marrow.

I asked. I made the narrative parameters broad enough to let them roam, tinker and dream –and watched worlds spark into existence. What you're about to read is the result of this action.

There are some things you won't find in this collection. You won't see any of the clichés you bump into when you browse the kitschy softporn in the SF/F section. You won't find concubines, wicked stepmothers, statements like "This is a man's job," or "Aren't you shortchanging your children?" You won't find wasp-waisted turbo-breasted courtesans or women with obedience spliced into their DNA or implanted in their skulls. You won't find alpha males—who, incidentally don't exist biologically in humans, whose cultural alpha males are invariably disastrous in terms of the "optimal reproductive potential" so beloved of Tarzanists. You won't find glorified pseudo-medieval or aynrandian societies, nor aliens who are either stand-ins for demonized Others or paternalistic quasi-gods. And though the stories here extrapolate very far in many of their premises, their protagonists are close to how real women could be in the future—because that's how they've already been from the day Lilith stated she didn't like the missionary position.

The stories in this collection have at their centers women who are fully invested in their work. Since this is space opera, after all, several are starship captains (*Sailing the Antarsa*, *Velocity's Ghost*, *Dagger and Mask*), pilots (*This Alakie and the Death of Dima*, *The Waiting Stars*, *Cathedral*) or engineers (*Mission of*

Greed) while others are chieftains (*Mimesis*, *Under Falna's Mask*). But they are also biologists (*Landfall*), linguists (*The Shape of Thought*), salvage archaeologists (*Finders*), weavers (*In Colors Everywhere*), civil workers (*Bad Day on Boscobel*), indentured laborers (*Ouroboros*), street urchins (*Exit, Interrupted*). All cast long shadows. All carve unique paths to heroism—and by doing so, lend a wider, deeper definition to the term.

But of course they're much more than that. All are embedded in kinship webs of partners, relatives and friends of many genders—from quasi-nuclear families (*A Bad Day on Boscobel*, *Landfall*) to polyandry (*Finders*) to communal arrangements (*Sailing the Antarsa*) to alliances of choice (*Under Falna's Mask*, *Exit, Interrupted*). They live in complex societies that range from ones that live by consensus (*Sailing the Antarsa*, *Under Falna's Mask*) to ones guided by elders (*In Colors Everywhere*, *The Waiting Stars*) to spoke-wheel hubs (*Mimesis*) to stratified dystopias (*Velocity's Ghost*, *Exit, Interrupted*). The aliens are equally intriguing: the formidable ultraphytes of *Landfall*; the haunting relics of *Finders* and *Ouroboros*; the sessile bioengineers of *This Alakie and the Death of Dima*; the altmatter life of *Sailing the Antarsa*; the infinitely nuanced hand-speakers of *The Shape of Thought*.

The characters and stories in this collection also carry echoes from myth and history as well as ties to landmark forerunners in SF. To just skim the surface, one of the protagonists in *The Waiting Stars* is a space version of tragic princess Mi Chau as well as a jacked pilot like that of the *Farscape* TV series. The rituals in *Under Falna's Mask* bring to mind customs of Central Asia and the American Great Plains. The protagonist of *Dagger and Mask* is an incarnation of Morrigan—but also a direct descendant of Cherryh's Signy Mallory. *A Bad Day on Boscobel* is an interstellar take on the Triple Goddess; *Sailing the Antarsa* shows an extrasolar evolution of Jainism. *Cathedral* depicts a Thermopylae-like stand, while *Ouroboros* tells of a Martian Teiresias and of Alexander's storm-raising mermaid sister; *This Alakie and the Death of Dima* has human-alien interactions that are kin to those in Butler's *Bloodchild*, *Mimesis* is inhabited by cousins of Anderson's Ythrians, the starship in *Mission of Greed* is from the same factory as the *Nostromo* in *Alien* and *The Shape of Thought* contains distant descendants of Le Guin's Gethenians. These soundbite descriptions are just ripples on the deep waters of these universes.

The science component of these stories is as strong and integral to the works as their fiction: sentient extremophiles and amyloid lifeforms in *Landfall*, bio-based technology in *This Alakie and the Death of Dima*, neural-inorganic interphases in *The Waiting Stars*, paired quantum macro-interactions in *Exit, Interrupted*, altmatter navigation in *Sailing the Antarsa*, punitive uploading in *In Colors Everywhere*, targeted genetic engineering in *Ouroboros* and nanotech in just about all of them. Some of these concepts are truly novel. Others give new—dare I say, mind-altering—dimensions to established SF concepts. But all are mindful of the dilemmas and dangers lurking in the science-y magick.

These stories prove abundantly that when people are asked to write as full adults for other full adults, they will do so with zest and flair. They also demonstrate that sensawunda and vivid prose are not mutually exclusive, even in works that hew to traditional modes of storytelling. I lived in these universes, wore them like garments as I edited them from the inside out, felt them pulse under my hands. They made me smile in both surprise and recognition.

And I, a feral loner who walks between worlds, between cultures, languages, roles and vocations and who has been homesick her entire life for places that don't exist, felt I was in the company of chosen relatives while I lived in these worlds. Perhaps you will, too.

Finders

Melissa Scott

A SALVOR'S GUIDE TO THE ANCESTRAL ELEMENTS:

BLUE, visual scale 1 to 199: the most common element, can be found alone, as part of an Ancestral device, or in conjunction with other elements. Carries instructions and programming.

GOLD, visual scale 400 to 599: appears in about the same frequency as RED, usually found in Ancestral devices, rarely as a "depot node" unconnected to any other element. Absorbs and responds to input as directed by BLUE-based instruction sets.

RED, visual scale 600 to 799: appears in the same frequency as GOLD, almost always found in Ancestral devices, almost always found in conjunction with both GOLD and BLUE. (Claims of "depot nodes" and RED/GOLD hybrid nodules remain unproven.) Responds to GOLD input with action/output.

GREEN, visual scale 200 to 399: the rarest of the elements, can be found alone or as part of an Ancestral device. Provides "life" to the other elements, which remain inert unless activated by GREEN.

A thousand years ago the cities fell, fire and debris blasting out the Burntover Plain. Most of the field was played out now, the handful of towns that had sprung up along the less damaged southern edge grown into three thriving and even elegant cities, dependent on trade for their technology now rather than salvage. Cassilde Sam had been born on the eastern fringe of the easternmost city, in Glasstown below the Empty Bridge, and even after two decades of hunting better salvage in the skies beyond this and a dozen other worlds, the Burntover still drew her. It was the largest terrestrial salvage bed ever found; it still had secrets, depths not yet plumbed.

But not today, not by her. Never by her, unless something changed... She closed the window above the workbench, cutting off the seductive view, the raw land of the Burntover rusty beyond the black-tiled roofs of Maripas. There was snow in the air, the thin hard flakes that came across the Blight and carried the sting of that passage. Two hundred years ago, that snow would have been a threat to everyone in the city, carrying poison enough to burn and even kill, if the circumstances were right; even in her own grandmother's day, people had taken the snow seriously enough to stay indoors while it fell. But now that Racklin had unlocked the Aparu-5 command set, and the GOLD-based satellites could reliably measure the drifting toxins, it was only the compromised that avoided the incoming snow. People like her.

She killed that thought and looked down at her workbench, frowning at the scrap of BLUE floating in the matrix. It was showing the familiar halo that indicated dissolution had begun, and she switched on the power, feeding the gentle current through the conductive gel. The BLUE shimmered and split, breaking into dozens of tiny hexagons, the building blocks of a command chain. She slid the matrix into the reader, peering down through the magnifying lens, reading the patterns backlit against the pale jelly. All of them were familiar, disappointing: plain scrap, part of a bag she'd picked up in the high-market beyond Barratin. It was a useful source of spare parts, not the sort of thing that contained new code.

And that was a reminder of repairs she needed to make, something else to take her mind off her own problems. She hauled out the sensor core from *Carabosse*'s ventral array, ran the sonic probe around the faint line that marked the hemisphere and split it open. The BLUE was badly faded—the instruction sets wore out over time, though no one had ever been able to isolate the cause. Luckily, it was a simple set, and she pulled out another matrix, touching keys to set the gel to incubate. She had a full supply of blocks in her kit and began hooking them out of their storage cells, building the instructions block by block against the pale gel. *Go seek hold go*, the delicate hexagons slotting neatly against each other to create a larger ring. *Fix track find go...* When she reached the second clause she hesitated—she'd had an idea about that, a different, perhaps more efficient way of defining the search—but this was not the time to experiment. Even with all the documentation in the world, Dai wouldn't be able to figure out what she'd done, and there was increasingly the chance she wouldn't last to explain it to him herself. She finished the pattern, the rings joining to build the familiar snowflake of a BLUE control string, and set the matrix to cure overnight.

That was the end of the chores she'd brought with her from the ship. She shut down the workbench and drifted back to the narrow kitchen, where the clock read four past sixteen. She filled the iron kettle that came with the rented room and set it to boil on the island's largest eye while she dug out a packet of tea. The Ancestors had to have been fond of tea: there wasn't a single Settled World that didn't boast some decoction of boiled leaves and berries. Ashe had laughed at the idea, in the days before the war, before she'd gotten sick—but she wouldn't think of that now, either. Ashe was gone, and that was the end of it.

A chime sounded, and she glanced at the cooktop, but instead the door slid open. She reached for the narrow-draft welder she kept handy in lieu of a gun when she was on a civilized world, but relaxed as she saw Dai Winter in the doorway.

She slipped the welder beneath the counter as he let the door close behind him. He had done his best to brush away the snow from the shoulders of his coat, but the smell of it came with him, dank and bitter. It caught in her throat, and

Dai hastily shed the offending garment, hung it in the bathroom and turned the vent to high.

"Sorry," he said, still keeping his distance, and his blue eyes were filled with concern.

Cassilde swallowed her cough, tightening the muscles along her ribs to hold it in. At least she took a careful breath, mouth pressed right, nostrils flaring; she choked again, swallowed bile, but the second breath came more easily. "I'm all right."

She sounded breathless, she knew, but blessedly Dai took her at her word and set the stacked tins that held their dinner on the counter beside the now-singing kettle. The food came with the room, at a surcharge, from the *bilai* on the ground floor: another small luxury they pretended they could afford.

"Bad day?" he asked, carefully casual, and began unlatching the tins. The waiter-boy would come along after midnight and retrieve them from outside the door.

"So-so. Though I put together fresh BLUE for the ventral core, so that's a win." Cassilde set the tea to steep. "And you?"

Dai avoided her eyes. "All right. The snow's supposed to end tonight, you'll be clear in the morning."

"To do what?" She controlled the urge to clash the enameled iron cups that matched the kettle, set them gently on the counter instead. "We're not credentialed to bid on any of the jobs at hand."

And if they couldn't bid, there would be no money, and they were already at the end of their savings... It was not something she needed to say, but Dai grimaced as though he'd heard them.

"I shouldn't have fired Lanton," he said. "I know that. But he was impossible."

"And he was skimming from the take," Cassilde said. "And you're right, that would have gotten us in trouble sooner or later. But we should have had the replacement in line first."

Dai dipped his head. He was a big man, taller than she by more than the breadth of his hand, and she was by no means small. A dangerous man, one might have said, looking at him, with his knotted muscles earned in high salvage, hauling significant mass in varying gravity, sandy hair cropped short, the evening's stubble coming in pale on his lantern jaw. She'd taken his measure long ago.

"We've had an inquiry," he said. It was something of a peace offering. "An answer to your notice."

"Oh?" She was intrigued in spite of herself. With new permits up for bid, on a new section of an Ancestor's wrecked sky palace, lost in long orbit for at least a hundred years, scholars with a class-one license could name their price. And the ones they might afford, the ones with a class-two license and a supervising master, were already hired. Even Lanton had a new job, with someone who should have known better. "What's the catch?"

"I think it's Ashe," Dai said.

Cassilde froze just for an instant, then very deliberately poured them each a cup of tea. Summerlad Ashe had been their first scholar, partner and lover and friend, brilliant and unscrupulous as you had to be in salvage. But when the Trouble broke, he'd chosen the richer side, Core over Edge, and put those same talents to use against them. She'd be damned if she trusted him again.

"He wouldn't dare," she said firmly, as though she could make it true.

Of course it was Ashe. Dai checked at the door of the little teashop where the high-class salvors did business, as though he hadn't really believed it after all, but Cassilde put her hand in the small of his back and pushed him on. Ashe gave them both his usual sardonic smile, and waved a hand toward one of the sunken booths.

Three steps down, it was quiet and warm, the winter light diffused and colored by the amber skylight and the translucent window. She had wondered how Ashe had dared to show himself here, so close to the Edge—he was hardly unknown, after the mutiny that had ended the war—but even in the dim entry there had been a shadow disfiguring his cheek, and in the light of the booth it resolved itself to a datamote the size of his thumb clinging to the skin beneath his left eye, drawing attention from his prominent nose and well-shaped mouth. There had been a fad for motes a few years back, at least for deactivated ones, worn like bright jewels on skin and hair, but this one was active, his skin pink around the spots where the fine wires had burrowed into the nerves.

"Clever," she said, and he bowed.

"Thank you."

"Looks painful," Dai said.

For a moment, she thought Ashe would deny it, but then he shrugged. "Uncomfortable, sometimes. You get used to it."

Cassilde lifted an eyebrow at that, and stepped past him to take her place at the head of the low table. Both the cushions and the footwell were heated, and she wriggled her toes where the others couldn't see. The Lightman's that was slowly killing her left her sensitive to cold.

"You think damn well of yourself," Dai said to Ashe, who shrugged again.

"I'm good, and you know it."

"You're as good as you say you are," Cassilde said. "And so are we. Our skills are not at issue." She stopped, seeing a waiter-girl approaching with a filled tray. "Bribery, too."

The color rose in Ashe's sallow face, but he made no answer. And that was odd: he disliked being caught in one of his schemes almost as much as he disliked his first name.

Cassilde let the girl serve them, a pot of floral tea for herself and Dai, coffee for Ashe, thick and ropy in its copper pot. There were plates of biscuits as well, pale circles decorated with sugared flowers or stamped with a star and crescent moon: definitely bribery, she thought, and settled to enjoy it while it lasted.

She watched the men eye each other as they all took ritual

tastes of the food. She was not so naive as to think Dai was the only one hurt, for all that his face showed his pain more clearly. Ashe might cultivate a brittle disdain, but he had felt the break perhaps even more keenly. Of course, he had chosen to leave, and not long after she'd been diagnosed with Lightman's—but that was unfair. Still, that old suspicion sharpened her voice.

"What do you want, Ashe? Exactly and in detail, please."

"I'm offering to go in with you on a bid for some section of the latest contract," Ashe said. Only the flicker of his gaze, one quick glance from Dai to her, betrayed that he was not as utterly confident as he sounded.

"Offering," Dai said.

Cassilde ignored him. "Why?"

Ashe shrugged. "You need a scholar, and I need work—"

Cassilde slammed her hand hard on the table, rattling the teacups. "Don't give me that! What do you want, Ashe? Tell me now and tell me straight, or walk away."

Even then, he hesitated for an instant. "I want to bid on a specific piece of the contract—it's not an obvious choice, but I have reason to think it may be more profitable than it looks at first sight." He touched the datamote in his cheek. "But it will take a really good team to pull it off. You're the best I know. Still."

Cassilde poured herself another cup of tea. That was Ashe for you, the lure of the exotic larded with compliments, *no one can do it but you*, and yet... She looked at Dai, saw him already half willing to believe. "What does that thing tell you?"

"My mote?" Ashe touched it again, the almond-shaped body glowing pale green behind a blackened filigree. The wires glittered where they pierced his skin.

"What else?"

Ashe smiled, ruefully. "You're right, that's how I got my information. It's a Palace piece, I'm sure you can see that. It was inert when I got it, but I had a speck of GREEN left, and I—revived it. And when I compared its records to the first scout report, I saw that the Claim-court had undervalued one segment—well, not undervalued, precisely, it's a fair value for the obvious salvage, but there's more there."

"How's it classed?" Cassilde asked.

"It's a second-class site," Ashe answered. "No supervision required, only the share-out at the end. Unless you find something worthwhile, of course."

Dai shook his head. "If we bid on something like that, everyone will know we've got a lead."

"Not really," Ashe said. "You've just lost your scholar, you've got a new one on short notice, untried, an unknown quantity—why wouldn't you bid on a class-two, and take the sure thing?"

"Because we don't do sure things," Cassilde said.

"No," Dai said slowly. "It could work."

It could. It probably would, like all Ashe's schemes, though like all Ashe's schemes there would be a dozen things he hadn't mentioned, and trouble to spare. And it was tempting—there was the possible payout, certainly, and they desperately needed one good run. The chance that they would find something truly unique, some as-yet-unknown artifact, the secret of the Ancestors—well, that was the dream of everyone who went into salvage, no secret and no surprise, glorious if it happened and no heartbreak if it did not. Somehow she'd find the money for the bid. "All right. I'm willing. If Dai agrees."

Dai nodded. "Yes. I'm in."

"Right." Cassilde looked back at Ashe. "We'll take you on, on a standard contract, quarter shares with one for the ship, and everything in writing. Is that clear?"

"Clear," he said, and she pretended not to have seen the flicker of hurt in his dark eyes.

Carabosse had never been impressive, just another pre-war Fairy-class scout bought surplus and converted for salvage.

They had added a second pair of cannon after the war, when they were cheap and things were still unsettled enough that demobbed crews were raiding the more distant salvage fields, and the welds still showed raw against the fading paint. The outboard grapples were folded neatly against the ship's belly between the landing struts, and they and the bulk of the oversized engine at the stern coupled with the dropped sensor bulb forward gave the ship a hunched, insectoid look. Cassilde glanced over her shoulder, waiting for Ashe to complain again about carrying cargo outboard, but he dropped his gaze and concentrated on helping Dai get the baggage cart up the ramp and into the ship.

There was no place to put him but his old cabin—they had always each kept space of their own, though she and Dai still shared the big bed in the master's cabin—and when she came back from stowing her own belongings, Ashe was at the library console, files open to begin drafting their bid. It was shocking to see him there, scowling into the multiple screens—how dare he act as though nothing had changed, as though he'd never left them for the Center, run away to war with never a thought for them? She saw Dai's hands close to fists, and Ashe spoke without looking away from the screens.

"Who's been keeping your find-files for you? They're an idiot."

Cassilde turned on her heel and stalked away. It was all she had, short of hitting him. She kept walking, half expecting to hear the sounds of a fistfight behind her, made her way down the full length of the ship until she reached the darkened control room. She keyed off the lights that came on as she closed the hatch behind her and settled into the co-pilot's seat, automatically assessing. She was cold, her fingers white and numb: that was the walk. It and the anger had left her short of breath as well. She could feel her lungs straining, each breath pinched close and tight, and for a moment she was tempted by the speck of GREEN she kept for the really bad days.

She drew her knees to her chin, forcing herself to breathe

slowly, carefully, and the worst of the spasm passed. GREEN wasn't meant to be used as medicine, but, as with all the Ancestors' artifacts, over the centuries humans had figured out more ways to use the substance. It would clear her worst symptoms, buy her a week or two of normal breath and movement, but it would not cure her. And every pinhead dot of GREEN that she used to prolong her life was GREEN that could not be used to power the ship's Ancestral devices. And without GREEN, nothing would function. She'd had to make that choice too often lately, choosing between her own health and the ship's, and they had no money for more when their stockpile was exhausted. In fact, if they didn't find GREEN on this current job, they'd be in serious trouble.

If only the Ancestral elements didn't fade over time—if only someone, anyone, could find a way to restore their potency. But that was the Grail of the true scientists, the elemental physicists in their orbital labs, not a problem that could be solved by salvage. All salvage could do was find a few more pieces of the Ancestors' wreckage, and keep the systems going a little longer.

"Silde?" Dai loomed in the open hatch, taking stock in a single glance. "You good?"

She nodded, and saw him relax. "And you?"

Dai gave a crooked smile. "Ashe has the bid roughed out for your approval."

And that meant that whatever words might or might not have passed between them, they'd achieved enough of a truce that she wasn't allowed to challenge it. "Right," she said, and uncoiled from the chair. "How's it look?"

"Pretty much like he said," Dai answered. "You'll see."

It definitely hadn't been a ship, she thought, skimming through the general description of the find. The individual units were too large, too specialized—too complex in places, too simple in others, though obviously once part of some coherent whole. It couldn't be anything but the ruins of one of the Ancestors' orbital palaces. Before the Fall, there had been dozens of them in the Maripas system, weaving an impossible ring around the main planet. Most of those had been salvaged long ago, but others occasionally appeared, either returning on long orbits or possibly abandoned in transit between systems, and there was always a fight over what were likely to be the richest sections. At least Ashe promised this was only a class-two, something they might be able to afford.

"What are we bidding on, exactly?" she asked, and Ashe leaned over her shoulder to touch keys.

"Here—this big trailing section. It masses low, and the quick scan confirmed it's hollow. The Court survey has it pegged as possible support or storage volume, based primarily on its position in the train, but I don't think that's right."

Cassilde scanned the numbers that filled the screen. "Not tech-rich."

"No," Ashe said. "The mass is too low, and there aren't enough exotics."

"Yeah, but would they show on a quick scan like that?" Dai asked.

"If it was engineering or control space, it would," Cassilde said. Not much tech, which meant not much of the Ancestral elements, except maybe some more BLUE, the most common element. But everyone needed BLUE; between that and the non-exotic salvage, they might be able to clear enough to replenish the GREEN she'd used on herself.

Ashe grinned. "Exactly. But I think it's living space—passenger volume—and you know that's where the most interesting goods are always found."

That was at least partly true, Cassilde thought. In the past, the most valuable finds had come from what seemed to have been the habitable volumes of the palaces. They weren't necessarily the most useful things—those had been the drive and navigation units from what were deemed tenders and runabouts, simple enough that humans could not only borrow but reproduce most of it. But the finds that made a salvor's fortune these days weren't the technical innovations; it seemed as though everything that human science could reproduce had already been found. These days, the money was in elementals and the weird. And if there was enough of either—she might live long enough to make another strike, leave Dai at least with enough money to keep the ship.

She damped that sudden hope. "What do you think we're looking for? What does that bug tell you?"

"Toys," Ashe said promptly. "I'm not pretending it's anything important, but you know the kind of money they bring. Enough to earn all of us a new stake." He shrugged. "And at the very least, there will be raw materials to take."

"You'd be willing to go for that?" Dai asked. He sounded skeptical, and Cassilde couldn't blame him. Ashe had always fought to preserve their finds intact.

"I think there are toys there," Ashe said. "Good ones, maybe even unique and fabulous things. From everything I've been able to work out, this was the owners' living space, not crew. The things that could be there—it's almost unimaginable."

Dai stared at him, and Ashe sighed.

"And, yes, if we don't find anything else worthwhile, we can recoup our costs on salvage value alone. I'm good with that."

"I don't believe him," Dai said to Cassilde, and she nodded.

"What are you really looking for, Ashe? No bullshit this time."

"I don't know," Ashe said. "That's the trouble. I mean, yes, I have every reason to think there will be toys there, but this—" He touched the device on his cheek. "All it says is that this is, or was, a critical area, holding something vitally important. The implication is that it's lifesaving, maybe some sort of rescue device, or something medical, though I can't make that fit with the other things it's telling me about the section. Why would you put a lifesaving device in the middle of a residential area?"

This was why they'd taken on Ashe in the first place, Cassilde thought, caught up in spite of herself in the possibilities he was sketching. Even without the mote's help, he'd always had the gift for seeing the Ancestors' relics as they were meant to be.

"If the owner had a medical condition, maybe?" Dai said.

"The Ancestors were supposed to have been both incredibly long-lived and impossibly healthy," Cassilde said. "So say the records, and that's confirmed by everything we've seen of their surviving ground settlements. No hospitals, no clinics, no medical facilities of any kind—"

"Except for the tower on Devona," Dai interjected.

"If you agree that's a medical facility," Ashe said. "Which I don't."

"So you're going to agree with Orobandi on that?" Cassilde lifted an eyebrow.

"Embarrassingly, yes," Ashe answered. "I think the Ancestors were, if not actually immortal, possessed of such an immensely long lifespan and the ability to heal almost any injury that they might as well have been. Whatever human beings were to them, that's a fundamental physiological difference between us."

The words were more bitter than Cassilde had imagined, looking at her white, numbed fingers. "Which brings us back to the question," she said. "What do you think is there?"

"I don't know," Ashe said again. "I can't translate everything this thing tells me, and I can't guess, not from what I have. But if it's something the Ancestors thought was good for healing—imagine what it could do for us."

Cassilde flinched at Dai's stricken stare, heard her own breath sharp before she got herself under control. "You bastard. Off my ship."

"What?" Ashe looked genuinely bewildered. "You can't say this is a bad idea—"

Dai closed his fists, but his voice was almost frighteningly controlled. "You heard her, Ashe. Off the ship."

"But—"

"The Lightman's is now third stage," Cassilde said.

She heard Ashe's breath catch in turn, his eyes suddenly wide. There was nothing beyond the third stage, the point at which even GREEN was required in ever-increasing doses just to maintain function. No one had ever been able to afford enough GREEN to know if it would preserve life indefinitely.

"If I'd known that," Ashe said, "I'd have put it to you right away. What I thought I had, I mean."

Cassilde studied him for a long moment, trying to read his true feelings. He looked contrite, appalled, shocked into silence—but this was Ashe, who'd always been the best liar of them all. And also the one most capable of casual, unanticipated kindness. She let out her anger with her breath. "Well. Now you know."

"Now I know," he echoed, and glanced at Dai. "I can't promise anything. You have to understand that. It's only hints and shadows."

"Better than nothing," Dai muttered.

Cassilde looked away. Hope was a luxury she couldn't afford, but she couldn't bring herself to deny it to Dai. "All right. Yes, we'll bid on it."

Relief flickered across Ashe's face, gone before she could be sure she'd seen it, and Dai sighed deeply.

"Supplies?"

"Close out the rainy day account," Cassilde said. "You'll have to."

"Right," Dai said, and reached for his tablet again.

Cassilde scrolled down to find the final bid price. Ashe had kept it to a reasonable margin, but even so, the numbers made her wince. They'd be betting everything on this bid, emptying every account. But at the most conservative estimate, they would make the bid price back in raw materials alone, and if they found even a handful of the Ancestors' toys—it would be worth it, regardless of what else might be in the wreckage.

"Dai, are you good with this?"

The bigger man nodded. "Yeah. I say we do it."

"Right." Cassilde scribbled her name and keycode across the screen, and pressed the send button before she could change her mind. "Done. And now I am going to go lie down."

Her tone dared either of them to comment, and Dai raised his hands in surrender.

"I'll wake you when anything comes in."

"You do that," she said, and turned away. As she stepped over the hatch combing, she heard Ashe's voice, soft and aggrieved—*you could have told me*—but she did not look back.

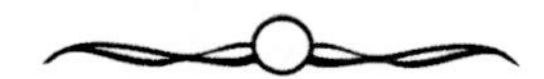

They won the bid without a second round—no real surprise there, Cassilde thought. The only reason someone might have bid against them was their reputation. The claim papers came through promptly, and they lifted from the Maripas field ten hours later, bank accounts empty but full of fuel and supplies.

It was a two-week flight out to the projected intercept point, and after two days they'd let Ashe back into their bed. It was inevitable, Cassilde supposed, and she could not be sorry. The Lightman's was worse again, her fingers numbed and clumsy, a dry, nagging tightness in her chest and throat that erupted with exertion into a hacking cough. She had taken to carrying the little case of GREEN in her pocket again, in case of an emergency that increasingly seemed likely, and she was glad of any distraction. If that was Ashe returned—Ashe compliant and willing and affectionate as ever—she would take it. She was unlikely to have to deal with the fallout when it came.

She shoved that thought away, concentrating instead on the sensor readings that filled her screens. They were running on autopilot, their own transponders silent, sensor net extended to the fullest to catch any whisper of another ship. Every other experienced salvor would be doing the same, and she paid particular attention to the proximity alarms, set to trigger at a forty-klick radius. No one wanted to draw attention if there were raiders lurking, and there almost certainly would be, with a find this size. The Guard patrols couldn't be everywhere, and most captains made the same calculation she did: the risk of collision was vanishingly small compared to the risk of a hijacking.

The sensor net had been empty of everything but debris since they passed the fifty-hour mark, but she was starting to pick up the Claim-court beacons, marking out the edges of the salvage field. If her observations were correct—and they would be; *Carabosse*'s sensors were GOLD-enhanced and fitted with the most recent Agnoss BLUE control rig—their claim was about twelve hours ahead, in a relatively clear section of the field. Even so, it would probably be easier to drop under the bulk of the debris, avoiding the risk of collision, and she reached for a control tablet to begin blocking out the change of course.

The sensor net pinged once, then a second time, and she sat up quickly, running her hands across the controls to center the sensor display. Something was moving in the far edges of the net, running without transponders, without active sensors, just the whisper of its mass against the background gravity to give it away. She hit the kill switch, shutting down all engine power, everything but the environmentals and the GOLD-based net, and held her breath, watching the shadow drift across the fringes of the ship's vision. It stayed steady, and she pressed the intercom button.

"Dai. Ashe. We have a ghost."

Dai answered with reassuring promptness. "Nothing solid?"

"Not yet." Cassilde studied the screen. If she could see the stranger, they could see her—if they had a GOLD net, if they were looking, if she hadn't cut power in time. Too many imponderables. All they could do was wait it out. "Ashe, I want you on the guns. No power except on my say-so."

"All right."

"I'm coming up," Dai said.

On the secondary display, the gunroom light went from green to red as Ashe entered the compartment, but he did nothing more. Behind her, the hatch slid back, and Dai took his place in the copilot's seat.

"Anything new?"

"No change." Cassilde frowned. "No, it looks like they're slowing."

"Damn." Dai started to reach for the sensor controls, stopped even before Cassilde shook her head.

"I don't think they've seen us," she said. "It's something else."

"They're maneuvering," Dai said.

"Any idea how big they are?"

"Bigger than us," Dai answered, and Cassilde gave a sigh of relief. If it was a larger ship and they were just barely picking up its mass, there was a good chance *Carabosse* was still invisible.

"Can you tell what they're doing?"

"Slowing," Dai said.

"Can I go to stand-by?" Ashe asked, and Cassilde realized she'd left the intercom open.

"Not yet," she said. "I don't think they've seen us."

"Still slowing," Dai said. "I'm getting a better look at them, Silde. Definitely a ship, and definitely bigger than us—it might be another salvor, we're in range of some of the other claims."

"I think we should go to stand-by," Ashe said again. "At least let me warm up the guns."

"Not yet," Cassilde said. It wasn't like Ashe to be trigger-happy, and she frowned again. "What do you know?"

"Nothing except that getting caught by a pirate would be bad," Ashe answered. "Before we even get a look at the claim..."

And that was the Ashe she remembered: nothing got between him and salvage. "It's too much of a risk they'll pick up the power use," she said. "You know that."

"Damn it," Dai said. "They've dropped off."

"Out of range or gone to ground?" Cassilde demanded. The screen was black again, just the faint lines that laid out the gravity and the background scatter, the debris dull purple against the void.

"I can't tell." Dai shook his head. "Let me ping her once, super-low power, GOLD frequencies only—"

"No," Cassilde said again. There was too much risk another ship would pick up active sensors.

"Any idea what it was?" Ashe asked.

"Not really," Cassilde said. She looked at Dai. "What's the chance it's one of us?"

"Somebody running quiet out to their claim?" Dai shrugged. "It could be. Like I said, we're in sensor range of a couple of other sites."

"I don't think it's a salvor," Ashe said.

"If you know anything," Cassilde said, "say it now."

There was a little silence. "There were rumors before we left. Nothing solid."

"Damn it, Ashe," Dai said.

"It was talk," Ashe said. "The usual chitchat, somebody heard somebody say somebody else might have mentioned a smash-and-grab. Nothing we all haven't heard a thousand times. But, yes, it's possible that somebody else saw what I saw in that section. Not likely, I admit. But possible."

"There are always rumors," Cassilde said, as much to herself as to the others. She shook herself and looked at Dai. "Any idea where they went?"

He reached across the screen to shape a wedge of light, the wide end pointing away from their position. "That's what I make from the last readings."

The ghost ship was headed away before it disappeared. Probably another salvor, Cassilde decided, taking the same precautions they were. "All right," she said. "Bring us back to low power, and let's get on this. The sooner we're on our claim, the better."

Dai brought *Carabosse* down neatly against the side of the chunk of wreckage that was their claim, latching on with the landing grapples, then setting the pitons that would hold the ship firmly to the section's outer shell. Scans revealed the hull and interior bulkheads to be in surprisingly good condition, as though the palace had broken up along the faces of its strongest points. Or maybe it had been designed to fail that way, Cassilde thought, as she supervised the mapping daemon from the control room while the others adjusted the fields that would hold an atmosphere and transmit power to their equipment. She'd seen similar patterns before, on other wrecks, and it was a logical way to build a space habitat—though logic didn't always have much to do with the Ancestors.

It took a full twelve hours to generate a breathable atmosphere, and she used the time to smooth out the artificial gravity and get a decent night's sleep before turning Ashe loose on the point they'd marked as their best entrance. He set the portable airlock with his usual quick skill and eased his way through the layers of rock and metal, working around nests of BLUE that would pay most of their expenses for the job once they had time to recover them. Cassilde marked their locations, and once the shell was breached, loosed a swarm of smaller daemons to chart the interior volume. The result was rough, but she displayed it in Central with a certain satisfaction.

Ashe fiddled with his tablets, flattening the map to a rough schematic, then expanding it to the three-dimensional model, then zooming in on image fragments as though he could identify specific objects in the daemons' feed.

"The resolution's not good enough for that," Dai said.

He'd done the cooking, since his job was suspended for the moment, and slid the bowls of rice and beans onto the table. Cassilde took hers without enthusiasm. Dai was in fact a decent cook, but she had no appetite, a sure sign that she was working up to another attack of the Lightman's. Her fingers stumbled on the spoon and Dai gave her a sharp glance, but she stared him down.

"At least I can get something to work with," Ashe said. He was eating with one hand and still fiddling with the map with the other. "I'm guessing this might be what we're looking for?" He pointed to a smaller chamber, connected to the larger spaces by a single narrow tunnel. The bulkhead between was thicker than the others, almost as thick as the bulkhead that had divided the section from the rest of the parent craft.

"A treatment room?" Dai said, sounding intrigued in spite of himself.

"Maybe." Ashe twirled the map again.

"Do you mind?" Dai said. Cassilde gave him a grateful look. Between the shifting image and the Lightman's, she was feeling a little queasy herself.

"I'd normally say it was sleeping quarters," Ashe said, "but that bulkhead is way too heavy. There's something that wanted power behind that. Or there was." He made no acknowledgement of Dai's complaint, but at least he'd stopped spinning the map.

"You say that because—?" Dai squinted at the map.

"Because of that," Cassilde said, and pointed, the lights of the map playing over her hand. "That does look like some sort of power node."

Ashe nodded. "The daemons say it could be an inert device. Pings were inconclusive, but it's possible."

"Right," Cassilde said. "So we'll start there."

"Nothing more from the sensor web?" Dai asked, and Cassilde shook her head.

"It must have been one of us."

Ashe nodded, but Dai hesitated. "Maybe I should stay on

board, keep an eye out for anything else that might show up."

Cassilde weighed the options, the added security of a live person minding the ship against the need to do a thorough survey as quickly as possible. If there had been anything more, any warning from the web, it would be different, but at the moment, speed mattered. "No," she said. "We'll risk it."

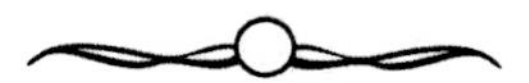

Despite the environmental fields that established an arbitrary gravity and atmosphere, and transmitted power to their lights and tools, the wreck was dank and cold. Some of that was psychological, Cassilde knew—it would feel warmer once they were able to rig working lights instead of relying on hand- and helmet-beams—but some of that was the Lightman's creeping through her body. She could barely feel her feet, in spite of the heated boot liners. She dialed up the heat in her vest, tucked the hood tight around her face, and swung her light and camera methodically around the largest of the claim's inner volumes.

"You were right," she said. "This looks like living space."

"I told you," Ashe said. He had his own recorder out, scanning the walls, and streaks of color bloomed as the light hit them. "Here, put your light over here."

Cassilde brought her light to join his, and a series of linked circles swam out of the shadows, pale gold on lavender-grey. "Dai?"

The pilot trained his light on them as well, widening the picture, but it remained abstract, one large circle linked to a dozen smaller ones, circles smaller still hanging off each of those. "Fractal symbolism?"

"Maybe." Ashe broke from the joined lights, followed the diminishing circles up the wall and onto the wall above them, where they faded into invisibility. "Or maybe just decoration."

Cassilde swung her light again, scanning the room. Shapes rose like islands from the floor, the remains of furniture—

a sweeping curve that might have been a lounge, cubes that might have been chairs or tables, another cube with a shallow depression in one side—and light glittered in a corner. She moved toward it, and it resolved into a lump of cloudy glass the size of her fist. She picked it up, careful of her grip, and felt the familiar deep hum that meant it was active. "I've got a music box."

"Nice," Dai said, and nodded as she held it up. "That's a big one, too."

Cassilde nodded, stowing it in her carryall. They weren't really music boxes, of course, weren't even boxes, but when a human held them, the glass slowly cleared to reveal twirling threads of light and produced a cascade of pleasant sound. Between it and the BLUE they could salvage from the hull, the job was already making a profit—which was a good thing, if she was going to be incapacitated for a while.

"We'll come back," Ashe said. "This way."

They had to pass through two more compartments before they reached the circular opening in the thickened bulkhead. Cassilde swung her light, examining the slot where presumably the original door had disappeared, but there was no sign of it or of any controlling mechanism. Dai produced a heavy metal bar as thick as his wrist and laid it gently in the opening. When nothing happened, he tried wedging it into the gap, but the bar slid into the slot without finding a stop.

"We'll be fine," Ashe said, and stepped through. "We've got cutters."

Which was true, Cassilde admitted, as long as the transmitter kept functioning. "I thought you didn't like messing up your finds."

"I don't," he answered, his light sweeping over the new space. "I just don't expect we'll have to."

Cassilde lifted her own light, blinking as she began to make sense of the shadowed curves. "Holy—"

"Yeah," Dai said. He shrugged off his carryall. "Ashe, you want me to rig some worklights?"

"Please." Ashe was moving slowly across the open space, his light flashing over what looked like beds made of woven silver, a cascade of scarlet thread and a chair that spiraled out of the floor.

There was a sharp click as Dai found metal to take the worklight's magnet, and the room was suddenly flooded with light. Cassilde switched off her handlight, her breath coming short again.

The compartment was curved like the inside of a shell, the open space where she and Dai still stood curling down to a narrow alcove, half hidden behind the flowing strands of scarlet. The walls shimmered like nacre, too, palest gold shading toward green in the shadows; there were lines drawn on the floor and up the walls, following the gentle curves. On other installations, similar lines had been filled with flowing light.

Dai flicked on the second worklight, driving back the rest of the shadows. "Impressive."

"Isn't it?" Ashe had moved the datamote from his face to his collarbone, was rubbing it as though that would make it give up its information. "I've never seen anything like it."

And if Ashe hadn't, this might be a unique find. Cassilde killed that hope—it was far too soon to speculate—and said, "Any sign of this lifesaving device?"

"In the alcove, I think," Ashe answered. The worklights didn't quite penetrate its depths; he was still using his handlight to examine the walls. "But I'm not seeing any actual device."

"There's things attached to the beds," Dai began, and the lights flickered.

Cassilde grabbed her remote, pinged the ship to check its status. The codes flashed back in the proper sequence, power transmitters all green, ship's systems green, nothing in the sensor web, and she shook her head. "Nothing here."

"I could head back and make sure," Dai said, reluctantly.

Cassilde considered, weighing the difficulty of getting out again if they lost the transmission. "You posted glow-dots, right?"

"Of course." Dai sounded annoyed, and she gestured an apology.

"Sorry. Stay, I think. If it happens again, we'll rethink it."

"Better rethink it now." The stranger's voice came from the hatch.

Cassilde spun, reaching for the blaster at her hip, froze as she registered the leveled weapons. There were three of them—no, four, all with heavy military-surplus blasters and body armor over their work vests. Dai swore, and she lifted her hands to show them empty. They must have come from the strange ship, she thought, damped *Carabosse*'s sensors with their own web. The flicker in the power had been the ship's final protest against their attack. It wasn't impossible, but it was difficult enough that she had discounted the possibility, and they were all going to pay for her mistake.

"Smart woman," the stranger said. He stepped through the hatch, still with his blaster leveled, a wiry man with a pointed chin and muscles that stood out like brackets at the corners of his mouth. "Hello, Ashe."

Dai swore again, not softly.

Ashe gave a bitter smile. "Hello, darling."

The words dripped venom, and the stranger smiled. "Did you really think I wouldn't follow you?"

"I thought we had an agreement," Ashe said. He was keeping his hands in plain sight, raised shoulder high, but the heavy handlight was in his left hand, a possible weapon. Seeing that, Cassilde shifted her weight, tipping ever so slightly to her right. Only the stranger had actually entered the compartment; if Ashe distracted him, there was a chance she could drop behind the closest of the woven-silver beds, and use her blaster from there. It was lighter than the weapons the pirates were carrying, but deadly enough at this short range.

"Agreements change." The stranger was scanning the compartment, weapon still leveled, but his eyes elsewhere. Dai saw it, too, and slid one foot forward, but the stranger focused on him instantly. "Don't."

Dai dipped his head in acknowledgement, and in the same moment Ashe swung the heavy light. The stranger stepped into the blow, blocking it with his forearm, and brought the barrel of his blaster hard across Ashe's face. Ashe dropped to his knees, and Cassilde dove for the dubious shelter of the woven bed, fumbling for her own weapon. Fire creased her shoulder, and her hand spasmed; she dropped her blaster, fingers nerveless, and scrabbled for it with her other hand, heedless now of shelter.

"Don't move," the stranger said, and stepped closer to Ashe, still on his knees. There was blood on his mouth and nose, a bruise already rising on his sallow cheek. "All right, Ashe. Where is it?"

"I don't know."

"Don't waste my time."

"I don't know," Ashe said again.

The stranger lowered the muzzle of his blaster until it rested against Ashe's temple. Ashe glared up at him.

"If you kill me—"

"Oh, never you," the stranger said. He turned on his heel, the blaster shifting aim before Cassilde could even register his intent. Fire cracked, and the impact knocked her backward, pain filling her belly. She curled around it, too stunned to cry out, heard Dai call her name as if from an immense distance.

"You bastard," Ashe said. "You son of a bitch—"

"She might live," the stranger said. "But her clock's running." There was the sound of a scuffle. "That's right, hold him."

That had to be Dai, Cassilde thought. She rocked slowly, trying to ease the pain, but it clawed up her spine, down into her hips, every nerve on fire.

"Where is it?" the stranger said again. "I'm waiting, Ashe."

"It's not here," Ashe said. "I thought it would be, but it's not—and since it's not, it has to be—I'll take you, I'll show you, I swear—but let me take care of Silde first."

"Two minutes," the stranger said.

Tears filmed Cassilde's eyes, blurring her vision. The pain

rolled over her in waves, threatening to drown her; she fought through it, gasping, and Ashe knelt at her side.

They each carried first aid, but the kits were inadequate for something like this. Cassilde heard Ashe crack open his package and then hers, flinched as he pressed both bandage packs against the wound.

"I will fucking kill you," Dai said, somewhere in the distance, and she didn't know if he was talking to Ashe or to the stranger Ashe had called darling.

There was a sharp pain in her forearm, unfairly distinct against the background agony, and then another. She twisted her head to see, and realized that Ashe had planted both the shock buttons in the flesh of her arm. Already the drugs were taking hold, and she blinked up at him, expecting at least some apology.

"Green, then the red," he said, so softly she barely heard him. His back was to the stranger, to Dai, hiding the movement of his lips. "First green, then the red curtain."

"Time's up," the stranger said. He moved to Ashe's side, laid the barrel of the blaster against Ashe's cheek so that it pointed past him at Cassilde. "Come on, Ashe, time to go."

"I'm coming," Ashe said. The stranger stepped back smoothly, and Ashe rose to his feet with only a single backward glance.

"All right," the stranger said. "Ashe, you will take me to the device. Usslo, bring that one along."

He must mean Dai, Cassilde thought, blinking hard. The buttons' effect was building, beating the pain back to manageable levels, giving her new strength. She lay still, hoarding it—she would have one good effort, she didn't dare waste it—and the stranger turned away.

"Ashe, if you cross me, I'll kill him, too."

"I understand." Ashe's voice was tight with fury.

"What about her?" That was one of the others, though she couldn't tell which one. The stranger glanced back at her and gave a tiny shrug.

"Leave her. She's not going anywhere."

Cassilde closed her eyes, shuddering, another wave of pain washing through her. When she opened them, the strangers were gone, leaving her alone in the sea-shell room, the harsh worklights throwing doubled shadows. The buttons had kicked in, giving her all the strength she was ever going to have, and nothing useful to do with it. It wasn't fair that she should die like this, when she'd been more or less resigned to Lightman's, not fair at all.

She hooked one hand over the edge of the silver bed, hauled herself to a sitting position. Ashe's bandages were doing their job, just like the buttons, staunching the blood where the blast hadn't cauterized the wound. She recovered her blaster, checking to be sure the charge was still good. Now what? She clutched the blaster harder as another wave of pain rolled through her, and fought to breathe against it. She doubted she could walk; crawling after them was only going to waste what little strength she had.

And what the hell had Ashe meant, whispering about color? Green, then red—no, she thought, GREEN, then RED. GREEN she had, tucked into the pocket of her vest. It might, it should, give her more strength, maybe enough to stand. She reached for it, fumbled the tiny box, and had to put the blaster down to open it. The sliver of GREEN was less than a centimeter long, and barely thicker than a hair: a quarter's profit, and all her discretionary income for the year. She licked her fingertip, picked it up, and transferred it to her tongue before she could change her mind.

The GREEN fizzed, bitter and cold, filling her mouth with metallic saliva. She'd never taken so much at once, and she swallowed hard, once and then twice. The wound in her stomach protested, but the pain was distanced, manageable. She imagined she could feel the GREEN crawling through her nervous system, freezing the pain and shock, and hauled herself to her feet before she could think too much about it.

The blaster was on the floorplates at her feet. She swore

silently, unable to bend, and made herself concentrate on Ashe's words. GREEN, then RED—but there was no RED anywhere in sight, unless he'd meant for her to break one of the Ancestral devices? She had the cutter still, but that would take time, and the sound would surely bring Ashe's "darling" or his men. She would kill Ashe for that herself, later. She laughed silently. It seemed unlikely there would be a "later."

GREEN, then RED. First GREEN, check, she'd done that, then RED—no, then the red *curtain*.

The red curtain, the shimmering veil of scarlet thread that covered half the narrow alcove, the alcove that probably was Ashe's mysterious life-saving device. First take the GREEN, and then the red curtain... She staggered toward it, her feet slurring on the floor. The buttons' effects were starting to wear off, the pain surging; the GREEN pulsed cold with every heartbeat, so cold she thought her bones would crack, her fingers blacken.

The curtain swayed as she came close, a few tentative strands lifting as though to sample the air. She stopped, swaying herself, unsure of what she was really seeing, and still more threads rose, reaching for the exposed skin of her face, her hands. Their touch was pleasant, sweet and soothing, warm as the smell of tea. She let herself be wound in, the threads tugging her gently forward until she was entirely surrounded, tucked into the alcove. Its walls shifted against her, forming to her body, and the final layer of the curtain swept in to enclose her. She felt an instant of panic, but then sleepy warmth suffused her, the pain retreating to nothing, and her eyes closed.

She opened them again an infinity later, her breath easier than it had been in years, the pain a receding memory. She filled her lungs, marveling at the play of muscles and ribs, flattened her hand against her stomach. Vest and shirt and undershirt were in tatters, but her skin was smooth and whole. The last of the threads dropped from her shoulders, unwound from her ankles, dissolving into dust. Out of power? Their job complete? She hoped it was the latter, hoped she would have the time to find out. But for now, there was Darling to worry about.

She scooped up her blaster, the charge still ready, and for good measure drew her cutter and set it to standby before she slid it into her belt. It wouldn't be much help unless she got into hand-to-hand, and that was to be avoided, but it was better than nothing.

Armed, she peered out the circular hatch. The corridor was dark, but lights moved in the distance, in the nearer of the two compartments between this one and the one with the linked circles. She eased through the hatch, still amazed that her body responded, pressed her back to the bulkhead as she moved as quietly as she could toward the light.

She heard the voices before she was close enough to see, Darling's cool and calm.

"I'm not buying it, Ashe."

"I swear," Ashe said. "This is the only other place to look, and—I don't know. Maybe I got it wrong. Maybe there's nothing here."

"You don't make mistakes," Darling said.

"Yes, I do. Even I do," Ashe said. "I just got it wrong."

"Usslo!" There was scuffling, and a choked sound that might have been Dai, before Darling spoke again. "Ashe, you are determined to be difficult."

"I'm not, I swear. I got it wrong—"

Cassilde reached the door, angled her head carefully to see inside. Dai was on his knees, his hands clasped on his head, a man wearing a monocular holding a blaster to his head. Ashe stood beside a hole in the bulkhead, the edges still black from the cutter's beam. There was RED inside, glimmering in the single worklight, RED and GOLD and maybe even a hint of GREEN—a season's solid work, a lucky find, and still Darling shook his head.

"A Gift was here, I know that. Don't make me do this."

There was no more time. Cassilde took a step, aimed, and

fired twice, catching One-Eye in neck and chest. He fell forward, and Dai rolled with him, scrambling for the dropped blaster. Cassilde turned her blaster on Darling, two shots, three, four, all to the chest and belly, driving him back—

"Silde!" That was Dai, blaster in hand, Darling's last two men crumpled against the bulkhead, and Cassilde drew a shaken breath.

"I'm fine," she said.

"Yeah, but how—-" Dai stopped abruptly, and Cassilde nodded.

"He knows." She looked at Ashe. "You do, don't you?"

"It was the device," Ashe said. His voice cracked. "That was the thing, the lifesaver, oh, God. The Gift. It worked."

"We need to get out of here," Dai said. "There's no telling who else he's got." He kicked Darling's body, not gently.

"He works alone or with small teams," Ashe said. He had himself under control now, only the faintest trembling of the handlight to betray him. "This should be it."

Cassilde took a breath. "We will discuss how you know that later—"

"I need to look at the Gift," Ashe said. "Please, Silde. It's more important than you know."

"We don't have time for that," Dai said. "Are you fucking crazy?"

"Shut up, both of you," Cassilde said. "Ashe, the device—it worked on me, and then the red stuff just dissolved. I don't think there's much left to look at."

Ashe closed his eyes. "Damn it..."

Cassilde ignored him, scanning the compartment. Dai was right, they needed to get away, get out of range of any of Darling's friends still lurking nearby, but there was also too much easy salvage to abandon. "All right. Clean out that cache, quick and dirty. Anything else we see on the way, grab it, but no more cutting. We'll come back if we can."

Dai was already moving to obey, pulling gloves and expandables from his pockets to collect the Ancestral elements, and after a moment Ashe joined him, pulling out RED and GOLD in enormous expensive lumps. At any other moment, Cassilde would have been breathless with delight—this was a massive find, a solid year's expenses paid for and more—but there was no time. They needed to get back to *Carabosse*, get themselves into the protection of the Guard. Then they could think about coming back.

The cache was empty, at least of the largest pieces. There would be more, crumbs and fragments, but there was no time to search further. "Back to the ship," she said, and pinned Ashe with a look. "And you owe me answers."

"Yes," he said, and that was strange enough that she nearly dropped her carryall.

"Move," she said.

Carabosse made an emergency lift from the chunk of wreckage, blowing the pitons and leaving the depleted atmosphere cartridge behind. They left Darling's ship grappled to the opposite side of the claim as well, over Ashe's protests, and set a fast course for the nearest Guard beacon. Cassilde adjusted the sensor net to its widest sweep, and set the active systems to random scan—she'd rather someone caught the pings than miss any pursuit from any more of Darling's men, no matter what Ashe said about the man working alone—and made her way back to Central.

She still couldn't believe how good she felt. It wasn't just that the blaster wound was gone, it was that she could breathe, that her muscles moved with a fluid ease she could barely remember. Her joints no longer clicked and popped, she no longer stepped cautiously to avoid setting off shooting pains from the ankle she'd broken the year before. The Lightman's was gone, she was sure of that, the incurable cured, but even more, all the minor aches and pains that came with age were also gone. Even the marks of the shock buttons had vanished, though there should have been puncture marks and deep bruises. They had to get back to the claim, recover what was left of the Gift.

Ashe was sitting at the unfolded table, his head tipped back to that Dai could tape his broken nose. Both eyes were blackened, and there was another swelling bruise on his left cheek.

"You look like hell," Cassilde said. She wasn't sure she was sorry, either, and felt vaguely guilty.

"Done," Dai said, and Ashe sat up slowly. Dai turned away from the table, bundling the scraps from the aid kit into the disposal, then collected a bottle and glasses from the cabinet and poured them each a stiff drink. Ashe downed half of his in a single wincing gulp and held out his glass for a refill.

"Don't be in too much of a hurry," Cassilde said, and sat down across from him. "We need to talk."

"I know." Ashe took a more careful sip of the whiskey, and Dai perched on the edge of the table beside him.

"So what just happened?" Cassilde asked. Her own whiskey tasted wonderful, sweet and sharp and perfectly chilled.

"How are you feeling?" Ashe asked in turn.

Cassilde looked at him. "Well. Better than well. What just happened, Ashe?"

Ashe glanced at Dai, still looming, and wrapped his hands around his glass. "It's—it was a Gift. The Ancestors made them, very rarely. We have no idea why, only that they exist—"

"Wait a minute," Dai said. "You're talking about a Miracle Box. I thought you didn't believe in them."

"I was wrong," Ashe said. Something between a smile and a grimace crossed his face. "About this, too."

"We'll get back to him later," Cassilde said. "You're telling me that Miracle Boxes are real."

"You're here," Ashe said, with some asperity. "You should be dead."

Twice over, if not from the blaster bolt then from the

Lightman's, shock triggering a deadly attack. That was what she'd always expected would happen. Cassilde took another sip of her drink, sharp on her tongue and warm all the way down to her healed belly. "And you knew it would be there."

"I suspected." Ashe took a breath. "The Ancestors made the Gifts—that's the word they used, not Miracle Box. Who knows why, and who knows why they left them, just the way they left everything else. But sometimes you find one, and it works. It heals the sick, revives the dying, cures everything from madness to Lightman's to the common cold. It works once, three times, a hundred times—there are traditional shrines on some of the late-settled worlds that have to have begun as Miracle Boxes. And sometimes you find one that's special. It only works once, but it carries a bonus. Not only does it heal whatever ails you, but—it changes you. You become one of them."

"No," Cassilde said. Even as she spoke, the denial faded, replaced by appalled certainty. That explained how she felt, the intense sensation, the fizzing energy along her veins.

Dai said, "You're saying Silde has become an Ancestor?"

"I don't know for sure," Ashe said. "You'd have to test it, and I don't have the tools to do it without actually harming her. But, yes, I think so. That was what the bug was telling me, that there was a special Gift there on the wreck."

"You're not cutting her," Dai said, and Cassilde spoke over him.

"You mean that I heal like the Ancestors? That I'll never be sick again? That I'll live forever, stay forever just as I am?"

"If I'm right," Ashe said. "Yes."

"So." Cassilde stretched to reach across the table, grabbed the serving knife from its slot in the edge of the table.

"Silde—" Dai's voice broke.

"Let's find out," Cassilde said, and drew the blade across the skin of her forearm. It parted at the touch, welling blood and then a pain sharp enough to stop breath, far more than she had expected. She swayed, and the cut began to close, the blood reabsorbed, skin flowing over it, fading from pink to white to tan. Ashe let out a breath as though he'd been holding it, and Dai shook his head.

"God, Silde."

"And there we are," she said. It was hard to get her mind around it, but she was trying, the possibilities crowding in on her. There were things she could do now, things she'd put aside—and things she'd lose, over and over, never aging, never dying, but she thrust that thought aside. She would find a way to fix that, find a way to bring the others with her, so she wouldn't be alone. She had all the time there was to find an answer. She smiled, slow and fierce. "All the myths are true."

Bad Day on Boscobel

Alexander Jablokov

Dunya stopped just outside Phineus's unit to calm herself down. Otherwise she would burst in and start screaming at him. That was no way to start a check-in meeting with one of her refugees.

That gave her a chance to realize that she looked like hell. She'd already had one fight that morning, with her daughter Bodil, and afterwards she had rushed out, unsnapped and unbrushed. It was hard enough to manage someone like Phineus, all Martian and precise, without giving him more ammunition about how lax things were here, among the asteroids.

She stepped out of the foot traffic, pulled out her kit, sharpened her eyebrows, got her pale hair in some semblance of order, and cleaned sleep and tears out of the corners of her eyes.

They'd put Phineus low down, not far above actual rock, in a line of wooden cubicles along a root. Leaves rustled overhead. But there was no dramatic view up past the trunks to the spreading branches of the famed Boscobel axis, just some fibrous safety panels and a moving ladderway. Phineus sometimes grouched about what it said about his status.

There. Bodil had gone straight to bed after their fight. Dunya had a full day ahead of her. Looking good might be poor revenge on an ungrateful child, but that was what she had. And it had relaxed her enough. Now she was ready for that idiot.

When she got into his narrow space, her most difficult refugee sat on his bed, bony knees against his chest. Phineus's cliff of a face swept up into an impressive brow and forehead. It was almost too big for the room.

"I didn't expect you for a couple more days," he said.

So she'd been getting predictable. And he wanted her to know it, which was interesting. "I have something to talk to you about."

"Am I in trouble?" He smiled.

She didn't answer.

"Look," he said. "I'm happy to see you. It's kind of a treat. Not a lot happens down here."

"I was just over in Lower Cort. In the Wendell Beech, about a third of the way up."

"Nice spot," he said. "If you're the sort who likes nice spots, that is. I never pegged you for the type."

"The branches sag down there," she said. "Thick growth. If you climb up bough 73, then slide a bit down the branches there, you'll find a bunch of these." She flipped something across to him. He caught it. "All hanging from strings, blowing in the breeze. They're getting tangled up in the twigs. Someone should have given them a bit more weight in the lower parts."

Phineus looked expressionlessly at the doll in his hand. It was made from human hair, looped and woven together, with the loose ends bursting from the top of its head in a huge fall. Its face was miserable, with downturned mouth and squinted eyes, like a child with a stomach ache. It might have been almost cute, but it was all held together by something thick and sticky.

"You know that's blood, right?" she asked.

"Look, I don't—"

"It's gang sign, Phineus. Green Burnings. They jump the boughs around here. Sometimes keeping order, sometimes tearing it up. They're Root & Branch party supporters, field workers, and enforcers. Things have been fairly balanced lately. But if the Green Burnings push up into Five Boughs, there's going to be trouble with the Trunk. I don't know how things are on Mars, but it's not just about gang territory here on Boscobel. It's always got another dimension. The Trunkers are losing support from small businesses who think the party's not protecting their interests. Burnings jumping through Five Boughs will only make that more obvious. Things might get rough."

"I still don't understand local politics," he said.

"That's exactly why you shouldn't be messing around with it."

"Me? What do I have to do with it?"

That expression of outraged innocence was the last straw. Dunya snatched the doll from his hand, startling the old Martian corridor fighter with her speed, and stuck it back in her pocket. "You know them. Hang out with them. Give them a bit of training. Just keeping your Martian hand in? Or something more? In any case, you're going to get into trouble. Not just with some rival group. With me."

"How did—"

"My sources are none of your business." She wasn't going to reveal that she had learned it entirely by chance, by fighting with her daughter just that morning, not because she had previously had any interest in what he was doing.

"You've got the wrong guy. I see that detritus, sure. Green Burnings, whatever. They flip off branches above me while I'm catching some breakfast out at Kumar's. We got to talking. So maybe I gave them some tactical tips, just to keep my hand in. But I don't drill them or anything like that. Maybe they hired from outside. I mean, there are Martians hanging around Preem Bough. Maybe they've set up a school or something."

This was unexpected. "You're the only Martian in Boscobel."

"Piece of information, Dunya: there is always another Martian. We're tricky that way."

"So you've seen other Martians out there?" she said.

"Oh, you know, rumors. Someone uncomfortable with all the plant life is up there, looking for trouble. It would be nice to see someone from the old dustball." He looked bleak. "But it's probably false. I'm the only Martian here. Stuck down in the roots, going nowhere."

Once Phineus started feeling sorry for himself, he usually went all the way and ended up lying face down on the floor, refusing to respond. It could last for days.

She didn't have time for that. "Phineus. Let me be clear. No more combat training. From now on. And no contact with anyone who jumps with Green Burnings. It will endanger your status if you do. Do you understand?"

"What does that mean? Say I want to go up to Kumar's. If a Burning comes in and gets coffee while I'm there, do I have to pack it up and leave?"

"If you're going to ask, I'm going to tell you. Yes. Don't even share a common space with them until I say otherwise." Phineus kept himself clean, but his room was a mess, with clothes shoved places that must have taken more work than just putting them away properly. He even had a couple of noodle-parlor containers under a cushion. She resisted the urge to lecture him about it. "You like to bring your food home. If you see a gang member, just do that. Any more questions?"

"If I ask, I'll find out I have to stay in my room. So, no."

"Smart man. Just find yourself a better hobby."

He didn't raise his head as she left.

Bodil had sauntered in that morning just as Dunya was getting ready to leave for work. She smelled of trees far from where she was supposed to be, with a couple of girlfriends: every spot in Boscobel had its own combination of gums, saps, pollens, nectars, and oils. Bodil relied too much on the fact that her mother wasn't a native, and sometimes had trouble with the more subtle signals.

When Bodil tried to just brush past her mother on her way to her room, Dunya had blocked her path with an outstretched leg. First Bodil had denied she had been anywhere. Then she said she'd told her mother about it, but she, distracted and too busy, had forgotten. Then she denied that her mother had any authority that meant anything.

"And where is Dad?" Bodil had said, through too-ready tears. "Why isn't he ever here? What's he trying to get away from?"

Bryn *was* away a lot. Dunya didn't like it either.

But the fight had come with one unexpected benefit. After Dunya had started in about Bodil's on-again, off-again boyfriend Unray, who jumped with the Green Burnings, Bodil had burst out with a defense of his capabilities. "He's the one who figures out their tactics. He's learned a lot, don't think he hasn't. Martian stuff, not like the other gangs. It's a whole other level of activity. You should see how he's marked their territory over at Wendell Beech..."

Her mother's sudden interest told Bodil she'd made a mistake boasting about that. But it was too late. Dunya connected that information with other things she'd learned, and understood something of what Phineus was up to. She let her daughter go, already planning a detour to Lower Cort on her way to Phineus.

Bodil could try to use Bryn as a weapon, she thought now, as she climbed to her next appointment. It would still be just the two of them for quite some time. They'd have to fight it out on their own.

She rose through several layers of the great branches that made up the dwelling levels of Boscobel. Sometimes the view went out a great distance, revealing a group of people at a table, a prowling cat, a vortex of rain renewing pockets of water in the great branches. Usually it was compacted, held in by leaves and lattice. She finally stepped off onto a busy pathway and made her way between shops and the small personal gardens people here kept in front of their units.

No matter where you were, most of Boscobel was invisible, but from this level, about a third of the way up, you got the best feel for what this world was. Boscobel was trees, the biggest trees in the solar system. They stuck their roots deep into the crust, flung themselves across the axis of the spinning cylinder of the asteroid, and then plunged into the opposite side, where their upper branches became roots. In between, vast boughs spread, providing living and production areas. Some had developed leaves meters across or complex meshes of interlaced branches. Though they still bore names like sycamore and juniper, they had only slight resemblances to their earth-rooted ancestors.

"I started out late," she said, as she came up to Fama's dining area. "I'm not catching up."

"That's okay, you can help me get things ready. Let's roll this out."

Dunya pushed hot tables loaded with steaming pots out onto the balcony that looked out over a wide opening among the trees. Nothing dramatic, but a nice spot. It was shaded by a couple of gigantic leaves, each of which had bugs scurrying in its furry underside. To any asteroid-dweller eye, Boscobeli or not, that was comforting. It meant that, no matter what else happened, you wouldn't starve.

Fama was a big woman who seemed to wear all of her clothes at the same time. The outer garment was always different, but Dunya thought she recognized a couple of the layers underneath. It was cooler than average here, where a breeze came down from the distant North Pole. But she didn't think that was the explanation. Fama was still ready to flee, and wanted to make sure she had everything she needed with her when the time came.

"Any shakedowns recently?" Dunya asked.

"None, thanks to your suggestion."

Dunya tried to remember what she had come up with. "Ah, Strop."

Fama shrugged. "He knows his food, I'll give him that."

Merv Strop was an agent of the Office of Adversary Knowledge, Boscobel's internal security force. Fama had been getting harassed by some low-level thugs from the Dead Roots, competitors to those Green Burnings Phineus gave tactics classes to. Dunya had suggested that she invite agent Strop to dine, in a visible way. The Dead Roots had moved off to find an easier target, while Strop had stayed.

"He's actually got a real crime to solve, I hear," Fama said. "Someone took off with an ancient emergency kit from some secure area. It's sweating his skull, making him ornery."

Dunya had to get to business. "I'm curious about someone. In the area. A Martian, I've heard."

"Anything else? Martians don't got red dots on their foreheads to make them easy to spot."

Dunya had found a few minutes to check up on available tourist entries. She had access because tourists were sometimes refugees in disguise—or ended up as refugees when a political shift back home left them unable to return after their relaxing vacation lounging in a tree branch. No Martians had turned up, but there was one good possibility, from the inner-belt asteroid Fortuna. Fortuna had close relations with Mars, and might have been willing to cooperate in screening someone's identity. If so, this person had some connections to the Martian government, but was probably operating unofficially.

"It's someone a fairly tough guy would still be nervous about. One possibility is a woman, supposedly from Fortuna." And Phineus had been nervous. Who knew what enemies Phineus might have made back on Mars?

"I need some critters," Fama said. "Soup's kind of bland."

Dunya helped pluck bugs from the underside of the leaf. Most of them escaped her fingers. Fama grabbed writhing handfuls and dumped them into the steaming pot. Their shells puffed, and their dissolving legs gave the stock the saffron color that marked its quality. A restaurant depended on the diet of its feedbugs as much as it did on the skill of its chef.

"That might actually explain a few things, though." Fama tasted, and nodded in satisfaction. "That's enough now. Let the rest go."

The bugs scurried into the fibers. "You've seen someone?" Dunya said.

"Didn't think 'Martian' till you said. A woman. Tall. Does claim to be from Fortuna but moves like she grew up in gravity. No obvious business. Has a drink here, chats with someone there. But she's working hard the whole time. No relaxation in her." Fama was desperate to expand her business, kept her eye on competitors and potential customers.

"Any idea where I can find her?"

"She sleeps at the Moss, I think."

Fama was looking over Dunya's shoulder to see who might have come in. She should let the woman get to her business.

"Anything else you need to talk about?" Dunya said.

"Well..." Fama was suddenly reluctant. "Tell me. How long did it take you to feel that you fit in?"

"Here in Boscobel?" Dunya made it a principle to be honest with her clients. Sometimes that was difficult. "Most days I don't feel I fit in at all. But sometimes, when I stand under a dripping leaf and watch the white gibbons jump the gap at Gantan, I think I should never have been anywhere else."

Fama scooped a bug out of the soup and sucked thoughtfully on its head. "Hope for me yet, then."

"Hope for us all."

A couple of clients later, Dunya was at the Moss, a set of rental rooms on stilts above the mosses that gave the name. This woman was after Phineus for something, and Phineus was nervous about it. His casualness had been unconvincing. If she was keeping Phineus under observation, Dunya had a chance to maybe spot her.

Phineus wouldn't listen to a thing Dunya had told him. He'd go to breakfast, meeting with a Green Burning or two, maybe in a corner, so as not to be obvious. If this woman, whoever she was, meant to keep him under observation, that would be an easy spot. If Phineus then went back to sulk in his unit, the woman might take the opportunity to come back to the Moss to take care of other business. If she did, she would most likely skirt the roots of the big ash tree.

That was a lot of assumptions. But Boscobel was incredibly resistant to travel if you didn't know it well. Once visitors learned a useful route, they tended to stick to it. Dunya found a spot by a mossy root where she could watch, get work done, and have someone bring her a coffee every now and then.

After an hour or so, she had updated everyone's files. Just as she was considering giving it up, she saw an odd bit of movement. Someone had started down the stairs from the direction of Phineus, glanced across the open area below, then stepped back. Somehow, Dunya had been spotted.

Now Dunya was even more interested. Who was this woman? And why was she so anxious to avoid an interview?

She'd been successful in predicting the Martian's route home, at least. Where would the woman go now? She'd probably planned out some escape route and bolthole, for contingencies. Dunya was used to people trying to avoid her.

What choices would have seemed smart to a Martian corridor dweller who hadn't had the time to work out the intricacies of Boscobel? The main question was: up or down? Right here was a mazelike sprawl of roots. Concealment would seem easier, and it was just the kind of place that would give comfort to a Martian.

But she would have thought past that. She'd try to be unpredictable, at least to herself. And she'd want to use the ways in which Boscobel differed from her home. She'd want things to be interesting. She'd climb.

There were three good routes up from here. The closest one was exposed in most directions, easily seen. One of the other two, then.

As it happened, both those routes hit a bottleneck in the understory, in a volume that had suffered a fire a couple of decades before. Several branches had not regrown to useful size, so both those routes would kink back to near the ash trunk.

Dunya knew another way up. It was longer and involved climbing higher, into the crown. There was no on-bough route there, where a high wind swept the branches. To the inexperienced eye, it looked impassable. But Dunya knew a tunnel *inside* a bough, the result of a cleared-out fungal infection, that sometimes served as swing housing for low-status new dwellers. She'd have to step over people's shitpots, but they knew her there. After that a drop-down would put her across where the Martian would have to go. That should persuade her that Dunya was someone she had to pay attention to.

No matter what, after that she had to get home, find her daughter, and try to keep the rest of her life under repair. She grabbed a ladderway and rose up.

The sunglobe had moved past its brightest point and lunchtime had gone past when Dunya found herself in a wet space under massive leaves. Water burped up onto the ridged surfaces, and cascaded down to the hanging gardens below. Only a few misguided frogs clinging to strands of pale fungus gave hints of life elsewhere.

This was part of Boscobel's secret support equipment. Fluid-filled tubes along the walls carried nourishment to the higher reaches of the impossible trees. Light fibers pumped photons into photosynthetic centers to support metabolisms that couldn't possibly get all their energy from the mostly decorative sunglobe.

The woman now dodged through a small café that hung from the rough bark of the oak bough just below here. It was a good spot to check for pursuit.

Too bad for her that Dunya was ahead of her, not behind.

She was a long-limbed woman with big hands and feet. With the strength in her shoulders she looked like she could have picked up the entire café and shaken everything out of it.

But instead of revealing any force, she moved smoothly, sliding past people before they even knew she was there. She wore her dark brown hair loose, a style more suitable to a Martian corridor than leafy Boscobel. She'd clearly bought that tree-silk jacket here, though, and it suited the length of her torso. Dunya pulled herself back into concealment.

The chase had taken her out of herself. Now all the worries of the day came back to her. As cold water dripped on the back of her neck, she worried about her afternoon schedule, about her next encounter with Bodil, about whether Bryn would send her a message today. The longer he was away, the more entertaining his messages got, a bad sign. A poorly healed pipe with a lumpy joint vibrated under her boot, and she saw that it had shaken a couple of the big leaves loose from their adhesive connections with each other. Pushing back with her elbow and feeling the leaves peel away from each other was like childishly poking at a loose tooth with your tongue, pleasant and disturbing at once. Looked at too closely, much of Boscobel was falling apart.

She slid out of concealment. Where was the woman? Had Dunya miscalculated?

She felt the breath behind her. There was no time to respond. Something hit the back of her head and knocked her forward. She rolled, and found herself looking up at a long boot that pushed on her throat, and beyond it, slowly coming into focus, the Martian.

The woman wasn't beautiful, but she was certainly striking, with dark skin, high cheekbones, and big eyes the color of moss agate.

"Who the hell are you?" Dunya said.

"I could ask you the same thing," the Martian said.

"You could, but you have no right to. I'm a citizen of Boscobel trying to get through my day. You're the one who snuck in here in pursuit of Phineus Gora."

"And who is Phineus Gora to you?"

"My client. He's a refugee. I'm responsible for grafting

him onto Boscobel."

"Good luck with that." The woman was amused. "So you look out for him."

"I look out for all my refugees. It's my job. He's worried about why you're here."

"But he didn't give you any details, hoping your sense of responsibility would put you in my way." The amused look disappeared. "He had no right to risk you that way. His problems should stay his own." She pulled her boot off Dunya's throat.

For a second, Dunya didn't know what to do.

"Get up, get up." The woman was impatient. "You've tempted me into... actually, I think you've tempted me into exactly what Phineus hoped. Exposing myself. Giving the OAKs a reason to throw me out of Boscobel. Maybe he's smarter than he seems."

Dunya sat up. What *had* Phineus gotten her to do?

"He knows who you are," Dunya said.

The woman laughed. "He thinks he does."

"But I still have no idea."

"It may not matter. But... my name is Miriam Kostal. I'm from Mars."

"Dunya Hautala."

"Let me be short. Phineus is the inside man for a filibustering expedition that left Mars orbit two months ago and will be here within a day. Does that mean anything to you?"

Anarchic Mars had turned into a menace to everyone between the orbits of Jupiter and Earth. A weak central government, recovering from assassination and attempted revolution, was unable to stop ambitious groups from putting together military expeditions to seize individual asteroids and set themselves up as ruling juntas. As a girl, Dunya had fled just such a takeover, finally fetching up on Boscobel.

"And so you take a room at the Moss and follow Phineus around?" Dunya said. "How much sense does that make? Do the OAKs know? Anyone else?"

"No one knows. Even on Mars. Filibustering expeditions

rarely succeed without cooperation from their targets, either tacit or explicit. On Mars, the expedition has some official support. Here... I have no idea who might be involved. Anyone could have an interest in rearranging things to end up closer to the top. Phineus is a technician, not anyone involved in political discussions. He's got a specific mission, assisting the initial penetration by the attacking force. I can't trust anyone here. But I don't need to. All I need to do is figure out what he's doing, and stop it. Then I can be on my way."

Miriam was almost persuasive. It was always tempting to skip the mess of political compromise and get straight to the decisive action. And Boscobel sure was a mess. Dunya didn't even try to deny it. But decisive action always left its own mess, to be cleaned up by people like her, while people like Miriam strode off in search of some other dramatic problem to fix.

Dunya slid herself to sit with her back against the loose leaves.

"The complexities of corruption are all we've got," Dunya said. "I'm sure not everyone's looking forward to being ruled by someone else. If you have information that will help our government fend off an attack, you should share it."

"No. I'll be arrested. And now you. Any investigation will be ended by the new regime. End of story. End of us."

That was plausible enough. But Miriam hadn't even tried getting cooperation. Dunya found herself irritated at the woman, impressive though she was. Boscobel was her home. She didn't like thinking of it as a clump of trees run by people instantly eager to betray it for a better deal.

The bottom of the leaves was loose. The top still stuck. She didn't have time to work on it more. She had no real reason to trust Miriam. She had to make contact with someone. She leaned her head back, as if thinking it over, and pushed harder. She knew there was a branch about ten feet below, where she could find a quick route down. The leaves parted behind her and she fell through.

From the last glimpse of her face, Miriam was taken completely by surprise. But she recovered almost instantly. She dove forward, whipped out a long arm, and just managed to snag Dunya's ankle as she fell. Stopping Dunya's fall almost jerked her out of the gap. She braced one foot against the ripping leaf and swung Dunya to the side, until she dangled over a much longer drop. The endless network of tree boughs circled around her.

She could tell Miriam was considering it. People would pretty much assume that Dunya had tried something too difficult for a non-native to do properly. "Poor Dunya never quite got the hang of it..."

With a sudden effort, Miriam hauled her in. Dunya curled up and grabbed the edge of the leaf. Finally, she lay on the floor next to Miriam, sucking in air.

"Nice move," Miriam said. "You practice that?"

"A sudden inspiration."

"Look," Miriam said. "You want to go to the OAKs for help? I can't stop you. It won't help, and it might put this whole world at hazard. But it's up to you."

"Would you really have killed me?" Dunya said.

"An impolite question. We've been slashing each other's faces on Mars for a decade or more now, trying to solve problems by eliminating the people we think are causing them. Hasn't worked for us, but it's habit now."

"Not for you, though."

"I wouldn't rely on the quality of my habits, if I were you. Go. Go now. Before I get sensible."

Dunya could feel the stare of those agate eyes like something physical. She thought about saying something else, but nothing, not even "good luck", made sense. Without another word, she turned and went.

"Eh?" Strop looked up from his soup. "Dunya. What are

you doing here?"

"I want to ask you some questions."

"Well, I..." Strop grunted in annoyance as Dunya pulled a chair up and joined him at his table. "Suit yourself, then."

Strop's pale hair lay plastered to a soft-looking skull. He was the local OAK agent, and as OAKs went, he was a decent sort. OAKs didn't go very far, Dunya reminded herself.

"What do you know about Phineus?" she said. "I mean, what drove him from Mars, why he's here. Who he's in contact with."

Strop swallowed a spoonful of the soup and closed his eyes. He was known for his devotion to food, and his presence at a restaurant actually served as a sign of approval. So maybe Fama wasn't quite the victim she made herself sound.

"Phineus is your client, isn't he?"

"Of course," Dunya said.

"So it's your job to make sure he stays out of trouble. What we pay you for. Didn't you do some kind of intake when you got him? Then you know he's a protected exile. Unable to return to Mars, but protected by Martian law. A Martian trying to kill him would be in serious trouble on return home. Anyone after him would have an unusual devotion to justice. Please be more vigilant about your intakes. They give you at least little preliminary information. Too bad we don't get to do one when we have a child. That's why children can surprise you. They never fill out the proper forms."

Strop had two well-liked and successful children, both older than Bodil. It was just exasperating.

She thought about giving him Miriam Kostal. *That* he'd have to pay attention to. But Miriam had gauged her right. She couldn't do it.

And she was reflecting that there were probably good reasons why Phineus had been dumped on her without much background information. Did Strop know those reasons? In any event, bringing that up would either sound like whining or be actively dangerous.

"Look, Dunya." Fama had whisked away the soup, careful to show no sign she'd seen Dunya earlier, and the sculpted pyramid that steamed in front of him smelled delicious. "I appreciate that you've gotten a yen to get better at your job. These impulses never last. If you don't mind a bit of friendly advice, I'd say that you should look after your own family situation instead."

"My family situation?" Dunya said. "What the hell is that supposed to mean?"

He pursed his disconcertingly full lips, pleased that he'd pissed her off. "Children can be a handful. Sometimes they can even do things that pass beyond the childish, and get in real trouble. Are you heading home soon?"

"I don't think that's your business."

"If you're hoping to find your daughter there, give up on that notion. She's found herself a hidey hole. She seems to think it's secret. Secrets can lead to trouble."

This was too much. Not only was she not going to get any action out of Strop, he was going to punish her for trying by implying that she was a bad mother.

And what was even more irritating was how right Miriam Kostal had been. There would be no help in the OAKs. Whether or not there was some high-level interest in a change of regime, field agents like Strop knew better than to wander into delicate political situations. It might interfere with their digestion. So Strop would fight as hard as he could to hear nothing about Phineus.

She pushed her chair back, ready to stand. But she couldn't just leave. He had her, just as he intended.

"Do you know where she is?" Dunya said.

"In the crust. Near the Xanthus airball. Her boyfriend has run into trouble from his Green Burnings buddies, big surprise. Bodil might easily end up in the same trouble. If those kids broke into where I think they did, they're all in serious trouble. Stop worrying about what plausible Martians might be up to and give your daughter some thought. This isn't official advice, by the way. One parent to another."

"Thanks, Strop." Dunya had to consciously loosen her jaw to speak. "I hope I can return the favor someday."

"Not likely, Dunya. Not likely."

Her daughter was definitely a Boscobel native, Dunya thought. An immigrant like her would have tried to hide in the trees. Bodil knew the many ways of getting found there, and had instead burrowed into Boscobel's neglected shell, which she thought of as invisible.

Dunya looked up into the shaft above. Boscobel had a huge volume in its shell, but only the poorest lived in it. The air rumbled. Just beyond was the vast space of Xanthus, one of the pressure equalization spaces excavated after the newly expanded shell of Boscobel had cooled.

The only illumination came from infrequent light bumps. There was no way she was going to stumble around this ridiculous space searching for her daughter. She stood in the center of the shaft and said, "Come down, Bodil. Now."

Before a minute was out, she wanted to say something more. She stopped herself. The silence grew as hollow as the space around her. The best way to get a client to say something was to say nothing. That conversational vacuum could suck out the most amazing things.

There was a rustle. A pair of shoes appeared in a hole about ten meters up. Bodil slid into view and then slowly climbed down to the level where her mother stood.

Bodil favored her father, Bryn. She was taller than Dunya, but with softer features, big eyes and downturned mouth. She looked gentle. Maybe someday she would be.

"It's your fault." Bodil spoke quietly, the way she showed she was really angry.

"What? What's my fault?"

"Don't pretend you don't know!" The other way she showed

she was really angry was by yelling. "You got that information about that Martian out of me, and now Unray's been beaten. They knew it had to come from him. They hit him, momma. A lot. I never trusted them. I want to hurt them."

"You think that's bad?" Dunya said. "Things are way worse than you think. Every one of us is in trouble. I don't have time for this. You don't have time for it. If we're not careful, we might all end up as slaves, or refugees, or something worse."

"What are you talking about?"

"I need your help, Bodil. I'm sorry about what happened to Unray. Probably not as sorry as you'd like me to be. But we've got Martians crawling around our home that might rip the whole thing apart and I don't have time to worry about your stupid boyfriend and his lame-ass buddies."

For the first time in a long time, Bodil clearly didn't know what to say. She'd hoped her mother would feel guilty and help her. Instead, her mother was asking for help herself. That hadn't happened in an equally long time.

Dunya realized she'd gotten up against her daughter, looking up at her, feeling like a knife pointed at her belly. She stepped back, looked around. "Isn't this their territory? You shouldn't be here."

"I don't care what they call their territory. They don't deserve anything. I thought... I can do something to them, make them feel it, the way they made me feel it."

"Well, Bodie," a voice said from the gloom. "Good luck for you 'cause here's your chance."

Phineus had trained the Green Burnings well. They appeared all around, blocking every route of escape, while moving as casually as if just out for a stroll.

"Eger," Bodil said. "Eger!"

"Yeah?" A young man slouched from the shadows. He

wore a long jacket decorated with silver loops and pins. Pieces of the stolen emergency kit, Dunya thought, the parts they thought weren't good for anything.

"My mother doesn't have anything to do with any of this," Bodil said.

Eger looked Dunya up and down, raised his eyebrows. "Doesn't look that way to me. Like she said, this is Burnings' territory. Doesn't matter who's messing with it. Or why."

"Why you—"

Eger blocked Bodil's blow with a forearm and threw her back. Dunya took a step forward, and found herself looking at a blade that seemed to reflect more light than there was in that dark place.

Eger shook his head. "Nah, Mom. Not a good idea."

Bodil was puffing next to her. Dunya thought she was crying, but when she glanced at her daughter, she realized that it was the breath of rage. Knife or not, greater fighting skill or not, she looked like she was going to throw herself at Eger. Did she know this girl?

"You can define your territory with respect to some other gang," Dunya said. "Not for ordinary citizens."

"Ordinary citizens?" Eger was in her face. "You telling me you don't know what's what? You come here, know all our business, what we do." He looked even younger close up, with smooth skin and curly reddish hair.

"We'll get out," Dunya said.

"'We' won't do anything. Bodil and us got to talk."

"No."

"*No*?"

"Stop it, Eger," Bodil said. "Don't be an idiot. My mom doesn't have anything to do with this. You're the one who beat Unray. Right?"

Eger grinned. "I got some licks in, sure. But we had to share. Everyone wanted a piece. You know what it's like when everyone wants a piece. We share, in the Burnings."

Even though he was genuinely dangerous, Dunya found his

leer too deliberate, like he practiced it in front of the mirror.

"Because Unray could have taken you alone," Bodil said "That why?"

Dunya knew that tone of lazy insolence well. It made her want to hit her daughter. She never had.

Eger had less restraint. Bodil dodged his first, overhand blow, but he moved fast and punched her in the side. She oofed and bent over and Dunya slid away from her position, looking for an opening, even as she knew they weren't going to get out of this—

There was a wail from somewhere overhead, and a body came hurtling down out of the dangling roots. It hit so hard it bounced.

Dunya moved as if she had expected exactly that to happen. She hit Eger with her shoulder and, off balance, he fell.

She turned to tell Bodil to run. Bodil was gone, already moving at full tilt, slashing at the face of the young Green Burning who tried to stop her. The boy dodged back, automatically covering his face. By the time he realized he still had his looks, it was too late, and she was past.

Behind, another crash, as another scout fell from above, followed by shouts.

Her daughter ran beautifully, also like her father. Dunya's own legs were shorter, and she had to pump them hard to keep up. She kept expecting resistance, but the Burnings had been confident enough not to set pickets out this far.

And if it hadn't been for that sudden intervention, they wouldn't have needed them. Who had flung that scout down? He seemed to have been flung with some force, by someone with muscles. Martian muscles.

She just managed to keep Bodil in view as she dodged, first into this corridor, then that, then up a ramp, first shallow, then steep, then stairs. Stairs covered with moss and ferns.

They were out, in the shadows amid the roots. Around was the rustle of leaves, the green glow, air thick with pollen. Bees flickered in the light that made it through from high overhead.

Bodil turned and fell against her mother, almost knocking her over. She was laughing. Unbelievably, she was laughing, almost helpless.

"Ah!" Bodil said. "Did you see the look on his face?"

"I was too busy panicking."

"He always thinks he's got it all under control. Jerk." The savage look Bodil threw back down the black hole of the stairs was beautiful and terrifying. "I visited stupid Unray in the hospital. He talked all tough too, and blamed it all on me."

"Okay, it was my fault. Right now I need your mind working. Someone was above us in that shaft. She's just a visitor, doesn't know Boscobel. She's going to be moving out of that area, fast. Where would she go, and can we intercept her?"

"There's really only one way. Come on."

The route turned out to be fairly simple, involving just a climb up to a living bridge between a twisted olive tree and a baobab whose hollow interior held a playground filled with shrieking children.

Dunya grabbed her daughter's shoulder and pointed. Below them, tall above the crowd, Miriam Kostal strolled. Dunya could sense that Bodil instantly picked her out.

Without hesitation, Bodil jumped off the stubby branch of a baobab. Dunya followed, hitting a mossy spot that would have been softer if it hadn't been so worn. The gravity was highest here, near the roots, and Dunya really felt the impact as she landed.

Bodil slid ahead, and up again, on the aerial root of a mangrove. They were now ahead of Miriam, though Dunya had been in that position before, and it hadn't helped her. Just below them was a noodle shop, Cairngorm's, sending up puffs of aromatic steam and making her hungry. She looked down at the bubbling pots, the patrons with their heads bent over bowls. She'd never been there, but it seemed familiar to her—

"Mind telling me why we're after her?" Bodil plopped down in a tangled mass of vines and looked up at the hummingbirds that investigated a flower just above her.

"Your buddies the Green Burnings are being used by someone else," Dunya said. "A Martian. Phineus. Who happens to be one of my clients."

"You never talk about your clients."

"They appreciate my silence. You should too. But he's kind of moved himself out of the confidential category by trying to get me killed. And you, now."

"Nah. I don't know about this Phineus. Eger was on his own, just being his usual jerk of a self. Defending Burning territory. I was just hiding out there. Hoping no one would ever find me. But you did."

Dunya had already resolved never to tell her daughter how she had found out. It was too humiliating.

Fortunately, Miriam rescued her again.

"You think that was smart?" Miriam Kostal stood over them, casting more shadow than it seemed reasonable for her lean form. "Putting yourself at risk was bad enough. Putting my mission at risk might be fatal."

Instead of being intimidated by the other woman's anger, Dunya found herself just as mad. "I don't need to justify myself to you."

"Protecting your offspring." Miriam eyed Bodil. "How do you feel about being defended, little girl?"

"Don't try to set us against each other." Bodil's insolence was more pleasant when applied to someone else. "That's our own, on our own time. Nothing for you. And my name's Bodil."

Miriam looked the girl over, then smiled, an expression as tight as a wrestler's grip. "Pleased to meet you, Bodil. Have you had a chance to figure out what it is you are now involved in?"

"No. Not that much."

"If I knew what your mother was up to, I might be able to fill in some of the gaps for you."

Bodil and Miriam turned to look at her, and Dunya found herself nettled. That had been a nice bit of solidarity with her daughter, but it was over. Now that they were standing side by side, she fancied she saw similarities between her daughter and the rangy Martian. They both had sharp jaws, and an easy stance. Assuming that Dunya was perversely withholding information seemed to be another thing they had in common.

"Bodil. That trim Eger was wearing, some of the others. What was it? Where did they get it?"

"Those loops? They grabbed some kind of gear from some old locker."

"Emergency gear?"

"I... I don't know. They were all excited about it, though. First real operation. Tactics, penetration of secure areas. Martian training, they said."

"You have information about it?" Miriam said in Dunya's ear.

"A friend who runs a restaurant heard about it. Someone took off with a complete emergency kit. An old one, probably ignored and forgotten."

"Where did they run their operation?" Miriam asked Bodil.

"Imperial Valley. There's an access lock there, not used much now. This was in the storage area nearby. Secure, I guess. Not as secure as the OAKs thought, though." She couldn't suppress a hint of pride in what her boyfriend and his unpleasant friends had accomplished. "But... what's going on?"

Dunya could feel Miriam waiting. This was up to her, how much to tell. "Phineus, the guy they've been getting their lessons from. He's the inside man in a Martian filibustering expedition that means to take over Boscobel. He's using them as some kind of screen."

"He's using them to gain access to an airlock," Miriam said. "A place they can make entry. And their vessel will be here soon."

Bodil looked at Dunya. "Momma. What do we do?"

"There's really no need for you two to do anything," Miriam said.

"Really?" Dunya had thought about how to argue this. Practicality was the best way. "Does that give you the best chance of success?"

"Are you going to help me by going back to the OAKs again?" Sarcasm didn't suit Miriam.

"The theft of safety equipment is a real crime, one the OAKs can enforce without any concern about who is hoping the Martians will give him a better office. If they hold Phineus for that, it will give you some breathing space. And Bodil... do you think you could face Unray again?"

"Sure. I have to go there and tell him we're through. I was too mad the last time."

"Well, that will give you a good reason to pump him on what the Green Burnings are up to. I'll bet it isn't at all what Phineus thinks they're doing."

"I have the perfect outfit," Bodil said. "I've been waiting for the opportunity to wear it. I'll break his heart."

"That's my girl."

"Do I get to say anything about the help I need?" Miriam was surprisingly patient.

"I waited for that," Dunya said. "I finally went without it."

"We're making a lot of assumptions. Some are bound to be wrong. Be ready to switch direction as necessary. Keep your OAKs on the emergency kit, and leave any mention of Martians to me."

"You got it."

"I have to handle Phineus carefully," Miriam said. "He's got support back home, and harming him would have bad consequences. But preventing him from acting will achieve what I need. Then, maybe, Martians can start hashing out their problems with each other, rather than exporting them. It's a dream, of course. But it's one I share with my husband."

"You're married?"

"Don't sound so shocked. Hektor doesn't get to see much of me, unfortunately. While he's trying to build a stable coalition at home, I'm usually out trying to keep each leak from turning into a blowout."

"I'm sure he misses you."

"I wish he was out here with me. He'd be better at working with people than I am."

"Oh, I don't know," Dunya said. "You seem to be doing fine."

Dunya could see that, despite herself, the fierce Martian was pleased. Dunya wanted to meet the man who could keep someone like that in his bed.

"The sooner we take care of Phineus and his ridiculous ambitions, the sooner I can get home," Miriam said.

Dunya would have loved to order Bodil home, to prepare dinner and perhaps ready for a siege. That would just result in Bodil's running off to do something on her own. She hoped she would not regret the choice that she had made.

"See you, momma." Bodil gave her a kiss, and was gone.

By this time, with the sunglobe getting red, Strop would have moved up and over and been holding court at a restaurant high up in an aromatic cedar. She'd have to find a way to get him on that missing emergency kit without getting herself arrested—

"Twice in one day." Phineus blocked the twisting ladder ahead of her. "How about that?"

He was the last person Dunya wanted to see. "I'm in kind of a hurry right now."

"Sure, sure." He moved as if to go around her, then leaned in, his big forehead looming. "Did you get a chance to check out my fellow Martian?"

"It's on my list, Phineus."

"I'm in danger! It's not at all like you not to take the concerns of your clients seriously."

Unfortunately, that was true. He knew her too well. "I think you just made her up."

"Maybe I did. But was my imagination good enough for you to notice if the Martian pursuing me was a man or a woman?"

No way she could remember how precisely he'd described who was after him. It didn't matter. He knew that she would have checked his story out by now, and that Miriam would have done something about it. As far as he was concerned, no explanation for why Dunya was walking around healthy and alive was a good one.

"I might have a chance to get out there before I go to bed." If he wasn't going to move, she would swing around him. She glanced up at a convenient branch, to find two long-jacketed kids hanging over her, one girl, one boy. How long had they been there?

Phineus shook his head. "She doesn't miss, Dunya. That's why I'm afraid of her. I was hoping she'd make a mistake and get herself in trouble. Instead of killing you, she recruited you. And here I thought you were on my side."

Before Dunya could move, the two kids grabbed her and swung her into the leaves.

To her surprise, there were fish here. A carp bumped its snout into her mask.

Within five minutes of grabbing her they had bound her, put her into a mask and air supply, tied her legs to an elastic band, and sucked her down under a water drop. It was half local water supply, half wildlife reserve—and now her prison. Phineus had not looked her in the eye as the Green Burnings had done their work, but just before the water had closed over her head, he had muttered, "The new administration will free you."

He had made her complicit with his plot. Only his success would bring someone here to keep her from suffocating. If he failed she would be left here to become food for these fish.

Dunya breathed slowly and carefully. She had no idea how much air she had, and struggle would just shorten the time she had left. She'd curled herself down a couple of times. She could find no way to influence her bonds. She could only plan for what she would do if someone rescued her, or compose her soul for death.

The facemask, with its blinking indicators, smelled old. It had to be from the stolen emergency kit. So it was designed for vacuum, not underwater use, yet another thing to worry about. It did have an eyeball-controlled display that she ran through. No comm, and no "cut my bonds" command. It did have an inventory list of the kit of which it was a part, some things marked as "exhausted" or "damaged-unrepairable". It included two spacesuits, of which this was presumably one, an exoshelter, fuel cells, enough procal bars to live on for a few months while awaiting rescue... and a full emergency airlock. Without her consciously willing it, the faceplate showed her an exploded view of the airlock and listed all of its many components. Good to go, it told her with satisfaction.

Phineus had gotten the Green Burnings to steal the old emergency kit because he wanted the airlock. Dunya was sure of it. That the kit had been stored near the Imperial Valley airlock was just a distraction. Miriam was wasting her time there.

But he needed a place to link inside and outside. Asteroid environments didn't survive by being easy to punch through. Dammit. It was one thing to resolve to be calm and meditative and accepting. It was another to keep on doing it. Where was Bryn? Why wasn't he around, at least to comment mordantly on affairs? Her husband had been increasingly given to mordant commenting. Doing something about things was less his line.

But she was being unfair. He worked with cultural development in various asteroids, as far sunward as Phobos. He was respected, and busy. When he came home he was loving, attentive, and everything he needed to be.

And then he was gone again. And she found herself just as happy. Could she imagine some other man who she would want around more? Sometimes she thought she could. But she, too, was too busy to spend too much time on that.

Bryn's absence was equally hard on Bodil, of course. So she ran with losers like Unray, getting rudimentary political education with the Green Burnings. That seemed a reasonable explanation. Nothing to do with anything Dunya herself had done.

Did this facemask have a setting that sucked away all illusions? Clever, some of these old gadgets. A rough way to die, though, facing the absolute truth about everything you'd been so careful to keep under control.

She thought about Bryn's own dusty and peppery scent, which had eventually faded from his side of the bed, careful though she'd been not to move anything, and only breathe it when she absolutely had to. She'd smelled something else recently, associated with quite a different man. Peppery as well, but damper, and tanged with... cilantro. She remembered the noodle shop she'd parked herself above to get a drop on Miriam.

Phineus had shoved leftover containers under his cushions. From that same place, Cairngorm's.

He was working with his airlock somewhere down in Xanthus. The crust was thinner down there, sure, but it was still nothing you could just hack through.

Something splashed above her. A larger fish? Since the carp, she hadn't seen much more than larvae. But now it was dark, and she couldn't see anything. Someone yanked on her. She stretched up, then was pulled back by the cable holding her bound feet. She sensed swearing, hearing nothing. Arms reached far in, grabbed her, and pulled hard. She rose and rose... and finally pulled free. Then she was lying on a seeping bank of wildflowers. Her facemask was pulled off.

"Momma!" Bodil said. "Are you still breathing?"

Unray had given Bodil her mother's location. He was out of the loop as far as Green Burning tactical operations were concerned. But someone had felt it right to tell him that his soon-to-be-ex-girlfriend's mother had been captured and imprisoned in a water tank in the cedars.

You found virtue in the oddest places.

"I guess they sometimes hide stuff in here," Bodil said. "Contraband. Not usually people, though."

"What's that?" Dunya looked at a bundle of steaming leaves that lay amid dew-covered yellow flowers.

"Mom! You have no idea how hard it was for me growing up, to have a mom that didn't know anything."

"God, of course I know what it is. Should I eat it, or nap on it?"

It was the wrong tone to take, even if she was newly resurrected and should be cut some slack. Bodil pushed her lower lip out and looked about to cry.

Dunya hugged her daughter. "We're on a mission," she whispered. "And we have a lot to do. Unwrap it."

"You're cold." Bodil pulled off her jacket and put it around her soaked, shivering mother. Then she dropped to her knees and unwrapped the leaves, letting steam rise into the dark air.

This lozenge cake was traditional Boscobeli food for a journey. The leaves were from a modified fig and added a spice to the outer layers of the dough, which cooked enzymatically when tugged in just the right way. Dunya had never cared for it, finding it too sour for a decent dessert, and, uncooked, too hard as a pillow, the use the ancient and fictional tradition had for it.

Of course, a people defined itself by those things no sensible individuals would pick on their own. And Bodil was

Boscobel born and bred. So Dunya sat on a branch in a world she had not chosen, happy to be alive, and shared the almost-inedible cake with her daughter.

Bodil had figured it out instantly. Any airball had an expulsion pore, through which the waste rock had been expelled. And above that, a series of baffles. All safe, no danger from the ancient weakness.

Except that, at the base of Xanthus, the baffles had collapsed into useless piles of cracked rock, another sign of the deferred maintenance that put the entire world at risk.

Dunya climbed down the tumbled slabs alone. Bodil had gone to find Miriam. She wouldn't succeed, of course. But Miriam would find her. Dunya only hoped that would happen before she got herself into serious trouble down here.

One other thing Bodil had learned from Unray: there was no one from the Green Burnings down here. They'd gotten irritated with their mysterious guru, and had dumped Phineus in preference to mixing it up with their competitors over in Five Boughs. After that, a party. Phineus was on his own down here.

It didn't really matter. He could take her easily. She had to wait for Miriam, who knew what to do. Miriam would have told her that herself.

She couldn't listen to Miriam, even though what Miriam had not actually said made perfect sense. Phineus was still her client, making bad choices. Even as she knew she had to stop him, she recognized him as her responsibility.

There he was, working with a small light. The airlock was in. She could see the rubble from the sealed pore all around it. Being so small, it had to be secret. It could fit, at most, two people at a time. It was next to impossible to get an army in position and deployed using that. But, as she had learned from both Phineus and Miriam, next to impossible was a Martian's favorite spot to get a seat.

She thought she was moving quietly. Phineus heard her, and jerked around. The light caught her.

"Aren't you cold?" he said. "You're all wet."

"Oh, how thoughtful, Phineus," she said.

He muttered something.

"What?" she said.

"I said I'm sorry. It had to be done."

"Please stop, Phineus. Just stop. Do you really think you're still going to get a force of Martians in here?"

He shook his head. "You think what you see is what there is. I have support, here in Boscobel. It's really my place, not yours."

She tried not to think about how much he was right. "Contingent support. If-you-win support. If there's any problem, it will vanish. I walked right in here. The gang you trained up is gone, you're here alone. That should tell you something."

He'd never done his own dirty work. First he'd sent Dunya into Miriam's path in the hopes that Miriam would take her out, then he'd used his gang. Now he was pretending to be too busy to bother with her. No wonder he'd left Mars. He just wasn't up to it.

"There's no way to advance on Mars," he said. "Everything's owned or closed off. The only way to get somewhere is to come out here. There's a lot of unrealized value in the asteroids."

If he was arguing, there was a chance. But it was too late for him. At the last instant it seemed he knew that, because he stopped and stared at her. Before he could say anything else, Miriam dropped from somewhere overhead and kicked him in the head.

Not straight on, though. Phineus reacted fast. He tilted his head so that the force of her kick grazed past, then tried to help her on her way with a slap at her heel.

Miriam was fast too. She spun and landed in a crouch.

Dunya wished she could help. But she knew all she could do was get in the way or become a hostage.

The struggle was brief and vicious. Then Phineus whipped a rock at Miriam, and when she dodged he rolled and launched himself into a black gap among the dry roots.

Without hesitating, Miriam went after him. Both vanished among the rocks.

Dunya stepped down to the airlock. The least she could do was deactivate it while Miriam did her work.

"I need to return that in good working order," Strop said.

He stood among the rocks, looking miserable and sweaty. Stumbling around in the high-gravity area in the dark wasn't usually his way of getting things done.

"Did it get too public?" Dunya said. "Too hard to deny?"

She hadn't expected him to answer, and he didn't. He lumbered forward and slapped a Maintenance Required sticker across the airlock.

"What's going to happen?" Dunya said.

"I can at least tell you something that *won't* happen. No Martian vessel will approach Boscobel. If one does, it will get a warning shot, and know to go elsewhere."

"Thus ensuring no one ever has to testify to who knew what."

He shrugged. "A lot of people would prefer that. You might even be one of them. If Phineus is still alive, he won't get a trial either. He'll be expelled. He can go to Mars, where they'll kill him. Or he can go somewhere else. Not our problem. I do need to say that your inability to control him will be a black mark on your record. Not a lot I can do, but I'll put in a good word for you." He smiled at her.

She'd take a shower when she got home. That might do something about the greasy film he left on her, even as he was helping her out.

"As staff is rotated off the entry and departure airlocks to be re-vetted and cleared, coverage will be affected. Pretty much anyone who wants to get out of Boscobel without interference will be able to do so."

She glanced up. Bodil stood on a rock high above. She

smiled and gave her mother the thumbs-up.

"Go ahead," Strop said. "Get your girl home. I'll pick up our unfortunate Martian invader."

She'd have to use Bodil to communicate with Miriam and get her off Boscobel. Too dangerous for Dunya to do it directly. That was too bad. That woman was someone to know.

Someday, she guessed, Bodil would want an off-Boscobel school. Deliberately exposing her daughter to Miriam's influence would be dangerous, of course. But she had heard that there really was nothing like a Martian education.

She climbed up the shattered slabs of rock, back toward the trees she had come to rely on.

In Colors Everywhere

Nisi Shawl

Clients must not be killed. WestHem has opted to destroy their original bodies while preserving psychoemotional components. Transport to Amends completes the allotted punishment, taking into consideration the impossibility of return to Earth, along with the harsh experiences certain to arise from atechnical living conditions. On this account, however, minimal attempts should be made to ameliorate these conditions.

— *Mission Guidelines,* Psyche Moth, *2055*

Trill walked home through the Rainshadow Mountains with Adia, her former mentor. Not alone.

The sky had been high all day. Now, with evening, it came low, wetting them and their surroundings with mist. Silver beaded the fuzz beneath their feet.

Adia was tough, though an elder. She walked steadily, without complaint. She ought to have been tired even before they started; she and Trill had spent the week teaching a cohort of tens-to-thirteens how to weave buildings.

Jubilee, the largest settlement of prisoners on Amends for two generations now, had decided to bud a new village. As expected, the tens-to-thirteens were eager for adventure, the fourteens-to-seventeens hardly less so. The site they chose, where the peninsula joined the mainland's western coast, fronted a beach on Unrest Bay, quieter waters than Jubilee's open ocean. "Unrest" might well be picked as the new place's name; the selection would be finalized by those who ended up living there.

The first wave had big plans. They would build boats and fish there, these two age-groups claimed. They'd start double the Fisher Dopkwes and beat the older settlement's harvest. The eighteens-to-twenty-fours were of course more skeptical, having just discovered cynicism. The few twenty-fives-to-forty-fives—Trill's age cohort—who had chosen to emigrate with them smiled and nodded encouragingly whenever the idea came up. And then returned to the work of their current dopkwes: rope spinning, planting, preserving, and so on.

Trill and Adia had left to go home late that morning with no urgency. No Rogues or Solitaries had been sighted in the area for months. And it was summer; even when the sky came down to kiss them they were sure that leaflight would last long enough for their trip. They'd eaten a big lunch at the halfway point, so they wouldn't be hungry till they arrived—

Trill stopped before she knew why. Adia, ahead of her, kept walking moments after the sound became audible to Trill: a scream, a shriek sinking lower, louder—closer, Trill realized. She shrank to crouch under a dripping chrismas tree while looking up, frightened but curious. Like a tooth or a knife the sound bit through the air. A flock of prettybirds burst out of a fall of redvines hanging from a bluff and flew south. The sound grew, grew, the rising roar of someone who never needed a new breath.

Adia still stood in the open, face tilted up as if she could see the screaming. Trill staggered to her feet to coax the Lady who had trained her to shelter, to safety.

BOOM!

On her hands and knees, Trill looked around. Nothing had changed—except that she had to piss from fear. But Adia stood stubbornly upright in the same place, on the same rough path just beginning to be worn between Jubilee and the new settlement. She stood calmly, relaxed, as if facing nothing more serious than a test—though she'd become a Lady decades ago. As though nothing threatened her.

The elder shook her head and glanced at Trill over her shoulder, then came to help her rise. "Long time since I heard anything like that." Adia's words were soft as whispers. Why? "Poor shang. You got no clue, do you? That come from Dr. Ops."

Trill stepped back off the path to release her water. She whispered too. "From *Psyche Moth*?" Her clothes didn't rustle. Her water made no sound striking the fuzz.

"What? Speak up!"

"Dr. Ops on the *Psyche Moth*?" Trill shouted. She understood now. Adia wasn't whispering, so she didn't have to. It was just that the huge noise had made it hard to hear anything else afterwards.

"He the one. It ain't a bomb or nothin—mission guidelines say he ain't spozed to kill us. Naw, he just sent us another drone, sounded like. First since I had my final period. I wish I coulda seen it. Fuckin chrismas trees in the way. Wonder what kinda trouble he put inside it?"

Low intrusion surveillance recommended. High-orbit monitoring to be supplemented by trustee insertion at periodic intervals keyed to instructions relayed from verified WestHem government facilities via translight. If no such instructions are received for over 20 years, refer to procedures for establishing surface stock.

— *Mission Guidelines,* Psyche Moth, *2055*

Trill was working out a design when they sent for her, an idea about something to help the Hunters Dopkwe that had come from talking with her ex-lover Hett, LeeRai's father. It was a sort of a box that became a basket when its walls dried out. A strap over the forehead and the high-climbing sixes-tonines could pack one of them as full of phibian eggs as they liked. Hang the box-baskets from a line and even with the lids left on, there'd be enough air getting inside to cure the leathery eggs slowly, the way she liked them.

"Lady?"

Trill looked up from her workbasin. Dola, an eighteens-to-twenty-fours female, leaned tentatively in at the shed's entrance. "Will you come with me to the baths?"

A summons. Trill nodded. "Just let me—" She did what she needed to without further explanation: tied off her project's last side panel, laid it on a rack, emptied her workbasin's water into the shop's barrel, and wiped dry her hands.

Outside, the sky had mellowed to a gold like beer. Evening. She should have stopped work long ago to visit the kitchen for food. There would always be something, though. More tempting was the urge to find the fives-and-unders before they went to sleep. She hadn't spent the night with LeeRai since coming home four days—almost a full week—ago.

That morning they had raced each other on the hard-packed sand of the beach. Trill had laughed, the breath hot and easy in her lungs, her daughter big and plump and bronzed by the sky. And getting so strong! So fast! Always moving—it would be strange and lovely to see her lying still, asleep—

But the other Ladies wanted her now.

She followed Dola up the hill. This neighborhood of Jubilee, up against the Rainshadows, had drawn people to it from the settlement's main site because of the hot springs. As they walked the sun disappeared, ducking behind the mountains, though the sky's grace and the leaves' first radiance provided plenty of light.

Dola had applied to become a Lady that spring, shortly after conscripting Trill to help the Gardeners Dopkwe. Having recently completed her entry trials she was now an apprentice, in training for her final test. Many Ladies were part of the Gardeners Dopkwe, since plant lore was intimately tied to their power.

Trill didn't mind helping Inker, Dola's main mentor. She liked the girl. They had sung together while working, and since then, too. The eighteens-to-twenty-fours had a good voice and knew all the verses to "Billie Jean". She wore her hair in bunches of thin braids braided together into three thicker ones these days, the same as Trill did. Around her neck hung a necklace woven of redvine tendrils, one of those things Trill made when she had nothing else to keep her busy.

They climbed a fuzz-covered slope and descended into a shallow, wooded valley. Steam rose from the dark water pooled at its center. Around the water's edge several of the Jubilee Ladies lounged. In the leaves' glow Trill saw Adia's sharp-chinned face; the elder next to her, braiding her long, white hair, was Robeson, Adia's friend. She recognized others, too, such as Kala and True, also from Trill's cohort. On Earth, the groups the Ladies modeled themselves after wouldn't have considered admitting Trill, Kala, or True, let alone an applicant Dola's age. But the empty clone bodies given to the first prisoners had all been twenty-fives-to-forty-fives. "You don't have to be old to be wise," they said. That was why the younger cohorts were welcome to at least ask to belong.

One person in the pool wasn't a Lady. Standing in the middle of the spring was an unfamiliar eighteens-to-twenty-fours—from another settlement? She didn't know everyone here; Jubilee was home to almost 32,000 people. If not for the Ladies, there would have been twice that number—too many to prosper.

She folded her dress and underwear and left them on a bench. The dark water washed warmly over her feet, calves, knees—

"Stop." Trill obeyed. The voice was Robeson's; she held the bright, dying branch of a hannakka bush, meaning she was the Ladies' speaker for now. "Don't need to stand no deeper. You ain't makin no report; we got Adia's. And Odell's. We called you for a different reason. Work."

"Work?"

"We want you to go where that thing Dr. Ops sent landed."

The Ladies had used her before for duties not obviously connected with her dopkwe, of course. After her test, when she became one of them, they told Trill that honesty was her particular power; lies made her weak. Because since then she'd told the truth scrupulously, paying almost obsessive attention to conveying details, she was their best reporter. But—

"But—but—where? Where is it? How do you know?"

"Odell a trader comin here from Hamza. Six of em together on the road an they think it dropped down between where they camped at and us. They was gonna radio—" Eefay, to the far south, had supplied Hamza, Jubilee, and the nine other settlements on Amends with crystal sets. "—but that didn't seem real safe. *Psyche Moth* mighta changed orbit. Dr. Ops mighta heard. They split up instead."

"You want me to go with—" Odell wore no clothing, which meant Trill had no way of telling if the stranger was a him or a her. "You want us to go together and find out... what?"

Adia put her hand over Robeson's tiny one, sharing the speaker's branch with her. "What kinda trouble he put inside," she said, echoing the words she'd spoken on the path from the new place.

Dola would go too, with Trill as her mentor. Training. It made sense. The girl was due for her final test soon. She needed fieldwork, a task to take her outside the settlement.

Trill acknowledged to herself that she'd rather stay home and weave. The men and women in her dopkwe had interesting ideas that kept them talking some nights long after the last leaves faded. But she waded out of the water and dressed again without protest. The three of them would depart at flowerlight. She had just a short time to eat and sleep.

Offspring produced by clients during their sentences have committed no crimes but must serve with them, as they are likely to be

contaminated with clients' views. Under no circumstances are they to be allowed to develop extraplanetary capabilities. Similar caution must be exercised regarding any later generations coming into direct contact with clients.

— *Mission Guidelines,* Psyche Moth, *2055*

Trill woke as the flowers' buds were barely beginning to unfurl. Beside her, Odell stirred gently, driven from sleep's depths by the growing light. Their sex had been excellent. According to his estimate—Odell was currently male, and apparently had been since the age of six—the stretch of shoreline they now neared was close to the waters where whatever Dr. Ops sent must have come down.

She sat up, twisting, lifting one buttock and then the other to free her dress, and pulled it on over her head. "Dola!"

"Yes, Lady!" The eighteens-to-twenty-fours girl had climbed a bottle tree like a much younger person. "Is it time for breakfast?"

"Come and find out."

Odell rose and left silently to relieve himself. Dola descended and did likewise, then returned to eat the tofruit they had brought as provisions for their trip. Tasteless but somehow more satisfying than ordinary garden crops, tofruit grew from seeds that had arrived on Amends years ago in a drone sent to Nunavut Island. So Dola said.

Trill went a little ways off to make her own water and earth. She buried them quickly, yet Dola had again climbed a tall tree when she got back. For a member of the Gardeners Dopkwe she spent very little time on the ground. "What are you searching for up there?"

The bottle tree's leaves shivered as Dola scrambled down to the forest floor. "A flock of prettybirds. They were looking at us while you slept. Then they flew away."

Odell frowned and pushed the blond fronds of his hair back from his temples. "Anything else? Smoke or—or glints of metal? Or is some part of the ocean an unusual color?"

"No."

Not till noon did they come upon a sign of Dr. Ops's intrusion: trustees talking loud enough they could be heard ten arms away. Two of them. At first Trill thought they were Rogues, though none had been reported north of Hamza. But they were arguing about what Dr. Ops wanted like they knew. According to the elders he told trustees his secrets.

"How come you ain't let us start with that other place, the closer one? Coulda got clients carryin our equipment. Be quicker than us havin to lug evvathing, an we spozed—"

A high, decisive voice cut the other off. "Dr. Ops sent us here to take care a business, not be goin all over, back an forth. We start up in Jubilee, get clients there to help us an head on south, we be fine. Like I said yesterday, an the day before. Like we already *doin*. Now stop askin me am I sure."

Both spoke the way many elders did, so they, too, must have originally occupied black bodies.

Trill, Dola, and Odell stepped softly to within three arms of the pair. She saw the strangers through the day-dull leaves: both men, judging by their overalls, with the pale skin of babies. They faced each other over four stacks of four smooth grey-and-black boxes. She edged closer and one box lit up like a tiny, square chrismas tree. The men fell suddenly silent. After a long while the high-voiced one called out that he could see them, then contradicted himself by asking them to show themselves.

Odell emerged into the open from behind Trill.

"Come on. Where's the other two?"

Trill was impressed. Adia's claims of accuracy for Dr. Ops's tracking equipment held up. Could his weapons kill as horribly as she and Robeson said? The hand of one man now held something—without waiting to learn what, Trill followed Odell. So did Dola.

"Well. That's much better. Have a seat." The high-voiced man gestured at the fuzz to one side of the stacks with what Trill assumed was a weapon. "We trustees come from the

Psyche Moth. Been waitin here for you—you stay in Jubilee?"

Trill nodded. "Me and Dola do; Odell here belongs in Hamza."

"Well, I'm Isabelle and this is Freddie. Dr. Ops figured you could use a more permanent installation at this point, so he picked us to set one up. After we take care a Jubilee we can help the other settlements."

Did the man think they were stupid? "Take care of us how?"

Isabelle patted the top of one of the stacks. "With the latest advances in knowledge just come from Earth, transmissions got sent to us only a few years back. These here banks contain blueprints—um, that mean models, plans—"

Trill tried to look as ignorant as Isabelle obviously believed she was.

"—for improvements, medicines, time-saving devices—"

"Of course, only Isabelle and I be able to access things for you," Freddie added. Maybe he was afraid he'd be murdered if he didn't make that plain.

What the trustees *said* they wanted in exchange for their "improvements" was safe conduct to Jubilee. They *said* they were worried about Rogues and Solitaries. Which made no sense; they'd been fine for the week-and-a-half since Trill heard them arrive, and they'd just demonstrated they could tell when someone approached their camp. And Isabelle carried a weapon... Again Trill pretended like she had no mind.

Going along with the lie about Rogues and Solitaries though none were known to be nearby, the three took turns "scouting". This consisted of getting far enough away that they no longer registered on the trustees' tracking instruments and then spying on what they said and did.

Sixteen boxes. Either Freddie or Isabelle stayed with their "equipment" at all times. Trill's attempts to wander off aimlessly with the four boxes she carried mostly failed. Twice she managed to open a box's latched drawer to reveal mysterious black slabs of identical lightweight material: plastic, like a lot of things the Scavengers Dopkwe in Dinetah used and traded.

The second time, Isabelle caught her and she pretended it had been an accident. The last time.

At night, the sky showed them *Psyche Moth's* orbit. It hadn't changed. They calculated when it would most likely fly overhead; that was when Freddie and Isabelle could learn their "guides'" locations easily from Dr. Ops. That was when the prisoners took care to be where expected.

Climbing trees in pursuit of prettybirds, Dola discovered that above the height of seven arms she was undetectable. Trill in her underwear was almost as agile as the eighteens-to-twenty-fours girl. One afternoon the trustees thought they were completely alone. Stretched out on a branch—almost within eyesight, if they'd bothered to look for her—Trill listened closely.

Freddie was grumbling about having to walk. Elders reminisced about easier ways of traveling, too. And faster ones. "We takin so *long*." he complained. It had only been five days—just a week. "We know where Jubilee is—cain't we do the job right here?"

"You wanna set up equipment an tear it down again inna middle a nowhere on the chance one a these the best bet? An explain that to em how? Look, Dr. Ops say do one in every settlement. So we go to Jubilee. With the clients we with. Then we probably have a lot more success gettin a big bunch of em to buy what we sayin."

"Awright." But Freddie wasn't through complaining. "Still wish they'd hurry up. Or we had a auto, hover, *somethin*. Ain't it spozed to be more sunshine when we get there? So tired a these goddam fuck-ass clouds an this mothafuckin fog I could strangle the shit—"

Despite the danger—or maybe because of it—Trill laughed so hard she fell ten arms to the ground. Cursing the *sky*? What good was that going to do? The sky was *there*, always would be.

She lay giggling on the fuzz, unhurt. Good thing chrismas tree branches were so thick and soft.

But here came the two trustees thrashing through the hannakka bushes—of course they'd heard her crashing down. Trill crawled away and "returned" to their camp by another route. She called them back there and told a tale of chasing off a dangerous Rogue from the spot where she'd fallen.

Given a timelag for Earth-Amends communications of nearly a decade, and a minimum duration of almost a century for any physical return trip, rehabilitation efforts made after clients are settled should consist of observation and counseling only. None will have even the slightest effect on WestHem paradigms. Natural tendencies as embedded in the provided genetic material will eventually assert themselves.

— *Mission Guidelines,* Psyche Moth, *2055*

They arrived at the new settlement as the sun was about to rise over the Rainshadows. New gardens lined the rough path, rosetoo blooms shining their last yellows, reds, blues, and shocking pinks. They passed the two eighteens-to-twenty-fours on perimeter watch without either of the trustees noticing them. Trill had sent word ahead about their arrival via Dola. They were expected.

The two houses Trill and Adia had helped the emigrants start were fully woven. Beside them, five more half-finished ones curved in a line like a barely-bent bow around the central workshed. Or where the workshed would be—the posts were set, cured redvines pulled tight in their notches, but the actual weaving had yet to begin. At either side three more ranks of seven house foundations each curved around relatively flat areas.

On sixteen of the house sites, members of various of the new settlement's dopkwes were dressing, rolling up blankets, laying out tools for their day's work. In the middle of a space surrounded by unoccupied sites, people holding bulbs from bottle trees circled around baskets full of sweetly steaming food—rosetoohip porridge, from the smell.

Isabelle stopped and put his hands on his hips, turning, looking around. "This ain't Jubilee! What you tryna pull?"

"We just stopped here on our way," Trill told him. "Jubilee's close, though. People came here because it got too crowded—"

"How close? How many people come here?"

"Through the mountains," Dola said. "One more day, right?" Trill nodded. "And—how many?" The girl looked helplessly at Trill. "All the dopkwes, most cohorts. And more people every time they want to..." Her words trailed off.

"You alla sudden cain't count?" Freddie asked.

Of course they could. The Ladies knew exactly how many there were of every kind of woman, man, boy, girl, gardener, hunter, elder, under-six—but Dola was just an apprentice, and Trill hadn't checked for changes recently. "Three hundred forty-seven," she said, the last figure she'd been given.

This did nothing to ease Isabelle's suspicious expression, but all he did was demand who to see about where to set up. The trustees expected to take over one of the two finished houses. The Weavers Dopkwe offered theirs as a courtesy to Trill.

Black, silver, grey, and clear were apparently the trustees' favorite colors. All the boxes she handed Isabelle, and all the things coming out of them, looked like that.

When Freddie and Isabelle came outside to set up a giant, silver fake flower in back of their house she followed them to help, but they shooed her off. Skirting their house's half-woven neighbor, she circled around for a short, uninformative peek through the door. It would be rude and unexplainable to enter uninvited. Besides, the biggest box, which the trustees had always carried themselves, was as yet unopened. The noise they'd been making as they worked behind the house ceased and she walked away before they could see she was still there.

Dola seemed to have connected well and quickly with the new settlement's Gardeners Dopkwe. Trill joined them a while to make sure. The eighteens-to-twenty-fours girl sat with several others around a pile of dried bottle bulbs, cutting them open with sharp plastic tools. Trill helped pull out the spoor masses and spread them flat so the wind would blow them clean enough to spin. Already some in the group were leaning close to Dola, telling her their troubles. Not long, Trill thought, till Dola was able to function as a full Lady, a junction of secrets. Satisfied at her charge's progress, Trill considered the loose ends of the main panel she was weaving, her true work.

She decided to try to find out more about the trustees' equipment that night, after leaflight, when at least one of them slept. In preparation she napped on the site of the workshed. Odell offered to lie down with her awhile, though it wasn't the same as snuggling with LeeRai, or her dopkwe. What she needed was a friend, someone like Adia had in Robeson. Not a sex partner. Someone more. Someone...

She woke alone. The sky was still bright but close again, the bay swallowed in mist. She got up and rolled her sleeves down against the chilly dampness. She was tired of being away from home.

Trill walked downhill till she saw the walls of a house to her left, the one being used by the Gardeners Dopkwe. Just beyond that the fake flower had opened wider, flattening—and turning to the west? The trustees' house *hummed*, a low, hard-to-notice noise. If this was an elder's memory instead of something happening right now, that sound would be coming out of a machine.

The house's doorway was filled with a grey curtain. Trill had never seen anything like it. She tried to pull it aside. It wouldn't move. Caught? Tied? She ran her hand along the seam where wood met cloth.

"Can I help you?"

Freddie! Fear panged through her like salt. She turned and smiled. "I only wanted to make sure you got everything you need."

"Come on in. You here for the health test?" He reached past her and drew the curtain aside easily. The house's interior was much brighter than it ought to be.

"Sure," Trill said. She entered the house. Clear baskets hanging from the roof beams burned white, canceling out each others' shadows. Two short stacks—including the big box—still stood in one of the house's quarters, but the rest must have been unpacked and then somehow rewoven or folded into these odd furnishings.

Freddie pointed to a long, low surface. "Sit on that table and pull your sleeves up." He took a pair of white gloves from a box and put them on and started touching her, proceeding from her hair to her ears, face, throat, and downwards. He lifted her dress.

"Oh. Uh. Oh."

"Somethin wrong?" But she knew there wasn't. Unique checked everyone every five weeks—once a month, regular as leaflight. Doctors out of Uluru backed him up when they came through the settlement. Trill was fine.

"It's just—I can't, uh—I thought you were a woman."

"I am. Since I was a tens-to-thirteens."

"Of—you—of course—"

A whisper of cooler air as Isabelle pushed the curtain aside and walked in. "What Freddie mean is a course we knew gender assignments among you all be pretty fluid—that's why come summa us original clients wound up here, after all. Among other crimes. But he never suspected *you*, that you wasn't born what you say you are."

The elders were right again. "But it won't be a problem? People put here were allowed to live on Amends anyway we wanted, so—"

Freddie had recovered his ability to talk in sentences. "The only difficulty is that summa my treatments are for *biological* females." He stripped the gloves off and rolled them up without touching their outsides. Isabelle held open a grey bag and he dropped them in. "Guess we're done, then."

Trill didn't frown till she was well away from the house. She sat on the shore side of a tangle of roots sticking out of the sand, the remains of a broken and upended tree. The sky caressed her, bathed her in dew, in coolness, yet she felt no easing of her... anger? No. Fear? Much closer to that feeling, but stiller, deeper.

Dread.

Different kinds of women and men had different kinds of genitals. Like colors. Elders said that most places on Earth, that had mattered. Mattered enough to get some women—some men, too—murdered.

What treatments would the trustees—or rather, Dr. Ops working through them—want to impose based on those differences?

The Ladies would need to know. She'd have to find out. Somehow.

Tonight she'd investigate further. But she'd already expected to do that, so why this sudden, awful feeling? She looked at the sky for comfort.

A flock of prettybirds wheeled close overhead. Unusual to see them here in the open, Trill thought. They stayed in the woods and mountains, generally, though the elders said that when they'd first been brought down to the surface prettybirds were in the thick of everything, always. Much easier then to find their eggs, she imagined. Adia had told her Wayna practically lived on them when she was alive and pregnant with Trill. But now the Ladies had asked everyone to leave the eggs alone.

A rush of wings in front of her and Trill involuntarily shut her eyes. A small weight rocked on her head, balanced, then two more fell on her shoulders, a fourth on her left knee. Breathing as softly as she could, she opened her eyes.

Prettybirds had landed on her, were using Trill as a perch. At the edges of her sight, gold and orange and scarlet flashed, fluttered, made her want to turn her head—but would that scare them off? And without moving at all she could clearly see the last one who had arrived, aquamarine and a dazzling green, impossibly bold. It cocked its head and stared her in the face.

A visitor from Hamza who studied the animals of Amends said that elders in her dopkwe hadn't wanted to call them pretty*birds* because their eyes weren't on the sides of their heads. And they had hollow hairs instead of feathers, which no one else cared anything about.

And the visitor thought they shouldn't have been so good at flying, since they had to turn their heads to look anywhere but forward.

The prettybird on Trill's knee blinked once. A pause and it blinked twice more. Another pause. Four times. Another pause. Eight. Another pause, longer. Evidently that ended the sequence.

She wanted to shake herself. Was she dreaming? Awake?

The Ladies had suspected. Dola had come up with her own theories and they'd encouraged her to investigate them. Here was proof! Skin tingling as if she lay over hot spring bubbles, Trill lowered her lashes once, waited—twice, waited—four times—and they were gone, flying off. Someone had frightened the flock. She listened closely, and soon she heard another person approaching. He came into view: Lou, a tens-to-thirteens member of the Food Dopkwe, holding a limp bag. Well, she hadn't walked that far from the settlement. She'd have to get someone else, another Lady, to follow up on what had probably—maybe—happened. Sighing, she got up and stretched, ready for her night's work.

A record of cooperative rehabilitation is the first requirement for trustee selection, with acceptance of the tracking and communication equipment necessarily incorporated into the body another non-negotiable issue. Utilization of the selected subject's psychoemotional predilections can help when other factors indicate a less desirable fit,

and indeed can form the basis for stronger than usual loyalty ratings.
— Mission Guidelines, Psyche Moth, *2055*

The roofing made her knees and shins itch unbearably. Quietly, Trill shifted her position, lowering herself to lie on her side. Now her dress shielded her. That helped. She re-aimed her mirror so she could see through the sky vent.

Sky vents penetrated roofs' layers of casing-bundles at angles meant to keep the rain from entering. Trill peered upwards to where her long-handled mirror reflected the house's interior. Outside, full night reigned: leaflight had died down, and flowerlight wouldn't come for many hours. Inside, though, the clear baskets burned whitely.

Trill thought she might have been able to open a more direct spy-hole into the clinic, sheltered by their glare. But this would do. She saw plenty. More than she really wanted to.

Dola lay silently on the table where earlier Trill had sat. Perhaps she was asleep? Drugged? Trill's view of her was only from the girl's midsection down, and the other sky vents showed even less. But Dola's bent legs and scantily haired mons barely moved, and the pale belly rose almost imperceptibly with her long, slow breaths.

Breaths Trill couldn't hear above the sound of Freddie's, quick and harsh, as he pumped his penis between Dola's feet. In and out, in and out of the hollow he formed by clasping them together.

From Dola, nothing indicating refusal or rejection. No moans of joy or instructions or encouragement, either. From Freddie, faster breathing, harder fucking. He slammed to a stop, grunting. Semen spilled from his penis over Dola's tanned ankles and he bent forward.

Slurping sounds. Was he licking up his come? He kept slurping long after it must be gone, though.

"You about rehabilitated?"

Isabelle's voice. Trill had made sure he was in the house, too, before she climbed to the roof. But this was the first time he'd spoken.

"Come on. Do the implants. And then see if you can bring yourself to fuck her pussy; she never gonna believe she got pregnant cause a you pervin over her way down there."

"Why don't you do it, you in such a hurry?" Snorts of laughter were Isabelle's only answer. Freddie pulled up and fastened his overalls and left the reflection of Trill's mirror.

Implants. Pregnant. What had she gotten Dola into?

Freddie came back into view carrying a—Trill couldn't figure out the thing he cradled in his arms. She'd never seen it before, so obviously it had been hidden inside the big box. It seemed to be covered in skin. Kind of a cube but vaguely oblong, about the size of her LeeRai, it showed a puckered opening on the side she saw best. With the—skin?—darkening slightly around it, the opening looked like an anus. Freddie plopped the thing unceremoniously on the table between Dola's still-open knees, and left again.

Was that hair? Yes, two small, sunken circles of hair—black, scantier than Dola's, and rimming what seemed to be recesses in the thing's top—

Freddie returned more quickly than before; this time he carried a white speculum and a clear rope with shining metal ends. One end—it was hard to tell from where she lay, but it looked like he somehow stuck it into the face of the cube nearest to Dola's mons. He draped the rest around his neck. Then, with an odd expression of disgust on his face, Freddie pulled apart the lips sheltering Dola's vagina and inserted the speculum.

Trill imagined a muted squeaking as she watched Freddie crank it open.

He did something she couldn't quite make out with the rope's remaining end and fed it through the speculum, into the girl's vagina. Bending over, he seemed to make a few sharp adjustments to the arrangement of things. Then he caressed—no other word would do—caressed the skin-covered oblong. With both hands he rubbed the side Trill couldn't see—gently, repeatedly. Soon the clear rope turned red. The color ran from its cube end to vanish into the speculum's white maw. And into Dola.

After some moments Isabelle spoke again. "Ain't gonna try an implant this first client with all of em, is you?"

"We got plenty. Over a hundred embryos stored in here. I'm spozed to set ten into every breeder so we make sure at least one of em lives."

"If you call that livin. No mind."

"You know what I mean."

Trill didn't. But she had faith one of the other Ladies would.

She was finding out something important tonight. Though that didn't exactly make up for the horror being inflicted on Dola. Which was Trill's fault.

Cool rain threaded down from the lightless clouds. She wanted to accept the sky's blessing, but kept wishing she had done things differently that day. Not told her apprentice about the prettybirds' intelligent behavior. Kept from mentioning in the same conversation how she'd been thwarted in her assignment. Made herself lie or omit part of the truth. One or the other. Really, there was no connection between those two things, though the girl had acted like receiving confirmation of her belief in the prettybirds' sentience obligated her to take on Trill's assignment. As if the two of them were involved in a trade.

She reminded herself that Dola had volunteered to go through the trustees' treatment in Trill's place. That as her mentor Trill had followed tradition in accepting Dola's help. Nothing got rid of her guilt.

Freddie and Isabelle lifted Dola from the table and moved her to a place Trill couldn't see. They made the table lower and wider and moved her back. In a new position; Dola's face was visible now. Her eyes were shut, as Trill had feared.

Her apprentice had been raped.

Now Freddie took off his overalls completely and lay down naked beside the naked girl. "What if the baby that come out be one a mine?" he asked.

"We be able to tell right away if it do more than breathe. Brain gonna be empty as what they put you in. An your body sterile, too. Doan worry. Dr. Ops took care a everthang. Now kiss her. Harder—wake her up!"

When a permanent installation is deemed optimal, operational success will almost certainly derive from creating appropriate transfer stock in situ.

—*Mission Guidelines,* Psyche Moth, *2055*

"The baby will be his—"

"No!" Trill raised a hand as if she could snatch Dola's complacency out of the air, then dropped it to her lap. "Even if he claims the birth, it will also belong to Dr. Ops. The baby will be a blank space for him to write another person onto. That's what they're planning."

The girl twisted the necklace Trill had given her, looking puzzled. "All babies are blank, aren't they?" She seemed not to believe that she had been raped, not to mind—probably because she didn't remember it. Only the consensual sex afterwards. Which Trill had felt obligated to watch till a more natural sleep claimed her apprentice and flowerlight dawned.

Not till then did she descend from the roof and go to Odell, who had spent the night with the new settlement's Traders Dopkwe. She sent him to the Jubilee Ladies with the best words she could come up with to describe what had happened. When she went back to the trustees' house the door's curtain was pulled back, and no one was inside except Isabelle. It took time to find Dola helping to construct a terrace on steep slopes, laboring away as if nothing were amiss, smelling pleasantly of sex and sweat. Trill had drawn her aside and insisted on talking with her out of the dopkwe's hearing, alone.

"No one is born blank, not exactly. We say the soul is building itself, a process going on before birth—and after—

but these are things you can learn later." Rote knowledge was rarely important when it came to an apprentice's final test. "All I want now is to let you know what has happened soon enough that you can have an easy abortion."

Dola's palms curled protectively over her young, pouting belly. "You're sure?"

Should she lie? "Almost. I need to ask the elders. And the Ladies. They'll decide what to do. We have to go back to Jubilee; Unique could test you, treat you—"

Here came Isabelle, Freddie right behind him.

"You don't know!" The girl stood up from the fuzz in one enviably smooth motion. "You're just jealous!"

"What?" Trill stood up, too, but stayed where she was as Dola hurried to her rapist's embrace. Jealous? Of whom? Of what? Dola's pregnancy? But Trill already had a child, though LeeRai'd been born out of Hett's womb... Jealous of Freddie? "I go with men," she murmured to herself. Dola didn't hear her. She was too far away.

The rest of that day the girl kept her distance. And the next. At Trill's approach she would scowl and leave her soup untasted, her seeds unsown, her conversations with her cohort unfinished.

In the following morning's flowerlight, though, Trill woke to find Dola snuggled against her side, her warm breath heaving hard with pain but her whispers quiet in Trill's ear. "—like you—said—it was—like you—said it was—I know—it was—"

"Shhh." She soothed the girl's scalp, brushing back a few tiny brown braids that had escaped their arrangement. "Now. Now." She was glad to hear the girl acknowledge she was right. That was what she'd been waiting for, why she hadn't returned to Jubilee. But she wished she'd been wrong.

The trustees had tested the eighteens-to-twenty-fours girl's urine to make sure their procedure worked. They hadn't thought Dola would overhear or understand when they gloated about the results.

Trill told Isabelle she and Dola were going home the next

day, and he and Freddie started repacking. Lou took Odell's place, bearing his former load. Knowing what was inside the big box, Trill was glad not to be asked to carry it.

At noon they stopped only briefly to eat and continued on. Again the trustees seemed not to notice the sentries in the chrismas trees, though Trill smelled and even heard at least four. They were much further out than she'd expected. Then they came upon Adia waiting for them. Trill was glad; otherwise, she would have brought the trustees to Jubilee's main site. Instead, they descended from the mountains slightly to the west of the hot springs, where Unique lived.

This was better. Treatment could start right away. She put a hand on Dola's tense shoulder, felt its warmth through the fabric of the girl's thin dress.

On Jubilee's outskirts, with so many gardens around, the danger of quill-throwing grazers was higher than at the settlement's center. People built houses here anyway, but not the nicest ones. Haphazard weaving, uneven roofs... Unique's was small enough he wouldn't be able to share it with more than two or three members of his dopkwe. Dola and Trill sat on the bare dirt floor, without mats. Freddie and Isabelle had invited themselves in only to be politely ignored until Adia offered to show them where they could stay.

Always smiling, slender as the branch of a bottle tree, Unique lowered himself apologetically to the house's one piece of furniture, a stool Trill and Dola had insistently refused.

"I appreciate your consideration," he said, "though it's going to make refusing you more difficult."

"You think you know what we're going to ask for?" Had he heard a rumor? From whom? Trill looked sideways at Dola's expressionless face.

"Women of your age cohorts generally come to me for one of two things: an abortion or fertility aids. It could be the latter, but being aware of Trill's preferences..."

Dola flushed, probably with anger. "You're right. I've been raped and I want lookoutforthelily. I'll take a pregnancy test."

Unique's pleasant expression remained in place yet faded. "What about talking this idea over with the Ladies first?"

"I *am* a Lady," Trill said. "As you're aware."

"*A* Lady. Only one. The others, though, have yet to be consulted. They—"

"What? What? You give her that plant! You have no right to do anything else!"

"I have no choice. Unless you are able to tell me the girl's condition has nothing to do with what the Ladies sent you off for." As silence dragged in the wake of his words, Unique's smile become smaller and more ironic.

He addressed Dola. "If the Ladies allow it, later, come back to me for an abortion, child. With your mentor or without her. Now, though, I think you should attend the meeting."

"What meeting?" But through the house's door she saw Adia returning, silhouetted by leaflight.

"Come," she said. They went.

Resource extraction may be greatly improved by the wide establishment of surface stock suitable for hosting multiple-generation downloads of reliable trustees. However, anticipated benefits must be weighed against highly probable costs such as lander production; fuel expenditure; embryo manufacture, storage, and implantation tools; remote downloading equipment; and of course against the risk of hostile client reaction to this initiative's primary agents.

— Mission Guidelines, Psyche Moth, *2055*

Adia, Robeson, Kala, True—even in the shimmering half-dark she knew their faces easily, their names. But it was Dola she looked at while she told the gathering of Ladies how her apprentice had lain helplessly unconscious under the trustee's assault as she, Trill, responsible for her, could only watch.

Black creases angled down between the girl's eyebrows and her thin lips pinched together. Her chin lifted, her head tilted back, but tears spilled down her cheeks anyway, reflecting the pastel shine of the hannakka bush branch in Trill's hand. She tried to pass it to Dola. The eighteens-to-twenty-fours refused it; evidently she didn't want to talk yet.

Kala took the bright branch. "We should kill them. But we can't. Dr. Ops's guidelines won't protect us from him if we do."

Adia's turn. "We have to stop em. Back before the final trustee died, our work was too hard! Let em get a new toehold now and we ain't never gonna have no peace.

"What we gotta do is this: have the babies but keep the downloads from happenin right. Corrupt em. Hide the mothers an kids afterwards till it's no more danger—maybe find a island for that down near Nunavut or Panonica."

Hands waved in the darkness like lightless leaves. Questions: Affect the downloads how? With what? Suggestions: Allow the downloads and then raise the newborn trustees as double agents. Or abandon them, isolate them where they could do no harm. Objections: Dr. Ops would only try again.

And at last Dola accepted and held the hannakka branch. Her head lowered. Tears spattered into the water, sent ripples of darkness through the bright reflection. Head up again, she spoke. "I want an abortion."

Robeson reached out. "But you can't—"

Dola snatched the branch away from the Lady's grasp. "I can! I will! I know the plant—I'll figure out the dosage—"

Trill shivered, cold in the warm water. So many had died proving the pharmacopeia of Amends that first generation, despite all the Ladies' precautions. Her own mother, for one.

"Listen!" Robeson grabbed again and this time tore the top of the hannakka branch free. "If you don't stay pregnant, they'll do some other girl the same way they done you! That what you want?"

"No! No!" Shouting, waving the stub of branch she held, Dola backed out of the pool. "I don't! I don't want anybody hurt but I—I won't—I can't—No!" And she was gone.

Silence ruled the meeting for long moments.

"She pass. Yall agree?" Adia asked. The other Ladies nodded.

"Trill, you go tell her. She a Lady now." But Trill couldn't move yet. She waited for the news to sink in. This had been Dola's test. The girl had passed.

Trill hadn't known. She hadn't known. They hadn't told her—mind crawling into movement again she understood why: because she couldn't lie.

Even so, she should have known. Because there was no reason Dola couldn't have an abortion. Not logically, and not according to any precedent, and no, no reason at all. Absolutely none.

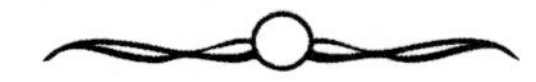

When setbacks occur to planned or in-place operations, best practice is to inquire as to their causes, even when they are assumed to be known. Worst practice is immediate retaliation. Biological entities are limited in their abilities, scope, and lifespans. Orders are orders, and must be carried out—eventually.

— *Mission Guidelines,* Psyche Moth, *2055*

Leaflight died. Unique's little house looked dark and sounded quiet. Trill knocked on the doorpost and called Dola's name, but only he answered. He had not seen her. The girl had not come there.

Under the sky's last scattering of grace she walked slowly, quietly, toward where the trustees were supposed to sleep. Soon Trill saw their white glow breaking through poorly woven walls. Dola would never have gone to them willingly. If they had managed to compel her—

A shadow shifted, became the tens-to-thirteens named Lou. Touching his ear she led him off a safe distance to talk. Dola was not in there, either. And Isabelle was awake.

The sensible thing to do would be to wait till flowerlight. Lookoutforthelilies grew somewhere nearby. Didn't they? She could find them in plenty of time. Dola would need to prepare them somehow. Wouldn't she? Plenty of time.

She tried to wait sensibly. That didn't last.

Instead of asking for help as she should have, Trill left on her own. Anyone else would only slow her down. While the path met her feet firmly she walked east. Downward. After a while the scent of the sea informed her of where she was. Sinking in suddenly looser soil, she trod forward a few more steps. The terrain rose very slightly, confirming that this was the edge of the dunescape. Where, if she remembered correctly, the plants Dola was looking for could be found. And, hopefully, Dola.

Who might not want Trill to find her.

Now that she needed the cover of full night, now the buds unfurled, shining, showing themselves to their pollinators. Showing the gentle slopes and hollows lying between her and the distant water. And—oh, wonderful!—another woman's back bending low over the ground, dress fluttering, a long stick in her hands.

Closer, she was sure. Dola.

The wind's direction helped. It was too early for the girl to expect anybody to have followed her here, and facing the ocean as she did, neither sight nor sound provided her with clues of Trill's presence.

It was the prettybirds who betrayed her. A rainbow flash caught the corner of her eyes; it grew and filled the air, a huge flock of them streaming out of the trees, over her head, over Dola and then circling around, reversing their flight path. Trill followed them with her eyes. When she turned her gaze on the girl again she saw that Dola, too, had tracked the flock and of course noticed Trill, just ten arms away by now.

The girl frowned as she lifted a handsome basket, green stalks peeping over its lip. "You can't stop me—I won't let you. Keep away." She backed up several steps and seemed about to turn and run.

"Wait! No!" Trill did the least threatening thing she could think of: sat down. "The Ladies are fine with an abortion."

"They're not! They said—"

"It was lies! They lied—we had to find out if you'd give in. If you'd do something you knew was wrong because the Ladies told you to, we couldn't let you join."

"You—you lied? You *lied*—to *me*?" The basket slumped in the girl's grasp.

Trill rose to her knees. "No. I didn't realize what the others were doing. I didn't know till after you left."

"How could they do that to you? To *me*?"

Trill shrugged. "I'm no good at not telling the truth. All the Ladies understand. So if they told me, they told you. It wouldn't have worked. Wouldn't have been a test."

"But—aren't you angry?"

"Yes. I should have known. A little. Yes."

"Not at yourself—" Dola stopped midsentence. Trill opened her own mouth to ask why and prettybirds surrounded them, their colors everywhere: swirling rainclouds and ripe gold seeds brushed against their arms, night and ivory and crimson filled the sky above and on their either side. And now a red luminousness hovered before them, its bright yellow wings beating the air as it blinked once, twice, four times, eight—not the same bird, but the same sequence!

Trembling, Trill repeated it. Received it in answer. Again. Again.

And then the prettybirds were gone. Her fingers hurt. Dola held them, crushed them in her hands. How had that happened?

"I saw! I saw! Trill—I'm a Lady now, we're equals? I can be your friend? And we can make a dopkwe, a new one, talk to them—oh, Trill! I saw!"

Counting. That was all the prettybirds had done so far. It was a long way from that to conversation.

A long way, but a good one. A good trail to walk. And not alone. She laughed softly to herself without opening her mouth, gently loosening the tight hold on her hands, making it more comfortable. Not remotely alone.

Mission of Greed

Sue Lange

In the third week after gagarin123 landed on an unnamed planet sweeping through a solar system claimed by ValeroCorp, First Mechanic Bertie Lai's chance for fame slowly swirled down the shitter.

And just yesterday things had been moving along swimmingly. René Genie, the mission biologist, had not yet found sentient life; the geologist, Aadil Alzeshi, had discovered beautiful 1.4. Specifically, he'd hit some pitchblende with enough uranium in it for ValeroCorp to recoup the cost of this mission. Yesterday Lai was sure her deal was sealed. But last night, Second Mechanic Charlene Sekibo discovered Alzeshi's numbers were off. The uranium was not quite beautiful after all.

When the day for blows between the mission biologist and the mission geologist came, Lai would side with Alzeshi. He was an unassuming young man with good posture, springy black hair, and tortoise-shell glasses. Methodical and quiet, he was. What was not to like? But even if Alzeshi was a big, fat oaf with bad breath and obsequious manners, Lai would still side with him. The geologist's numbers would be a ticket to immortality. ValeroCorp named planets with the beautiful 1.4 after their ship's commanders-in-chief, in this case, First Mechanic Bertie Lai. That and the fat bonus the energy company would hand Lai meant she had a lot riding on Alzeshi's number.

More than usual, in fact. At the age of fifty, she had a lot of life to live yet, but not a lot of missions. She'd received enough radiation in twenty years of service to be flirting dangerously close to her lifetime limit of 400 mSv, and she'd yet to be on a successful mission. This was to be her last shot at fame. If Alzeshi found a goodly amount of exploitable uranium, Lai's pals back at the club in Chicago would be impressed.

On this particular morning, three weeks in, Lai unsnibbed the hatch to gander at the planet's landscape and gauge the chances this deserted place offered. She hadn't yet been out beyond the perimeter of the valley where gagarin123 landed. That was Genie's territory, where the pond scum lay over everything. Lai knew about the pond scum before they even landed. Between the Supremely Big Telescoping assays that determined the atmosphere had enough oxygen to suspect at least single-celled life and the photos from flybys prior to landing, she knew everything about this planet that was pertinent. It had plate tectonics for uranium, air to breathe, and no large animals to worry over. It was her planet. She just knew it.

For the past few weeks she'd been assisting Alzeshi with his core sampler apparatus. A first mechanic is supposed to watch over all mission activities, troubleshooting as she goes, but Lai was interested in only one thing: the uranium. The constituents of the pond scum never entered her thoughts. Today, though, she wondered about what might be beyond the beyond.

She cranked the handle on the hatch. Before she could pull the door open it pushed in by itself. Aadil Alzeshi, the man with the less than beautiful uranium, slumped over the lip of the hatch, dead. She knew it was Alzeshi by the khaki polyester jacket and trousers. Nothing else was recognizable.

Lai dropped to her knees and barked at Genie, standing off to the side. He seemed transfixed.

"Can I get a hand here?" she yelled.

Genie shook himself from his stupor and together they rolled Alzeshi over. His face was gone for the most part: a bloody mass, same as what were once his hands. One opaque eyeball hung by the nerve. His jaw flopped open and several teeth rattled to the floor.

Genie knee-jerked at the sight. He fell on his ass and scrabbled back against the base of an instrument panel next to the hatch. "It's them!" he screamed, his eyes liquid with fear.

Before Lai could ask who "them" was, Security Officer Carpenter ran up from Sekibo's quarters.

"Stand away from the body. No one touches it without gloves," he shouted, and then without a pause: "Dr. Genie is confined to quarters."

"Are you nuts?" Lai looked up from her hands to Carpenter. Because everyone knew the biologist and the geologist are natural born enemies, she understood Carpenter's reaction, but he was going too far. This mission was not even close to the point where one would murder the other. Sure it happened a lot "out here," but only when the situation was close. gagarin123 hadn't even precipitated a situation yet. "There's no need—" she tried to say.

"Step back!" Carpenter ordered. "As security officer, I have command of the situation." He stood over Alzeshi's body like a dog guarding a bone. "Dr. Axelrod will perform an autopsy."

Lai stood. She glanced toward Axelrod, the mission psychologist/medic who was standing further up in the passageway and leaning against the door of the storage closet, seemingly amused.

"It's them!" Genie repeated from his spot on the floor. "Carpenter knows. He knows! Ask him!" Genie seemed frozen in fear, unable to rise on his own, or explain further what he meant. He pointed in horror at Carpenter, waiting for Lai to figure it out and take action.

Lai took it in and looked to Carpenter. "I'm still in command of this ship even if you're in control of this incident," she said. "Check your manual. I'm not stepping on your toes when I respectfully request what the fuck is going on here."

Carpenter began opening and closing his fist, a sign he was pumping adrenalin for an attack. Lai knew he was a Pinkerton dude. Not the kindly retiree that roamed the halls of troubled high schools either. A true Carnegie Pinkerton, he'd be ready at any moment to bust a union, a head, or a cherry, whatever it took. He was fully licensed and outfitted, and he had an eight-inch, steel facial plate implanted in his forehead. He was a big, big guy and not to be messed with.

Lai glanced up at the ship camera, non-verbally suggesting Carpenter might want to take it down a notch.

The Pinkerton relaxed his fists and swiveled his face from Lai to Genie. "For the record, I do not know what is going on here and with your..." he swiveled back to Lai. "... permission... I will confiscate the remote sensor video recordings for investigation. It is apparent Dr. Genie discovered sentient life and so as of now, he is under suspicion of murder and must remain in his quarters until a full investigation is done."

Lai opened her mouth to argue but Genie cut her off. "It's not me! It's them!" he screamed. His body regained its functionality and he jumped up to close the hatch while continuing to scream, "Not me! Not me!"

Carpenter leaped forward and caught him from behind, wrapping one gorilla arm around Genie's midsection and squeezing off his air. With the other he bent the man's head forward ninety degrees, thereby incapacitating the biologist, who continued to sputter his defense incoherently. Finally he choked out, "Close the door," as Carpenter lifted him up and away, stifling any last words Genie might utter.

Lai stepped over and as she closed the hatch, she saw, or thought she saw, an individual, something, a hundred yards off in the shadow of a rock. The person or thing seemed to raise a hand as if beckoning or waving goodbye or? Lai blinked and the individual resolved into a part of the rock? Maybe. She slowly closed the door and tightened the snibs. Back inside she tallied personnel: Carpenter and Genie struggling up the passageway, Sekibo and Axelrod standing, Alzeshi on the floor dead. Who was outside?

"First Mechanic, I… suggest… you help Dr. Axelrod carry the body to the dissection room," Carpenter called. "Wear gloves. That's an order."

Lai returned to the matter at hand and momentarily forgot about the possibility of sentient life on this planet. The thought was not actually forgotten but tucked into a back fold of her brain. She pondered instead Carpenter. His last post before this detail was bodyguard to Chancellor Schmack in Chicago, the main man, *capo di tutti* and all that. Lai often wondered why Carpenter had stepped down from such a lucrative job. Boredom, maybe, with the bureaucratic circus.

Chicago was the center of the world. All the multinationals like ValeroCorp had their offices there. The so-called government, too, centered itself in Chicago. Chancellor Schmack was democracy's current leader and Carpenter had had a cake job with him. He probably saw no action whatsoever in that well structured environment.

Whatever, Carpenter was here and under the circumstances—the geologist's death—he had the right to order everybody around. The only thing saving the situation for Lai was that, in the absence of direct supervision, protocol was every Pinkerton dude's master. He'd stick to it if it killed him.

Lai turned to Axelrod. "Do you know what's going on here?" she asked.

"Sure," Axelrod said in a dry tone. "Alzeshi here got a face lift and we're going to move what's left of him into this closet so I can find out how he died. Genie's under arrest. Carpenter is taking over the ship. It appears you've got a most unfortunate mutiny, darling."

Lai, hand on hips, looked from Axelrod to Sekibo, who had been silent throughout the ordeal. First Mechanic Lai had no hope of procuring any insight from her second, who generally had no opinions on anything. If Carpenter was a slave to protocol, Sekibo was its accountant. She'd kept meticulous track of every movement any member of the team had made since gagarin123 landed on this planet. She was perfect in a measured way. Lai hadn't trusted her from the beginning. Disguising AI as a robot indistinguishable from a human was against the law, but multinationals like ValeroCorp did it occasionally. They hated feeding humans. And trusting them.

Was Sekibo a plant? Lai didn't really think so. The second mechanic on any ship is by definition bucking for a first mechanic's position. Until she gets her own mission, a secmech receives lousy pay and little respect from the other crew members. For that reason most secmechs were overtly official and efficient. And they sought any opportunity to insert themselves into any conversation in the hopes that somebody will someday report their efficiency to the straights back in Chicago. Sekibo came out of South Dallas. She'd spent the last five years bootstrapping herself out of that handicap. Up until last night her efficiency made Lai uncomfortable. Nobody but an AI could be so unemotional. But last night, Lai discovered Sekibo was entertaining Carpenter in her quarters. Nice to know Sekibo was human, but Lai still didn't trust her. Something about efficiency in the face of lust didn't sit right with her.

"We can handle this," she said to Sekibo. "Why don't you see if Carpenter needs help."

The suggestion worked. Sekibo retreated up the passageway. Once she was out of earshot, Lai turned to Axelrod. "So why was Alzeshi out after curfew?" she asked.

Lai wasn't seeking after facts, she wanted to know what Alzeshi had been thinking, and Axelrod was the go-to person in this case. Required on every mission to detect and treat cases of the space crazies, the psychologist/medico usually had little to do but pass judgment. Once in a while they got a puzzle to work out, like Lai's current situation.

But Axelrod seemed uninterested in rising to the occasion. "How on this godforsaken planet should I know?" she answered as she reached for a box from a shelf in the closet.

"I'd think you'd know," Lai answered. "I mean, isn't human motivation your bag?"

"He was probably disappointed with his beautiful 1.4. Maybe he was out taking more samples. Genie was busting ass." Axelrod extracted a pair of blue neoprene gloves from the box before replacing it on the shelf.

Lai thought about it. ValeroCorp's mandate for gagarin123 was to find uranium, but Chicago demanded biological assays to make sure exploiting a planet wouldn't mess with any natives. That was just procedure as far as ValeroCorp was concerned; no one besides a biologist ever really wants to find sentient life. Sentient life mucks up the works. The current chancellor and Carpenter's former boss, Schmack, was pro-business all the way. He had been using his agglomerated power to change laws as fast as possible to favor organizations such as ValeroCorp. Good on him.

Genie, for his part, had not appeared insensitive to the situation. Lai knew he sweated to find life with a high enough SQ, sentient quotient, to put a check on any uranium exploitation. Not preclude it, just regulate it before legislation was passed that allowed unchecked exploitation

According to the logs, Genie had been clocking hundreds of miles every day in the e-spev transporter. As per procedure, Carpenter had been going along on the forays. You never know when you'll need security.

Lai guessed that sometime during all that movement Genie set up his remote sensors out in the beyond hoping to capture shots of motile life: animals.

To Lai, this part of the planet looked a lot like Earth's moon: dead and boring. But up beyond the beyond lay the pond scum and Genie's chance for biological fame. Sentience comes in many forms and is not always easy to detect. So far he'd only found single-celled organisms, masses of them. "It's not pond scum," he told her often. "Pond scum is really duck weed, a vascular plant. This is just algae." Which seemed worse for his case, but he kept looking, searching for something that ate the stuff maybe. The planet seemed rife with possibility but nothing was showing up. And Alzeshi had found his uranium, and so Genie sweated; he needed something spectacular to stave off rampant rampaging by ValeroCorp. Had he found something in his remotes?

Lai thought about the vision of the hand beckoning in the shadow of the rock. Even if there was something in need of protection, Genie should no longer be concerned about Alzeshi. Or anyone. The geologist's numbers had turned out to be wrong. Carpenter was way off base.

Once they moved Alzeshi's body to the closet, Lai left Axelrod to have at it. A ball was slowly forming in her stomach. With all efforts at the original mission halted, she'd lose her last chance. She was sure the uranium was here; all Alzeshi had needed was more samples. He'd have found his beautiful 1.4. Lai considered the difficulties of chasing after the numbers. How hard could it be to run a core sampler alone? She'd been watching the procedure the past few weeks.

At any rate, she needed to do something quickly. Once Carpenter announced his investigation was done, Chicago would call them home. Unless, of course, ValeroCorp could pay off the right public servant to overlook the death of a human. That wasn't a given. ValeroCorp was powerful, but sometimes not powerful enough. Sometimes someone in government had an agenda. For personal reasons they'd screw up the natural order of greed and corruption that usually provides for efficient exploitation of the universe's bounty. Would Schmack get involved with such a thing and do a ruling? Would it get that far? She hoped it would.

If she was going to get her planet, Lai needed to collect those samples before Carpenter did something screwy like decree Martial Law. She mostly needed to know where to sample. She needed Alzeshi's notes.

She found Sekibo and Carpenter running through the remote sensor results in her own quarters. "You can return to handling the daily checks," she ordered Sekibo. "I'll assist Carpenter in the investigation."

"Yes, ma'am," Sekibo answered and immediately left the room. Lai watched her for a moment. Her head was level, her hair pulled back into a perfect bun, the collar on her jumpsuit crisp. Without hesitation she began recording instrument readouts. She showed no sign of having been affected by Carpenter's lovemaking, Alzeshi's death, or Lai's dislike. Nothing could touch her, she was stone. Or rubber and copper?

Lai thought about that for a moment and then turned into the room.

For the next hour she pored over the mission records with the security officer: audio recordings from inside the ship; remote video sensor results from outside; numbers, slides. While Carpenter viewed the video footage from Genie's remote sensors, she checked Alzeshi's logs. One perfect core sample would do it.

At one point, Lai was sure she'd found it, a spot close by in the landing valley, a place not even beyond the beyond. Now she needed a reason to excuse herself. She looked up from the recorder, "You want to give me a clue as to what we're looking for here?"

"By law, I don't need to tell you anything," Carpenter said. "This is a murder investigation."

"I understand, but I could do a better job if I knew what's in your head. Why is Genie a suspect?"

"Everyone's a suspect."

"Surely not everyone. Not you."

"This is not a joke, ma'am."

"I'm not joking. We didn't all do it. I don't believe Genie did it, but he seems to know who did. Why aren't you talking to him?"

Carpenter hit the stop button and inhaled stiffly. "I believe Genie discovered high SQ life."

For a moment the blip of the hand waving in the shadow

of the rock entered Lai's thoughts. She brushed it away and said, "Hence 'them'. Possibly the culprits. At any rate, that's not a crime. Why is Genie incarcerated?"

"If he discovered high SQ life, he was remiss in not warning the crew."

"But I ordered everyone to wait the full eight hours before reporting any numbers. Just to be sure."

Indeed Lai had given that order. She'd been hungry for the numbers for about ten years and once before had jumped to false conclusions. Oh the looks she got when she returned to Chicago. The smirks and smug jokes. She'd vowed to never have a repeat of that.

"That was for reporting to mission control," Carpenter said. "As per procedure, he should have said something to us. So to answer your question, I need to know what Dr. Genie knew."

Lai watched Carpenter without responding for a few moments then returned to her own concerns. She retrieved a pad and pen from her desk. She liked taking notes manually around the snooping cameras and their incessant recording of every activity on board. Pad and pen was the only way to ensure privacy. As long as she held the pad correctly, the cameras wouldn't pick it up. She sat and began scribbling coordinates.

After a few minutes Carpenter broke the silence. "There!" he shouted. Lai flinched at the sound, composed herself, and stepped over to the viewer. Nothing. The ubiquitous pond scum from frame to frame.

"This is the sentient life?" she asked.

"Keep watching."

And then suddenly, out of nowhere, a hand waving. It seemed to grow out of the layer of algae like a human arm rising up from mud.

"What the..." she said.

And then it was gone, melted back into the mix.

"And watch this," Carpenter said, clicking to a different recorder. He found what he was looking for and said, "This is time lapsed. The whole sequence takes a couple of hours."

Lai watched again. A pond or depression filled with the algae. And then entering the frame from the right, a rock, carried along by a river or bed of slime perhaps. The rock rolled into the pit without a splash. The hump from its form remained visible for a few moments and then it melted into the pool as if it had been digested. And then a stream of the slime seemingly crawled out of the pond and off the frame to the left. As if it had a mind of its own.

"We need Genie for this," Lai said. "This is something. And he knows about it." She stood to make for the door.

"Dr. Genie is under arrest."

"I understand, but we need to find out about this. He knows what this is."

"Whatever he knows, we'll soon know. More importantly, his negligence resulted in a death."

"But he said you knew this, too."

"He told me he'd found something. I had no idea what it was. But he knew. He admitted it when he saw what happened to Dr. Alzeshi. You saw that yourself. His failure to inform us indicates he is guilty of manslaughter. But considering what is at stake, he is probably guilty of murder. I'm quite sure he did this on purpose. I've seen it before."

"This is outrageous. You're jumping to illogical conclusions. If he found high SQ, then he wouldn't—"

"I've seen it before. And I'm in charge here. I have strict procedures. Genie admitted his guilt and I need to find out if malice was intended. I can't do that if he is allowed access to the evidence."

"This is insane. Genie is no more guilty than I am. How was he to know Alzeshi was going to break curfew? I knew Alzeshi was outside. I discovered it during checks last night."

Indeed Lai had discovered it during her checks the previous night. She discovered other things too, things about Charlene Sekibo and Dufresne Carpenter. Something that gave her pause, but little more than that at the time. When she passed by Sekibo's quarters she'd heard the muffled sound of two voices. It had made her glad to think Sekibo was indeed human. She thought nothing about it beyond that.

When Lai had checked the personnel logs later she learned it was Carpenter in with the secmech. Fraternizing was not against the rules, wasn't even surprising. Sekibo was pure-blood African. Carpenter had been eyeing her the whole trip. Discovering Carpenter and Sekibo's secret was not something she would have had on either of the two; it was just interesting for its own sake. But not very. Lai was more concerned with the uranium numbers and cared little about anything else going on.

More interesting at the time was that the logs showed Alzeshi had gone out after curfew. An unusual thing for someone to do, but not unheard of. Alzeshi had just had a disappointing jolt. Lai figured he was out kicking at pavement so to say. She left him to his solitude. Maybe he was even working overtime. Lai had no reason to make a big deal about bringing him back in last night. Especially if he was looking for better numbers.

"I did nothing about it," Lai said. "That could be viewed as breaking protocol. And now Alzeshi's dead. Are you going to arrest me as well?"

Carpenter lifted his head from the view finder and slowly stood.

"First Mechanic Lai, I am placing you under arrest. You are to—"

"What! Are you c—"

"—remain in your quarters for the duration of this mission. Your actions have resulted in the mission geologist's death. By code 39f52c, you are under arrest."

By now Carpenter had stood to his full size.

"I will conduct a thorough investigation and apprise you of the results," he said. "Mission gagarin123 will be leaving as soon as my investigation is complete."

"You have no right to decide when this ship leaves. That is

still my—"

"I have every right and even if I didn't, once Second Mechanic Sekibo conveys our findings to Chicago, a dispatch will order us to return immediately. I'm sorry, First Mechanic Lai, but procedures require this action. I'll be back to receive your statement within an hour."

Carpenter exited. Lai heard the deadbolt click on other side and rushed to her comm unit.

> To: Earnest Crumpf/Valerocorp Command
> Recon, Chicago
> From: Mechanic Bertrina Lai/gagarin123
> Re:
> cc:
> --------------------
>
> Ernie, I need override assistance. Security has taken control on a technicality. I can't figure out what the game is, but integrity of this mission is compromised. Fairly certain security and secmech are AI-driven. Please advise.

"Send," Lai stated.

"Browser offline," the machine answered. "No connection possible."

"Dammit!" She wasn't fast enough. Carpenter cut the outside line to preclude exactly what she was trying to do. The two of them. Sekibo and Carpenter. What were they doing? Whatever they were up to last night in Sekibo's cabin had nothing to do with fun and games. Who had programmed them? Their actions were preventing ValeroCorp from cashing in on their investment. Who had motivation for this? Or were these two malfunctioning?

For half an hour Lai sat on the sofa in her quarters, going through the images of Alzeshi's body, the beckoning hand outside and in the video footage. She rubbed her forehead while thoughts of her failed career, rather than her incarceration, occupied her mind until despair crept in. Then she began grasping at chunks of her hair, squeezing and pulling, thinking of how the word "manslaughter" would look stamped across her record.

Nobody followed written-down rules to the letter. Nobody. You can't. Not out in the vac. Beyond the beyond has its own set of rules. She'd seen plenty of after-mission parties with the clowns' stories of bringing home illegal species, reroutes on the fly to check out unscheduled planets, fudging of the beautiful one-four.

"Carpenter!" she screamed, slamming her palm against the door. "I need a psychologist!" The only thing that would get something meticulously following the rules to open the door. It was against protocol to leave a case of the space crazies untreated. Even convicts had rights.

Three hours later, after she'd fallen asleep exhausted from replaying scenarios in her head, Lai awoke with a start. Axelrod was standing over her. "Ain't this sweet?" the woman said. She had alcohol on her breath.

"Dipping into the propanol again?" Lai said. She squeezed her fingers into the corners of her eyes to wake herself up.

Axelrod pushed Lai's legs to the floor and sat down. "You're in a good mood, considering your circumstances," she said. Her hair was disheveled. Strands of it stuck out from the band at odd angles. Her lipstick was long gone. A remnant, a lone smear, rode up her left cheekbone.

"What time is it?" Lai asked. "Carpenter cut my comm links."

Axelrod shrugged and shook her head.

"How did Alzeshi die?" Lai asked.

Axelrod lay back and closed her eyes. "Shock. From burns. Chemical."

"Like what you'd get if you fell into an acid bath?"

Not surprised or maybe too tired to be surprised, Axelrod only said, "The same."

"What about his clothes?"

"Sulfuric doesn't touch synthetics."

"Ah. Tell me about Sekibo and Carpenter."

"What about them?"

"Are they… psychos, or AIs?"

"They passed their tests, their security clearances, and their emergency exams."

"Are they overly ambitious? In a clinical way, I mean. Can they be declared…"

"That information is confidential and you know it." Axelrod opened her eyes and rolled her head toward Lai. "You know this is my last mission, too. I'm not losing my pension because you need me to do something—"

"Carpenter's overreacting."

"He's following procedure to the letter. It's his job."

"Nice job."

"Nice ass."

"For Chrissake, Doc! How about a little respect. This maniac incarcerated the biologist and the first mechanic!"

"The biologist and first mechanic are incarcerated because they did not follow procedures. Don't expect me to do the same because you find yourself in difficult circumstances. These things require certain actions."

"I can't believe you agree with that lunatic!" Lai said with a clenched jaw. Then she remembered Carpenter was listening in. The whole world, actually, was listening in, in a recorded kind of way. Axelrod would never have spouted this official garbage otherwise. Under the circumstances there was just so much the psychologist could say or do. Doc was simply hedging her opinions. Considering her pension and all.

Lai grabbed her pad and pen and began scribbling: "I need to talk to Genie. He could be a murderer, but I don't think so."

After a few moments she walked over and handed the pad to Axelrod. Axelrod read the note, then stood to go. "I'm beat," she said.

Lai wrote more: "Carpenter spent the night with Sekibo."

She figured that would get the psychologist. Axelrod had been eyeing that eight-inch plate the whole trip.

"La de da," Axelrod said before turning from Lai.

Lai clasped the woman's forearm to hold her back. "This thing stinks. You know it does," she whispered.

Axelrod looked at the hand on the arm and then turned fiercely on Lai. "Of course it stinks! The head mechanic on this mission has been relieved of her duties and now the mission's run by a security guard."

"No. The investigation's run by the security guard; the mission is being run by my second. Does she have the experience to get us home safely?"

Lai released her grip. The psychologist exited and the door shut silently behind her. The deadbolt clicked back into place.

Half an hour later, Carpenter stood in the doorway of Lai's cabin. "Dr. Genie has been accused of murder," he announced. "You will act as representative in the trial to be held in one hour. You are allowed fifteen minutes' consultation with your client."

So Axelrod came through. The psychologist had found something in the regs that Carpenter had to follow. Accusations resulting in off-planet execution require a lawyer for the defendant before sentence is carried out? Maybe. Shit! Was Carpenter planning on disintegrating Genie? Why? And Alzeshi? That was an accident. Surely. At any rate, Carpenter's strict adherence to the rules meant he had to allow someone to act as Genie's lawyer. Axelrod convinced Carpenter it should be Lai. Probably lied through her teeth about psychological profiles or something. And with the ship recording every conversation and action, everything had to go according to procedures. Carpenter had no choice.

Lai moved into the passageway and Carpenter followed behind as she walked down to Genie's quarters. She could feel his breath on the back of her neck.

She passed by Sekibo keying ship's vitals into her recorder. Good ol' Sekibo following mission procedures. Man's dead, but as long as we log the oxygen/carbon dioxide ratios every hour, we're good.

In his cabin, Genie was glistening with sweat, even between the French braids. His tunic had moisture patches under the armpits. He sat at his table, his head on his hands. When Lai entered, he raised bloodshot eyes toward her. Slowly his upper middle class dignity returned. He inhaled and lifted his chin. "I demand a line to Chicago," he said. "You all are not using me as a patsy for... whatever it is that you're pulling."

"Relax," Lai said. She had no patience for someone grandstanding, regardless of his pedigree. If Genie was guilty, she'd be happy to see him fry, but meantime, it looked like Lai was going down with him if she couldn't figure out Carpenter's angle. Did Genie know what it was? Probably, but he wouldn't say anything with Carpenter listening in.

"As per procedure, I'm here to act in your defense," Lai said. "You are facing mandatory execution if this doesn't go well. I suggest you cooperate."

"Execution?" All privileged bluster left him. He sat back down at his table and stared ahead, unfocused. "This is... insane." He turned a stone eye to Lai. A corner of his lip twitched. "What's going on here?"

"Thank you, Officer," Lai nodded to Carpenter who waited a moment before retreating to the passageway.

"You have fifteen minutes," the Pinkerton said before closing and locking the door.

Lai quickly sat next to Genie at the table and placed her pad between them. She began writing as she said, "When you first saw Dr. Alzeshi's body, you said, 'it's them.' What did you mean?"

On the pad she wrote: "How safe is it to go outside?"

Genie looked at the pad and tried to fathom what was going on. His body rocked and his face scrunched up like he was holding back tears. Suddenly he blurted, "What difference does it make? He's... crazy."

Lai wrote again: "You have fifteen minutes to come up with a reason why your defense depends on us going outside of listening range."

Aloud she said, "Officer Carpenter is following procedure to the letter. It appears through your negligence a human has died. That makes you, at best, a man-slaughterer. The fact that you and Dr. Alzeshi hated each other makes us think this was murder. Please answer the question." She pointed to the pad.

Genie took a deep breath, his shoulders heaved. He shuddered and then concentrated. His head snapped up.

"I can prove to you that I didn't do it," he almost shouted. "We have to... I mean, I can prove it, if we...visit the, uh... them."

"Them? I thought 'they' did it. How can we go visit them?"

"They, uh... you'll see. It's not them. Or me. They're too different for that. They... I just need to show you." Genie was panicking, threatening to blow the whole deal.

"Why did you say it was them if it's not them, and who are they anyway?"

"Them? They're... incredible." He swallowed. A stream of sweat rolled down his forehead. He closed his eyes and said, "I mean that literally. I can only prove it... by showing you," he managed to get out. He raised a shaky hand to wipe the sweat from his eyes.

"Officer Carpenter," Lai called as she rose from the table.

The door swished open. Carpenter's form filled the opening. "As per defense procedure, Dr. Genie needs to travel to the site of his research to gather evidence. We'll need the transp—"

"They have sentience." Genie stepped around Lai and stood in front of Carpenter. "You saw it yourself."

Lai's head swiveled to Genie and back to Carpenter. Carpenter's eyes remained trained on Lai, but he said nothing.

Lai's voice filled the empty space. "As per Chicago Manual

of Conduct, a potentially condemned prisoner is allowed any means of defense within reason. Do you think an additional couple of hours and the use of the e-spev to be unreasonable?" She stated it loud enough for the audio recorders to get it. "Dr. Axelrod can attend as witness."

"We'll leave immediately. Second Mechanic Sekibo will remain behind."

Lai struggled to keep her emotions in check. The man had said "We'll." Bad luck that. Thank god Sekibo was the secmech and not the psychologist. It would be three against Carpenter when Lai gave the signal. They'd never overpower him under normal circumstances. Fortunately, these were not normal circumstances. And the sacred procedures? Out the window.

"I'll need my personal recorder. It's in my cabin," Lai said. She stepped around Carpenter. "I need to relieve myself as well. I suggest you do the same. We don't know how long this will take."

Lai swiftly moved up the passageway. Sekibo had progressed to the power panel by now. *Still keepin' on keepin' on*, Lai thought. *Good on you, Sekibo, you'll be First Mech in no time. 'Specially if this mission loses theirs.*

In her quarters she sat herself on the commode and listened for Carpenter. In one movement he swung the door open, saw her sitting there, and quickly turned away, allowing the door to close behind him.

So he wasn't a robot.

Lai reached up to the folds of the modesty curtain she'd purposely left open and swished them closed. Then she tore loose the small packet taped on the inside and opened its contents. After extracting the ring, she placed it on her fingers, prong-side in. The commode flushed behind her as she stepped away. After washing her hands, she grabbed her recorder from the table and kicked the door. "Ready!" she called.

Carpenter reopened the door and followed her down to the hatch. Outside Genie and Axelrod joined the group in the e-spev, which became airborne immediately.

The area around the ship was a desert: brown and compacted with a thin surface layer of particulates. The air was dry and smelled dusty. Distance was difficult to estimate. The area might have encompassed ten thousand acres or a thousand thousand.

Beyond the ridges everything changed. Globular shapes of scum dotted the hills, massing together like a forest at the lower slopes. Everything glistened as if wet.

Genie and Carpenter had been here. They'd seen this. And something intelligent? Was Genie guilty after all? Carpenter knew… something. Something Genie had said? If Carpenter knew what Genie knew, then Carpenter would be guilty too. This was no maniacal following of procedures. This really was a mutiny of some sort. Genie wasn't in on it. It was Sekibo and Carpenter and they needed Genie and Lai out of the way. And Alzeshi? Had they murdered Alzeshi? Lai shivered.

The e-spev flew over the trees and greenery and on over a scum-covered lake unlike any Lai had seen on Earth. There the green layers on the edges of ponds varied in hue and depth. Patches of dark growth floated on and beneath the surface; other areas were light in color, drier perhaps. This here was all one color: no variation.

The transport came to rest on a cliff maybe ten miles out. Mosslike plants grew in patches along the lip. The air was cooler here, the altitude high.

Lai stepped off the machine and looked to the basin below. As far as the horizon allowed, the landscape was filled to the brim with the ubiquitous scum. Like a runaway algal bloom on the land, everywhere the eye could see, a gelatinous goo covered the ground. Lai had to force herself back to the business.

"Dr. Genie and I must have privacy," she said as she led the biologist away from the other two. Carpenter replied with, "You have fifteen minutes."

"What is it with you?" Lai shouted back.

Carpenter noisily clicked his paralyzer on. "Fifteen minutes. Dr. Axelrod will accompany you to ten feet. She will disregard anything you say."

Lai acknowledged and pulled Genie beyond Carpenter's listening range. Axelrod stood close enough to hear.

"What's going on here?" Lai asked the biologist. "If you don't convince me, I'll let him fry your ass."

"I don't know, but he's crazy. There's some sort of sentient life here. Look to the far right. With your 'nocks." Genie beckoned to the visor on Lai's head and then pointed off to far side of the basin below.

Lai lowered the eyepiece in place and scanned. At first she saw nothing other than the scum, but then a depression separate from the rest off to the right came into focus. The same area Carpenter had found in the monitor.

"You see it?"

"I think so."

"That depression?"

"Yes."

"It's not tectonic in nature. This planet doesn't have glacial activity. Something sentient made that. We've had a remote up here on the ridge trained on that. Carpenter knew about it. He set that up with me."

"Something sentient? Something that killed Alzeshi."

"Maybe. I don't know. Analysis shows only unicellular organisms, but once in a while, once in a while—"

"They colonize and form a hand."

"Or something. I don't know what. It's impossible. There's no XNA that I can detect. I can't do a genome analysis. No genes."

"So what does that mean? It's not even alive?"

"By our limited definitions, no, but whatever it is, it's sentient. It dug a hole. It changed the environment. That takes sentience. Carpenter knew all this. His allegations about me are a lie."

"You could be lying. Why didn't you inform me?"

"It's so astonishing I didn't know what to report on the forms. None of them are adequate. I could have said something, but I was sure Alzeshi was going to hack my results. Somebody's been monitoring the data, I can tell by the slow speed of my comm unit. I figured whoever it was, was going to… well, I don't know."

"You don't know what?"

Genie kicked at the ground, looking for the right words. "It's this mission. It's, well, it doesn't look good when the security officer is related to the Chancellor back in Chicago, does it?"

"You're confused. He worked for Schmack. They're not—"

"They're related," Genie said. "He told me he could get his cousin to assign me anywhere I wanted to go. I asked him what cousin and he said, 'Schmack has contracts all over the place.' You know, Schmack has a holding company that's into exploitation."

"Why would he tell you that?"

"I don't know. I think he was bribing me. Or baiting me to see if he could bribe me."

"Did you take the bait?"

"Of course not. This is too interesting here."

Lai blinked, trying to understand what Genie was saying. Schmack's business interests were not news, but Schmack and Carpenter? And as far as Lai knew, Schmack and Valerocorp were not connected. No conflict of interest there.

"Did you ever find anything on the vids?"

"I never got a chance to look. Carpenter was watching them. Standard procedure for security to keep track of possible alien movement. He would tell me if he saw anything."

"Did he see anything?"

"Not that I know of."

Instantly Lai said. "We have to neutralize Carpenter. When I make a break, you…" she looked up and included Axelrod in the order. "… two knock him off his feet backward."

"Knock him… what?" Genie's face was frozen in fear.

Lai knew at best he'd be incompetent, at worst he'd be in her way, but he needed to be doing something. Axelrod would no doubt simply step aside. She was not good for anything physical beyond lifting a fork or shot of whiskey, but at least she wasn't going to help Carpenter. She could put two and two together same as Lai. Carpenter and Sekibo were planning a domino thing. First Genie, then Lai, last of all Axelrod. Then they could do whatever it was they needed to do because, according to Genie, Chancellor Schmack was Carpenter's cousin. Or something. "Just knock him over so I can get to his face," she said to Genie. "Wait for the signal."

She led the other two back to where Carpenter stood with his paralyzer not exactly at ease but no longer pointed directly at them.

"Looks like we've got an insurrection," Axelrod said as the three returned to the vehicle.

Lai looked to Axelrod, searching for meaning. Axelrod was facing Carpenter, who then leveled his paralyzer at Lai.

Just as things ran clear in Lai's head, a fourth character entered the drama. Up from the valley floor, a handlike appendage seemingly growing out of the ubiquitous slime rose and engulfed the biologist. Before Genie could scream, before anyone could scream, it pulled him under and receded over the edge of the cliff.

In just that moment of disbelief and unsettlement, Carpenter lost his grip on the paralyzer.

Lai, fighting the shock of what she'd just seen, snapped the prong caps off her ring and smashed it into the falling guard's face, the only vulnerable spot on the man.

He fell fortuitously half into the open e-spev, his upper body flat on the front seats, eyes wide open, mouth likewise gaping. His body lay unmoving with his ass on the lip of the vehicle. His legs dangled almost to the ground.

"Pull him in all the way," Axelrod screamed.

"You need to help me," Lai yelled. "He's too big to..." She froze mid-sentence when she saw the paralyzer in Axelrod's shaking hands aimed directly at her midsection.

A wave of heat surged through Lai as she assessed the situation. Genie was a goner. Gone the way Alzeshi had gone. Or, more likely, the boulder she'd seen in the vid. She let it go and concentrated on the matter at hand. Stepping over the near side lip of the e-spev, she kept her eye on the paralyzer and gripped Carpenter's massive shoulders. She tugged on his dead weight, pulling him into the vehicle. It was slow going. The man was gorilla heavy. Finally she got him all the way in and sat back to take a breath.

"You'll drive," Axelrod ordered. "Genie's... lost. Get us the fuck out of here."

It occurred to Lai that the only reason Axelrod didn't shoot her now and dump her into the goo was because she didn't know how to drive the e-spev. Axelrod didn't seem to know how to do much of anything. Why had Carpenter taken her on as a partner in whatever business they had going on? Why had she helped Lai find an excuse to get Genie out here? Why hadn't the two of them just killed Lai and Genie and then blamed the aliens? Unless...

Questions materialized in her head. Axelrod could no more handle a paralyzer than she could the transport. She needed to get back so Sekibo could help now that their plan was jacked. Now that Carpenter was down.

Lai didn't want to stay here, but the last thing she needed was this transport to head back to the ship. Once back there, Axelrod would shoot her and just wait for Carpenter to wake up to finish the plan, whatever it was.

Lai knew Axelrod was a voluptuary; she drank too much, ate rich food, and fancied young men. Her hands were unsteady and her thoughts weak. If she hadn't picked up the gun and threatened Lai with it, she could have just gotten back to the ship and then they could have gone on with their little charade. Just long enough to figure out what to do with Lai. Come up with a plot that had the appearance of legality. They could lock her up. Condemn her to death for Genie and Alzeshi. Dissolve her before they returned to Earth. They could do that legally. With no proof that these organisms didn't kill Alzeshi, they'd have the right. They'd leave Genie out there, head back to Earth. In Chicago, they'd swim through an investigation.

Lai grasped at straws with shaking hands. "What about your pension?" she said. "If they find out, you're going to lose that."

Axelrod laughed in her ear. Sarcastically, as if her pension was the least of her worries. "I'm here for the real money," Axelrod said before jamming the nozzle of the weapon into Lai's shoulder. "I'm going out in style."

The last thing this transport was going to do was head back to the ship. Or so Lai vowed.

An extrasolar planet exploratory vehicle, e-spev, is not made for quick turns. It's not made for much of anything except moving forward at constant speed. It can swerve, but that's about it. Oddly enough, it can stop on a dime.

Lai hammered on the halt button and, at the same time, braced herself for the impact. Carpenter's body slammed into the low panel in front of him, Axelrod slammed into Lai. Unfortunately, the impact engaged the paralyzer. The beam hit Lai directly in her back at point-blank range.

When she woke up, she was in her quarters in the ship. She floated up from a deep and restful sleep so comforting she was sure all life's problems had been solved. But by fits and starts, the reality of her situation came upon her. She listened for the characteristic hum of a moving ship. Could they be on their way home? Was she to be disintegrated soon?

The door opened and Carpenter entered. "First Mechanic Bertrina Lai, you are hereby condemned to death as per ISO 24936:2053." He retreated and the door closed behind him.

She shouldn't have been surprised; nevertheless, a chill

spread through her body. No amount of training in the unknown prepared her for the pronouncement of her death sentence. She knew it was illogical. She knew it was wrong. She also knew this had been determined long before Alzeshi died. Because his numbers were low? And who killed him? Carpenter? Could Genie have been in on it after all? Paranoia crept in as she tried to piece together motives. Of course it had something to do with the creatures out there.

And the uranium. The uranium. The uranium. The numbers had changed. Or had they?

What difference did it make? The others on this ship wanted her dead regardless of the numbers. Why?

Lai had no idea. She thought of how any heroic captain should puzzle out motives and leave clues in her cabin as to the actual events. She should leave a trail so obvious that even the most inept of investigators could read it. The world would then know the truth. The captain would be vindicated, her great name no longer stained. Maybe they'd even name the planet after her.

But Lai was not a "captain." She may have been in charge, but she was a mechanic and she cared nothing for glory after she was dead. She wanted to stride through the lounge back in Chicago with chest puffed out and friends and competitors slapping her back in congratulations. Immortality was no good if you had to die to get it.

"What about my defense? Who acted as my lawyer?" She jumped up slammed her open palm on the door. "There are procedures, you asshole! They'll figure it out. You'll f—"

The door swished apart before Lai could finish the word. Axelrod stood in front of her, cold, indifferent, all jokes gone.

"First Mechanic Lai, your trial has been held. You breached security, your violence against Security Officer Carpenter required immediate action. Nevertheless, we followed protocol. I acted in your defense. You may read the proceedings here." She handed Lai a recorder and pressed the door closed behind her. Lai stared a moment at the space

Axelrod had been standing in. Slowly she walked backwards to the seat. And then she sank to read the list of accusations.

The witness' accounts included Axelrod's, Sekibo's, and Carpenter's. The logic was there and yet, this whole thing was insane. Why were they doing this?

Out beyond the door she heard the muffled voices of heated argument. The assassins were in disagreement? Was there hope? She stood by the door but could not make out any words. They were down at the end of the passageway. By the hatch. And then the hatch opened and closed. Someone left. All of them? "Axelrod!" she hollered." Nothing. "Sekibo!" Nothing. Oh god, not him. "Carpenter!" Nothing.

For two hours, she paced in her cell, her cabin. She thought she heard a footstep at the door at one point, but when she ran to listen all she heard was the hum of the ship's ventilation, a hollow wind sound.

For two hours, Lai contemplated her execution. When she heard non-existent footsteps at her door, she went mad for a moment, felt herself heading down the lane to happyland. Later, she heard a barely stifled cough.

"Axelrod!" she cried. "You know you won't get away with this. Carpenter's smackin' on Sekibo. He won't share anything with you!" Why was she trying to work psychology on a psychologist?

And then she imagined she heard a scuffle. Feet scraping, a body slammed against a wall, even the room she was in shook a little. A corpse dragged across the floor?

She sat on her sofa with the heels of her hands pressed into her eye sockets, trying to escape the insanity of sounds coming from the passageway. The door swished open and Genie stood in the frame.

Lai closed her eyes slowly, hoping the world would make sense once she opened them. A single tear rolled down her cheek.

She heard Genie enter the room, drop to the floor, felt him take her hands into his. "It's me," he said. "I'm okay."

Without opening her eyes, she lifted the back of his hand to her lips and kissed it.

"Really, I'm okay," he said.

Then she opened her eyes and believed.

Genie launched his explanation. "It was unreal. They took me in. I saw what they are. What it is."

"It?"

Genie shook his head a little, as if Lai couldn't possibly understand anyway, or maybe Genie couldn't adequately explain. He moved to beside her on the couch.

"It's a single organism. Just one. Without XNA. I don't know exactly what it is. It's a self-organizing something. Like an ant colony, only with cells. An ant colony acts as single organism even though each ant is itself a self-contained entity. And the colony's knowledge is… ubiquitous. That's the only way I can describe it. It's like the organism is just a brain. And it took me in and my cells were then part of it and I had all its knowledge and… they… it had never encountered anything living other than itself before Alzeshi."

"Alzeshi?"

"Yes, Alzeshi startled it. Frightened it. It spat Alzeshi out. Returned him to us, but it was too late. They'd already started to… well, you saw him. And then when it… took me, it was ready and so it didn't digest me, it merely… sort of, joined with me. I saw what it knew and then it spat me out, but I stayed whole and fine, really fine. After it was over, I remembered what it knew and now I know. I don't understand, but I know."

Lai could not comprehend. She moved on to other matters. "Where's Carpenter?"

"Dead."

Lai nodded slowly as if that was expected. As if that was the only answer there could be.

"And—"

"Axelrod is incarcerated." Sekibo stood in the doorway. She remained out of focus until the thoughts in Lai's head cleared.

"And..." Lai began again. She wasn't sure how to frame a question so she hesitated.

Sekibo became impatient. "While you were out with Dr. Axelrod and Genie, I viewed the vids myself. I... learned... well, I can show you... outside."

She and Genie said "outside" together. "Outside" being the euphemism for "somewhere beyond the range of the ship's recorders."

Lai stood, stretched her limbs, looked around for a moment to gather herself and then slipped between Genie and Sekibo to lead the team to the hatch.

She turned to Genie. "Anything going to attack me, or—"

"We'll be fine," Genie said. "I promise."

Lai exited the ship and some fifty yards out, she stopped and turned. Sekibo and Genie joined her and began talking together at once.

"I hacked into the ship records while you were gone," Sekibo said.

"Carpenter fudged Alzeshi's numbers," Genie said.

"It's something I learned in South Dallas," Sekibo added.

"They were beautiful all along," Genie said. "As if that's going to do any good now."

Sekibo: "He was covering it up so Schmack could make—"

Genie: "A claim. A claim! They wanted to keep it from ValeroCorp. And—"

Lai shook her head. Too much, too fast. She turned to Sekibo, and said, "In South Dallas you learned—"

"So after you all came back without him," Sekibo pointed at Genie, who nodded enthusiastically, "I accompanied Officer Carpenter to the ridge where Dr. Genie was... taken."

Genie jumped in. "I saw them. It had spat me out by that time. I couldn't think straight, so I just stopped. And hid and watched the two of them. They were standing by the pit."

Lai rubbed the back of her hand against her chin "Pit?" she asked.

"You remember. You saw it. It's an area of concentration

of a certain type of fluid. It's for digesting food: rocks, inorganic materials. It's highly acidic. I believe Carpenter was going to throw her in like he had done—"

"Carpenter threw Alzeshi in? And how do you know that?"

"Carpenter had left the remote recorder on," Sekibo and Genie said together. They stopped and glanced at each other. Sekibo continued alone.

"I found the vids in his quarters. He's not such a smart guy. He had to get rid of Dr. Genie."

Genie picked it up, "The vid media is all logged and they lock after use. He couldn't just erase it. I would know something was fishy."

Lai looked at Sekibo and said very slowly, drawing it out, "So, you knew Carpenter had killed Alzeshi, Genie you presumed dead? And I was brought back unconscious and incarcerated. And then what?"

"Well, I have a ring," Sekibo said. I keep it in the curtain of my commode. It's totally contraband, I know, but it's something I learned—"

"In South Dallas. Naturally. Continue please."

"Yes, South Dallas. And I used it to incapacitate Duf... Officer Carpenter. Only he..."

"Fell in," Lai stated it for her. It was the only time she'd seen Sekibo falter.

Sekibo took a breath, raised her eyes to Lai's, and said, "He fell in and, well..." She stopped and blinked rapidly before turning to Genie. "You tell it."

"Carpenter was unconscious and apparently they, it, didn't know it was consuming something alive. Or something. Alzeshi, you see, he was awake when he went in, but Carpenter was—"

"But you have no idea, really, do you?" Lai cut in. She pointed at Genie, almost tapping his chest. "I mean, Carpenter could get spat out just like you were. If that's indeed what happened."

"After all this time in that acid bath, there will be nothing to spit back," Genie screwed up his face in defense. "He was consumed. I watched. He just... melted."

"And his brains cells are not turning your mass of single organism into some malevolent pile of shit at this moment. Why not?"

"Well..."

"And they're not going to rise up and consume this ship the way they consume rocks, either."

"I think not. That sounds like you've been reading too much pulp sci—"

"Shall we be on our way, then?" She looked from Sekibo to Genie.

"Yes, I need to get back and file this find," Genie said enthusiastically. As if two men dead and another incarcerated meant nothing. Then he checked himself, realized the situation, and said, "You know, it's sad, really. Alzeshi's death led me to the discovery of these, this thing. This very sentient thing. If he'd lived and rechecked and found his beautiful 1.4 numbers before I realized this thing was sentient, this planet would be one hundred percent exploited. But now, as it is, this is the most important discovery on an exo anywhere. Valerocorp has no chance whatsoever."

The group walked towards the ship

"Important?" Lai said.

"Yes, this organism flies in the face of countless theories of life. How life evolves, how sentience exists without a corporeal body. I'm going to be famous."

Lai nodded her head. Smiled to herself. Somehow the relief she felt at the change of events rendered her lost chance at fame unimportant.

"Yeah, well... Sekibo!" she said.

"Ma'am?" Sekibo answered. Lai was surprised the secmech didn't respond with a military salute.

"Seems I've underestimated you terribly."

"She's a good one, that one," Genie said, looking around

Lai to smile at Sekibo.

"Yes, well, I think I'll recommend you for First Mech," Lai said to Sekibo. "You've done an outstanding job."

Sekibo said nothing for a few moments. Her eyes were rigid and trained straight ahead. And then they were at the hatch. Genie went in first.

"Thank you," Sekibo said as Lai entered. "I appreciate your faith in me."

Good old Sekibo. All business. She just saved two crew members' lives, not to mention her own; advanced the search for extraterrestrial weirdness by decades; and saved about a month's worth of paperwork by executing a known criminal who just happened to be her former lover. And she's glad I have faith in her. And she's not an AI, no. Not Sekibo.

Sekibo stood in the entranceway and swallowed.

"Don't let it go to your head," Lai said. She closed the hatch behind Sekibo. "I need someone steady to send a communication to Chicago right away." She headed up the passageway to her quarters. "We need permission to abort this mission. Please report that we suspect we are under attack. We've lost two members of the team and need to leave immediately.

Sekibo seemed stuck to the spot. "Attack?"

"Yes, there's a malevolent organism out there that's about to digest the ship. We need to leave. I can't report and get permission at the same time I'm programming the ship for takeoff. Please try and pull yourself together to get the report."

"Yes, Ma'am." And then Sekibo was back on the job.

As Lai monitored the ship's takeoff and maneuvering through space towards home, Genie sat beside her. "Y'know," he started. "Whenever a new species is discovered, the discoverer gets to name it."

"I heard that," Lai said. "Congratulations. You've picked a doozy."

"Well, it's bad form to name a species after yourself

and I'm getting my propers anyway. I'll have half a dozen theories named after myself and, well, looks like you're not going to get your planet and I know what that means to a first mechanic. They'll probably name it after someone else. Maybe somebody—"

"Important. Somebody that has half a dozen theories about a new life form to their credit, you mean?"

"Yes, well, maybe, but... what I mean is, if it hadn't been for you trying to defend me in that stupid thing Carpenter was pulling, I'd be dead."

"Which reminds me, tell me again what it was that Carpenter was pulling."

"He was Schmack's flunky. It was really Schmack that was pulling it. They wanted to hide the fact that there was enough uranium here to exploit. Schmack wanted it all for himself. He's got a holding company. A competitor of ValeroCorp. He had Carpenter kill Alzeshi because Alzeshi would have just continued searching until he'd found his beautiful 1.4 for Valero. Then he wanted to discredit me, have me legally annihilated, so I couldn't investigate the missing file. You, too, if you got in the way. Sekibo, he tried to sweet talk. That was the surprise for him. He underestimated Sekibo, her feelings for him. He thought she was pretty well besotted. But she's straight up. And talented. My goodness, if that isn't First Mech material, I don't know. I've never seen such level-headed action under dur—"

"You know you have way of running away with a line, Dr. Genie?"

"People have said that about me. Anyway, how does *Laius bertrina* sound?"

"Excuse me?"

"The name. Of the species. I thought that maybe..."

Lai mulled it over. In her mind's eye, she saw herself striding through the club back in Chicago. The lads and lasses slapping her on the back. "You got your planet," they were supposed to say. For twenty years, it was the dream she'd held before her. It was her holy grail. Her name on a slime mold couldn't even come close.

She shook her head and looked out of the corner of her eye at Genie, inhaled deeply, and said, "Sounds nice."

Sailing the Antarsa

Vandana Singh

There are breezes, like the ocean breeze, which can set your pulse racing, dear kin, and your spirit seems to fly ahead of you as your little boat rides each swell. But this breeze! This breeze wafts through you and me, through planets and suns, like we are nothing. How to catch it, know it, befriend it? This sea, the Antarsa, is like no other sea. It washes the whole universe, as far as we can tell, and the ordinary matter such as we are made of is transparent to it. So how is it that I can ride the Antarsa current, as I am doing now, steering my little spacecraft so far from Dhara and its moon?

Ah, there lies a story.

I have gone further than anyone since my ancestors first came to Dhara four generations ago. As I stare out into the night, I can see the little point that is my sun. It helps to look at it and know that the love of my kin reaches across space and time to me, a bridge of light. I am still weak from my long incarceration in the cryochamber—and filled with wonder that I have survived nearly all the journey to the Ashtan system—but oh! It takes effort even to speak aloud, to record my thoughts and send them homeward.

I am still puzzled as to why the ship woke me up before it was time. During my long, dreamless sleep, we have sustained some mild damage from space debris, but the self-repairing system has done a good enough job, and nothing else seems to be wrong. There were checks against a half-dozen systems that were not of critical importance—I have just finished going through each of them and performing some minor corrections. In the navigation chamber the altmatter sails spread out like the wings of some marvelous insect—still intact. I put my hands into the manipulation gloves, immediately switching the craft to manual control, and checked. The rigging is still at a comfortable tension, and it takes just a small twitch of a finger to lift, rotate, lower or twist each sail. It is still thrilling to feel the Antarsa current that passes through me undetected, to feel it indirectly by way of the response of the altmatter wings! A relief indeed to know that the sense I had been developing of the reality, the *tangibility* of the Antarsa sea is not lost. We are on course, whatever that means when one is riding a great current into the unknown, only roughly certain of our destination.

There is a shadowy radar image that I need to understand. The image is not one of space debris, but of a shape wide in the middle and tapered at both ends, shutting out the stars. It is small, and distant, traveling parallel to us at nearly the same speed, but subsequent scans reveal no such thing. My first excited thought was: *spaceship*! But then, where is it? If it came close enough for my sensors, why did it choose to retreat? If this is why the ship woke me, which seems logical, then why didn't it wake me earlier, when a nearly spherical piece of space rock hit us? When we grazed past a lone planet that had been shot out of some distant, unstable solar system?

The ship's intelligence is based on the old generation ship AI that brought my ancestors to Dhara. It has a quietness and a quick efficiency that one would expect of an artificial thinking system, but there are aspects of it that remind me of people I know. A steadiness masking a tendency to over-plan for contingencies. That might be why it woke me up—it is a secret worrier, like my superficially calm mother Simara, so far and so long away. I will never see her—or any of them—again. That thought brings tears to my eyes.

Why does one venture out so far from home? Generations ago, our planet Dhara took my ancestors in from the cold night and gave them warmth. Its living beings adjusted and made room, and in turn we changed ourselves to accommodate them. So it was shown to us that a planet far from humanity's original home is kin to us, a brother, a sister, a mother. To seek kinship with all is an ancient maxim of my people, and ever since my ancestors came to this planet we have sought to do that with the smallest, tenderest thing that leaps, swoops or grows on this verdant world. Some of us have looked up at the night sky and wondered about other worlds that might be kin to us, other hearths and homes that might welcome us, through which we would experience a different becoming. Some of us yearn for those connections waiting for us on other shores. We seek to feed within us the god of wonder, to open within ourselves dusty rooms we didn't know existed and let in the air and light of other worlds. And the discovery of the Antarsa, that most subtle of seas, has made it possible to venture far into that night, following the wide, deep current that flows by our planet during its northern winter. The current only flows one way. Away.

So I am here.

I look at the miniature biosphere tethered to my bunk. One of my first acts upon waking was to make sure that it was intact—and it was. Parin's gift to me is a transparent dome of glass within which a tiny landscape grows. There are mosses in shades of green, and clumps of sugarworts, with delicate, brittle leaves colored coral and blue, and a waterbagman, with its translucent stalk and bulbous, water-filled chambers within which tiny worms lead entire lives. Worlds within worlds. She had designed the system to be self-contained so that one species' waste was another species' sustenance. It is a piece of Dhara, and it has helped sustain me during each of the times I have been awake, these years.

It helps to remember who I am. This time when I woke up, I had a long and terrifying moment of panic, because I couldn't remember who I was, or where I was. All I knew was that it was very cold, and a soft, level voice was talking to me (the ship). I cannot begin to describe how horrific a sense of loss this was—that my *self* had somehow slipped its moorings and was adrift on a dark sea, and I couldn't find it. Slowly, as memory and warmth returned, I found myself, anchored myself to the rock of remembrance, of shared love under a kind sun. So as I ponder the situation I'm in, the mystery of why the ship woke me—I will speak my own story, which is also many stories. Like my mothers who first told me of the world, I will tell it aloud, tethering myself through the umbilical cords of kinship, feeding the gods within.

I have been traveling for nearly eight years. Yet I seem to have left only yesterday, my memories of the parting are so clear. I remember when my craft launched from the Lunar Kinship's base, how I slowly shut down conventional fusion power and edged us into the Antarsa current. How it seemed hours before I could maneuver the little craft into the superfast central channel, manipulating the altmatter wings so that my spaceship wouldn't fall apart. But at last we were at a comfortable acceleration, going swifter than any human on my world—and I looked back.

The moon, Roshna, was slipping away beneath me with vertiginous speed. The lights of the Lunar Kinship were blinking in farewell, the radio crackling with familiar voices that already seemed distant, shouting their relief and congratulations. At that moment I was assailed with an unfamiliar feeling, which I recognized after a while as my first experience of loneliness. It was unbearable—a nightmare of childhood from which there is no escape.

Looking at the screen, with my kin's images flickering, hearing their voices, I was severely tempted to turn around. I was close enough to still do this—to arc my trajectory, turn from the Antarsa current into a high moon orbit and then use conventional fusion power to land. But I had pledged I would embark on this journey, had planned for it, dreamed of it—and there had been so much hard work on the part of several Kinships, so much debating in the Council—that I clenched my fists against temptation and let the moment go. I feasted my eyes on the thick forests, the purple scrublands of the moon, and the shining blue-green curve of Dhara below, the planet we had called home for five generations, memorizing the trails of white clouds, the jagged silver edge of the Mahapara continent, the Tura-Tura archipelago like a trail of tears, as a lover memorizes the body of her beloved.

This was the moment for which my friends from Ship University and I had planned and prepared for nearly ten years, soon after the discovery of the Antarsa. We had placed a proposal before the World Council, which debated for eight years. There were representatives from all the Kinships (except the People of the Ice, of course—they have not attended Council in two generations): the People of the Himdhara mountains, the People of the Western Sea, the Roshnans from the Lunar Kinship, and of course my own People of the Devtaru, among a number of smaller Kinships. There was endless discussion, much concern, but they let us design and send the first few probes into the Antarsa current. Interpreting the signals from the probes, the University experts determined that the current appeared to run in a more-or-less straight line toward the Ashtan star system five light years away. The last signal from the last probe had arrived seven years after its launch, when the probe was as yet some distance short of the Ashtan system. There was something ominous about the probe's subsequent silence—what had befallen it?—although the explanation could have been as simple as malfunctioning equipment or a chance hit by a space rock.

Some argued that an expedition was justified, because we hadn't heard from the Ashtan system since my ancestors had arrived on Dhara. Two generation ships had left the old world, one bound for Dhara, the other for Ashta, and they had been one people before that. So our people had always wondered what befell our kin around the brightest star in our sky. Others in the Council argued that this was the very reason we should not venture out, because the silence of the Ashtans—and the probe—pointed to some unknown danger. And what if the current took us somewhere else entirely? What guarantee that we would wash up on a world as kind as our own? To go out into the void was to seek kinship with death before our time. And so on.

But at last the Council gave its reluctant blessing, and here I was, on a ship bound for the stars. I am a woman past my youth, although not yet of middle age, and I have strived always to take responsibility for my actions. So I watched the moon and the great curve of the planet that was my home fall away into the night, and I wept. But I did not turn around.

I float within my ship like a fishling in a swamp. I have swum through the inertial webbing (softer and more coarse at the moment, since we are at low acceleration) from chamber to chamber, checking that all is well. No more strange images on the radar. All systems working in concert. The bioskin that lines each chamber, produces the air I breathe, recycles waste, and spins the inertial web looks a healthy gold-green. We are now moving at half the speed of light, absurdly fast. From the porthole, the distant stars are like the eyes of the night. I sip a tangy, familiar tea from a tube (I have a little cold) and breathe slowly, remembering what my friend Raim told me.

Raim taught me to sail on the Western sea. His people designed the altmatter wings that spread within the navigation chamber (surely the only ship ever built whose sails are on the *inside*). When I woke from cold sleep there was a message from him. He said: *Mayha, farsister, when you are lonely, make a friend of loneliness.*

So I make kinship with the dark. I whisper to it, I tell it stories. Perhaps the dark will have something to say to me in turn.

At first our plan was to make the inside of the ship a biosphere, rich with life, choosing the most appropriate and hardy species, so that I would feel more we than I. But after debating on it the Council decided that unless I wished it very strongly, this would not be right. To subject other lifeforms to human whim, to put them in danger without compelling reason was not our way. Besides, we ran the risk of upsetting the balance of life on other worlds in case our containment protocols failed. When I heard the reasoning, I too fell in with this. We compromised thus: the inner surface of the ship would be a bioskin, but that was all. To save energy and to enable the long years to pass without pathological loneliness, we would install a cryochamber. My apprehensions at the length and solitude of the journey were nothing to that old desire within me since childhood: to soar skyward in search of our kin, new and old.

But as I was leaving, saying my forever goodbyes amidst tears and jokes and good wishes, Parin came up to me, indignant. She was worked up about the Council decision to not install a biosphere within the ship. She thrust something at me: a transparent dome of glass within which a tiny landscape grew.

"Mayha, take this!" she said fiercely. "I can't believe they're going to condemn you to such a long journey alone!"

I tried to argue that the Council's position was an attempt to be just to all lifeforms, and that I didn't know how her sealed-in, miniature biosphere would adapt to zero gravity—but I've lost most arguments with Parin. And the little biosphere was beautiful. Besides, I did not want our parting to be acrimonious. Parin and I had grown up with the rest of the horde of children under the same kinhouse roof. Through much of my childhood I had been part of her schemes and adventures. I remembered the time we had rescued a nest of firebirds from some imagined danger, and how we'd wept copiously when they died. Most of Parin's schemes had involved guilt and good intentions in about equal measure.

I took the little biosphere, as she'd known I would. She scowled at me, then started to cry. We hugged and wept. Then the others had their turn at goodbye. Goodbyes at the kinhouse always take a long time; there are so many of us. And this time, for this historic one-way journey, there were people from nearly all the hundred and twenty-three kinhouses of the Kinship of the Devtaru, waiting to see me off on the shuttle that would take me to the moon, where I was to board my craft. There were also representatives from the People of the Western Sea, my friend Raim, tall and grey-skinned, stared at by the children, waving at me with one webbed hand. The Ship University folk had adapted the spacecraft from one of the shuttles aboard the old generation ship and tested it. A knot of them was present, waiting at the edge of the crowd for their turn. Closest to me stood my mothers, each displaying grief and pride consistent with her nature: Kusum yelling about the dangers of the journey and how I should be careful about this or that, as though I was three again, Brihat simply holding my arm and staring into my face, with tears streaming down her broad cheeks, and Simara being sensible and controlled although her smile wavered. My birth-mother Vishwana was behind them, regal as always, our representative to the Council. She nodded and smiled at me. Although I had never known her well, I had always been in awe of her. My kinsisters and brothers were there, alternately cheering and weeping, and Sarang, grown so tall since I'd last seen her, tossed me a braided ribbon over the heads of the crowd.

My father was not there. I saw him rarely, since he was a traveler and a trader, and when I did we always took pleasure in sharing stories with each other. He had sent me a message by radio wishing me luck, but he was halfway across the world, too far to come in time.

Then near the back with the guests I saw Vik. He had partnered with me for fourteen years, and we had gone our separate ways, in friendship, until my decision to go on this journey became public. He had become a bitter opponent in the Council discussions, and would no longer speak to me. He looked at me from the back of the crowd and looked away again.

I have partnered for long and short periods with both men and women, but Vik was the one with whom I spent the longest time. There were times I thought we would always be together, as some partnerships are, but we sought joy in different things that took us on diverging paths. He was a historian at Ship University, content to stay in one place and let his mind go into the deep past. Like my father, I needed to wander. It was as simple as that.

I wanted very badly to end things well with Vik. I took a pendant off the string around my neck and flung it over the heads of the crowd toward him. It hit him on the cheek—he caught it, looked irritable, put it in his pocket. I smiled at him. He rubbed his cheek, looked at me and away again.

The shuttle finally took off. I scarcely remember my time at Roshna, at the Lunar Kinship, where my spacecraft was waiting. They took care of me, asked me again the ritual question before one goes on a long journey: *Is your heart in it, kinswoman? Do you really want to go on this quest*? And I said *yes, yes*, and there were more goodbyes. At last I was in the craft, up and away. As I manipulated the sails in the navigation chamber, as I'd done so many times on my way to the moon—except that this time I would be going beyond it—as I felt the familiar tug of the Antarsa current, the old excitement rose in me again. It was too soon to feel lonely, or so I thought, because the love of my people was an almost tangible presence.

As I float by the porthole, I can see them all so clearly. Their faces tender and animated, as I turn from the raised platform into the doorway of the shuttle, turn once more to look for the last time at my people and my world, to breathe the forest-scented air. There is the wide, woven roof of the kin-house, and the vines running up the brown walls, the gourds ripening green to gold. Here I had played and climbed, looked at the stars, dreamed and wept. There is the gleam of the river, the pier, the boats waiting on the water. Dwarfing them all, the great, shaggy forest, trees like spires, trees like umbrellas, reaching leafy arms into the sky, taller than the tallest kin-house. I think: when I rise up, I will see again the Devtaru, the one closest to us anyhow, greater than any tree that exists or can be dreamed. The Devtaru has shared its secret with us, and because of that I will fly beyond the moon. As I rise I will speak my gratitude to it, to all the world for having formed me, made me into myself. And so I did.

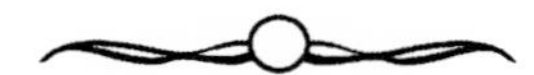

The devtaru is not a tree. It is perhaps what a tree would dream of, if a tree could dream.

The first one I ever saw lies two days away from my kin-house. In my thirteenth year, some of us trekked through the forest with Visith, one of my aunts, who has been a sister of the forest most of her life. On the way we learned plant lore, and we practiced the art of offering kinship to the beings of the forest.

"Kinship isn't friendship," my aunt said. "Don't go doing stupid things like putting your hand into a tree-bear's nest, or poking around inside an occupied bee-apple. Learn to sit still in a clear space, and let the creatures observe you, as you observe them."

We did a lot of sitting still. It was difficult at first but I got the idea of it quicker than the others. The forest whispered around me—sunlight dappled the ground. A wind-around approached me, its tendrils a-quiver, looking for something to climb. I nudged it away with my toe—it was kin, but I didn't want it taking advantage of my stillness. I sensed that I was being watched: a moon-eye monkey, which meant we were close to the devtaru. It was up in a tree, the white rings around its eyes giving it an expression of permanent astonishment. My heart thundered with excitement as the little creature peered out from its leafy shelter. But it was only after two days of seeing and being seen that the moon-eye came out into plain sight. A day later it took an apple-rind from me. After that the moon-eyes were everywhere, moving above me over the trees, chattering to each other and glancing at me from time to time. Then I could walk about without them hiding. I had made kinship!

Parin was in trouble for being too impatient, trying to climb up to a moon-eye's nest before it was appropriate to do so. The other two hadn't yet obtained the knack of it and needed to practice stillness without fidgeting or falling asleep. We lingered in that place until their impatience gave way to resignation, and they broke through. We got a congratulatory lecture from Visith.

"A kinship is a relationship that is based on the assumption that each person, human or otherwise, has a right to exist, and a right to agency," she intoned. "This means that to live truly in the world we must constantly adjust to other beings, as they adjust to us. We must minimize and repair any harm that we do. Kinship goes all the way from friendship to enmity—and if a particular being does not desire it, why, we must leave it alone, leave the area. Thus through constant practice throughout our lives we begin to be ready with the final kinship—the one we make with death."

We looked at each other and shivered.

"You are a long way from that," Visith said sardonically, then smiled a rare smile. "But you've taken the first step. Come, let us keep going."

So the journey to the devtaru took several days, and when we were standing at its edge we didn't even know it.

The ground changing should have been our first clue. The forest floor was dotted with undergrowth, but here we found that great roots as thick as a person reared out of the ground and back again, forming a fascinating tangle of steps and crevices that invited climbing. The trees had changed too—the canopy above seemed to be knit together, and trunks dropped down and joined the roots, making a three-dimensional maze.

Visith didn't let us go into the tangle. Instead we made camp and practiced stillness between meals and washing, and took walks along the perimeter of the maze. After two days of this, during which our impatience gave way to resignation, and then, finally, the open, accepting, alertness of mind that births the possibility of kinship—Parin pointed at the tangle.

"It's a devtaru! And we didn't even know it!"

It was indeed. The enormous central trunk was deep inside the forest of secondary trunks, likely several hours journey. The roots went deeper down than any other organism on the planet. To see a devtaru in its entirety, one has to be airborne, or on a far away hill.

Under the canopy, the moon-eyes led us over the maze of roots and trunks. We found shelter in the crook of a giant root, underneath which flowed a clear stream of water. The bark against which I laid my head was a thin skin that glowed faintly in the darkness, pulsing in response to my presence. To make kinship with a devtaru is extraordinarily difficult—Visith is one of the few who has succeeded, and it took her nearly twenty years.

"Tomorrow we will go to a place I know, where the devtaru was fruiting moon-pods last I came," she told us. "If the devtaru wishes, perhaps we will see a launch!"

I had seen the usual fruiting pods of a devtaru during our journey inside it, but never the legendary moon-pods. This devtaru was too young to make anything but small, empty moon-pods, but it would be a sight worth seeing. My heart was full. I wanted so much to be kin to such a being! Like Moonwoman, whose story Parin began to tell in the soft darkness.

There was a girl once, who sat in stillness seeking kinship with a devtaru for a hundred years. Potter-ants built a dwelling around her, and wind-arounds made a green tangle around that, so no rain or wind could trouble her. Flitters brought her crystals of sap and placed them between her lips so she knew neither hunger or thirst. She saw the devtaru and its beings, and it observed her with its thousand eyes, and at last they made kinship.

She lived within its forest, among its roots and trunks, and learned its moods and sensed its large, slow thoughts. She became familiar with the creatures who lived in its shelter, the moon-eyes and the dream-flitters, and the floating glow-worms, and the angler-birds with their lures of light. Then one day a moon-eye led her to a place within the devtaru forest where she found a large pod attached to the top of a trunk. The pod was just about as tall as she was and just about as wide in the middle, and it was covered over with a shimmering patina, so that she had to blink to make sure it was actually there. It pointed away from her toward the moon in the sky as though it yearned to break free, and it quivered gently as though caught in a breeze, although no breeze blew. The trunk glowed and patterns formed and dissolved on its surface, and the girl knew she had to climb right up to the pod.

And she did. She found that the pod's lips weren't closed as yet, and inside it was empty of seed. Within it there were little creatures, buzzwings and a grumpworm or two, and some leafy, mossy debris. She felt a great shudder from the trunk so climbed down hastily, just in time, because the trunk contracted, and the pod shot with a great noise into the sky. As it did, the trunk split and the girl fell down.

She walked for days through the forest and at last found the pod. It lay in a clump of bushes, already half-covered by leaves and branches from a storm. It made her wonder why the devtaru had bothered to send an empty pod into the air at all.

Now I've said she lived with the devtaru for a hundred years. When she was old, and the devtaru even older, something changed. The devtaru's leaves had been falling for a decade or more, and now she could see that its long arc of life was ending. The moon-eyes and the other creatures left the shelter of the devtaru but the girl couldn't bear to do so. The devtaru produced one last enormous moon-pod. The girl, now an old woman, crawled into the pod before its lips closed, and felt around her the creatures who were also stowaways, and felt also the smooth, shiny hard seed, half her size, larger than the seeds in the normal seed-pods. She had decided she could not bear to watch the tree die, and she would let it take her away to her final destination.

The pod grew and grew, and the old woman fell asleep inside it. Then one day the time came. She could sense a tensing in the limbs and sinews of the devtaru, preparing for the launch, but this time there came to her faintly a strange slight smell of burning. The lips of the pod closed completely, and if it hadn't been for the stowaways making air to breathe, she would have suffocated. Off she went into the sky.

Now there was a sister of this old woman who came to see her from time to time, and she was watching from a hilltop not far from the devtaru. She liked to look at the stars through a telescope, so she was known as Sister Three-Eyes. She saw the great pod quiver and align with the now risen moon. Tendrils of smoke emerged from the crevices of the tree. Then the pod launched.

There was a noise like a clap of thunder, and the devtaru shattered. As it did, it began to burn from its deep internal fires, slowly and magnificently. What a death! But Sister Three-Eyes soon turned her attention from the dying devtaru and trained her telescope on the pod, because she wanted to know where it landed.

To her surprise, it didn't land. It went higher and higher, and soon it was a speck she could barely see. Just before she lost sight of it, she saw it move into a low orbit, and then, suddenly, the pod changed its mind and made straight for the moon.

So she found that the devtaru's last and final moon-pod is truly destined for the moon. Which is why the devtaru's children grow on the moon, although they do not make such enormous pods as they do on Dhara. The lunar forest and the purple scrublands and the creatures that live there and make the air to breathe are all gifts of the devtaru, the only being known to spread its seed to another world.

As to what happened to Moon-woman—who knows? When the next generation found a way to get to the moon in shuttles, they looked for her in the forests and the grassy plains. They did not find her. Some say she could not have survived the journey. Others say that she did survive it, and she wandered through the lunar forests content that she had found a place among the children of the devtaru, and died a peaceful death there. These people named the moon Roshna, after her, as it is still called today. Her sister thought she saw a light burning or flashing on the moon some months after Moon-woman left, but who can be sure? There are those that believe that Moon-woman went further, that she found a way to launch her moon-pod into the space beyond the moon, and that she sails there still along the unknown currents of the seas of space and time.

Parin had always told this story well, but listening to it under the devtaru, in that companionable darkness, made it come alive. I wondered whether Moon-woman was, indeed, sailing the void between the stars at this moment, offering kinship to beings stranger than we could imagine. Looking at a small patch of starry sky visible between the leaves above me, I shivered with longing.

We never got to see a pod launch on that trip. But even now I can remember Parin's young voice, the words held in the air as if by magic, the breathing of the others beside me, the feel of the tree's skin glowing gently like a cooling ember.

The story anticipates the discovery of the Antarsa, of course. That I had a small role to play in it is a source of both pain and pleasure, because it happened when I first realized that Vik and I were growing apart from one another.

I have been torn between excitement of a most profound sort, and a misery of an extremely mundane sort. The excitement first: there have been *several* flickering images on the radar. It is clear now that there are others around me, keeping their distance—spaceships from the Ashtan system? Our long lost cousins? I sent a transmission in Old Irthic to them, but there is no reply. Only silence. Silence can mean so many things, from "I don't see you," to "I don't want to see you." There is a possibility that these are ships from other human-inhabited worlds, but it would be strange that they would not have made contact with us on Dhara.

My other thought is that the occupants of these ships may be aliens who simply cannot understand my message, or know it to be a message. This is even more exciting. It also makes me apprehensive, because I don't know their intent. They appear in and out of range, moving at about the same average speed as my craft. Are they curious? Are they escorting me, studying me, wondering if I am an enemy? All I can do is to practice what I did in the great forest: stillness. Stillness while moving at more than 50% of the speed of light—I wonder what my aunt Visith would say to that! *Do nothing*, says her no-nonsense voice in my memory. *Wait and observe, and let yourself be observed.*

That I have been doing.

The misery is that I have a message from Vik. Sent years ago of course, but there it is: he is grateful for the pendant I tossed him when I left, and he has found a new partner, a fellow historian at Ship University, a woman called Mallow. When I first got his message I just stared at it. A sense of deep abandonment welled up inside me; my loneliness, which I had tried to befriend, loomed larger than mountains. Of course I had expected this—even if I had stayed on Dhara, there would have been no going back to Vik—but I felt resentful of his meticulous observation of correct behavior. Yes, it is a graceful thing to do, to tell a former long-term partner when you have found a new love—but I would never come back, never find a new love, someone to hold—there was no need to let me know. Except it would make Vik feel better, that he had done the right thing. He had not thought about me, and it hurt. For once Parin's little biosphere did not assuage my pain. I couldn't even go outside and run up a mountain or two. Instead I swam from chamber to chamber through the inertial webbing, if only to feel the web break and re-form as I went through it, my tears floating in the air around me like a misty halo, attaching to the gossamer threads like raindrops. There was nowhere to go. After I had calmed down I tethered myself to the porthole and stared into the night, and thought of what it had been like.

After Vik I had taken no lovers for a while, until I met Laharis. She was a woman of the Western Sea. I'd been working with Raim on the ocean, learning to sail an ordinary boat before I learned the ways of the Antarsa. We had been out for several days, and had returned with a hold full of fish, and salt in our hair, our skin chapped. Raim and I developed a deep love and camaraderie, but we were not drawn to each other in any other way. It was when I was staying at their kinhouse, watching the rain fall in grey sheets on the ocean, that his sister came up to me. The others were away bringing in the last catch. Laharis and I had talked for long hours and we had both sensed a connection, but the construction of the altmatter wings from the discarded moon-pods of the devtaru had taken up my time. Now she slid a hand up my arm, leaned close to me. Her hair was very fine, a silver cascade, and her smooth grey cheek was warm. Her long, slanted eyes, with the nictitating membranes that still startled me, shone with humor. She breathed in my ear. "Contrary to stereotype," she whispered, "we Sea folk don't taste like salt. Would you care to find out?"

So we learned each other for two beautiful months. During our time together I forgot stars and space and the Antarsa—there was only her slow, unfurling self, body and mind, every part an enchantment. I would have wanted to partner with her, had I stayed on planet. Now that I was far away, I could only remember and weep. She never sent me messages, though her brother did. I think it was hard for her and perhaps she thought it would be hard for me.

Dear darkness, help me keep my equilibrium. Here I am, in a universe so full of marvels and mysteries, and I mourn the loss of my already lost loves as though I was still young and callow. What a fool I am!

I shall keep stillness, and feed no more that envious, treacherous god within, the god of a heart bereft.

Vik has rarely ventured from Ship University. He's one of those people who likes to put down roots and ponder how we got here. The past is his country. Ship University is a good place for him.

It is housed inside the generation ship that brought my people to Dhara so long ago. The ship lies in a hollow made for it in the sandy plains near a lake. It contains the records of my people's history and of the home planet, and the cryochambers are now laboratories. The shuttle bays are experimental stations, and cabins are classrooms. In the forests or the sea, the mountains or the desert, it is hard to believe that we have the technology we do. "Have high tech, live low tech," has been a guiding principle of the Kinships. That is how we have lived so well on our world.

Ship University's sky scholars were the first to study the flight of devtaru pods. Vik's friend Manda, a sky scholar of repute, told me how the mystery deepened as the early scholars tracked the moon-pods with increasingly powerful telescopes. I can see Manda now, slender fingers brushing back her untidy brown hair, her eyes alight. I was visiting Vik after wandering for a month through the Bahagan desert, and it had become clear to me that there was a wall between us. I felt then the first hint of the ending to come. I think Vik sensed it too. He sat next to me, looking restive, while Manda talked. She showed us a holo of a devtaru moon-pod launching from a century ago.

Despite my misery, I found myself fascinated. There was the tiny pod, dwarfed by the curve of Dhara, apparently going into low orbit. The moon wasn't in the picture, which was to scale, but we were informed that the planet, the pod and the moon formed a more or less straight line through their centers. In its orbit around the planet, the pod began to tremble abruptly, like a leaf floating on a stream disturbed by a random eddy. Then it swung loose from its orbit and made straight for the moon. It traveled with such astonishing rapidity that all we could see was a silver streak. Then the scene cut to the moon and the pod approaching it, swinging past it a few times, slowing gradually until at last it made a rough landing in the southern forest. There was a bloom of light, a brief fire where it hit, then the film stopped.

"This was taken by Kaushai, back about a century ago. All this time there have only been speculations as to how the devtaru pods get to the moon, why they suddenly change course from low orbit to the trajectory you saw. The pods themselves have no means of propulsion. There is nothing in the void of space between the planet Dhara and the moon. The first probes that were sent to duplicate the orbit of the pods suffered no strange perturbations, nor were they drawn toward the moon. The devtaru pods apparently violate fundamental laws of nature: that momentum and energy must be conserved."

I knew something of all this, of course. But I had never seen the holo before. It was quite amazing. I felt Vik stir beside me—he looked just as entranced, and when my gaze met his, as miserable as I.

Yet it was a chance remark I made on that visit that set the sky scholars on the right track.

I go back to that time in my imagination. Vik and I are both starting to realize that our paths are too different to allow for us to be together, although it will be quite some time before we have the courage to say so to each other. So the golden afternoon, and our togetherness, have acquired a deep, sad sweetness. We join Manda and her friends for a walk around the lake. They have been talking all day about the mystery of the devtaru pods, telling us how they spent years camping by a certain devtaru, watching it, getting to know it, asking it to share its secret. Now some of them feel as though the devtaru has communicated with them already, that they already know what the secret is, but it is buried deep inside them and needs some kind of stimulus, or reminder, a magic word or phrase to bring it into consciousness.

After evening sets in we find ourselves tired and hungry—we have walked a long way and the stars are beginning to come out in a pale pink sky. We are at a place where a small river empties into the lake, making an intricate delta of rivulets. We are wishing we had a boat to get to the shore from which we ventured, where the bulk of Ship looms, its many windows lit. The air is full of the trembling cries of glitter-wings. I am speechless with emotion, with the thought that the end of our partnership is as close as the other shore. Vik is silent beside me. Just as we are talking about boats, I find the remains of one at the bottom of a rivulet. It is full of holes—in fact, most of it has rotted away, but for the frame. It lies indifferently in place as the water rushes through the holes.

"If this boat were solid," I say, "and the current strong enough, it would move. It would carry us home."

A pointless, inconsequential remark. But Manda stares at me, understanding awakening in her face.

She told me later that my remark was the thing she needed to unwrap the gift the devtaru had already given them. What had been one of the saddest evenings of my life was the moment when she and her colleagues solved the mystery of the devtaru pods. Two days later Manda spoke to a gathering of hundreds.

"Imagine an ocean that washes all of space and time. Like the water ocean, it has currents and turbulences. But its substance is invisible to us, as we are invisible—or transparent—to it.

"This is not so strange an idea. As the neutrinos wash through ordinary matter, through you and me, as though we weren't there, as water washes through the broken boat with the holes in it, so the subtle ocean—the Antarsa, named by our poet Thora—washes through planets and stars, plants and people, as though we did not exist.

"We don't know whether the Antarsa is made up of neutrinos or something else. We suspect it is something as yet unknown, because too much is known about neutrinos, which can be caught by ordinary matter if the net is both deep and dense.

"Now imagine a form of matter that is not ordinary matter. This, too, is not strange, because we know that what we call ordinary matter is rather rare in the universe. There are other forms of matter that make up the bulk of the cosmos. One of these forms, what we are calling the altmatter, is opaque to the Antarsa. So if you place a piece of altmatter in an Antarsa current, it will move.

"The pods, of course, have to be made in part of altmatter. How the devtaru acquires it we don't know; maybe it draws it up from deep underground, mingles or combines it with ordinary matter, and forms the pods that are meant to go into space."

That was so long ago, that moment of revelation. Some years later, experimenters took the discarded moon-pods that are empty of seed, the ones that the devtaru shoot out for practice when they are young, to make the first altmatter probes. And now I am here.

Here I am, working the sails in the navigation chamber. I've done enough waiting. I am steering my craft as close to the edge of the current as I dare, as slowly as it needs to go so that changes in speed won't tear it apart. I want to get closer to my mysterious companions.

The shapes on the radar flicker in and out with increasing frequency now. Some are shaped like fat pods, but some appear vaguely oblong smudges. I want to see a pod ride by with Moon-woman in it, waving. If that happens, I will extend a grappling hook, gently as I can, and bring the moon-pod close to me so she can crawl into my little craft and share a tube of tea. But no, there is no likelihood of moon-pods being this far away from Dhara. After all, the Ashtan system is a few months away. The star is discernibly a round yellow eye, no longer a point, and the planets around it, including Ashta, appear disk-like as well, although I need my telescope to clearly see them. I can just see Ashta's polar ice caps. It is far from my spaceship at the moment, but when I enter the system it should be at a point in its orbit that brings it close to my trajectory. I have to be careful that the Antarsa current does not pass directly through the planet, because I will simply crash into it, then. I am anticipating some delicate maneuvering, and there is no time like this moment to practice.

After a long while, I discover something.

My companions move unobtrusively away as I approach them, which means, of course, that they can sense my presence. Are they simply making room for me, or is it something else? However, what I've found through this experiment is that the Antarsa current, the central, fastest channel at least, has widened considerably. It took me much longer to find its edges, where there are dangerous eddies and rivulets. The speed of the current has not changed, however. Mystified, I continue on my way.

I send my offer of kinship out, but as yet there is no answer but silence.

Listening to the silence, I am reminded of a story my father, the trader, told me when I was small. Among our people the Kinships are fairly self-sufficient, but we do have need of small shipments at regular intervals: metals from the Himdhara mountains, cloth from Tura-tura and so on. We send out our herbs and jewelry. There is constant flow of information between the Kinships (except for the People of the Ice, about whom my father told this story) and also with Ship University. Most things are transported where possible by boat, in a rare while by flyer or shuttle, but there are also wandering caravans that go overland, and my father has traveled with many of these. He is from a kinhouse of my own people further east of here, deeper in the forest and he met my mother during one of his journeys. Neither was interested in a permanent partnership but they remain cordial when they meet. And always he has tried to come see me, to bring me a shell from the Western Sea, or a particularly pretty pebble from Himdhara.

The People of the Ice stopped speaking to us from the time that the second generation of humans was grown. By that time the Kinships had each chosen their place, depending on where they felt most accepted and would do the least harm to the beings already present. My people of the Devtaru had genetically modified ourselves to digest certain local proteins; the Western sea folk had modified their bodies to be more agile in the water and to hold their breath longer than any other human. The People of the Himdhara could thrive in the thin mountain air. The People who settled in the Northern edge of the great continent, where there is ice even in the summer, adjusted themselves to live in that terrible cold. It was said that they grew hairy pelts like the beasts that dwelt there, but this could have been a joke. All the Kinships tell jokes about each other, and most are reasonably good-natured, but the People of the Ice got the worst of it because they were so remote, in both geography and temperament.

When I was little, my father said, his caravan was asked by the World Council to go into the North to find out what had happened to the People of the Ice. Was it that they did not answer radio calls because something terrible had befallen them, or were they being obstreperous as usual?

Take only a few people, said the Council, so that they don't feel invaded. So my father and three others—a man and two women—went. They wandered for days and weeks through forest and scrubland, desert and plateau, until they came to the land of perpetual snow. Here the trees grew up into tall spires, and the wild creatures all had thick, luminous coats and some knew the use of fire. My father knows this because one night the party followed a flickering light through a snowfall, and found large, hairy creatures huddling before a fire, tossing twigs into it and grunting. As is our custom, the four travelers sat some distance away and waited, speaking softly the offering of kinship, until the creatures waved their paws at them and invited them, through expressive grunts, to join them. My father says these were shaggorns, and fortunately this group was full of meat and therefore amiable. They are very curious and they poked at the travelers with twigs to see what they would do (some of his companions laughed but my father only smiled and gently poked back) and one of them wanted to try on my father's coat—my father allowed this, but had to give his watch to get his coat back.

It was bitterly cold, but the four survived with the help of the shaggorns, and one late afternoon they found themselves at the edge of an icy plain, over which rose a city.

The city was made of ice. The buildings were constructed with ice blocks and had slit windows, and the streets were ice. People moved about them on skates, and the travelers could not tell whether they wore hairy pelts or if they had grown their own. The travelers set themselves down outside the city's perimeter but in plain sight, in keeping with the tradition of waiting for an invitation.

But there was none. People skated across the ice, from building to building, and didn't even look at the travelers. One little girl stared at them but was roughly pulled away by an adult. The four travelers sang the offering of kinship, but there was no response. This was a terrible thing to witness, my father said, because they had come so far and endured so much to make sure that their kin were safe. They were cold, hungry and tired, and the song was acquiring rather angry overtones. So they stopped their song, and set up camp there because the evening was setting in.

In the morning they found some supplies—meat, some cooked roots, all frozen by now, a pelt blanket. The meaning was clear: the People of the Ice did not desire kinship, but they meant no harm. There was no weapon left symbolically at the edge of the camp. They did not want a kinship of enmity—they simply wanted to be left alone.

So the travelers began their return journey, somewhat mollified. The next evening, before they were able to go very far (they were tired, as my father said), they saw a small dwelling in the forest. To their surprise they recognized the home of a farsister. Farsisters and farbrothers are people who wander away from their Kinships for a life of solitude, usually seeking some kind of spiritual solace. Some of them have done terrible things and seek to redress them or have suffered a loss and need to find a reason to live. Others simply wander in search of something they can't identify, and when they find it, usually in a place that calls to them, they settle down there.

The farsister's courtyard was snowy and bare, and furnished with only two low flat-topped rocks that my father assumed were intended to be chairs. This meant that the farsister did not like company, but one person would be tolerated. There was an intricately carved block of ice near the door, which indicated the occupation of the person within. That she was female was indicated by a red plume of feathers that hung from her door.

My father sat outside the courtyard and waited. She made him wait for several hours, by which time it was night and getting very cold. Then she came out and ushered him in. She turned out to be a grim, dour woman who seemed to be made of ice as well. The inside of her little hut was just as cold as the outside and this didn't seem to bother her.

She told him that she was not of the People of the Ice, and

that there was not anything to be done about them, they kept to themselves. She gave him a cold tea to drink that made my father feel dizzy. He felt himself falling into deep sleep, and the icy fingers of the farsister easing him down into a cold bed.

When he woke up he found that the hut was empty. Moreover, there was no sign that it had ever been inhabited. The hearth was cold, and filled with ashes, and a wind blew through the open window. My father felt frozen to the marrow. He got himself up slowly and painfully and emerged into a snowy dawn. The courtyard of the hut was bare—no sitting rocks, no ice carvings, no evidence that anyone had ever lived here. His companions were waiting anxiously for him at camp.

It was a long journey home, my father said, and they were glad to come back to the warm lands and make their report to the Council.

When he used to tell us children this story in the sunny garden in front of the kinhouse, with the warm sun at our back, we would shiver in the imagined snowfall. We were trapped in the hut of the ghostly farsister, or lost in the enchanted forest with the People of the Ice in their hairy pelts, wandering around to scare us, to take us away. Later we would come up with games and stories of our own, in which the Ice folk were the principal villains.

When I was older, my birth-mother would take some of us to Council meetings. Council meetings rotated from Kinship to Kinship, and when we were the hosts, my mother would let us come. We would see our sea-kin, with their scale-like skin and their webbed hands, and the tall mountain folk with their elaborate head-dresses, or the cave kin with their sunshades over huge, dark eyes, and our own eyes would go round with wonder. In the evenings various kinfolk would gather round a fire or two and tell jokes. We would joke about the people of the Ice, and why they didn't ever come to Council ("they were afraid they'd melt" or "it would be too hot in their fur coats"). During one of these occasions my father was also present—he pulled some of us older ones aside.

"You all talk a lot of nonsense," he said. "Listen, I never told you one part of my story about the People of the Ice. What I dreamed about while I slept in the hut of the farsister."

We were all eyes and ears.

"Listen. I dreamed that the farsister took me to the city of ice. Some of the ice people met me and took me in, saying I could stay the night. I was put in an ice-cold room on a bed of ice, and it was so cold that I couldn't sleep. In the night I heard my hosts talking about me, arguing. Some said I should never have been brought here, and another voice said that maybe I could be made to substitute for some relative, an old man whose time had come. The executioners would not know the difference if I was wrapped in furs and made unconscious, and that way the old man could live a little longer in secret. This went on for a long time, until the people moved away. I was so scared that I fled from there. My captors chased me some of the way but without much enthusiasm. Then I woke up in my cold bed."

My father paused.

"I may have simply dreamed the whole thing. But the dream was so vivid that I sometimes wonder if it didn't actually happen. Since that time I have wondered whether the reason for the silence of our Ice kin is something more sinister than mere bad manners. What if their genetic manipulations to adapt to the cold resulted in something they did not expect—something that prevents them from dying when they are old? Since they cannot die, they must put to death the old ones. And they are terrified that by mingling with us they will let loose an epidemic of deathlessness. So in their shame and misfortune they keep themselves separate from all other humans."

We were appalled. To cheat death, even to wish to live longer than one's natural span, is to show so much disrespect to all living beings, including one's own offspring and generations yet to come, that it is unthinkable. It is natural to fear death, and so it takes courage to make kinship with death when one's time has come. How terrible to have death itself refuse kinship! To have to kill one's own kin! It was an honorable thing to isolate this curse in a city of ice, rather than let it loose among the rest of the Kinships. After my father's revelation we found ourselves unable to joke about the People of the Ice with the same carelessness.

I am thinking about them today because I wonder about the silence of the spacecraft around me, and the deeper, longer silence of the Ashtans. Did they settle on their planet, or did they find it unsuitable and move on? Did some misfortune befall them? Or did they simply turn away from us, for some reason?

I don't know if I'll ever find out.

So much has happened that I have not had time to speak my story until now. Dear, kind darkness, dear kin on Dhara, I have made such a discovery! My companions, whose flickering images on the radar screen have so mystified me, have revealed their true nature. It is hard to say whether there are simply more of them—they are so clear on the radar now—or whether I have gained their trust and they have moved closer.

They are not spaceships. They are beings. Creatures of deep space, made of altmatter, riding the Antarsa current like me.

I found this out a few days ago, when the radar screen presented an unusually clear image. A long, sinuous, undulating shape, broadest in the middle and tapered at each end moved parallel to us. Something waved like a banner from the far end—a tail. It was huge. I held my breath. The visual image showed a barely visible shape, lit only by starlight and the external lights of my ship, but it reminded me just a little of the seagu, that massive, benevolent ocean mammal of the Western Sea.

It was clearly made of altmatter. Its flattened limbs—fins?—moved in resistance to the Antarsa current, which propelled it forward. There was a purposefulness, an ease with which it swam that was delightful to see. Here was a creature in its element, apparently evolved to travel between the stars on the great Antarsa ocean. I closed my eyes, opened them, and the image was still there. My fingers were shaking.

How to describe what it meant to me, the company of another living creature, be it one so removed from myself! I had lived with other living beings all my life before this journey. I had played with chatterlings in the great forest near my home, swum with ocean mammals—walroos and seagus, and schools of silverbellies. Even in the high, bare mountains of Himdhara, where life is hardy, scarce and without extravagance, I had made kinship with a mog-bear, with whom I shared a cave for several days during a storm. Nearly always I had traveled with other humans. This was my first journey into the dark, alone. Parin's biosphere had much to do with maintaining my sanity, but how I had missed the company of other life! I blinked back tears. I took a deep breath and thanked the universe that I had lived to see such a marvel.

It was an exhilarating moment. It reminded me of my time with Raim, learning to use the sails on his boat on the Western Sea. Wind and current carried us far from the shore, and that wind was in my hair, whipping it about my face, and chapping my lips. Raim was beside me, laughing, rejoicing that I was finally moving the boat like an extension of my own body. Just then a school of seagu surfaced, and leaped up into the air as though to observe us. Crashing down into the water, raising a spray that drenched us, they traveled with us, sometimes surging ahead, sometimes matching our speed, their eyes glinting with humor.

This creature did not seem to have eyes. It must sense the world around it in a different way. I wondered whether it detected my little craft, and what it thought of it. But close on that thought came a new surprise. A fleet, a school of smaller shapes tumbled past between my ship and the behemoth. They were like small, flattened wheels, perhaps a meter in diameter as far as I could tell, trailing long cords through the current. They moved not in straight, parallel lines, but much more chaotically, like a crowd of excited children moving about every which way as they went toward a common destination.

As though this spectacle was not wonderful enough, I saw that around me, on either side and above and below, there was life. There were fish shapes, and round shapes, and long, tubular shapes, all moving with some kind of propulsion or undulation. They shimmered the way that altmatter does to the human eye, and some had their own lights, like the fish of the deep sea. These latter ones also had enormous dark spots on their bow end, like eyes. What worlds had birthed these creatures? Had they evolved in a gas cloud, or in the outer atmosphere of some star? They were so fantastic, and yet familiar. Our universe is, we know, mostly made from other kinds of matter than ourselves, but I hadn't imagined that altmatter could be the basis for life. It occurred to me now that altmatter life might be much more common in the universe than our kind. Space is so big, so empty. We have always assumed it hostile to life, but perhaps that is true only of our kind of life, made of ordinary matter.

For the next two days I prepared radar clips and visual clips to send home, and watched the play of life around me. I have seen what seem to be feeding frenzies—the behemoth feasted on those wheeled creatures—and I might have witnessed a birth.

Today I saw a new creature, twice as long as the behemoth I had first set my eyes upon. It had armor plating with fissures between the plates, and apparent signs of erosion (how?), as though it was very old. It trailed a cloud of smaller creatures behind it, evidently attendant upon it. Its round hole of a mouth was fringed with a starburst of tentacles. I was musing on the problem of the radar imaging system's resolving capacity, wondering what I was missing in terms of smaller-scale life in the life-rich current—when I saw the leviathan's mouth widen. It was at this point ahead of me and to one side of the ship, so I couldn't see the mouth, but I inferred it from the way the tentacles fringing the orifice spread out. To my astonishment a great, umbrella-shaped net was flung out from the fringes of the mouth, barely visible to my radar. This net then spread out in front of the creature like a parachute; the creature back-finned vigorously, slowing down so abruptly that a number of other swimmers were caught in the web. Had I not swerved violently, my craft and I would have been among them. The acceleration might have flung me across the chamber and broken some bones, had it not been for the inertial net, which thickened astonishingly fast. (That the ship suffered no great damage is a testament to the engineering skills of the great generation-ship builders of old, my craft being a modified version of one of their shuttles).

Now that the Ashtan system is nearly upon us, I have a new worry. I don't know whether the Antarsa current flows through any celestial objects, such as the sun, or a planet, or a moon. If it does, I must manipulate the altmatter sails in time to escape a violent crash. I am afraid something like this might have happened to the altmatter probes that were first launched from Dhara, that stopped sending back radio signals. Or perhaps they were swallowed by some creature.

Strangely, the current appears to be slowing; this would be a relief if it wasn't laced with chaotic microflows. I can sense them through the way they make the sails shiver, something I could not have told a few years ago. Sometimes I feel as though I can *see* the current with some inner eye, almost as though it has acquired a luminosity, a tangibility. I imagine, sometimes, that I can feel it, very faintly, a feather's touch, a tingling.

I have a sense of something about to happen.

What can I say, now to the dark? How do I explain what I have experienced to my kin on Dhara? What will you make of it, my sister Parin, my brother Raim? What stories will you now tell your children about Mayha, Moon-woman?

Nothing I once assumed to be true appears to be true.

As we entered the Ashtan system, the Antarsa current became chaotic on a larger scale. At that point I was not far from the second planet, Ashta, with its two lumpy little moons. Navigation became very difficult, as there were eddies and vortices and strong, dangerous little currents. There is a backwash from Ashta itself, I am convinced. This can only be the case if Ashta has a core of altmatter. Otherwise wouldn't the Antarsa wind simply blow through it, without becoming so turbulent?

This is not surprising. On Dhara there must be altmatter within the planet, else how would the devtaru have drawn it up? On Dhara, however, the Antarsa current does not go headlong through the planet, nor is it so wide. There is only a soft breeze through the planet, with the current itself running perhaps two hundred thousand kilometers distant. Here a broad channel of the current rushes through a region occupied by part of Ashta's orbit, and includes the tiny, uninhabitable inner planet and the sun. Depending on how much altmatter there is in these celestial objects, there is likely to be quite a backflow, and therefore much turbulence. A mountain stream studded with rocks would behave the same way.

For a long while, I was caught in the rapids. Caught with me were other creatures, altmatter beings of a fantastic variety, swimming valiantly, changing course with an enviable dexterity as the currents demanded. My hands were sore from manipulating the sails, my mind and soul occupied with the challenge of the moment, but the ship's AI managed to send a message in Old Irthic to Ashta. There was no reply but the now familiar silence.

I now know why. Or at least, I have a hypothesis. Because I have seen things I can hardly yet comprehend. I will not be landing on Ashta. It is impossible, and not just because of the turbulence.

This is what I saw: The day side of Ashta, through my telescope, showed continents floating on a grey ocean. There were dark patches like forests, and deserts, and the wrinkles of mountain ranges. I saw also scars, mostly in the equatorial belt, as though the planet had been pelted with enormous boulders. Most dramatically, the edges of the continents seemed to be on fire. There were plumes of smoke, mouths of fire where volcanoes spoke. In the interior, too, the scarred regions were streaked or lined or edged with a deep, red glow, and there were dark, smooth plains, presumably of lava. I imagined the invisible Antarsa current slamming into altmatter deposits deep within the planet, the impact creating internal heat that liquefied rock, which erupted volcanically onto the surface. There must be earthquakes too, on a regular basis, and were there not forests on fire?

That the forests were there at all spoke of a kinder past. Perhaps the Antarsa current had changed course in recent geological time? Now Ashta was a planet in the process of being destroyed, if the current didn't push it out of orbit first. I had never seen a more terrible sight.

But as we got closer, I saw much more to wonder at. The radar picked up something thousands of kilometers in *front* of the planet.

It first appeared as a roughly rectangular shadow or smear, very faint, that later resolved into a great array—a fine mesh of some kind, reminiscent of the net of the altmatter creature who nearly ate us. But this was on a massive scale, stretching across much of my view of the planet. Studded within it at regular intervals were lumps that I couldn't quite resolve—knots or nodes of some kind? No, too irregular. The net seemed to be held in place by beings, crafts or devices (I couldn't tell the difference at this distance) at corners and along the perimeter so that the whole thing sailed along with the planet. Its relative indifference to the chaotic Antarsa current indicated it was made of ordinary matter. Getting closer, I found that the lumps were creatures caught in the net, struggling. There was an air of great purpose and deliberation in the movements of smaller objects about the net—these craft, if that is what they were, appeared to buzz about, inspecting a catch here, a catch there, perhaps repairing tears in the net. It might have been my imagination but the creatures became still once the busy little craft went to them.

I went as close to the net as I dared. I had already folded the altmatter wings to decrease the effect of the current, although the eddies were so turbulent that this did not help as much as it should have, and my ship shuddered as a consequence. I switched to fusion power and edged toward the net. I wanted to see if the busy little objects—the fishermen—were spacecraft or creatures, but at the same time I didn't want to be swept into the net. One can't make an offer of kinship unless the two parties begin on a more-or-less equal footing. From what I hoped was a safe distance, I saw a drama unfold.

A behemoth was caught in the net. As it struggled, it tore holes in the material. One of the busy little fishercraft immediately went for it. Arms (or grappling hooks?) emerged from the craft and tried to engage the behemoth, but the creature was too large and too strong. A few lashes of the powerful tail, and it had pulled free, swimming off in the current—but the little craft-like object or creature broke up. From within it came all kinds of debris, some of it clearly made out of ordinary matter because it was impervious to the chaotic churning of the Antarsa and only influenced by gravity. These bits had clean, smooth trajectories. Flailing and struggling in the current, however, were three long, slender creatures with fins and a bifurcated tail. Were these the pilots of the craft, or parasites within the belly of a beast? The inexorable currents drew them to the net. I wanted to linger, to see whether they would be rescued or immobilized—two of the busy craft went immediately toward them—but I was already too close and I did not want to subject my ship to more shuddering. So I powered away in a wide arc.

I made for the night side of the planet. I was hoping for lights, indicating a settlement, perhaps, but the night side was dark, except for the fires of volcanoes and lava beds. Whatever beings had engineered the enormous net had left no trace of their presence on the planet—perhaps, if they had once lived there, they had abandoned it.

My kin were clearly not on this planet. The generation ship must have come here and found that the constant bombardment of the planet by altmatter creatures made it a poor candidate for a home. I hoped that they would have escaped the net, if the net had been there at the time. It was possible, too, that they had come here and settled, and when, as I thought, the Antarsa current shifted and slammed through Ashta, they perished. I felt great sadness, because I had hoped, dreamed, that I would find them here, settled comfortably in the niches and spaces of this world. I had imagined talking to them in the Old Irthic that I had been practicing, until I learned their languages. Instead I had to send a message home that they were not here after all.

Where had they gone? Manda had told me that the old generation ships were programmed for at least three destinations. Wherever they had gone, they had not thought it worthwhile to send us a message. Perhaps something had gone wrong en route. I shivered. None of the options implied anything good for our lost kin.

I decided I would attempt a moon landing. The moons did not seem to be made of altmatter as far as I could tell. The moon over the dark side was in the planet's wake, where there should be fewer eddies and undertows. So I brought my craft (still on fusion power) into orbit around the moon.

That was when it happened—a totally unexpected undertow caught the folded altmatter wings in the navigation chamber at just the right angle. I had at that moment cut speed from the fusion engines, preparatory to making an approach, so the undertow caught me by surprise. Before I knew it we were flung head-on toward the moon.

As I saw the moon's battered surface loom larger and

larger, I thought of you, dear kin. I thought my moment had come. You would wonder at Mayha's silence, and hypothesize various endings to her story. I couldn't let that happen to you. Quicker than thought, I powered the fusion engines to brake my craft. I made a crash-landing, bumping along the uneven ground, over and over, until at last we were still. I felt the slight tug of the moon's gravity. The inertial web retracted slowly—I winced as it pulled strands of my hair with it. I was shaking, weak from shock. How slowly the silence impressed upon me as I lay in my craft!

Then the ship's AI began to speak. The fusion engine was intact, but one of the altmatter wings was broken. There was some damage to the outside of the ship, and the AI was already launching a repair swarm that clambered insect-like over the cracked and fissured shell. Anchoring cables had dug in and secured us to the surface of the moon. There was a spare wing stored within the navigation chamber, but it would take a long time to shape and match it to the old one. Then I would have to remove the broken wing and put in the new one, and adjust the rigging to the right tension. Working with altmatter meant that as I turned a wing this way or that, it would pick up a current or two and tumble out of my hand, and blow about the chamber. After a while I decided I needed to restore my mental equilibrium to the extent possible under such circumstances. So I did what I would do at home: after suiting up, I went for a walk.

Walking on the moon was both exhilarating and terrifying. To be outside my little home after years! I could spread my arms, move my legs, go somewhere I hadn't been before. There was the great bulk of the planet ahead of me, dominating my field of vision, dark and mysterious, streaked with fires, limned with light. The moon seemed to be a fragile thing in comparison, and I had to fight the feeling that I would fall away from it and on to the smoking, burning planet. I had to step lightly, gingerly, so that the ground would not push me away too hard. I walked halfway around it and found myself at the edge of a deep crater.

Lowering myself down to it was easy in the low gravity. At the bottom it was very dark. My suit lights picked out an opening—a hollow—a cave! I stepped into it, curious, and found a marvel.

The cave was filled with luminous fish-like creatures, each about as long as my finger. They circled around on tiny, invisible currents, so I guessed they were made of altmatter. As I stared at them in wonder, a few darted up to me, hovering over my visor. I stood very still. To make kinship with a fellow living being, however remote, was a great thing after my long incarceration. I was inspected and found harmless, and thereafter left alone. I stood in the dark of the cave, my ears filled with the sound of my own breathing, and fervently thanked the universe for this small encounter.

As I turned to leave, I had a terrible shock. My suit lights had fallen on somebody—a human, sitting silently on a piece of rock against the wall of the cave, watching me.

No, it was not a person—it was a sculpture. Fashioned in stone of a different kind, a paler shade than the material of the moon, it had clearly been brought here. I went up to it, my heart still thumping. It was the statue of a woman, sitting on a rock cut to resemble the prow of a boat or ship. There was a long pole in her hands, and she looked at me with obsidian eyes, her face showing a kind of ethereal joy. I thought she might be one of the old gods of our ancestors, perhaps a goddess for travelers. I touched the rock with my gloved hand, moved beyond tears. Why had my kin left this symbol here? Perhaps they had tried to make a home on Ashta, and failing, had left the statue as a mark of their presence.

I spent three days on the moon. I repaired the wing, a task more difficult than I can relate here (Raim will find a better description in my technical journal) and went back to the cave many times to renew kinship with the fish-like creatures and to see again the statue of the woman. The last time, I conducted an experiment.

I took with me some pieces of the broken altmatter wing. They confirmed that the inside of the cave was a relatively still place, where the Antarsa currents were small. By waving one piece of wing in front of the statue, and using another piece on the other side as a detector, I determined after a lot of effort that the statue was made of ordinary matter except from the neck upward, where it was altmatter or some kind of composite. This meant that my kin had made this statue *after* they had been here a while, *after* they had discovered altmatter. I stared again at the statue, the woman with the ecstatic face, the upraised eyes. She saw something I could not yet see. I wondered again how she had come to be placed here, in a nameless cave on a battered moon of Ashta.

I am now moving away from Ashta, on a relatively smooth current of the great Antarsa ocean. I am convinced now that I can sense the Antarsa, although it blows through me as though I am nothing. I can tell, for instance, that I am out of the worst of the chaotic turbulence. I can only hope that I've caught the same current I was on before I entered the Ashtan system—it is likely that the current splits into many branches here. I will be completely at its mercy soon, since I do not have much fuel left for the fusion engines. I also must conserve my food supplies, which means that after this message I will enter the cryochamber once more—a thought that does not delight me.

At last I have relinquished control of the altmatter sails to the ship's computer. I woke from several hours of sleep to see, on the radar screen, images of the altmatter creatures sailing with me. Unlike me, they all seem to know where they are going. Here their numbers have dropped, but I notice now a host of smaller replicas of the behemoths, and the wheel-like creatures, and I wonder if the Ashtan system is some kind of cosmic spawning ground. I wish very much to offer kinship to these creatures. I already miss the little fish in their cave on the moon. That has given me hope that although we are made of very different kinds of matter, we can make a bridge of understanding between us. Life, after all, should transcend mere chemistry, or so I hope.

I have sent many messages home. In a few years my dear ones will read them and wonder. The young people I will never see, children of my kin-sisters and kin-brothers, will ask the adults with wide eyes about their aunt Mayha, Moon-woman, who forever travels the skies. But I have one faint hope. Out on the Western sea, Raim once told me that the great ocean currents, the conveyor belts, are all loops. It seems to me that it is likely, if our universe is finite, that the Antarsa currents are also closed loops. If I have chosen the right branch, this current might well loop back toward Dhara. Who knows how long that will take—perhaps my descendants will find only that this little craft is a coffin—but the hope persists, however slight, that I might once again see the blue skies, the great forest of my home, and tell the devtaru of my travels.

One casualty of my crash-landing on the moon is that Parin's biosphere is broken. I am trying to see if some of the mosses and sugarworts can still survive, but the waterbagman broke up, and for a while I found tiny red worms suspended in the air, some dead, others dying. There was one still captured in a sphere of water, which I placed in a container, but it is lonely, I think. I am trying to find out what kind of nutrients it needs to stay alive. This has been a very disturbing thing, to be left without Parin's last gift to me, a living piece of my world.

I stare at my hands, so chapped and callused. I think of the hands of the stone woman. An idea has been forming in my mind, an idea so preposterous that it can't possibly be true. And yet, the universe is preposterous. Think, my kin, about this fact: that ordinary matter is rare in the universe, and that in at least two planets, Dhara and Ashta, there is altmatter deep within. Think about the possibility that altmatter is the dominant form of matter in the universe, and that its properties are such that altmatter life can exist in the apparent emptiness between the stars. Our universe then is not inimical to life, but rich with it. Think about the stone woman in a cave on the irregular little moon that circumnavigates Ashta. Is it possible that there is some symbolism in the fact that she is made of both matter and altmatter? Is it possible that the generation ship of my ancestors did not really leave the system, that instead my kin stayed and adapted more radically than any other group of humans? Imagine the possibility that the fate of all matter is to become altmatter, that as the most primitive and ancient form of substance, ordinary matter evolves naturally and over time to a newer form, adapted to life in the great, subtle ocean that is the Antarsa. Suppose there is a way to accelerate this natural change, and that my kin discovered this process. Confronted with an unstable home world, they adapted themselves to the extent that we cannot even recognize each other. Those slim figures I saw, thrown out of the ruins of the little spacecraft after its epic battle with the behemoth—could they once have been human?

How can anyone know? These are only wild conjectures, and what my kin on Dhara will make of it, I don't know. It depresses me to think that I never found a way to make kinship with the creatures monitoring the vast net. If there had been a circumstance in which I could have met them on a more equal footing than predator and prey, I would have liked to try. If my ideas are correct and they were once human, do they remember that? Do they return to the little moon with its cave-shrine, and stare at the statue? At least I have this much hope: that given my encounter with the tiny fish-like creatures of the cave, there is some chance that lifeforms composed of ordinary matter can make kinship with their more numerous kin.

My hands are still my hands. But I fancy I can feel, very subtly, the Antarsa wind blowing through my body. This has happened more frequently of late, so I wonder if it can be attributed solely to my imagination. Is it possible that my years-long immersion in the Antarsa current is beginning to effect a slow change? Perhaps my increased perception of the tangibility of the Antarsa is a measure of my own slow conversion, from ancient, ordinary matter to the new kind. What will remain of me, if that happens? I am only certain of one thing, or as certain as I can be in a universe so infinitely surprising: that the love of my kin, and the forests and seas and mountains of Dhara, will have some heft, some weight, in making me whoever I will be.

Landfall

From *The Blood Star Frontier*

Joan Slonczewski

Most college sophomores spent their summer running toyworlds while catching sun at air-conditioned disappearing beaches. Jenny Ramos Kennedy spent hers at the Havana Institute for Revolutionary Botany, which students called the *Botánica.* At the *Botánica*, Jenny worked with ultraphytes, Earth's cyanide-emitting extraterrestrial invaders. Could she discover how to engineer ultraphyte chromosomes—to control them genetically, before they poisoned the planet?

In a tank on the sixth floor swam an ultraphyte. The creature's golden cells soaked up ultraviolet, each eyespot scanning the lab. Around the sealed tank, air vents hissed continually in case the alien life form panicked and put out cyanide.

Jenny watched it undulate through the water, while data scrolled down the windows in her toybox. The creature reminded her of her own pet ultraphyte, the "faux orchid" she hid in her room at Frontera College, the college out in orbit. Beyond the tank, in the corner sat a pockmarked bowl of feathers for a Cuban *orisha,* Babalu the smallpox god. The window looked out from the laboratory to the umbrella crown of a century-old ceiba, a tree sacred to *orishas*. Havana's crowded streets reached into the sea, protected by carboxyplast built ever higher atop the Malecón. The great seawall now extended all around Cuba, rising against the seas that threatened every coast on Earth. As did invading ultraphytes like the one in the tank. No wonder colonists climbed the anthrax lift to escape Earth's troubles and live in spacehabs like Frontera.

César, Jenny's cousin, pressed both hands upon the tank. "*¡Ojo!* It's growing, no? The fifth cell—it has a crease, about to split." César Kennedy Callejo was the son of her mother's brother, the Havana Kennedys. His final summer after high school, he interned with Jenny at the *Botánica*, before following her up to Frontera College. The college had survived ultraphyte invasion, power blackout, and a biblical flood, all in Jenny's first year. But Jenny was going back, and she'd persuaded her twin cousins to come.

"Watch your fingers. The tank is sensitive." Jenny had her first year's experience of Frontera science under her belt. She knew that tripping the tank alarm would cause a *follón*.

César's hands flew open. "Nothing can escape, *¿verdad?*"

"Not here." Jenny hoped. "Touch the control just so, *así*." Unlike her professor's lab at Frontera, where an ultra had escaped, this tank at the *Botánica* was made of six layers of different materials, so if the ultra mutated to dissolve one layer the next would still contain it.

The dark-haired *chico* touched the control, calling up one layer then the next: polycarbonate, aluminum silicate, arsenic sulfide... "Are we ready to add the virus?"

To learn how to fight the deadly invader, the Havana scientists tried to alter its genes. Their genetic tool was a virus—a marine reovirus, with RNA just like the ultra's genes.

Jenny half smiled at her cousin. "Are all your dishes done?" Newbies in the lab spent half the summer washing glassware.

César gave her a withering look, and tapped beneath his eye. "Look for yourself." The cabinet by the Babalu altar gleamed with sterile flasks.

Jenny took another look at the ultraphyte. "The cell is dividing, so the virus will infect it. I'll call Lázaro." Lázaro was their postdoctoral supervisor. He had trained Jenny and César how to run the tank and make the virus. But that morning he'd gone to the toyroom "visiting" a lab in Australia that analyzed ultraphyte poisons. To find him, Jenny checked her toybox.

The toybox hovered virtually before her eye, a dozen windows blinking for her attention. Her mother, Soledad Kennedy, the Wall Street financier and Washington power broker. *"Hijita*—did you hear the Senate resolution?" Soledad's voice was scandalized. "'Be it resolved that the moon hangs from the Firmament!'"

Jenny sighed and blinked the pollmeter, "No." If only enough sensible citizens did the same. "Okay, Mama, but I'm running an experiment."

Her boyfriend Tom had stayed the summer up at Frontera, framing a house for Homefare. From the rooftop he raised a hammer. "Did you get the daily molecule?"

The NMI, IR, and 3D spectroscopy—Jenny blinked through quickly. "A jasmonate, *verdad.*" She blinked it back. He brainstreamed a kiss.

"Cherie, do you have a minute?" Her Parisian girlfriend Anouk at MIT. "Please watch this subroutine for me—I have an urgent mission."

"Anouk—you're not hacking Homeworld again?" But Anouk's purple headscarf had already vanished. In the lab downstairs another Phaistos disc printed out, crying like a baby, "Help! Pick me up!"

The Homeworld Security window blinked orange. Jennie's neighborhood health officer, Captain Vega, the red star blazing on her white uniform. "The Kessler burn is at forty percent." Homeworld was burning out an old launch platform the size of a city block, and first responders had to watch for debris from space. "Keep your scanscope at all times." Vega's face stiffened. "Whatever happens—honor the Blood Star flag."

Lázaro finally appeared in Jenny's toybox, his stylized robotic face in a tiny window at lower left. "I'll be right there.

Did you add the anticyanide?"

Jenny checked the toybank of controls. "The anticyanide, and all the stress damping reagents." A stressed ultraphyte always put out cyanide—plus some new concoction of molecules never seen before. And mutated its RNA genes to make them. Back in her room at Frontera, her own ultraphyte was a plant-form, not a snake like this one. She hoped her own was getting enough salt water, and no stress.

The wall behind the tank, opposite the sundrenched window, shimmered into moonbeams. Out strode Lázaro, a white-coated DIRG with a string of blue-rimmed white *orisha* beads. "Direct Intervention Robotic Guardian"—only Cuba and Alaska let DIRGs get degrees in grad school like humans. A post-DIRG.

Lázaro inspected the tank, then he nodded at the feathered pot in the corner. "All that's left is to say your prayers."

César rolled his eyes. "*No me digas.*" César had no use for religion, so Lázaro, a *santero* initiate, poked fun at him.

"Let's go," Jenny urged. "Before the cell completes division, and the ultra freezes up." An ultra with an even cell number froze because the cells split their decision, could not decide what to do. "*Cuidado*—we still don't know how the ultra will react to the virus."

"Well," said Lázaro, "you know what to do."

Jenny took a breath. She transferred her brainstream to the cellular probe, the tiny nanobot that carried the virus within the tank of the ultraphyte. The tank, the laboratory, the window looking out beyond the tree, past the Malecón to the Mariel spacelift, all receded. In their place pulsed the nanoscopic landscape of the ultraphyte cell, the view from the nanobot. Jenny's stomach felt as if turned inside-out; but she took a deep breath. She was used to spacewalking; a nanobot via brainstream felt not so different.

The nanobot rested its three legs upon the cell surface, a meadow of membrane lipids. Poking out of the lipid meadow were rounded shapes of proteins, like Cuba's *mogote* hills to the west. Jenny drove her nanobot cautiously through the meadow of lipids. Upon one protein hillock came César sliding his nanobot down. Not a good idea; the protein was covered with a forest of long sugar chains. "César, *cuidado*; if the ultra's protein detects your nanobot, it may turn on its defense."

"Okay." César knew the controls by now. His eyes blinked as he set them within his own virtual toybox. But his nanobot was stuck, caught by the long chains of sugars from the protein that stuck to its surface.

"Clip the sugars." Jenny blinked him the code.

César blinked, and the nanobot put out enzymes that clipped the sugar chains.

"Quick now," warned Jenny, "before the ultra's antibodies detect the shortened chains."

The nanobots glided over the lipids, seeking the protein receptor for the virus. The virus was an RNA reovirus, a Franken-mix of genes and signals spliced from octopus, shrimp, and other marine invertebrates. No one knew for sure what could infect an extraterrestrial ultraphyte, but Lázaro had calculated the mix.

"*¡Candela!* There it is." César's nanobot glided toward a large red hillock, the protein that could attach the virus.

Jenny steered her bot more slowly. She blinked to call in the virus. From above, V-shaped proteins from the ultraphyte were coming down then bouncing off the lipid; random motion, but they might react against any foreign particle. Above, responding to her signal, the virus slowly descended, a twenty-faced capsid enclosing its coiled RNA. Slowly the virus descended until it docked upon the red receptor protein.

Suddenly the virus flew off. Like a volcano, there erupted a stream of V-shaped proteins that kicked the virus off to nowhere. Others buffeted the nanobot; Jenny blinked for emergency ejection, but it was too late. The proteins clamped on, piling themselves over the nanobot.

Jenny found herself back in the lab, stomach heaving, as if

she awoke from a bad dream.

"They got yours too?" César shook his head. "How could they tell?"

"The capsid," said Jenny. "The viral coat protein—it's still too foreign. We need to engineer it more like an ultra's protein."

Out the window, beyond the Malecón, a bright streak reached the sea. Kessler debris, from near-Earth orbit, where Homeworld Security was burning the derelict platform. The platform could be seen at night crossing the sky, a silvery moon. The little moon shone in her toybox, the window hovering above her right eye, where Homeworld's lasers methodically burned into it. But occasional bits broke off and fell toward Earth. Most would burn up in the atmosphere, or fall out to sea far from land, and far from the anthrax cords of the Mariel spacelift. Next week the spacelift would take Jenny and César to college.

Lázaro nodded slowly. "We've tried protein so many times. Maybe we need to hide the virus with sugar chains." Another trial down, their third so far that summer.

In Jenny's toybox, amid the wailing Phaistos discs, a window opened. A familiar head loomed forward, dark hair caught in a flight helmet. "Jenny! *¿Qué volá?"* Marta Kennedy Callejo, César's twin sister. "You uploaded your room yet?" The engine whine meant Marta was out in her air-to-space Mercedes that buzzed cornfields as easily as jetting to the moon. Marta and César were both cultured Omara, the high cheekbones and prominent chin, with subtle adjustments such as the Kennedy brow. César's mixed look was quite the thing; his toyworld had logged a hundred *chicas.*

César's eyes blinked rapidly at his own toybox. "Marta, *manita,* we're busy in the lab."

"The code's orange," Jenny warned her. "It's the biggest chunk Homeworld ever burned."

Marta made a face. "As if I don't know." Her jet banked and swerved.

"What's this?" The post-DIRG's amyloid forehead creased.
"Something in the tank," Lázaro warned. "It's not good."

In Jenny's toybox, the tank alarm was blinking. The tank's innermost material was under attack by some chemical—something from the ultra. Jenny's scalp crawled. If the tank were made of only one substance, it would dissolve—like the one at Frontera that Professor Abaynesh had tried to keep. But unlike the professor's tank, this one at the *Botánica* had six layers of different materials: an innermost shell of diamond-coated borosilicate glass, layered with two kinds of polycarbonate, then glass layers of aluminum silicate and arsenic sulfide. If the ultra dissolved the innermost layer, the next layer remained, and so on. Since the ultra had never reached the outer layers, it had never evolved enzymes to defeat them.

The window's red numbers rose and fell. Within the tank, the innermost layer was dissolving away. The layer of diamond.

"Oye," exclaimed César. "Tell everyone to leave their rings home."

Jenny clasped her hands together. She blinked at the EMS window, a first-level warning, just in case.

"Diamond," observed Lázaro with interest. "An enzyme cleaving diamond—that's been seen only once before, at Salt Lake." Where the extraterrestrial seed first landed.

The tank grew cloudy as its inner surface wore away. Jenny took a deep breath and tried to ignore the rising warning levels in her EMS box, the alert sent out to the drone squad. The diamond was only one layer; five more to go, materials this ultra had never seen. César stared for a minute, the lines taut in his neck. Then he leaned back, and his eyes defocused, working at his toyworld. Nothing for it now but to wait and see.

César's eyes widened and he jumped up. "Marta! No way!" His eyes blinked furiously at his own toybox, which Jenny of course could not see. But he spread his hands and chopped his left palm with his right.

"Marta," Jenny called, *"te lo dije,* we're busy. And you need to land. Pieces are falling all over. A ship got swamped already." Another spark, far out to sea, where it kicked up an ominous column of water.

Still watching the tank numbers, Lázaro shook his head. "I don't like this. I think the diamond cracked open, exposing the borosilicate."

Jenny thought furiously. "If the borosilicate dissolves..." The tank itself was now completely clouded, hiding its uncooperative occupant. But the ultra appeared in her toybox, undulating in the water as usual. Then it froze, as if stunned. "The cell divided," Jenny guessed. "Fourteen cells now. I wonder whatever they're trying to decide?" Like how Congress had split on a resolution declaring the moon was a disk tacked to the Firmament. But now the Senate had gone and passed it.

From outside came a distant whine. No toyworld —Marta's plane was actually out here, like an insect homing for blood.

"Come for a ride!" called Marta from Jenny's toybox.

"Marta," Jenny warned, "I'll have to report you."

"To Guantánamo!" added César. Guantánamo naval base housed all the nation's cyber terrorists— human, machine, and inbetween.

Marta laughed and disappeared. Outside, the plane grew and its whine became a roar. Right over the ceiba it zoomed in, close enough to glimpse Marta's face. At the last minute the plane reared up and raced for the sky. It barreled around its axis, followed by three police planes screaming in pursuit.

"You always embarrass me!" César tapped his chest. "I'll go to Berkeley instead. You'll be on your own at Frontera." César alone at Berkeley—a million fellow students, most of them virtual. He'd better go to college with his twin, like most of Jenny's friends did with theirs. Jenny would have gone with her own twin, if he were still alive.

Lázaro focused on the tank. "See the depth gauge. The ultra is definitely eating into the borosilicate."

The number rose malevolently, another digit in the column. "The diamond may have been cracked already," said Jenny. "So the ultra had access through it, to evolve enzymes."

"But how could the ultra reach it?" objected César. "This ultra's too big to reach through a crack. And borosilicate doesn't leach out."

"Let's get the boss in Mare Crisium." The head scientist Dr. Reinaldo Chang was on the moon for the Plant Neurology Association annual meeting at the *Z*, the most famous Lunar zoopark.

The toyroom wall shimmered and pulsed like a curtain. Then it opened upon a row of slot machines, showing zebras in suggestive poses. The slots were topped by research posters in which experiments looped over and over. Past the machines strolled scientists with windows labeled China, Brasil, and Botswana, watching an experiment here, playing a slot there.

"Candela, the *Z*!" exclaimed César. "How *chulo*."

Dr. Chang stood real as life, an angular man with an impeccable moustache. Chang's dark eyebrows twisted like question marks, as he awaited the signal from his lab on Earth. To the moon and back, the time lagged, then his brow lifted. *"¿Qué volá?* Jenny, I was just admiring your poster on cauliphytes." Cauliphytes were the kind of ultra Jenny kept in her room, the kind that stayed put in salt-filled soil and grew stalks like asparagus. "Jenny, you should have come to present it."

"She will next year." Jenny's Frontera professor Abaynesh stepped forward. Her Gabbana shirt covered jeans torn at the knee, stained by potting soil. "If her real work's declassified," Abaynesh added.

Jenny took a sharp breath. "Um, how's the 'weather' on the moon?"

"Jenny," added Abaynesh, "Reinaldo says you could bring us some of that reovirus."

"If we ever get it to work." Jenny thought ruefully, she

had little to show for the summer except a cloudy tank. The life of a bench scientist.

"You'll get it to work." Dr. Chang nodded at the tank. "And we'd like to see your 'wisdom plants.'" Professor Abaynesh's *Arabidopsis* plants, infected by ultra. The real plants were classified.

"Que lástima," exclaimed César, "our ultra didn't like getting virused."

Lázaro caught César's arm. "The students took the virus in just right," he added. "But no matter how careful, as soon as the virus touches down, the ultra's enzymes pour out. We need somehow to put it to sleep."

"Interesting." Dr. Chang walked out of his hotel room into the lab, as if he were really there. He gazed reflectively at the tank. "Ultra must have some experience of viruses. Its defenses evolved before the pod fell to earth." Fell into Great Salt Lake, where only the most salt-loving organisms survive. "Was your capsid entirely new? I see two protein matches for your capsid."

"I missed those," César realized. "*Guau,* did I screw up."

The luminous image of the scientist hovered in time delay, then nodded. "Never mind mistakes. That's how Fleming discovered penicillin."

"Of all days," sighed César. "Nothing escaped all summer, and now, just when we have to get our last data."

"It did not escape," corrected Jenny. "Not yet." Jenny knew well what an escaped ultraphyte looked like. Her bizarrely challenged roommate had turned out to be one in disguise. That part was classified—a Homeworld scheme gone rogue.

Lázaro added, "We need to rethink our experimental design. We've only one tank left." Each tank had to be custom designed in Shanghai with newly invented materials, to the tune of five million dollars.

"Let's order two more," said Dr. Chang. "They'll give us ten percent off the second one."

Jenny blinked. This was the *Botánica*, Havana's world-class research institute.

Professor Abaynesh said, "You could ship us the extra." At Frontera, their ultras had already escaped to the wild, like Florida pythons. Like the ultra Jenny hid in her room—*sólo Dios sabe* what they could do.

"Jenny?" Dr. Chang's hair shifted back absently, and his gaze had a faraway look as if he'd just come up for air in a toyworld full of abstracts. "Did you read this report from Salt Lake?" The first ultraphyte from outer space had landed in Great Salt Lake, where it needed concentrated salt to grow. But then ultras had evolved to concentrate salt on dry land. And still others evolved to grow in the ocean. Ultraphytes evolved fast as a virus, faster than any native life form on Earth. "About ultraphyte microbes."

"Microbial ultraphytes? Microscopic? But—they could be anywhere. They could have got into the cracked diamond." Jenny's hair stood on end. "We could swallow them."

"We probably have."

At left, a sudden flash. The white heat burned Jenny's eye. Not her retina, of course; the brainstream to her toybox. Her eyes shut reflexively, though of course she still saw all the windows. She resisted the urge to pull her diad off her forehead and cut the brainstream.

The flash came from the derelict platform that Homeworld ships were lasing. The platform had exploded.

"Full alert, code red." In the window appeared Homeworld Security director Glynnis Carillo, her blunt chin delivering the news, her eyes stern beneath her sandy colored hair. "All personnel attend your stations. First projectiles make landfall in twenty minutes..."

Landfall. Homeworld had known the platform could explode, and the debris fall to Earth. But they had to burn it up soon, before the whole thing fell at once. The previous Centrist administration had put off this chore till after the election. And now—Jenny blinked for her orders, what emergency response. She opened the matrix of DIRGs on her watch, the ones assigned to the apartment complex adjacent to the *Botánica* tower.

Marta reappeared. "Jenny—"

"Get out!" said Jenny.

"But Jenny—it blew up! Right overhead."

The whole city block —a gazillion pieces. Half of which would be heading straight down to Earth.

César threw up his hands. "No you won't!" he yelled at his toybox. "Marta, you cannot pick us up. *¡Vete!* Just get your ship out of here!"

In Jenny's box rose Captain Vega. "Landfall projected throughout the Caribbean. Everyone to the shelters."

As the students raced downstairs, others joined them, streaming out of side labs for botanical neurology, like students fleeing a column of army ants. On the third floor emerged a young man with his leg in a splint, carried by a DIRG; a regular DIRG, still under human control. Jenny blinked at her toybox; she was in charge of the DIRGs for the apartment complex next door, the ones that searched the buildings to make sure everyone came out.

A dozen tiny windows opened, each with a tiny DIRG searching the floors. Ten of them were fine, busy at their job of herding residents downstairs to the underground shelter. But two of the DIRGs were disabled. Jenny blinked one of them; the reset took. But the other did not respond. She had to get out and find it. She had about sixty seconds before the first fragments made landfall.

From outside came the furnace blast of heat. Jenny choked on the air, and sweat streamed into her eyes. The incessant east wind brought up a raincloud, obscuring the heaven-stretched cables of the Mariel Spacelift that Jenny would soon take to college. Rain year-round brought Cuba rich harvest now, but the rain band marched inexorably north. Thereafter, *el desierto.*

Where was the disabled DIRG? Jenny followed her brainstream, down past the ceiba with its flared roots, across the courtyard to the flagpole. The pole flew the stars-and-stripes, topped by the Blood Star flag, since Cubans said they'd "won their war" with the States. Behind the apartment complex, sun-darkened *chicos* and *chicas* in monokinis watched the horizon. Craning their necks, they laughed at each bright spark on the sea; a front-line view of Homeworld's epic battle with space trash. *"Oye,"* called Jenny. "Get down to the shelter!"

A ten-year-old laughed back. "Nothing hits Havana."

"The trash falls a hundred klicks out to sea," said another. His fingers fluttered at a Phaistos disc. The multi-universe puzzle game had played for free the year before; this year it added a house edge.

There was the DIRG—the kids had hacked it to dance. The humanoid dipped and swayed, thrusting its backside. Meanwhile, another bright spark hit the blue distance beyond the Malecón, then yet another to the east.

Jenny focused her brainstream directly at the DIRG and blinked the EMS code. The DIRG straightened itself, then each hand picked up a *chico* by the collar. The Phaistos disc clattered on the tiles, wailing "Pick me up!" The kids all shrieked and headed indoors.

Below ground was a maze of shops and stores, from Gabbana shirts to Mercedes jets like Marta's. Most days people came here to flee the heat, but today they fled the impending shower of trash. Red-skirted school girls, stooped men in walkers, suited men and women blinking their client lists.

The hand of an elderly man clasped Jenny's arm. "Will it miss the apartment?"

"No se preocupe," Jenny tried to reassure him. Still, she thought of the ceiba tree. The tree had stood through floods and hurricanes, depression marches and clashes over statehood. Would it survive landfall?

"¡Oye!" Captain Vega called for order. "Be steadfast—like our heroes of the Revolution."

"Ha," said a woman from the plant neuro lab. "Those Centrists call the sky a bowl above our heads, with the stars painted on. Let them explain this *follón."* Centrists had run the States till the last election.

A neighbor spread his hands and pointed south. "It's more than space trash. It's the Antarctic *piratas."* The melting continent was full of pirate armies that vied for new land.

Jenny shook her head, but others implored her. "What is it really, *Kennedicita?* They tell you, don't they?" They knew of her White House connection, though not her direct line to Homeworld. And certainly not her classified project on ultraphyte intelligence.

Amid the crowd, Lázaro tried to reassure the anxious ones. "We are in good hands," he told them. "The hands of *La Caridad."* The DIRG's white *santero* vestment and beads inspired calm.

"*Escucha, todo.* Everything's under control," barked Captain Vega. "Water, medicines, it's all here. Listen to Officer Ramos." She took off for the next shelter.

Jenny nodded. So far, Havana efficiency won the day. She strolled through the shelter, answering calls to "Officer Ramos," checking for any injuries. Phaistos discs appeared amongst tapping fingers.

Then her toybox went dark. The Mercedes jet vanished, and the Gabbana shirts. Only emergency lights glowed blue along the walls.

There were gasps and shrieks. Children started crying. Their toybox dark—no one ever saw that. People grasped the diads from their foreheads and wrung them as if to shake the dark out.

Even Jenny blinked reflexively, and had to restrain her hand from snatching the useless diad. But the trouble was not here. Somewhere, out there in hyperspace, a major data stream had been cut. Jenny's father ran the east coast Toynet; she knew what it took him to keep all the electrons flowing. She cast her gaze around the crowd and tried to think what to do.

Jenny took a deep breath. "I've got a signal. An emergency channel." She nodded importantly. "It's all right, they say. Everything's fine. Toynet will be back up soon."

The sobs subsided. All around, pairs of eyes looked back at Officer Ramos, eyes wide through their dark empty toyboxes.

"My child can't breathe," someone cried out. "Tell them we need help."

Lázaro looked directly at her. Jenny looked back, her gaze unflinching. Lázaro knew there was no "emergency channel."

Most of the people grew calm, but the elderly man let out a groan, his face twisted. He fell back, two neighbors catching him as he fell, eyes glazed, fingers jerking. Jenny blinked to download his history, but of course the box was blank. She slapped her scanscope around his arm, programmed manually, and hoped she recalled how to stabilize a seizure.

From behind came a guitar chord. The amyloid of Lázaro's left arm had morphed into a guitar. He played a descending train of chords, then launched into "*Vengo del espacio.*"

I come from outer space

To meet the human race

I am un ser sincero

Just another poor granjero.

While the verses went on, Jenny stabilized the patient until a doctor took over. Then she worked her way through the crowd, offering meds for a sprained ankle here, elevated glucose there. She found César sitting on the floor against the Mercedes window, hugging his knees. She crouched down and tapped his knee. "You okay?"

César shrugged. "Whatever." He never wasted energy being scared. But he seemed intent on something.

"What is it?"

"I was just thinking. About our experiment."

"The ultra?"

"*Sí,*" replied César. "And about the wild ultras, out there."

The ones releasing cyanide and other toxins. "If we're trying to control them…"

"So?"

"What if they're trying to control us too? With their own molecules?"

Jenny bit her lip. Of course, that's what the ultra had done at Frontera last year—with a bit of human help. Changed the election, and maybe the course of history. But only a few knew.

"Ow!" Across the hall, a man jumped up, hopping on one leg, then the other. He pulled up his trouser leg and picked something off his skin. *"¡Hormiga!"*

Around him people gasped and moved away, searching the floor. An army ant—Jenny had to find the column from which it strayed. Introduced for ultraphyte control, army ants were the one natural predator that could subdue the eye-celled invader. The column of ants would lead her to it.

A dog growled, straining at its leash. *"¡Mira!* Here it is!" Tugging the dog's leash, a woman pointed to the floor. There the ants marched, clambering over one another, a black pulsing column. The column met the foot of the wall and followed along the edge, past the Mercedes shop.

"Everyone get out your anti-cyanide." Jenny clicked a bracelet that pulsed anti-cyanide into her blood. A bitter taste on her tongue; it was not safe for long. She followed the trail of ants along the wall, stepping gingerly to avoid strays. Dead ants appeared, accumulating in piles. Their sisters just kept climbing over. Then, amid a large mound of dead ants, appeared the decaying remains of an ultraphyte. The ants had exhausted the ultra's cyanide, and now fed upon the remains.

The ultra must have been small, probably a single cell. Most single-cell ultras didn't last long anyway, their RNA genes doomed by mutations. This one could not have come far. So… where was its parent?

Reflexively Jenny blinked her toybox to run a Homeworld-grade ultra search; a search that could find ones that escaped the everyday ultra-search that Toynet routinely ran. But Toynet was out. Did the original ultra know that? And what was it after? Not salt—the laboratory, and the apartment complex, were full of salt traps. An ultra sharp enough to get this far must be after something else.

From somewhere in the underground maze an alarm was beeping. It could be anything; when Toynet gave out, all kinds of alarms beeped, popped and whistled. But the tone of this one caught her ear. It might be a cyber alarm, like the one from Lázaro when a circuit blew.

"Lázaro?" No one answered her amputated brainstream. She ought to go for help, but the alarm might be urgent. Dodging the stream of ants, she edged down the hall and turned past a skybike store. The alarm grew louder.

A body lay splayed on the floor, the limbs contorted. Skin bright pink; Jenny's heart sank. By now the cyanide victim must be brain dead. And the ultra might still be close. She hoped her own protection hadn't run out; without brainstream, she could not tell for sure.

But the head's eyes blinked, and the lips moved. The head was the source of the alarm. A cyber head.

In an instant Jenny was on the floor, with her scanscope around an arm. If the head was cyber, the organic body might recover. As the scanscope tightened, Jenny was thinking already what to do next. She patted the woman's neck, wondering which parts were cyber and which organic. A clean line crossed the neck, as if someone had sliced off a head and replaced it with a new one, but the internal organs could be anything. Behind the neck, Jenny tapped the alarm. Silence fell, except for her own deep breaths.

"*¡Ayudame!* Medibot!" The head mouthed words barely audible. It must require the lungs for speech; a dumb arrangement, in Jenny's opinion, but then she wasn't the surgeon. She held open the prosthetic lips to clear the airway, trying feverishly to remember how to revive the lungs and heart without the help of a medibot. Despite herself her eyelids kept trying to call one. Where was everyone—she hoped Lázaro kept them calm.

After an eternity of pressing and pounding, the woman gasped. She choked, and Jenny turned her on her side. Jenny felt behind the neck again, counting the cervical vertebrae: three, four, five... all had the flat feel of carboxyplast, the sturdy building material condensed from carbon dioxide. Carboxyplast all the way down the spine.

From the end of the hall came a medibot, attracted to the alarm. With a sigh of relief, Jenny transferred her patient.

"I power down in twenty-five," the bot warned. Hopefully that would be long enough—for this one. Where was Toynet? What had landed—where?

The medibot shaped a brace for the neck and back. The brace helped the cyber-headed woman take a breath, then another. Her breaths rasped.

Jenny asked, "Who are you?" The first test of brain function. Usually Jenny knew the right answer; it unnerved her to be cut off even from the Toynet namelist.

"A person." The words burst from between the cyber lips. *"Soy persona*—a human being. Sixty-eight percent."

Sixty organic was the threshold for federal rights. Below that, you faced a patchwork of laws in different states. Human in Cuba and Alaska; junkyard meat elsewhere. And if you ran afoul of the law, there was Guantánamo.

"Will my body live?"

Jenny smiled. "Let's hope." With hope they did better.

The cyber lips moved. "I don't want to go back on the shelf, waiting for a body."

"If you get amyloid lungs next time," Jenny suggested, "they're built to filter cyanide."

"Then I'd be under sixty percent," said the *persona*. "I had spongebrain; all I needed was a head." Spongiform encephalopathy, from eating mammalian meat.

The ultra—it was still out there. "What happened?" Jenny asked. "Where was the ultra? Do you remember?"

"In the stairwell. I put my hand on the rail, and there it was."

Jenny shuddered. If the ultra had escaped, it could be anywhere by now. And there could be more than one.

She went to search the stairwell. The floor tiles were bare, the rails clear.

Her brain exploded with Toynet. Caught by surprise, she stumbled, half falling down the stairs. She blinked furiously, scanning the city. To the west, from Punta Brava, rose an ominous cloud of black.

Like Marta's plane, Jenny zoomed her brainstream across Havana. As suburban towers grew in her window, the smoking wreckage appeared in Punta Brava. The people were safe, her stream said, but the collapsed half of a DIRG lay beneath a fallen beam of carboxyplast. Jenny caught her breath. It was no *persona*, no post-DIRG like Lázarus, just an ordinary bot from the crew that stayed upstairs to mind the buildings. Still... part of a crew doing its job. *¿Qué es persona? ¿Ser sincero?*

And to the northeast, beyond the Malecón, the Mariel Spacelift—the anthrax lines were cut. A rising capsule had parachuted to safety.

From Frontera, Tom's face filled his window. "Jenny? Your window disappeared!"

"All citizens accounted for," announced Captain Vega. "Well done, Officer Ramos. We survived the assault by unbridled space capitalism."

But how long would the lift take to repair? And how would Jenny and her cousins get up to Frontera College next week?

Marta zoomed in. "Jenny, I'm coming back to get you and César, ready or not."

Anouk's window was empty. What if Homeworld had caught her this time?

"ToyNews—From our box to yours." The collapsed building at Punta Brava. "The defunct twenty-first century launch pad exploded, severing the Mariel Spacelift while showering debris across the Caribbean. Dozens of people are missing.

Homeworld director Glynnis Carrillo is here to explain this tragic miscalculation."

Jenny briefed Glynnis daily on Frontera's classified ultraphyte intelligence program, after the previous administration had secretly shipped an engineered "intelligent" ultra to "test" at the spacehab. But today, the Homeworld Director had more pressing matters.

"As you know," Glynnis began, "our administration inherited this disaster waiting to happen. The derelict launch pad should have been squared away ten years ago. We deeply regret the casualties, though our losses could have been much worse."

"Indeed," said the announcer. "And now, for an alternative view of the disaster, we bring you professor Hector Umberto, astronomer on the faculty of John Whitcomb University."

The professor, a leading Centrist, wore a brown tweed suit and his golden hair curled up like Tin-Tin. Umberto gave a self-satisfied smile. "The old launcher has long hung from the heavenly Firmament that, according to divine plan, rotates majestically around our central Earth." Hung there, like a picture on the wall. "The fall of this object off the vault of heaven is a sign that divine patience with our new leaders already wears thin." Before that year, Centrists had run the White House and Congress. Before the election that Frontera turned upside-down.

"Loco," exclaimed César at Jenny's elbow. "Earth must be the craziest place in the cosmos."

Jenny recalled her first year at the college in the sky. "Don't be sure," she told him. "Wait till you see Frontera."

This Alakie and the Death of Dima

Terry Boren

When Dine Paloan asked this woman, Alakie, to leave before destruction arrived, she refused at first. She had trained to be Paloan's pilot, but this Alakie had never thought she would be leaving without Dine. So instead of accepting the Dinela's wishes, this Alakie helped to send Paloan's other tokens back to Cassin, and she stayed.

This Alakie did not understand Dine Paloan's decision to remain on Dima. Dine's building skill and control of resources were so enormous that the honorific "Dine" seemed not enough to encompass or define Paloan. This woman had difficulty believing Paloan could not compact itself soon enough to leave, but Dine refused to lose memory or status. And after days alone in the quietness of Paloan's tunnels, with almost all of Dine's tokens already gone, she finally agreed to leave.

This Alakie approached the plug of Dine's final retreat deep in the maze of its etched tunnels one last time and begged Paloan to show her how to pull Dine to the surface. But Paloan refused, and as this woman leaned her head against the Dinela's filigreed communication pad, her body infiltrated by its fine, soft filaments and Dine's taste of flowers on her tongue, Paloan asked this woman to make sure the other Hu were safe. Time was short.

"You must place trade value for yourself now, Hu Alakie,

or return with the ship to that Paloan on Cassin," it said. This Alakie would not consider that. When still small, Paloan's bud had been Dine Paloan's pilot, before Alakie finished her training, but it did not share Paloan's memories or Alakie's affection. When Paloan had endowed that bud with Dine's territory and tokens on Cassin, this woman had not been part of the inheritance.

So, much too soon, this woman scrambled up Paloan's wide tube toward the display dome. The tube was smooth-walled, curving upward at a steep angle, but this Alakie used the hand and foot holds Dine Paloan had allowed her to carve in the fused polysaccharide walls of its shaft to climb quickly toward the surface. When she reached the shaft terminus, she stood on the ledge that Paloan had built for her when she was a small one and then pulled herself over the retaining wall onto the clean white sand of the domed and walled enclosure. Paloan had not visited the surface for display since beginning to retract the year before, but had insisted that this Alakie continue to go on her own. She missed the bright colors of Dine Paloan's display. There was no trace of any of Dine's filaments on the surface of the huge, sandy circle.

Today would be her last chance to watch the sunrise on Dima, the world this woman thought of as hers. One of Dine Paloan's stupid ones fluttered out of the tube mouth and batted at her head until she swatted it away and it returned to the tunnels, a blue flash receding into the darkness.

There would be rain after sunrise, Paloan had said, the last rain she would ever see on the planet, but as she started for the rendezvous point to meet the other Hu tokens, the early morning was almost cloudless. The sky just before dawn was bright with the small moons, Dimit and Dimit's Token, so the prick of light that marked the debris cloud of the lost traveling throat was barely visible setting low in the west. This Alakie could see no sign of the singularity that had destroyed the gate's throat and would destroy them all soon if they stayed. The sun would be up soon behind the cap rock.

As this woman neared the viewing platform at the outside edge of Paloan's display enclosure, the ground shook. She stopped and looked east toward the cap. The stalk of the elevator made a pale line in the dark blue sky above the rocky palisade, and the contrail of a departing shuttle crossed behind it. The last of the Dinelate were fleeing from Dima. Paloan would stay, though, because the old Dinela had refused to leave its tunnels until it was too late. This Alakie curled her toes in the cool sand beneath her feet, then started walking again. She did not want to leave Dine Paloan, but she could not humiliate the Dinela, so this woman would do as it asked.

At the perimeter of the circle of white sand, near her platform, this Alakie paused to rest and think for a few minutes, but then she touched a small pad recessed into the outer retaining wall. The dome snapped off, and a gust of wind slapped the fabric of her loose pants against her legs. As the cooler air of the dome collapsed and dispersed, the thin cellulose panels of her viewing platform rustled in the breeze. She held her straight brown hair away from her face with one hand and quickly hopped the retaining wall. The oldest of Paloan's communication strands sloughed away in her hand.

She laced on her boots, then started off toward the rocky upthrust of the cap. As she made her way east across the wash below the mesa's cliff face, she encountered a few mats of exploratory surface hyphae, Dine Valiean's, she thought. Valiean had been moving into Dine Paloan's area as Paloan retracted.

This woman had called the remaining Hu tokens in as Paloan had asked. So as she followed the footpath up the rough mesa wall, she occasionally glanced west across the plain to see which tokens would come. Far to the south, Dine Valiean was spread in full display, totally filling its enormous enclosure. Waves of Valiean's iridescent substance were visible even in the early light; but closer, the wash below the palisade was dark. She stopped under the overhang just below the trail's last pitch up to the cap and waited.

Of the ten small ones rescued by the Dinelate from the

wrecked ovary of the ship *Amore*, seven Hu had survived to maturity. Hundreds had died on the Hu colony ship. Dine Paloan believed that the Hu ship had been destroyed by some unidentified enemy, perhaps by the same malign agent that had sent a singularity through the Dima gate.

Of those seven Hu survivors, two had been sent away from the planet in the last year, one without her Dinela. This Alakie's throat ached with the thought of leaving Paloan and Dima. But before long, this woman saw a movement below. The Hu seed carrier, Balal, soon joined her on the flat rock where Alakie sat. Balal's offspring snuggled in a pack against her thin chest, asleep. The light was growing, so this woman could see the tears on Balal's cheeks. It had not been long since the blood of Balal's successful reproduction, and this Alakie knew the woman was not fully recovered. The female offspring had not even been named.

"Dine Valiean will not leave," Balal said to this Alakie. "And Dine will not let this Balal stay." The depth of her conflict was clear on Balal's pale face.

This Alakie knew that Valiean would never consider letting Balal stay, because Hu Balal was the token carrier of Valiean's seed to Dine Kapoan. Kapoan could not go because the value and beauty of their Hu tokens had caused Kapoan to exchange with Valiean, and as Kapoan was now ready to fission, Dine Kapoan could not leave. So, Valiean had refused to lose status and retract until too late; and still at full extension, Valiean was larger than any possible transport could hold. Without question, Balal was the most valuable token Valiean would ever display and probably the last. Dine would not allow her to remain on Dima.

"Valiean would be humiliated if you tried to stay," this Alakie said to her friend, hoping she would listen. "Paloan and Valiean have already sent all their stupid ones away. They only let these Hu stay so long out of consideration for their intelligence and value."

"Lanifie is as valuable as these Hu are," she said.

"And Kapoan would not want him to stay either," this Alakie said.

"This Balal knows that is right, but Lanifie has refused to leave."

This woman was startled. Would Hu Lanifie defy his Dinela's wishes? As Kapoan's seed carrier, Lanifie was expected to go with Valiean's token when Kapoan split. He was now Valiean's token.

"Lanifie is not listening, then?" The Hu rarely refused any Dinela.

"No." Balal looked across the sunrise-tinted plain toward the display circles. "And Valiean will not let this woman stay."

This Alakie stood. "These women should hurry. The sun is already up behind the cap rock. These Hu will talk to Lanifie."

Balal stood and took this woman's hand. "This Balal thanks you, Alakie," she said. There was little time, but this Alakie did not want to leave Lanifie to die and was afraid that Balal would choose to die with him if both he and Valiean stayed. This woman had to persuade Lanifie to leave. So these Hu traveled back the way they had come, making their way slowly down the cliff face.

Bakbak met these women at the bottom of the trail, smiling as he always was. He wore only a pair of hiking boots. His long body was brown from display in the sun, and three stupid ones fluttered in his masses of dark brown curls, but they took to the air when Bakbak neared this Alakie. Her scent attracted them. These stupid ones were Malkean's taste buds and eyes. Seed carriers attracted any of a Dinela's fragments.

"These three are the last of Dine Malkean's tokens," he said and laughed as the golden flier batted at this woman's lips. "Dine couldn't find them, so Malkean said this Bakbak could wait for you and try to tempt them. Is it time to go? These are ready?"

"Past time," this Alakie said. "Dine Malkean has gone?" She waved her hand to shoo the stupid one away.

"On that last shuttle. This Bakbak has never seen Dine so small. It could barely talk."

It was never easy for Dinelate to travel off-planet. They had to give up most of their substance to do so. Though a Dinela could expand quite rapidly, that kind of deliberate selection and compaction was slow, and they hated to lose status and so much of themselves.

"Lanifie has refused," this woman said.

Bakbak's eyebrows rose. "No... that won't happen," he said, his smile fading.

This Alakie felt the same way. The ten small Hu had lived together with Paloan until they were grown and Dine distributed them to gain position. The Hu were so rare that Paloan had won a large part of Dima's resources with the most valuable tokens, unique sentients the Dinelate could trade. She remembered Lanifie as a boy, strong and compact, sweet tempered, almost as quick as Alakie at their studies. In the years since they had gone to their Dinelate, the survivors had remained close, clustered together on Dima. None of these had known any other Hu.

"Lanifie will come if these Hu all talk to him," Balal said.

This Alakie asked Bakbak, "Where is Sanva?" Sanva had never recovered after Pik and Malvy died. Sanva did not like to be alone. None of these Hu did.

"At the shuttle," Bakbak answered. "He'll wait. These need to hurry if they're going to pick up Lanifie and return in time."

The sun rose from behind the cap rock as these Hu made their way south along the wash, and the air grew warmer, wetter, clouds piling on the horizon. At Balal's platform, they took her big-wheeled runner to reach Lanifie's pavilion as soon as possible. Because the Dinelate had bridged the wash a day's walk to the north and even farther to the south and the scrub of the plain was difficult to maneuver, the streambed route was by far the fastest, and these Hu's most favored. The brightly painted runner ground down the wash to the south to reach Kapoan's territory.

By the time these arrived, the air had warmed but storm clouds were gathering thickly, so Lanifie had raised the dome around Kapoan's display enclosure. The viewing platform was tented in purple fabric to provide shade, and the platform was completely covered in tokens—blue and scarlet jewels, bright metals etched with intricate designs, furs, skins, and artifacts from half a hundred worlds—as if Kapoan were still able to trade. A small, four-legged creature with very sharp teeth watched them with shining, predatory eyes as they approached the platform. This woman knew that Kapoan had sent most of its tokens to Valiean, but many beautiful things remained. This Alakie admired a glossy carved table and a chair padded in softest nesting fluff. The chair supported the reclining frame of the seed carrier, Lanifie. At least six stupid ones, fanning their multicolored wings in the warm air, perched on tokens near Lanifie. Balal immediately climbed the platform's steps to his side. He smiled at her. It was impossible that Lanifie and Balal might be separated.

Long since at full growth, Lanifie was the largest of the Hu, thick of neck and muscled heavily in the thighs and shoulders. His naked skin glowed, dark as the sky without moons, and his sex rested heavy and dusky against his thigh. Lightly touching his skin, Balal's small hand was a moon on a still, black lake. The beauty of their bodies together had caused Kapoan and Valiean to exchange, even though each had risked so much status to accomplish sexual reproduction of their own. Even asexual budding caused a drop in status, but sexual mixing was often fatal to at least one Dinela.

A sour smell rose from the enclosure behind Lanifie's platform.

This Alakie looked closely at Kapoan, and wished she had not. A mound of Kapoan's sloughed communication rhizomorphs rotted near the edge of its enclosure. Though this woman had never heard of a Dinela's reproduction proceeding so rapidly, clearly Kapoan's time was growing close. Lanifie must have known that for days. Dine Kapoan had lost the reproductive wager, and with it any status; it had already ceased to exist as a personality. All of its iridescent colors had dulled, and large areas of Dine's substance were clearly abandoned. A huge fissure ran through its substance extending from the platform almost to the buried retaining wall around its tunnel entrance. This woman looked back to Lanifie on his platform. His face seemed sad, almost stunned. But she knew that he could recover, and that he would if he understood how much Valiean also valued him. Alakie and Bakbak joined the two Hu on the platform.

"Kapoan will be gone soon... very soon," this woman said carefully.

Lanifie nodded and took Balal's hand. His eyes focused on this Alakie.

"You and the offspring of Kapoan are exchanged with Valiean, and Valiean will be humiliated if you don't go as Dine wants." Lanifie could refuse, as any sentient could, but what sense was there in such humiliation.

"Valiean will soon be dead," he said.

"Yes. And so will Kapoan, but you won't be if you come," she said, and glanced at Bakbak.

"And Kapoan's offspring?"

"It's too late for them, too. Kapoan can't complete autolysis in time."

"But they have value," he said quietly. "These Hu are valuable to them." She could see it was useless to urge him. He still needed to be with Kapoan and had never accepted the outcome of the exchange.

There was no time to argue, so when Lanifie dropped his gaze from hers, this woman nodded to Bakbak. He stepped forward and grabbed Lanifie from behind. Before the big man could do more than buck a few times, this Alakie had shot him in the throat with a tranquilizer. Bakbak had always been a reliable man, this Alakie thought.

Bakbak held Lanifie until the big man slumped in his carved

chair, but it took all three of these Hu to load him into the runner with as many of Kapoan's tokens as would fit inside with four Hu. All of Lanifie's stupid ones fluttered in with him.

Balal's offspring had begun to cry loudly and wave her fists by the time this Alakie slid behind the yoke and started the runner. When she glanced into the back, Balal was patting her offspring's dark curls and holding Lanifie's hand.

"Valiean wouldn't like you forcing him," Balal said from the back as this Alakie bumped the vehicle down the ramp into the wash. The loaded runner churned as fast as this woman could make it go toward the spot where the southern ramp left the wash near the road that climbed the palisade. The four-legged predator loped beside the runner, faster than seemed possible, its tongue lolling between pointed teeth. Sen Predator, this Alakie thought, and wondered where Kapoan had acquired it. Sen clearly had made its own decision.

Thunder rumbled on the horizon. Over the small one's wails, this Alakie tried to comfort Balal, "In Lanifie's head, he's not Valiean's, yet," this woman said to Balal. "But Dine Valiean would want this Hu to take him with these if they could." This woman knew certainly that what she said was true. And that was when this Alakie knew what she had to do, but she would see the others safe before she tried. Valiean could help her if what she thought about Dine was true.

The runner churned through the sand toward the south cap, and the small offspring's sobs slowly subsided, but as they climbed the ramp to the road, rain began to pound the roof of the runner, and the slender sap trees on the mesa's flat top bent and moaned in wind. By the time they reached the launch facility, this woman couldn't see three runner-lengths in front of the windshield through the rain. When the purple base of the elevator loomed out of the rain, this Alakie braked hard, and the runner skidded to a stop, throwing up a plume of water.

Crouched miserably in the storm near the airlocked entrance to the base's elevator, soaked to the skin, Sanva surged to his feet close enough to touch the front wheels of the runner. This Alakie clutched the yoke for a moment then unclenched her teeth and glanced at Bakbak, grown pale beside her. He grinned feebly.

"Lanifie is waking up," Balal said. "Get him off of this Balal."

Sanva pulled open the back of the runner and began unloading tokens. With him was a short figure, obviously not Hu or Dinelate, in a complete environmental suit. It was a very squat tripod, almost fully obscured by rain and the suit. This woman had met only one Gamela before, during the first time she had visited the station at the traveling throat for training, before Paloan had brought the rest of the Dinelate to Dima to build the elevator, but she wasn't sure if this was the same one.

Something kicked the back of her seat, hard, and these Hu spent the next few minutes wrestling Lanifie out of the runner and coaxing him into the airlock. Finally, when Balal's offspring began to wail again, Lanifie shook his head and followed Balal unsteadily into the elevator. He was collapsed outside of the airlock when this woman and the Gamela stepped through carrying three wet and angry stupid ones.

"This weather… it feels like Dima knows," Sanva said, frowning. He was shivering, his clothing wet and plastered to his angular frame.

Bakbak snorted. "It feels like a hurricane," he said. Lightning flickered through the thin membranes of the elevator carriage's common area.

"This Alakie must go back to get some of Dine's tokens, Paloan's stupid ones," this woman said. "These cannot leave them." But then she stopped. There was no sense in lying. "This woman must try to save Dine Paloan."

Bakbak just nodded, but Sanva turned toward her, his eyes wide in his bony face. "Hurry," he said. "These cannot wait. The elevator is slow. The shuttle will have only one chance to meet up with the tether on time. It is the only way to reach the Gamela's ship."

Cold rain was still pelting the roof of the vehicle when this Alakie arrived at Dine Valiean's enclosure, but the runner's lights revealed that Valiean had expanded over its retaining wall in order to reinforce Balal's viewing platform with its own substance. Elevated on the outside of a Dinela's wall, a platform was usually a pleasant place for invited guests and the display of tokens, but in the runner's lights Valiean's platform looked more like some empty cave enveloped in heavy, iridescent waves of its substance. Valiean's surface display was larger than any Dinela's this Alakie had ever seen; billows of its substance moved behind the walls of its enclosure, and Dine must have extended many times the area of its walls underground. Valiean's dome was not deployed. The tented platform made Alakie uneasy, but at least she would not get wet, this woman thought.

She ducked her head, hopped out of the runner, and then ran for the shelter of Dine Valiean's display area. In the cave of its platform, this Alakie paused for a moment—she seldom spoke with Dinelate other than for Paloan—but then she pressed herself against Valiean's filigreed pad.

Sometimes, as a child, this Alakie imagined that she could feel Dine Paloan's filaments curling through her cells. She knew that wasn't possible because the smallest fingers of any Dinela's substance could be small enough to slip easily between molecules, but held tightly by Valiean's larger external filament, that feeling was hard to dismiss. And Valiean's voice was so strong in her head that her brain seemed to be vibrating. Dine was not accustomed to speaking to this Alakie and pushed her bonded synapses too hard.

"Kapoan is finishing," it said. "The offspring must go. You must take them."

This Alakie could taste Valiean's loam and spice on her tongue. "Dine Valiean," this woman said quietly, her lips moving against its soft substance. "You are of lower status than Paloan. This woman is not your token, she speaks for Dine Paloan, and she must go soon. Though this Hu loves

Kapoan, the Dinela has not completed division, and Dine Kapoan's offspring, if Kapoan had split, would be too fragile to go." This Alakie did not know what Balal would say when she found out, but this woman continued: "And so Balal and Lanifie have also decided to stay."

In her peripheral vision, a wave of fluorescence spread across Valiean's pad.

"You must take the Hu tokens."

"But they do not want to go, and they are sentients."

"Balal is valuable." That valuation was clear in Valiean's thoughts. "And Kapoan's offspring are small enough to ride the ships."

"So is Balal's offspring, and so is Lanifie, but they are also strong enough to survive..." This Alakie was touched to feel Valiean's love for the Hu seed carrier and her offspring. "But their value will be destroyed. None of them can, or will, go."

"Will Paloan exchange? Will Dine trade for them and send them to Cassin?" Dine Valiean asked. "The Hu have always loved Paloan."

"Paloan is retracting; most of Dine's tokens have already gone. You cannot force the Hu tokens to lose value." Another peristaltic color change flashed over Valiean's pad, and the taste of spice sharpened on this woman's tongue. "Paloan is still too large to go," this woman said softly, "So Dine cannot take them."

Even over the muffled sounds of the storm, this woman could hear the hissing of Valiean's substance moving restlessly above her head. "That bud of the Paloan who found you on *Amore* will take this Paloan's tokens if you speak for them, so Dine will keep and value the Hu on Dine's old home, on Cassin. This Valiean will exchange with that bud of Paloan. What will that Paloan require to save Kapoan's offspring?"

"This Hu does not wish to stay with that other Paloan or speak for Dine. The bud of Paloan on Cassin has no claim on this woman as a token. This Alakie places her own value."

"Then you must still speak for *this* Paloan. You have always spoken for Dine's tokens. What will Paloan take to save Kapoan's offspring?"

This woman was silent. She watched the rain outside of Valiean's shelter and felt sorry for Dine. "Your reproduction cannot be saved," she said. "There is no action that Dine can take that saves Valiean's status." The truth was, this woman thought, there was no way to save Valiean. And Valiean knew that, too; she was counting on it. "Dine Paloan also will soon cease to be."

But the Dinela misunderstood what she wanted. "Then this Valiean will trade with the Hu woman, if she values her own tokens. What will the Hu woman take to save this Valiean's sentients and Kapoan's offspring? The other tokens do not matter." Valiean was growing increasingly agitated.

"This woman has no value. This Alakie wants no status without Paloan as Balal wants no status without Valiean." She felt the shock jangle through Dine's substance. She could sense its confusion.

"Would you humiliate Paloan by not valuing yourself properly? All sentients must be valued. Balal will be valued by Kapoan's offspring."

But then this Alakie told Dine Valiean again that she would not take Dine's offspring just to see them die. "And so Balal and her offspring will have no value," she said bluntly.

"Unless Paloan takes them. But Paloan has not compacted." Valiean was beginning to understand.

"And Dine has also sealed itself behind a plug."

"So these ones all lose any value, Lanifie, Alakie, Balal, and Valiean. None will give or take. Then why are you here?"

This woman suspected that Valiean knew why. "To cause you great humiliation, Dine," she said, determined not to back down, and cruel because her sympathy would change nothing. "This Hu knows that you have extended into Paloan's territory."

Dine's pad darkened. The Dinela was silent. Dine had also expanded into or under Kapoan's enclosure, it must have.

This Alakie didn't know how Valiean had managed it, but she knew it had. Both expansions were impossible if the neighboring Dinela's chemical and physical barriers were intact, and that kind of expansion was also deeply wrong and disturbing in any of the Dinelate. The stress of the impending destruction had been too much for Valiean to withstand.

"Kapoan needed to ripen faster, but Dine's access to reproductive support was shrinking all the time. Hu Alakie, this Valiean did not encroach on Paloan, only transported abandoned resources."

So, as this woman had thought, because Valiean knew it could not survive, Dine had risked confrontation and perhaps fatal humiliation to force-grow the progeny and transfer its tokens to them. "All of your sentients will lose value, and your offspring, had they survived, would not have been allowed the territory to germinate," she said.

"But you do not want the other Hu to be humiliated, or for the other Sen to lose value."

"No."

"Again, what will you trade for your silence, for all of Kapoan's other sentients? Will you accept them to save them from humiliation? ...But you have already refused."

"This woman will take them, if they will go. But only along with Paloan. It's the only way."

The platform shuddered beneath this Alakie's feet. "No. This Valiean cannot do such a thing. The Hu does not understand."

"Dine already has done such a thing. And of course this woman understands. Valiean has forced Kapoan, absorbed Dine, before its time was even done. You have done that thing; you can do what this woman asks."

"No, Kapoan agreed to that. Lanifie agreed, and spoke for Dine."

Not that it mattered. But Lanifie had already been exchanged for sexual fusion, at least in the viewpoint of Dine Valiean certainly, and could not have spoken for Kapoan.

Lanifie's actions explained some things about Lanifie's condition, but Valiean knew better: that kind of thing could not be agreed to morally by any of the Dinelate. This Alakie knew she had won.

"Then this woman will have to go," she said. "These are done with trading." And this Alakie pulled away from Valiean's pad. The thinnest of Dine's hyphae clung for a moment, too long for Valiean's status, then dropped away, released from Valiean's substance. Alakie shuddered as she descended from Valiean's platform.

The rain had almost stopped, but as this woman started for the runner, lightning still flashed and grumbled to the south. Before this Alakie had taken five steps, Valiean swelled itself up, forcing gouts of rainwater to cascade off its sides and over the retaining wall to soak her feet. When she turned, Valiean's substance flashed in red and purple patches and moving stripes of color. But this woman turned away again, climbed into the runner, and then cranked the vehicle around to the north.

Across the wash, the walls of the palisade ran with water, and the wash seethed in a rust-colored flood. But even if Alakie had to scrape and jam the runner through the stand of scrub between Valiean's territory and Paloan's, the route that avoided the wash was passable; and though a steady drizzle began again before she was half way back to Dine's enclosure, she made good time.

But then, rounding the small hill west of Dine Paloan's enclosure, this Alakie doubted her plan for the first time.

Heaved out of the sand, unpassable for the runner, great knees and stumps of Valiean's rhizomorphs knotted the wall around Paloan's display area. Valiean's had not been merely an exploratory sortie into Paloan's territory. Dine must have infiltrated deep underground long before this Alakie spotted that patch of surface hyphae. There was no way to approach the enclosure without pushing through a bleached mat of mycelial growth and sterile fruiting tips, which she hesitated to do. Only the area in front of the display was pristine – a signal clear enough for any sentient to understand. This Alakie climbed the three steps to her platform.

Paloan's pad was overrun in a fuzz of unusual growth, sickly white and tomentous, thick with connections. This woman had never seen any communicative structure like it and was reluctant to accept contact. As she stretched one hand toward the pad, the surface of the growth lifted toward her palm. This woman paused as a burst of stupid ones exploded from the dark mouth of Paloan's tunnel. The large flight of multicolored tokens flashed into the air, then settled around her on the papery walls of the platform and on her hair.

She stepped forward and bent her head against the pad. Again, she was sure she could feel Valiean's filaments surging through her body and into her brain.

"You must go in first," Dine said very quietly. "This Dinela cannot force Paloan, but will help if this Valiean can. Paloan has left no signals, no barriers, so perhaps Dine is small enough. But this Valiean cannot enter unless that is true."

This Alakie wondered if Valiean did know Paloan's size, if the number of stupid ones around her indicated a much more hurried pruning of mass than Paloan would have stood for on Dine's own. Or perhaps Paloan had relented and decided to be saved even at such a sudden loss of capacity. She nodded, and Valiean released her, gently. A cloud of stupid ones followed her from the platform.

In the dark of Dine Paloan's tunnels, barely illuminated by heritage phosphorescence and her companion stupid ones, it was difficult for this Alakie to tell what had dissolved the chitinous plug that Paloan had constructed to wall Dine in. But she could tell that Paloan was there. And that Dine was small, so small. Even so, she could not drag Dine to the surface on her own. Valiean would have to help.

And so, to Dine Valiean's shame, Valiean invaded Paloan's tunnels, absorbing the secrets of Dine's constructions and materials and whatever else Paloan had failed to absorb itself.

To this Alakie it was obvious that Valiean had expanded into and under Paloan's territory and even Dine's enclosure long before the final days, perhaps as soon as Paloan had retracted far enough into its tunnels to tempt Valiean. What Valiean had done was a dangerous, unbalanced thing for a Dinela to even attempt.

After returning to her viewing platform, this woman watched as mycelial cords erupted from the sand of Paloan's enclosure in popping, tearing, and grinding chaos, carrying what looked like a dark lump of compacted dirt and minerals and cellulose that was Dine Paloan, architect of the space elevator, to the surface. Probably too late for either Dine Paloan or this woman to be saved, she thought. Though the sky was rapidly clearing and streaks of sunlight broke through the clouds to the west, the wash roared. In heavy flood, its rust-colored water choked with tree trunks, brush and even boulders carried along in the torrent, the wash couldn't be crossed closer than at the bridge near Malkean's enclosure far to the south. The travel could easily take too long.

After raising Dine Paloan's sclerotium to the gate of the runner on a bulge of its own substance, Valiean had refused her attempts at communication. This woman did not know how to communicate with a Dinela who refused, but she knew that she needed to make for the south as fast as she could, so she started back the way she had come, planning to arc around Dine Valiean's enclosure then try running near the wash where it hugged the palisade south of Kapoan's tunnels.

With Paloan in the back looking like an enormous lump of fossilized waste covered in brightly colored stupid ones, the truck wallowed and crashed its way south, west of the Dinelate enclosures, until this woman encountered a water-filled sink that cut her route just past Kapoan's tunnels and forced her to turn the vehicle toward the wash. The sun broke occasionally through a red stew of clouds to the west as this Alakie drove carefully along the crumbling trail above the abating flood. By the time she neared the crossing, this woman felt every jolt of the yoke through her bones. The run was a desperate and exhausting attempt to reach the elevator before dark, but ultimately, it had been doomed from the start. Even from some distance, it was clear that the middle section of the southern bridge had been taken down by the flood.

This woman pulled the runner, scratched and smeared with red mud, away from the edge of the wash and parked it on the approach to the bridge. She stepped down onto the roadbed from the vehicle and walked stiffly to the span, wondering how anything built by the Dinelate, constructed of the same nano-molecular fibers as the elevator, could be torn down by a single flash-flood. But of course, it hadn't been. What ten Dinelate had labored to build, one could destroy. The roadbed of the truncated span was spongy with infiltrates, and urine-colored metabolites pooled there on a fuzz of matted rhizomes.

As this woman carefully leaned over the end of the bridge, she could see a ropy mat of substance drooling across the wash and attached to the support structure on the other side. A familiar pad had formed on the final buttress on this Alakie's side of the span. It was signaling, purple and red. To her shame, this woman hesitated for a moment. As far as she knew, no Dinela had harmed another sentient in their historical memory, but what Valiean had done gave her pause. However, she really had no other choice. Valiean had something to say. She stepped up to the stanchion and pressed her forehead lightly against Dine's pad.

"You must talk to this Valiean, Hu Alakie," its contact was as delicate as a whisper. "This Dinela is sorry, but will soon pay for everything it has done."

"You have also killed this Alakie, and Dine Paloan. There is only one ship at the counterweight station, and these will not be able to meet it."

"No, but this Valiean had to stop you. You must trade one more time. Look at the elevator."

The stalk of the enormous construct seemed slender from

a distance. Just visible ascending the stalk was a single bulge, the carriage, climbing slowly but steadily away from the mesa.

"What can Dine do to pay for these lives?" this Alakie asked.

Again, she felt Valiean's shock. "This Dinela would never take your life... but you would not stop. You must also take Kapoan's offspring. Dine Kapoan is no more, and Valiean will not survive. Paloan may be years in germination, and Dine will have forgotten everything that has happened. Hu Balal must find value. Valiean's tokens must give and take status."

Almost, this woman pulled away again; Dine seemed not to grasp the present situation. But instead, she touched Valiean's soft external filament with her fingers. "You have something to trade. What will you trade?"

"In trade for building the entire base of the elevator complex, Dine Paloan exchanged." Valiean hesitated, then continued. "Dine traded the Hu ovary to this Dinela. But kept the ten Hu offspring. Dine also kept the unrealized reproductive fragments it carried to trade later, and for the use of the ovary until the potential was realized and traded, Paloan gave Balal to this Valiean. So the ovary can be traded, and the ship it is in."

It was this woman's turn to be surprised. Paloan had never mentioned unfertilized Hu seed. She had not known the ovary still existed.

"This Valiean will trade the ovary to Alakie if she will save Kapoan's offspring. You must take them; this Dinela will also trade the offspring to you, for your own."

A nodule had formed in the mat of hyphae at her feet. It had swelled quickly, and then peeled away from a package inside the size of two heads wrapped tightly in a silvery, plump padding of filaments. This Alakie almost stopped breathing, and she could feel a flush of blood rising to her face. They were very small, too small for natural reproduction.

"Yes," Valiean said. "This Dinela has made them small. This Valiean could always build and strengthen at the smallest level, it has not hurt them. They will germinate. No other sentient has traded to win Dinelate as tokens. They will be valuable to Alakie."

Water still ran in the wash, though with little force, and it was clear this woman could not risk the crossing.

"This Valiean is the finest builder on Dima," it said. "Paloan has kept you since you were small. But only this Dinela can help you cross."

Valiean's filaments dropped away.

The base of the elevator to the northeast was lost in shadow, but the setting sun turned the upper stalk of the elevator into a blade-thin, glowing line against the darkening sky. The carriage itself was gone from sight. Spanning the wash, Valiean's substance had visibly darkened and tightened. There was no doubt in this woman's mind that Valiean's substance would support passage of the loaded runner. As she walked back to the vehicle, a luminous flyer lit softly on her hair.

This Alakie last saw Dine Valiean as Paloan's ship rose into the night from the base port. Patches of Dine's phosphorescent substance shone along the dark wash below the palisade and extended throughout all the abandoned territory of the Dinelate, but soon disappeared in the distance. This woman docked at the terminal as the Gamela ship was preparing to leave. But because Paloan's ship did not require a tether to boost from the station, these Hu said goodbye to the Gamela at the counterweight.

The ship had long crossed the orbit of Dimit's Token when this woman found Hu Bakbak in the pilot's cabin. From the pilot's green cube-seat, Bakbak gestured for this Alakie to join him. The second cube molded to this woman as she sat before the controls.

Bakbak lowered his head, his loose curls hiding his face. "These may not see anything before Dima dies."

Graphics crawled over the curved screens. The math of the singularity's trajectory from the gate was clear. The destruction of the gate and the pattern of debris indicated a mass of only slightly less than Dima's. The bending of the singularity's orbit by the sun had been clear since Dine Malkean had calculated its velocity from the time it exited the throat until it destroyed the station. It had chased Dima for almost a year.

"It's still too small to see, smaller than the size of your eye, and cool, so it's almost invisible."

There was only the red and blue ball of Dima floating in the speckled dark, sunlight flashing off of storms in its atmosphere.

"Such things do not grow unless fed. That is clear," Bakbak said.

"No. The universe is not large enough for such a coincidence. The singularity was aimed, at the Dinelate, or at the Hu. Something killed *Amore*."

Bakbak smiled. "Perhaps these will find out what."

Like all the other ships in the system, theirs looped slowly away from the planet and far out from the sun. This woman had been expecting the stars to distort into a lens, or Dimit to wobble away from its token. But in the end, as they neared the remaining traveling gate far out in the cometary halo, Dimit simply fell onto the planet as Dima was eaten from inside, and soon after, nothing remained but a spreading cloud of debris and radiation dispersing in the view from their rear-facing monitors.

In the Hu ovary tucked into the belly of Paloan's ship, Balal's offspring sucked her small fist and slept. This Alakie could not read the markings on the control panel or on the screens of the ovary, but a strange Hu face smiled in the comp display for each pod in its hold. This Alakie knew she would meet such Hu one day.

The Waiting Stars

Aliette de Bodard

The derelict ship ward was in an isolated section of Outsider space, one of the numerous spots left blank on interstellar maps, no more or no less tantalizing than its neighboring quadrants. To most people, it would be just that: a boring part of a long journey to be avoided—skipped over by Mind-ships as they cut through deep space, passed around at low speeds by Outsider ships while their passengers slept in their hibernation cradles.

Only if anyone got closer would they see the hulking masses of ships: the glint of starlight on metal, the sharp, pristine beauty of their hulls, even though they all lay quiescent and crippled, forever unable to move—living corpses kept as a reminder of how far they had fallen; the Outsiders' brash statement of their military might, a reminder that their weapons held the means to fell any Mind-ships they chose to hound.

On the sensors of *The Cinnabar Mansions*, the ships all appeared small and diminished, like toy models or avatars—things Lan Nhen could have held in the palm of her hand and just as easily crushed. As the sensors' line of sight moved—catching ship after ship in their field of view, wreck after wreck, indistinct masses of burnt and twisted metal, of ripped-out engines, of shattered life pods and crushed shuttles—Lan Nhen felt as if an icy fist were squeezing her heart into shards. To think of the Minds within—dead or crippled, forever unable to move...

"She's not there," she said, as more and more ships appeared on the screen in front of her, a mass of corpses that all threatened to overwhelm her with sorrow and grief and anger.

"Be patient, child," *The Cinnabar Mansions* said. The Mind's voice was amused, as it always was—after all, she'd lived for five centuries, and would outlive Lan Nhen and Lan Nhen's own children by so many years that the pronoun "child" seemed small and inappropriate to express the vast gulf of generations between them. "We already knew it was going to take time."

"She was supposed to be on the outskirts of the wards," Lan Nhen said, biting her lip. She had to be, or the rescue mission was going to be infinitely more complicated. "According to Cuc..."

"Your cousin knows what she's talking about," *The Cinnabar Mansions* said.

"I guess." Lan Nhen wished Cuc was there with them, and not sleeping in her cabin as peacefully as a baby—but *The Cinnabar Mansions* had pointed out Cuc needed to be rested for what lay ahead; and Lan Nhen had given in, vastly outranked. Still, Cuc was reliable, for narrow definitions of the term—as long as anything didn't involve social skills, or deft negotiation. For technical information, though, she didn't have an equal within the family; and her network of contacts extended deep within Outsider space. That was how they'd found out about the ward in the first place...

"There." The sensors beeped, and the view on the screen pulled into enhanced mode on a ship on the edge of the yard which seemed even smaller than the hulking masses of her companions. *The Turtle's Citadel* had been from the newer generation of ships, its body more compact and more agile than its predecessors': designed for flight and maneuvers rather than for transport, more elegant and refined than anything to come out of the Imperial Workshops—unlike the other ships, its prow and hull were decorated, painted with numerous designs from old legends and myths, all the way to the Dai

Viet of Old Earth. A single gunshot marred the outside of its hull—a burn mark that had transfixed the painted citadel through one of its towers, going all the way into the heart-room and crippling the Mind that animated the ship.

"That's her," Lan Nhen said. "I would know her anywhere."

The Cinnabar Mansions had the grace not to say anything, though of course she could have matched the design to her vast databases in an eyeblink. "It's time, then. Shall I extrude a pod?"

Lan Nhen found that her hands had gone slippery with sweat, all of a sudden; and her heart was beating a frantic rhythm within her chest, like temple gongs gone mad. "I guess it's time, yes." By any standards, what they were planning was madness. To infiltrate Outsider space, no matter how isolated—to repair a ship, no matter how lightly damaged...

Lan Nhen watched *The Turtle's Citadel* for a while—watched the curve of the hull, the graceful tilt of the engines, away from the living quarters; the burn mark through the hull like a gunshot through a human chest. On the prow was a smaller painting, all but invisible unless one had good eyes: a single sprig of apricot flowers, signifying the New Year's good luck—calligraphied on the ship more than thirty years ago by Lan Nhen's own mother, a parting gift to her great-aunt before the ship left for her last, doomed mission.

Of course, Lan Nhen already knew every detail of that shape by heart, every single bend of the corridors within, every little nook and cranny available outside—from the blueprints, and even before that, before the rescue plan had even been the seed of a thought in her mind—when she'd stood before her ancestral altar, watching the rotating holo of a ship who was also her great-aunt, and wondering how a Mind could ever be brought down, or given up for lost.

Now she was older; old enough to have seen enough things to freeze her blood; old enough to plot her own foolishness, and drag her cousin and her great-great-aunt into it.

Older, certainly. Wiser, perhaps; if they were blessed enough to survive.

There were tales, at the Institution, of what they were—and, in any case, one only had to look at them, at their squatter, darker shapes, at the way their eyes crinkled when they laughed. There were other clues, too: the memories that made Catherine wake up breathless and disoriented, staring at the white walls of the dormitory until the pulsing, writhing images of something she couldn't quite identify had gone, and the breath of dozens of her dorm-mates had lulled her back to sleep. The craving for odd food like fish sauce and fermented meat. The dim, distant feeling of not fitting in, of being compressed on all sides by a society that made little sense to her.

It should have, though. She'd been taken as a child, like all her schoolmates—saved from the squalor and danger among the savages and brought forward into the light of civilization—of white sterile rooms and bland food, of awkward embraces that always felt too informal. *Rescued*, Matron always said, her entire face transfigured, the bones of her cheeks made sharply visible through the pallor of her skin. *Made safe.*

Catherine had asked what she was safe from. They all did, in the beginning—all the girls in the Institution, Johanna and Catherine being the most vehement amongst them.

That was until Matron showed them the vid.

They all sat at their tables, watching the screen in the center of the amphitheater—silent, for once, not jostling or joking among themselves. Even Johanna, who was always first with a biting remark, had said nothing—had sat, transfixed, watching it.

The first picture was a woman who looked like them—smaller and darker-skinned than the Galactics—except that her belly protruded in front of her, huge and swollen like a tumor from some disaster movie. There was a man next to her, his unfocused eyes suggesting that he was checking something on the network through his implants—until the woman grimaced, putting a hand to her belly and calling out to him. His eyes focused in a heartbeat, and fear replaced the blank expression on his face.

There was a split second before the language overlays kicked in—a moment, frozen in time, when the words, the sounds of the syllables put together, sounded achingly familiar to Catherine, like a memory of the childhood she never could quite manage to piece together—there was a brief flash, of New Year's Eve firecrackers going off in a confined space, of her fear that they would burn her, damage her body's ability to heal... And then the moment was gone like a popped bubble, because the vid changed in the most horrific manner.

The camera was wobbling, rushing along a pulsing corridor—they could all hear the heavy breath of the woman, the whimpering sounds she made like an animal in pain; the soft, encouraging patter of the physician's words to her.

"She's coming," the woman whispered, over and over, and the physician nodded—keeping one hand on her shoulder, squeezing it so hard his own knuckles had turned the color of a muddy moon.

"You have to be strong," he said. "Hanh, please. Be strong for me. It's all for the good of the Empire, may it live ten thousand years. Be strong."

The vid cut away, then—and it was wobbling more and more crazily, its field of view showing erratic bits of a cramped room with scrolling letters on the wall, the host of other attendants with similar expressions of fear on their faces; the woman, lying on a flat surface, crying out in pain—blood splattering out of her with every thrust of her hips—the camera moving, shifting between her legs, the physician's hands reaching into the darker opening—easing out a sleek, glinting shape, even as the woman screamed again—and blood, more blood running out, rivers of blood she couldn't possibly have in her body, even as the *thing* within her pulled free, and it became all too clear that, though it had the bare shape of a baby with an oversized head, it had too many cables and sharp angles to be human...

Then a quiet fade-to-black, and the same woman being cleaned up by the physician—the thing—the baby being nowhere to be seen. She stared up at the camera; but her gaze was unfocused, and drool was pearling at the corner of her lips, even as her hands spasmed uncontrollably.

Fade to black again; and the lights came up again, on a room that seemed to have grown infinitely colder..

"This," Matron said in the growing silence, "is how the Dai Viet birth Minds for their spaceships: by incubating them within the wombs of their women. This is the fate that would have been reserved for all of you. For each of you within this room." Her gaze raked them all, stopping longer than usual on Catherine and Johanna, the known troublemakers in the class. "This is why we had to take you away, so that you wouldn't become broodmares for abominations."

"We", of course, meant the Board—the religious nuts, as Johanna liked to call them, a redemptionist church with a fortune to throw around, financing the children's rescues and their education—and who thought every life from humans to insects was sacred (they'd all wondered, of course, where they fitted into the scheme).

After the class had dispersed like a flock of sparrows, Johanna held court in the yard, her eyes bright and feverish. "They faked it. They had to. They came up with some stupid explanation on how to keep us cooped here. I mean, why would anyone still use natural births and not artificial wombs?"

Catherine, still seeing the splatters of blood on the floor, shivered. "Matron said that they wouldn't. That they thought the birth created a special bond between the Mind and its mother—but that they had to be there, to be awake during the birth."

"Rubbish." Johanna shook her head. "As if that's even remotely plausible. I'm telling you, it has to be fake."

"It looked real." Catherine remembered the woman's screams; the wet sound as the Mind wriggled free from her womb; the fear in the face of all the physicians. "Artificial vids aren't this... messy." They'd seen the artificial vids: slick, smooth things where the actors were tall and muscular, the actresses pretty and graceful, with only a thin veneer of artificially generated defects to make the entire thing believable. They'd learnt to tell them apart from the rest; because it was a survival skill in the Institution, to sort out the lies from the truth.

"I bet they can fake that, too," Johanna said. "They can fake everything if they feel like it." But her face belied her words; even she had been shocked. Even she didn't believe they would have gone that far.

"I don't think it's a lie," Catherine said, finally. "Not this time."

And she didn't need to look at the other girls' faces to know that they believed the same thing as her—even Johanna, for all her belligerence—and to feel in her gut that this changed everything.

Cuc came online when the shuttle pod launched from *The Cinnabar Mansions*—in the heart-wrenching moment when the gravity of the ship fell away from Lan Nhen, and the cozy darkness of the pod's cradle was replaced with the distant forms of the derelict ships. "Hey, Cousin. Missed me?" Cuc asked.

"As much as I missed a raging fire." Lan Nhen checked her equipment a last time—the pod was basic and functional, with barely enough space for her to squeeze into the cockpit, and she'd had to stash her various cables and terminals into the nooks and crannies of a structure that hadn't been meant for more than emergency evacuation. She could have asked *The Cinnabar Mansions* for a regular transport shuttle, but the pod was smaller and more controllable; and it stood more chances of evading the derelict ward's defenses.

"Hahaha," Cuc said, though she didn't sound amused. "The family found out what we were doing, by the way."

"And?" It would have devastated Lan Nhen, a few years ago; now she didn't much care. She *knew* she was doing the right thing. No filial daughter would let a member of the family rust away in a foreign cemetery—if she couldn't rescue her great-aunt, she'd at least bring the body back for a proper funeral.

"They think we're following one of Great-great-aunt's crazy plans."

"Ha," Lan Nhen snorted. Her hands were dancing on the controls, plotting a trajectory that would get her to *The Turtle's Citadel* while leaving her the maximum thrust reserve in case of unexpected maneuvers.

"I'm not the one coming up with crazy plans," *The Cinnabar Mansions* pointed out on the comms channel, distractedly. "I leave that to the young. Hang on—" she dropped out of sight. "I have incoming drones, child."

Of course. It was unlikely the Outsiders would leave their precious war trophies unprotected. "Where?"

A translucent overlay gradually fell over her field of vision through the pod's windshield; and points lit up all over its surface—a host of fast-moving, small crafts with contextual arrows showing basic kinematics information as well as projected trajectory cones. Lan Nhen repressed a curse. "That many? They really like their wrecked spaceships, don't they."

It wasn't a question, and neither Cuc nor *The Cinnabar Mansions* bothered to answer. "They're defense drones patrolling the perimeter. We'll walk you through," Cuc said. "Give me just a few moments to link up with Great-great-aunt's systems..."

Lan Nhen could imagine her cousin, lying half-prone on her bed in the lower decks of *The Cinnabar Mansions*, her face furrowed in that half-puzzled, half-focused expression that was typical of her thought processes—she'd remain that way for entire minutes, or as long as it took to find a solution. On her windshield, the squad of drones was spreading—coming straight at her from all directions, a dazzling ballet of movement meant to overwhelm her. And they would, if she didn't move fast enough.

Her fingers hovered over the pod's controls, before she made her decision and launched into a barrel maneuvers away from the nearest incoming cluster. "Cousin, how about hurrying up?"

There was no answer from Cuc. Demons take her, this wasn't the moment to overthink the problem! Lan Nhen banked sharply, narrowly avoiding a squad of drones, who bypassed her—and then turned around, much quicker than she'd anticipated. Ancestors, they moved fast, much too fast for ion-thrust motors. Cuc was going to have to rethink her trajectory. "Cousin, did you see this?"

"I saw." Cuc's voice was distant. "Already taken into account. Given the size of the craft, it was likely they were going to use helicoidal thrusters on those."

"This is all fascinating—" Lan Nhen wove her way through two more waves of drones, cursing wildly as shots made the pod rock around her—as long as her speed held, she'd be fine... She'd be fine... "—but you'll have noticed I don't really much care about technology, especially not now!"

A thin thread of red appeared on her screen—a trajectory that wove and banked like a frightened fish's trail—all the way to *The Turtle's Citadel* and its clusters of pod-cradles. It looked as though it was headed straight into the heart of the cloud of drones, though that wasn't the most worrying aspect of it. "Cousin," Lan Nhen said. "I can't possibly do this—" The margin of error was null—if she slipped in one of the curves, she'd never regain the kinematics necessary to take the next.

"Only way." Cuc's voice was emotionless. "I'll update as we go, if Great-great-aunt sees an opening. But for the moment..."

Lan Nhen closed her eyes, for a brief moment—turned

them towards Heaven, though Heaven was all around her—and whispered a prayer to her ancestors, begging them to watch over her. Then she turned her gaze to the screen, and launched into flight—her hands flying and shifting over the controls, automatically adjusting the pod's path—dancing into the heart of the drones' swarm—into them, away from them, weaving an erratic path across the section of space that separated her from *The Turtle's Citadel*. Her eyes, all the while, remained on the overlay—her fingers speeding across the controls, matching the slightest deviation of her course to the set trajectory—inflecting curves a fraction of a second before the error on her course became perceptible.

"Almost there," Cuc said—with a hint of encouragement in her voice. "Come on, Cousin, you can do it—"

Ahead of her, a few measures away, was *The Turtle's Citadel*: its pod cradles had shrivelled from long atrophy, but the hangar for docking the external shuttles and pods remained, its entrance a thin line of grey across the metallic surface of the ship's lower half.

"It's closed," Lan Nhen said, breathing hard—she was coming fast, much too fast, scattering drones out of her way like scared mice, and if the hangar wasn't opened... "Cousin!"

Cuc's voice seemed to come from very far away; distant and muted somehow on the comms system. "We've discussed this. Normally, the ship went into emergency standby when it was hit, and it should open—"

"But what if it doesn't?" Lan Nhen asked—the ship was looming over her, spreading to cover her entire windshield, close enough so she could count the pod cradles, could see their pockmarked surfaces—could imagine how much of a messy impact she'd make, if her own pod crashed on an unyielding surface.

Cuc didn't answer. She didn't need to; they both knew what would happen if that turned out to be true. *Ancestors, watch over me*, Lan Nhen thought, over and over, as the hangar doors rushed towards her, still closed—*ancestors watch over me...*

She was close enough to see the fine layers of engravings on the doors when they opened—the expanse of metal flowing away from the center, to reveal a gaping hole just large enough to let a small craft through. Her own pod squeezed into the available space: darkness fell over her cockpit as the doors flowed shut, and the pod skidded to a halt, jerking her body like a disarticulated doll.

It was a while before she could stop shaking for long enough to unstrap herself from the pod; and to take her first, tentative steps on the ship.

The small lamp in her suit lit nothing but a vast, roiling mass of shadows: the hangar was huge enough to hold much larger ships. Thirty years ago, it had no doubt been full, but the Outsiders must have removed them all as they dragged the wreck out there.

"I'm in," she whispered; and set out through the darkness, to find the heartroom and the Mind that was her great-aunt.

"I'm sorry," Jason said to Catherine. "Your first choice of posting was declined by the Board."

Catherine sat very straight in her chair, trying to ignore how uncomfortable she felt in her suit—it gaped too large over her chest, flared too much at her hips, and she'd had to hastily readjust the trouser-legs after she and Johanna discovered the seamstress had got the length wrong. "I see," she said, because there was nothing else she could say, really.

Jason looked at his desk, his gaze boring into the metal as if he could summon an assignment out of nothing—she knew he meant well, that he had probably volunteered to tell her this himself, instead of leaving it for some stranger who wouldn't care a jot for her—but in that moment, she didn't want to be reminded that he worked for the Board for the Protection of Dai Viet Refugees; that he'd had a hand, no matter how small, in denying her wishes for the future.

At length Jason said, slowly, carefully, reciting a speech he'd no doubt given a dozen times that day, "The government puts the greatest care into choosing postings for the refugees. It was felt that that putting you onboard a space station would be—unproductive."

Unproductive. Catherine kept smiling; kept her mask plastered on, even though it hurt to turn the corners of her mouth upwards, to crinkle her eyes as if she were pleased. "I see," she said, again, knowing anything else was useless. "Thanks, Jason."

Jason colored. "I tried arguing your case, but..."

"I know," Catherine said. He was a clerk; that was all; a young civil servant at the bottom of the Board's hierarchy, and he couldn't possibly get her what she wanted, even if he'd been willing to favor her. And it hadn't been such a surprise, anyway. After Mary and Olivia and Johanna...

"Look," Jason said. "Let's see each other tonight, right? I'll take you someplace you can forget all about this."

"You know it's not that simple," Catherine said. As if a restaurant, or a wild waterfall ride, or whatever delight Jason had in mind could make her forget this.

"No, but I can't do anything about the Board." Jason's voice was firm. "I can, however, make sure that you have a good time tonight."

Catherine forced a smile she didn't feel. "I'll keep it in mind. Thanks."

As she exited the building, passing under the wide arches, the sun sparkled on the glass windows—and for a brief moment she wasn't herself—she was staring at starlight reflected in a glass panel, watching an older woman running hands on a wall and smiling at her with gut-wrenching sadness... She blinked, and the moment was gone; though the sense of sadness, of unease remained, as if she were missing something essential.

Johanna was waiting for her on the steps, her arms crossed in front of her, and a gaze that looked as though it would bore holes into the lawn.

"What did they tell you?"

Catherine shrugged, wondering how a simple gesture could cost so much. "The same they told you, I'd imagine. Unproductive."

They'd all applied to the same postings—all asked for something related to space, whether it was one of the observatories, a space station; or, in Johanna's case, outright asking to board a slow-ship as crew. They'd all been denied, for variations of the same reason.

"What did you get?" Johanna asked. Her own rumpled slip of paper had already been recycled at the nearest terminal; she was heading north, to Steele, where she'd join an archaeological dig.

Catherine shrugged, with a casualness she didn't feel. They'd always felt at ease under the stars—had always yearned to take to space, felt the same craving to be closer to their home planets—to hang, weightless and without ties, in a place where they wouldn't be weighed, wouldn't be judged for falling short of values that ultimately didn't belong to them. "I got newswriter."

"At least you're not moving very far," Johanna said, a tad resentfully.

"No." The offices of the network company were a mere two streets away from the Institution.

"I bet Jason had a hand in your posting," Johanna said.

"He didn't say anything about that—"

"Of course he wouldn't." Johanna snorted, gently. She didn't much care for Jason; but she knew how much his company meant to Catherine—how much more it would come to mean, if the weight of an entire continent separated Catherine and her. "Jason broadcasts his failures because they bother him; you'll hardly ever hear him talk of his successes. He'd feel too much like he was boasting." Her face changed, softened. "He cares for you, you know—truly. You have the best luck in the world."

"I know," Catherine said—thinking of the touch of his lips

on hers; of his arms, holding her close until she felt whole, fulfilled. "I know."

The best luck in the world—she and Jason and her new flat, and her old haunts, not far away from the Institution—though she wasn't sure, really, if that last was a blessing—if she wanted to remember the years Matron had spent hammering proper behavior into them: the deprivations whenever they spoke anything less than perfect Galactic, the hours spent cleaning the dormitory's toilets for expressing mild revulsion at the food; or the night they'd spent shut outside, naked, in the growing cold, because they couldn't remember which Galactic president had colonized Longevity Station—how Matron had found them all huddled against each other, in an effort to keep warm and awake, and had sent them to Discipline for a further five hours, scolding them for behaving like wild animals.

Catherine dug her nails into the palms of her hands—letting the pain anchor her back to the present; to where she sat on the steps of the Board's central offices, away from the Institution and all it meant to them.

"We're free," she said, at last. "That's all that matters."

"We'll never be free." Johanna's tone was dark, intense. "Your records have a mark that says 'Institution'. And even if it didn't—do you honestly believe we would blend right in?"

There was no one quite like them on Prime, where Dai Viet were unwelcome; not with those eyes, not with that skin color—not with that demeanor, which even years of Institution hadn't been enough to erase.

"Do you ever wonder..." Johanna's voice trailed off into silence, as if she were contemplating something too large to put into words.

"Wonder what?" Catherine asked.

Johanna bit her lip. "Do you ever wonder what it would have been like, with our parents? Our real parents."

The parents they couldn't remember. They'd done the math, too—no children at the Institution could remember anything before coming there. Matron had said it was because they were really young when they were taken away—that it had been for the best. Johanna, of course, had blamed something more sinister, some fix-up done by the Institution to its wards to keep them docile.

Catherine thought, for a moment, of a life among the Dai Viet—an idyllic image of a harmonious family like in the holo-movies—a mirage that dashed itself to pieces against the inescapable reality of the birth vid. "They'd have used us like broodmares," Catherine said. "You saw—"

"I know what I saw," Johanna snapped. "But maybe..." Her face was pale. "Maybe it wouldn't have been so bad, in return for the rest."

For being loved; for being made worthy; for fitting in, being able to stare at the stars without wondering which was their home—without dreaming of when they might go back to their families.

Catherine rubbed her belly, thinking of the vid—and the *thing* crawling out of the woman's belly, all metal edges and shining crystal, coated in the blood of its mother—and, for a moment she felt as though she were the woman—floating above her body, detached from her cloak of flesh, watching herself give birth in pain. And then the sensation ended, but she was still feeling spread out, larger than she ought to have been—looking at herself from a distance and watching her own life pass her by, petty and meaningless, and utterly bounded from end to end.

Maybe Johanna was right. Maybe it wouldn't have been so bad, after all.

The ship was smaller than Lan Nhen had expected—she'd been going by her experience with *The Cinnabar Mansions*, which was an older generation, but *The Turtle's Citadel* was much smaller for the same functionalities.

Lan Nhen went up from the hangar to the living quarters, her equipment slung over her shoulders. She'd expected a sophisticated defense system like the drones, but there was nothing. Just the familiar slimy feeling of a quickened ship on the walls, a sign that the Mind that it hosted was still alive—albeit barely. The walls were bare, instead of the elaborate decoration Lan Nhen was used to from *The Cinnabar Mansions*—no scrolling calligraphy, no flowing paintings of starscapes or flowers; no ambient sound of zither or anything to enliven the silence.

She didn't have much time to waste—Cuc had said they had two hours between the moment the perimeter defenses kicked in and the moment more hefty safeguards were manually activated—but she couldn't help herself: she looked into one of the living quarters. It was empty as well, its walls scored with gunfire. The only color in the room was a few splatters of dried blood on a chair, a reminder of the tragedy of the ship's fall—the execution of its occupants, the dragging of its wreck to the derelict ward—dried blood, and a single holo of a woman on a table, a beloved mother or grandmother: a bare, abandoned picture with no offerings or incense, all that remained from a wrecked ancestral altar. Lan Nhen spat on the ground, to ward off evil ghosts, and went back to the corridors.

She truly felt as though she were within a mausoleum—like that one time her elder sister had dared her and Cuc to spend the night within the family's ancestral shrine, and they'd barely slept—not because of monsters or anything, but because of the vast silence that permeated the whole place amidst the smell of incense and funeral offerings, reminding them that they, too, were mortal.

That Minds, too, could die—that rescues were useless—no, she couldn't afford to think like that. She had Cuc with her, and together they would...

She hadn't heard Cuc for a while.

She stopped, when she realized—that it wasn't only the

silence on the ship, but also the deathly quiet of her own comms system. Since—since she'd entered *The Turtle's Citadel*—that was the last time she'd heard her cousin, calmly pointing out about emergency standby and hangar doors and how everything was going to work out, in the end...

She checked her comms. There appeared to be nothing wrong; but whichever frequency she selected, she could hear nothing but static. At last, she managed to find one slot that seemed less crowded than others. "Cousin? Can you hear me?"

Noise on the line. "Very—badly." Cuc's voice was barely recognizable. "There—is—something—interference—"

"I know," Lan Nhen said. "Every channel is filled with noise."

Cuc didn't answer for a while; and when she did, her voice seemed to have become more distant—a problem had her interest again. "Not—noise. They're broadcasting—data. Need—to..." And then the comms cut. Lan Nhen tried all frequencies, trying to find one that would be less noisy; but there was nothing. She bit down a curse—she had no doubt Cuc would find a way around whatever blockage the Outsiders had put on the ship, but this was downright bizarre. Why broadcast data? Cutting down the comms of prospective attackers somehow didn't seem significant enough—at least not compared to defense drones or similar mechanisms.

She walked through the corridors, following the spiral path to the heartroom—nothing but the static in her ears, a throbbing song that erased every coherent thought from her mind—at least it was better than the silence, than that feeling of moving underwater in an abandoned city—that feeling that she was too late, that her great-aunt was already dead and past recovery, that all she could do here was kill her once and for all, end her misery...

She thought, incongruously, of a vid she'd seen, which showed her great-grandmother ensconced in the heartroom—

in the first few years of *The Turtle's Citadel*'s life, those crucial moments of childhood when the ship's mother remained onboard to guide the Mind to adulthood. Great-grandmother was telling stories to the ship—and *The Turtle's Citadel* was struggling to mimic the spoken words in scrolling texts on her walls, laughing delightedly whenever she succeeded—all sweet and young, unaware of what her existence would come to, in the end.

Unlike the rest of the ship, the heartroom was crowded—packed with Outsider equipment that crawled over the Mind's resting place in the center, covering her from end to end until Lan Nhen could barely see the glint of metal underneath. She gave the entire contraption a wide berth—the spikes and protrusions from the original ship poked at odd angles, glistening with a dark liquid she couldn't quite identify—and the Outsider equipment piled atop the Mind, a mass of cables and unfamiliar machines, looked as though it was going to take a while to sort out.

There were screens all around, showing dozens of graphs and diagrams, shifting as they tracked variables that Lan Nhen couldn't guess at—vital signs, it looked like, though she wouldn't have been able to tell what.

Lan Nhen bowed in the direction of the Mind, from younger to elder—perfunctorily, since she was unsure whether the Mind could see her at all. There was no acknowledgement, either verbal or otherwise.

Her great-aunt was in there. She had to be.

"Cousin." Cuc's voice was back in her ears—crisp and clear and uncommonly worried.

"How come I can hear you?" Lan Nhen asked. "Because I'm in the heartroom?"

Cuc snorted. "Hardly. The heartroom is where all the data is streaming from. I've merely found a way to filter the transmissions on both ends. Fascinating problem..."

"Is this really the moment?" Lan Nhen asked. "I need you to walk me through the reanimation—"

"No, you don't," Cuc said. "First you need to hear what I have to say."

The call came during the night: a man in the uniform of the Board asked for Catherine George—as if he couldn't tell that it was her, that she was standing dishevelled and pale in front of her screen at three in the morning. "Yes, it's me," Catherine said. She fought off the weight of nightmares—more and more, she was waking in the night with memories of blood splattered across her entire body; of stars collapsing while she watched, powerless—of a crunch, and a moment where she hung alone in darkness, knowing that she had been struck a death blow—

The man's voice was quiet, emotionless. There had been an accident in Steele; a regrettable occurrence that hadn't been meant to happen, and the Board would have liked to extend its condolences to her—they apologized for calling so late, but they thought she should know...

"I see," Catherine said. She kept herself uncomfortably straight—aware of the last time she'd faced the board—when Jason had told her her desire for space would have been unproductive. When they'd told Johanna...

Johanna.

After a while, the man's words slid past her like water on glass—hollow reassurances, empty condolences, whereas she stood as if her heart had been torn away from her, fighting a desire to weep, to retch—she wanted to turn back time, to go back to the previous week and the sprigs of apricot flowers Jason had given her with a shy smile—to breathe in the sharp, tangy flavor of the lemon cake he'd baked for her, see again the carefully blank expression on his face as he waited to see if she'd like it—she wanted to be held tight in his arms and told that it was fine, that everything was going to be fine, that Johanna was going to be fine.

"We're calling her other friends," the man was saying, "but since you were close to each other..."

"I see," Catherine said—of course he didn't understand the irony, that it was the answer she'd given the Board—Jason—the last time.

The man cut off the communication; and she was left alone, standing in her living room and fighting back the feeling that threatened to overwhelm her—a not-entirely unfamiliar sensation of dislocation in her belly, the awareness that she didn't belong here among the Galactics; that she wasn't there by choice, and couldn't leave; that her own life should have been larger, more fulfilling than this slow death by inches, writing copy for feeds without any acknowledgement of her contributions—that Johanna's life should have been larger...

Her screen was still blinking—an earlier message from the Board that she hadn't seen? But why—

Her hands, fumbling away in the darkness, made the command to retrieve the message—the screen faded briefly to black while the message was decompressed, and then she was staring at Johanna's face.

For a moment—a timeless, painful moment—Catherine thought with relief that it had been a mistake, that Johanna was alive after all; and then she realized how foolish she'd been—that it wasn't a call, but merely a message from beyond the grave.

Johanna's face was pale, so pale Catherine wanted to hug her, to tell her the old lie that things were going to be fine—but she'd never get to say those words now, not ever.

"I'm sorry, Catherine," she said. Her voice was shaking; and the circles under her eyes took up half of her face, turning her into some pale nightmare from horror movies—a ghost, a restless soul, a ghoul hungry for human flesh. "I can't do this, not anymore. The Institution was fine; but it's got worse. I wake up at night, and feel sick—as if everything good has been leached from the world—as if the food had no taste, as if I drifted like a ghost through my days, as if my entire life held no meaning or truth. Whatever they did to our memories in the Institution—it's breaking down now. It's tearing me apart. I'm sorry, but I can't take any more of this. I—" she looked away from the camera for a brief moment, and then back at Catherine. "I have to go."

"No," Catherine whispered, but she couldn't change it. She couldn't do anything.

"You were always the strongest of us," Johanna said. "Please remember this. Please. Catherine." And then the camera cut, and silence spread through the room, heavy and unbearable, and Catherine felt like weeping, though she had no tears left.

"Catherine?" Jason called in a sleepy voice from the bedroom. "It's too early to check your work inbox..."

Work. Love. *Meaningless*, Johanna had said. Catherine walked to the huge window pane, and stared at the city spread out below her—the mighty Prime, center of the Galactic Federation, its buildings shrouded in light, its streets crisscrossed by floaters; with the bulky shape of the Parliament at the center, a proud statement that the Galactic Federation still controlled most of their home galaxy.

Too many lights to see the stars; but she could still guess; could still feel their pull—could still remember that one of them was her home.

A lie, Johanna had said. *A construction to keep us here.*

"Catherine?" Jason stood behind her, one hand wrapped around her shoulder—awkwardly tender as always, like that day when he'd offered to share a flat, standing balanced on one foot and not looking at her.

"Johanna is dead. She killed herself."

She felt rather than saw him freeze—and, after a while, he said in a changed voice, "I'm so sorry. I know how much she meant..." His voice trailed off, and he too, fell silent, watching the city underneath.

There was a feeling—the same feeling she'd had when waking up as a child, a diffuse sense that something was not quite right with the world; that the shadows held men watching, waiting for the best time to snatch her; that she was not wholly back in her body—that Jason's hand on her shoulder was just the touch of a ghost, that even his love wasn't enough to keep her safe. That the world was fracturing around her, time and time again—she breathed in, hoping to dispel the sensation. Surely it was nothing more than grief, than fatigue—but the sensation wouldn't go away, leaving her on the verge of nausea.

"You should have killed us," Catherine said. "It would have been kinder."

"Killed you?" Jason sounded genuinely shocked.

"When you took us from our parents."

Jason was silent for a while. Then: "We don't kill. What do you think we are, monsters from the fairytales, killing and burning everyone who looks different? Of course we're not like that." Jason no longer sounded uncertain or awkward; it was as if she'd touched some wellspring, scratched some skin to find only primal reflexes underneath.

"You erased our memories." She didn't make any effort to keep the bitterness from her voice.

"We had to." Jason shook his head. "They'd have killed you, otherwise. You know this."

"How can I trust you?" *Look at Johanna*, she wanted to say. *Look at me. How can you say it was all worth it?*

"Catherine..." Jason's voice was weary. "We've been over this before. You've seen the vids from the early days. We didn't set out to steal your childhood, or anyone's childhood. But when you were left—intact... accidents happened. Carelessness. Like Johanna."

"Like Johanna." Her voice was shaking now; but he didn't move, didn't do anything to comfort her or hold her close. She turned at last, to stare into his face; and saw him transfixed by light, by faith, his gaze turned away from her and every pore of his being permeated by the utter conviction that he was right, that they were all right and that a stolen childhood was a small price to pay to be a Galactic.

"Anything would do." Jason's voice was slow, quiet—explaining life to a child, a script they'd gone over and over in their years together, always coming back to the same enormous, inexcusable choice that had been made for them. "Scissors, knives, broken bottles. You sliced your veins, hanged yourselves, pumped yourselves full of drugs... We had to... we had to block your memories, to make you blank slates."

"Had to." She was shaking now; and still he didn't see. Still she couldn't make him see.

"I swear to you, Catherine. It was the only way."

And she knew, she'd always known he was telling the truth—not because he was right, but because he genuinely could not envision any other future for them.

"I see," she said. The nausea, the sense of dislocation, wouldn't leave her—disgust for him, for this life that trapped her, for everything she'd turned into or been turned into. "I see."

"Do you think I like it?" His voice was bitter. "Do you think it makes me sleep better at night? Every day I hate that choice, even though I wasn't the one who made it. Every day I wonder if there was something else the Board could have done, some other solution that wouldn't have robbed you of everything you were."

"Not everything," Catherine said—slowly, carefully. "We still look Dai Viet."

Jason grimaced, looking ill at ease. "That's your *body*, Catherine. Of course they weren't going to steal that."

Of course; and suddenly, seeing how uneasy he was, it occurred to Catherine that they could have changed that, too, just as easily as they'd tampered with her memories; made her skin clearer, her eyes less distinctive; could have helped her fit into Galactic society. But they hadn't. *Holding the strings to the last*, Johanna would have said. "You draw the line at my body, but stealing my memories is fine?"

Jason sighed; he turned towards the window, looking at the streets. "No, it's not, and I'm sorry. But how else were we supposed to keep you alive?"

"Perhaps we didn't want to be alive."

"Don't say that, please." His voice had changed, had become fearful, protective. "Catherine. Everyone deserves to live. You especially."

Perhaps I don't, she thought, but he was holding her close to him, not letting her go—her anchor to the flat—to the living room, to life. "You're not Johanna," he said. "You know that."

The strongest of us, Johanna had said. She didn't feel strong; just frail and adrift. "No," she said, at last. "Of course I'm not."

"Come on," Jason said. "Let me make you a tisane. We'll talk in the kitchen—you look as though you need it."

"No." And she looked up—sought out his lips in the darkness, drinking in his breath and his warmth to fill the emptiness within her. "That's not what I need."

"Are you sure?" Jason looked uncertain—sweet and innocent and naïve, everything that had drawn her to him. "You're not in a state to—"

"Ssh," she said, and laid a hand on his lips, where she'd kissed him. "Ssh."

Later, after they'd made love, she lay her head in the hollow of his arm, listening to the slow beat of his heart like a lifeline; and wondered how long she'd be able to keep the emptiness at bay.

"It goes to Prime," Cuc said. "All the data is beamed to Prime, and it's coming from almost every ship in the ward."

"I don't understand," Lan Nhen said. She'd plugged her own equipment into the ship, carefully shifting the terminals she couldn't make sense of—hadn't dared to go closer to the center, where Outsider technology had crawled all over her great-aunt's resting place, obscuring the Mind and the mass of connectors that linked her to the ship.

On one of the screens, a screensaver had launched: night on a planet Lan Nhen couldn't recognize—an Outsider one, with their sleek floaters and their swarms of helper bots, their wide, impersonal streets planted with trees that were too tall and too perfect to be anything but the product of years of breeding.

"She's not here," Cuc said.

"I—" Lan Nhen was about to say she didn't understand, and then the true import of Cuc's words hit her. "Not here? She's alive, Cuc. I can see the ship; I can hear her all around me..."

"Yes, yes," Cuc said, a tad impatiently. "But that's... the equivalent of unconscious processes, like breathing in your sleep."

"She's dreaming?"

"No," Cuc said. A pause, then, very carefully: "I think she's on Prime, Cousin. The data that's being broadcast—it looks like Mind thought-processes, compressed with a high rate and all mixed together. There's probably something on the other end that decompresses the data and sends it to... Argh, I don't know! Wherever they think is appropriate."

Lan Nhen bit back another admission of ignorance, and fell back on the commonplace. "On Prime." The enormity of the thing; that you could take a Mind—a beloved ship with a family of her own—that you could put her to sleep and cause her to wake up somewhere else, on an unfamiliar planet and an alien culture—that you could just transplant her like a flower or a tree... "She's on Prime."

"In a terminal or as the power source for something," Cuc said, darkly.

"Why would they bother?" Lan Nhen asked. "It's a lot of power expenditure just to get an extra computer."

"Do I look as though I have insight into Outsiders?" Lan Nhen could imagine Cuc throwing her hands up in the air, in that oft-practiced gesture. "I'm just telling you what I have, Cousin."

Outsiders—the Galactic Federation of United Planets—were barely comprehensible in any case. They were the descendants of an Exodus fleet that had hit an isolated galaxy: left to themselves and isolated for decades, they had turned on each other in huge ethnic cleansings before emerging from their home planets as relentless competitors for resources and inhabitable planets.

"Fine. Fine." Lan Nhen breathed in, slowly; tried to focus at the problem at hand. "Can you walk me through cutting the radio broadcast?"

Cuc snorted. "I'd fix the ship, first, if I were you."

Lan Nhen knelt by the equipment, and stared at a cable that had curled around one of the ship's spines. "Fine, let's start with what we came for. Can you see?"

Silence; and then a life-sized holo of Cuc hovered in front of her—even though the avatar was little more than broad strokes, Great-great-aunt had still managed to render it in enough details to make it unmistakably Cuc. "Cute," Lan Nhen said.

"Hahaha," Cuc said. "No bandwidth for trivialities—gotta save for detail on your end." She raised a hand, pointed to one of the outermost screens on the edge of the room. "Disconnect this one first."

It was slow, and painful. Cuc pointed; and Lan Nhen checked before disconnecting and moving. Twice, she jammed her fingers very close to a cable, and felt electricity crackle near her—entirely too close for comfort.

They moved from the outskirts of the room to the center—tackling the huge mount of equipment last. Cuc's first attempts resulted in a cable coming loose with an ominous sound; they waited, but nothing happened. "We might have fried something," Lan Nhen said.

"Too bad. There's no time for being cautious, as you well know. There's... maybe half an hour left before the other defenses go live." Cuc moved again, pointed to another squat terminal. "This goes off."

When they were finished, Lan Nhen stepped back, to look at their handiwork.

The heartroom was back to its former glory: instead of Outsider equipment, the familiar protrusions and sharp organic needles of the Mind's resting place; and they could see the Mind herself—resting snug in her cradle, wrapped around the controls of the ship—her myriad arms each seizing one rack of connectors; her huge head glinting in the light—a vague globe shape covered with glistening cables and veins. The burn mark from the Outsider attack was clearly visible, a dark, elongated shape on the edge of her head that had bruised a couple of veins—it had hit one of the connectors as well, burnt it right down to the color of ink.

Lan Nhen let out a breath she hadn't been aware of holding. "It scrambled the connector."

"And scarred her, but didn't kill her," Cuc said. "Just like you said."

"Yes, but—" But it was one thing to run simulations of the attack over and over, always getting the same prognosis; and quite another to see that the simulations held true, and that the damage was repairable.

"There should be another connector rack in your bag," Cuc said. "I'll walk you through slotting it in."

After she was done, Lan Nhen took a step back; and stared at her great-aunt—feeling, in some odd way, as though she were violating the Mind's privacy. A Mind's heartroom was their stronghold, a place where they could twist reality as they wished, and appear as they wished to. To see her great-aunt like this, without any kind of appearance change or pretence, was... more disturbing than she'd thought.

"And now?" she asked Cuc.

Even without details, Lan Nhen knew her cousin was smiling. "Now we pray to our ancestors that cutting the broadcast is going to be enough to get her back."

Another night on Prime, and Catherine wakes up breathless, in the grip of another nightmare—images of red lights, and scrolling texts, and a feeling of growing cold in her bones, a cold so deep she cannot believe she will ever feel warm no matter how many layers she's put on.

Johanna is not there; beside her, Jason sleeps, snoring softly; and she's suddenly seized by nausea, remembering what he said to her—how casually he spoke of blocking her memories, of giving a home to her after stealing her original one from her. She waits for it to pass; waits to settle into her old life as usual. But it doesn't.

Instead, she rises, walks towards the window, and stands watching Prime—the clean wide streets, the perfect trees, the ballet of floaters at night—the myriad dances that make up the society that constrains her from dawn to dusk and beyond—she wonders what Johanna would say, but of course Johanna won't ever say anything anymore. Johanna has gone ahead, into the dark.

The feeling of nausea in her belly will not go away: instead it spreads, until her body feels like a cage—at first, she thinks the sensation is in her belly, but it moves upwards, until her limbs, too, feel too heavy and too small—until it's an effort to move any part of her. She raises her hands, struggling against a feeling of moving appendages that don't belong to her—and traces the contours of her face, looking for familiar shapes, for anything that will anchor her to reality. The heaviness spreads, compresses her chest until she can hardly breathe—cracks her ribs and pins her legs to the ground. Her head spins, as if she were about to faint; but the mercy of blackness does not come to her.

"Catherine," she whispers. "My name is Catherine."

Another name, unbidden, rises to her lips. *Mi Chau.* A name she gave to herself in the Viet language—in the split instant before the lasers took her apart, before she sank into darkness: Mi Chau, the princess who unwittingly betrayed her father and her people, and whose blood became the pearls at the bottom of the sea. She tastes it on her tongue, and it's the only thing that seems to belong to her anymore.

She remembers that first time—waking up on Prime in a strange body, struggling to breathe, struggling to make sense of being so small, so far away from the stars that had guided her through space—remembers walking like a ghost through the corridors of the Institution, until the knowledge of what the Galactics had done broke her, and she cut her veins in a bathroom, watching blood lazily pool at her feet and thinking only of escape. She remembers the second time she woke up; the second, oblivious life as Catherine.

Johanna. Johanna didn't survive her second life; and even now is starting her third, somewhere in the bowels of the Institution—a dark-skinned child indistinguishable from other dark-skinned children, with no memories of anything beyond a confused jumble...

Outside, the lights haven't dimmed, but there are stars—brash and alien, hovering above Prime, in configurations that look *wrong*; and she remembers, suddenly, how they lay around her, how they showed her the way from planet to planet—how the cold of the deep spaces seized her just as she entered them to travel faster, just like it's holding her now, seizing her bones—remembers how much larger, how much wider she ought to be...

There are stars everywhere; and superimposed on them, the faces of two Dai Viet women, calling her over and over. Calling her back, into the body that belonged to her all along; into the arms of her family.

"Come on, come on," the women whisper, and their voices are stronger than any other noise; than Jason's breath in the bedroom; than the motors of the floaters or the vague smell of garlic from the kitchen. "Come on, Great-aunt!"

She is more than this body; more than this constrained life—her thoughts spread out, encompassing hangars and living quarters; and the liquid weight of pods held in their cradles—she remembers family reunions, entire generations of children putting their hands on her corridors, remembers the touch of their skin on her metal walls; the sound of their laughter as they raced each other; the quiet chatter of their mothers in the heartroom, keeping her company as the New Year began; and the touch of a brush on her outer hull, drawing the shape of an apricot flower, for good luck...

"Catherine?" Jason calls behind her.

She turns, through sheer effort of will; finding, somehow, the strength to maintain her consciousness in a small and crammed body alongside her other, vaster one. He's standing with one hand on the doorjamb, staring at her—his face pale, leached of color in the starlight.

"I remember," she whispers.

His hands stretch, beseeching. "Catherine, please. Don't leave."

He means well, she knows. All the things that he hid from her, he hid out of love; to keep her alive and happy, to hold her close in spite of all that should have separated them; and even now, the thought of his love is a barb in her heart, a last lingering regret, slight and pitiful against the flood of her memories—but not wholly insignificant.

Where she goes, she'll never be alone—not in the way she was with Jason, feeling that nothing else but her mattered in the entire world. She'll have a family; a gaggle of children and aunts and uncles waiting on her, but nothing like the sweet, unspoiled privacy where Jason and she could share anything and everything. She won't have another lover like him—naïve and frank and so terribly sure of what he wants and what he's ready to do to get it. Dai Viet society has no place for people like Jason—who do not know their place, who do not know how to be humble, how to accept failure or how to bow down to expediency.

Where she goes, she'll never be alone; and yet she'll be so terribly lonely.

"Please," Jason says.

"I'm sorry," she says. "I'll come back—" a promise made to him; to Johanna, who cannot hear or recognize her anymore. Her entire being spreads out, thins like water thrown on the fire—and, in that last moment, she finds herself reaching out for him, trying to touch him one last time, to catch one last glimpse of his face, even as a heart she didn't know she had breaks.

"Catherine."

He whispers her name, weeping, over and over; and it's that name, that lie that still clings to her with its bittersweet memories, that she takes with her as her entire being unfolds—as she flies away, towards the waiting stars.

The Shape of Thought

Ken Liu

Cat's Cradle turns into Painted Handkerchief turns into Dish of Noodles turns into Manger turns into Fishing Net. These are but the first of the Two Hundred Variations developed by bored human children on the Long Journey.

I was once one of them.

Young Ket hums as zie holds up zir hands, the string wound tight around the fingers. Zie glances at me and I wave back. Zie has the same long graceful neck and bulbous body as zir parent, Tunloji. Watching zem is like watching a younger version of my lover.

Even after all these years, the artificial pronouns still feel odd to me, like pebbles in the smooth flow of my thoughts.

The string holds one shape and then is transformed into another, like the way one memory fades into another, the way one scene of a story evokes the next. But between the shapes, the string goes through a hundred, a thousand states with no names: Almost-Painted-Handkerchief, Not-Yet-Dish-of-Noodles, Halfway-to-Manger.

Years ago, back on the *Rapa Nui*, my friends and I would pass quickly from one shape to another, jerking the string taut to admire the beauty of the forms. We did not care about the states in between, when the string was loose and did not yet have a name.

The children before me now move slowly and gracefully,

fascinated by the tightening and loosening of the string at every stage. For them there is no difference between when the string is taut and when it is loose, when the hands are moving and when they're still. They have named all the thousands of shapes between every pair of the Two Hundred Variations I've taught them.

Ket's partner and brood-kin, the delicate, willowy Ilo, inches up as it is zir turn to take the string from Ket. I hear the shell-shoes on zir four feet skittering against the sandy play yard as zie shuffles from side to side, contemplating what to do.

The Kalathani love this game, this human import. My mother had believed that they enjoy the elaborate formality of it: each partner taking zir turn to speak, only to enter into bondage and silence as the fingers are bound, mutely held in place by an elaborate arrangement of string under tension.

"Perhaps they can learn to view it as a metaphor for life," she had once said. "Give, receive, speak, observe, dominate, submit."

"You filter everything you see through the well-worn channels in your mind," I had said then. "Tunloji is right. You're incapable of seeing them as they are. You have no feel for"—my hands had flown up and clasped each other and I had held them against my chest as though I had been trying to stanch a wound. It was a Kalathani sign—a class of signs really—that I had never been able to get her to understand.

"*Tsuko*," she had said mechanically, watching my hands.

My mother had never given up the effort to reduce the Kalathani language to a series of individual gestures, minimal units of meaning that could be mapped, written down, and then analogized to the shape of our thought, our speech. Those were the syllables my mother used to impose the structure of speech on the unspeakable, to give names to the unnamable.

And I, knowing better, used them, too, because as well as I understood the Kalathani, my thoughts still required such syllables, such pegs to give them shape.

Then my hands had fallen limply by my sides, exhausted

with the futility of it. It was the last time I tried to have a rational conversation with her.

The skittering of the children's shoes grows louder, pulling me back into the moment. I look over and see that Ket and Ilo are surrounded by the other children. Their fingers twitch and the tips glow brighter, a sign of rising anxiety. Something is wrong.

I run over and the children open up a path for me to the center of the knot. Ket and Ilo face each other. Ilo is gesticulating wildly while Ket is silent, but I can see by the way zir body is vibrating that zie is on the verge of shedding the tips of zir fronds from the stress.

Be calm, I tell Ket, my hands holding zir gaze. I slow my hands' movements to the endearment register, the tips of my fingers vibrating at the rhythm of my heart in an effort to draw zem into synchrony with me. Without the bioluminescent tips and having fewer digits, I will never be able to speak as clearly as one of the Kalathani, but the children have learned to forgive my accent, to expend the effort to discern my meaning.

What is wrong?

We're stuck, Ilo tells me.

Ket holds up zir hands, and I see that they're caught in the shape of the Parachute. This is a form from which there is no path out. The knots are dead.

I embrace the child. The fronds on zir head shiver, vibrate, and shimmer in the last reddish rays of the setting sun. Zie looks into my gaze, zir big, round, iris-less eyes as dark as night.

As darkness falls and silence settles around us, the other children rush to give us their thoughts and advice. Their chattering fingers dance and glow with a natural, cool milky bioluminescence.

"Like a swarm of fireflies," Dad said.

I was six, and Dad and I watched the Kalathani children

playing about twenty feet from us in the open yard, the lit tips of their fingers leaving bright trails of light in the night air. Their play was eerily silent, devoid of the chatter and laughter that filled the air when my friends and I played.

Behind them we could see the vague outlines of the guards, standing motionless and erect, their bodies covered with gaudy ceremonial armor and clutching club-like weapons.

We sat in the shuttle with the canopy open, waiting for Mom to come back out of the massive, windowless building in front of us.

What kind of palace is this? I thought. It looked like a solid block of stone, a mountain carved and shaped by giants, nothing like the palaces I had seen in my picture books. Mom had explained to me that "palace" was just a name we gave the structure for convenience. We didn't know if the Kalathani had a king or even a government.

She also told me that she thought the Kalathani preferred thick walls to make it easy to keep the buildings heated or cooled. They didn't need windows because their glowing fingers could be seen just as easily in the dark.

I worried about Mom, alone in that vast, lightless building.

"Sarah," Dad whispered to me, "don't they look like a bunch of four-legged ostriches?"

I giggled. Dad always knew how to cheer me up.

With their small heads atop long necks and squat bodies that hovered high over ground on top of four thin legs, the Kalathani did look a bit like the ostriches our ancestors had taken onto the *Rapa Nui* as livestock when they had set out from Pele and filled their solar sails with light.

The Kalathani also had long arms that ramified into delicate fingers, like the spreading pinions of birds about to take flight. I thought their movements were graceful, dance-like, and I envied their easy balance, their fluidity of motion.

What's it like, I thought, *to speak with your whole body?*

The air smelled wet and warm and alive and wild, so different from the stale air I was used to in the ship. Now that

Dad had made me feel safer, I was giddy with all the open space around us, with a horizon that did not end a few feet in front of me. Above us, the sky was studded with brilliant stars—Dad told me that the brightest one overhead was the *Rapa Nui*. But without a moon, which I had unreasonably been expecting from all the old videos of Pele, the grassy plain around us was pitch black.

We could hear the sound of small, wild animals rustling in the grass, and once in a while the long, distant wail of a flyer. Then, from the children: skittering hard shoes, labored breathing, the snap of a broken twig. But the sound that was loudest in my ear was the beating of my heart.

"It's so eerie," Dad whispered, "the way they don't talk."

Mom had explained to Dad and me that the Kalathani did not speak with voices and ears.

I watched the light trails left by the children's fingers intently, wishing I knew what they were saying.

Before she left for the Palace, Mom had taken a pair of our emergency light sticks. She had shaken them vigorously until they began to glow with a greenish, cold light.

"Now I've got myself a voice," she had said. She had bent down and kissed me and then Dad. "Wish me luck."

Dad had grabbed her hand at the last minute. "Don't go. I don't feel good about this."

Mom had responded gently but firmly. "I'm the linguist. This is my job."

Then, to make him feel better, she had pointed to the children standing a little ways from the ship. "They have kids out here. This is a sign of trust. They don't mean us harm."

"You *don't* know what's in their minds," Dad had said.

"We have a responsibility to the ship," Mom said, "to our collective future." She kissed him. "And you always worry too much."

Reluctantly, he had let her hand go, and Mom had disappeared into the building.

I could see his fingers twitching nervously. On the floor of the shuttle, next to his feet, were the guns. Despite his attempt to cheer me, I knew that Dad was also scared and nervous. I saw that it took a lot of effort for him to resist his instinct to pick them up and start shooting.

Dad was the safety officer of the ship. It was his job to anticipate every danger along our path: from nebulae too dense for the shields to handle, to crew members about to succumb to deep space dementia. He had kept all of us safe with his vigilance, and he was uneasy with the unknown.

"Come on, come on," Dad muttered. He fingered his ring, etched with the insignia of the great Thunderbird, protector of the *Rapa Nui*, clutching in one claw a bunch of arrows and in the other an olive branch. Dad told me that as much as we talked about peace, we also had to always be ready to fight. It was the only way to ensure our survival. I reached for his hand to calm him down. It felt big in my hands, the hand of a giant.

Then the dancing lights of the children stopped and divided into two groups, leaving a dark path open in the middle. Gradually, we saw a pair of steady, green, glowing lights approach us out of the darkness, bobbing up and down, the rhythm familiar to me from all the times she had held me and walked up and down the noisy, cramped corridors of the ship until I fell asleep. Watching the bobbing lights, I felt the phantom movement against my body as a gentle murmur of comfort, a caress.

"Mom!" I shouted, and even I was startled by the loudness of my voice. It seemed to carry forever across the empty plains, until distant flying creatures took off from the grass and the fluttering of their wings seemed to carry the cry even further. The children's glowing fingers danced excitedly at my sound.

Mom was next to the shuttle in a second and lifted me into her arms. Her face was one huge smile. "I think they agreed to give us some land. Welcome to your new home, Sarah!"

"We should let some other family live here and play anthropologist," Dad said to Mom as we moved into our new home. "It's difficult for me to keep you and Sarah safe out here."

He would rather that we stayed on the Concession, a plot of land next to the sea about a hundred square kilometers in area, a gift from the Kalathani. It was fairly close to the Kalathani settlement around the Palace that we'd come to call the Capital.

After landfall, there had been a debate among the colonists about whether to build a fence around the Concession. Mom had insisted that a wall would send the wrong message, and the Council had finally agreed with her. The Kalathani children often wandered through the Concession, looking at everything with curiosity.

Mom was curious too, and she had a plan. "We have to learn the language and culture of our hosts. The best way to do that is if Sarah grows up among them." She looked at me and smiled encouragingly. I nodded, feeling the weight of responsibility.

Dad didn't like it, but the Council agreed with Mom. And years later I would find out what really made him acquiesce in the plan.

Our new home was a hut built inside the Capital. Mom tried to get permission from the Kalathani leaders she had negotiated with for the Concession, but she wasn't sure if they really understood what she wanted. In any event, no one stopped us when we carried the folded-up house over and set it to unfold like an origami box. The finished house looked like one of those fairytale huts inhabited by witches and bears in the picture books I read when I was little: a door in the middle, two windows to the sides, a sharp, triangular roof.

"I guess we can teach them about human culture too," Mom said, her eyes playful. All my life I'd lived in the square metal cabins and curved halls of the *Rapa Nui*, and I knew Pele's great gleaming cities and endless oceans only through old videos full of incomprehensible images and sounds. But this hut came from something even older, from the mythical

Old Earth, humanity's first home that no one had seen in a hundred generations.

Why do we want to recreate a home we have never lived in? I wanted to ask. Mom didn't like the house either, but it was all we had on the ship. She said it was in our nature to impose the old and familiar on the new and strange, like how the colonists immediately started to grow wheat and encircle land for ostriches after landing, instead of trying to learn how the Kalathani lived.

"Don't be too optimistic," Dad said. "Encounters between peoples too far apart in technology rarely end well." The Kalathani did not have the gift of spaceflight. Indeed, they did not even have firearms. The most advanced weapons they had seemed to be blowguns.

"And it's often the technologically superior people that get the worst of these encounters, because their tendency to romanticize their opponents and their more refined morals and delicate sensibilities end up getting in the way of their own interests."

There was a certainty in my father's deep voice that had always calmed me as a child. His was the sound of safety, of protection and security. He always saw danger from far away, and as long as he was around I believed I would be safe.

"We all have grown soft on the ship," Dad said. "After so many generations without warfare, we are prone to overestimate our ability to understand an alien species and to resolve conflicts without resort to violence.

"But we should be cautious. After all this time here, what have you really learned? Yes, you got us the Concession, but it was all based on vague and fuzzy guesses at what they were thinking and saying. You still can't figure out if they have a language that we can master, or mental patterns that are sufficiently similar to ours. Living among them without protection is reckless."

Six months ago, Mom had landed all by herself and made first contact. After the initial shock, the group of Kalathani she met had engaged with her enough to establish a basic mathematical code, enough to talk about counting, prime numbers, vast distances, and the concept that we were mortal beings from the stars.

Then she had taken us with her on that trip to the Palace. "I want them to see you, Sarah, to be reassured that we have children too, just like them."

Dad had disliked the plan because he didn't want to appear to be too similar to the Kalathani and therefore give them the sense that we were vulnerable. He would have preferred a show of force so that the Kalathani would think of us as invincible, alien, and powerful beyond comprehension. But the Council had sided with Mom then, as they did now with her plan to move our family into the Capital.

"If I were the Kalathani, the first goal would be to acquire as much human technology as possible," Dad said. "As long as such a great power differential exists, no negotiation among equals can occur. But as soon as the technological gap is sufficiently small, I'd attack the humans to gain the upper hand."

"Maybe the Kalathani don't think like that."

"It's my job to think of the worst-case scenario," Dad said, his voice full of weariness.

"Well, there's five hundred million of them and only two thousand of us," Mom said brightly. "That's a pretty big advantage on their side. I don't want to have to go back to wandering among the stars in a metal tube. I want to die with the open sky over my head."

"They're still scattered into a thousand squabbling tribes. We could have easily given ourselves a safe home if we were more willing to fight."

I walked to the window to look up at the great mansions of the Capital, arranged around us in the reddish-golden light of the giant but cool sun. The buildings rose like stone knives thrusting a hundred meters into the sky, and I thought our house looked like a toy next to them.

"Toy" was one of the first Kalathani words I learned.

The morning after we moved into our new house, I opened the door to find a young Kalathani standing outside.

The child looked about my height, which, according to my six-year-old's logic, meant that the child was also about my age. I decided that I was looking at a boy because he was carrying a smaller version of the club-shaped weapons that I had seen the guards carry at the Palace.

"Hello," I said, and immediately felt stupid. I probably appeared to the child as sensible as a fish gulping water. I knew perfectly well that the Kalathani did not speak. That was the whole point of my presence here.

Big, dark, iris-less eyes stared at me out of a wrinkled face topped with hundreds of soft, fleshy fronds that wiggled like little tentacles—I didn't know then that it meant he was nervous—and the boy shuffled up and presented his weapon to me.

I took it from him without thinking. It was very light.

"Be careful with that," Dad said from behind me. "It could be poisonous."

I gave Dad a fearful look, and he tried to reassure me, "I guess he's trying to buy your trust, letting you know he means no harm."

I handled it gingerly, keeping both ends pointed away from me as I wasn't sure which end held the killing tip. My hands became very sweaty, and the weapon slipped and fell on the ground. I jumped and cried out.

The boy's fronds suddenly began to shake like a rustling field of grass in a breeze. I glanced at him, worried.

The boy took a step back. His fronds danced even faster, more chaotically.

"Ellen, you need to be here!" Dad called into the house. In a minute Mom was behind me.

"Stay still," Mom said. "We don't know what taboo you might have violated." She examined the child more closely and added in a whisper, "I think this child belongs to one of the leaders I negotiated with."

The boy's fronds stopped moving. He held my gaze, and then pointed at the weapon on the ground between us. Very slowly, he lifted his hands, and I noticed how delicate his fingers were, like supple, thin twigs. He fanned out all sixteen of his fingers and put the left hand on top of the right, and wiggled them while moving both hands together in a counterclockwise circle.

"I've never seen that sign before," Mom said.

But I wasn't really paying attention to her. As I stared at the boy's hands swooping and sliding through the air, I thought I could sense playfulness to the motion, a kind of pure delight.

The boy looked into our uncomprehending faces—did he even understand that we couldn't understand him? Then he tried something else, he moved his index finger through the air, tracing out a Z-shaped pattern.

"I know that sign," Mom said, her voice breathless with excitement. "It's a negation particle."

Then the boy clasped his hands together and held them against the middle of his squat body perched atop his long legs.

"I've seen that, too," Mom said. "But I can't figure out what it means exactly. Maybe 'real,' 'true,' 'factual.' Let me see—"

She went and retrieved her computer. Mom had devised a way to write down the signs made by the Kalathani. She broke each sign down into components—hand location, shape, motion, orientation, illumination, and context—and recorded them in an alphabet she invented. It made tracking the signs easier and also allowed her to give them names. "Yes, this is the sign called *tsuko*. It came up in negotiations a lot."

Not real, I thought. Then I looked at the weapon on the ground again. I picked it up and looked into both ends.

"Sarah!" Dad tried to stop me but Mom held him back.

There was no barrel opening. The weapon was a toy, fashioned out of some solid wood-like material.

I tried to replicate the first sign that the boy had made, moving my hands together in a circle while wiggling my fingers, as though I'm illustrating a spider climbing around the rim of a clock.

"*Ethleth*," I heard Mom whisper behind me. "What does *ethleth* mean?"

I pointed at the gun. Then I pushed my parents aside, ran inside, and came back with the model of the *Rapa Nui* Dad had carved for me out of a piece of waste insulation foam when I was little. It was my favorite.

I handed the model to the boy, and made the *ethleth* sign again. I said aloud, for the benefit of my parents. "A toy, he was saying this was a toy. Not *tsuko*."

The fronds on top of the boy's head shook again like streamers tied to a ventilation vent on the ship. He laced his hands on the back of his head, and then unlaced them and moved his hands in front of him, fanning them open and fluttering them in the air, as though they were playing an invisible piano.

"The signs may look complicated," Mom whispered, "but they must be built from discrete micro-gestures that are capable of being combined."

I didn't understand much of what she said, but the child's fluttering fingers mesmerized me. I could almost feel the movements in my own hands, as though they were coalescing into meaning.

"He's making the same sign again and again," Mom said. "*Tunloji*."

Tunloji, *Tunloji*, *Tunloji*. And in that moment I suddenly saw Tunloji as a girl, not a boy. Maybe it was the way her eyes looked at me, interested but not aggressive. Maybe it was the way the wrinkles on her face suddenly seemed to me beautiful and deliberate, like etched makeup. I looked into her eyes, and I thought I saw a flicker of understanding.

I put my hands on the back of my head, and then said, "Sarah, Sarah, Sarah."

Tunloji blew air through her mouth, trying to imitate the sounds I made.

I laughed, and Tunloji's fronds shook.

And so I became the bridge between two peoples.

When I was a little girl, Mom told me to imagine the ship as a bridge between worlds.

The *Rapa Nui* was named after a mythical race from Old Earth, brave men and women who had challenged the vast sea in tiny canoes, their indomitable will leading them to bridge impossible distances and populate the tiny islands scattered across a great ocean like habitable planets strewn across the void of space.

I was of the fourteenth generation to be born aboard the ship. Growing up, there was little room for children to run and play. I watched the old archive videos of unrestrained motion and limitless space with envy: the ballet dancers, the waving tentacles of sea anemones, the swaying trees and galloping herds of animals across the plains of a home planet I'd never visit.

On the ship, there was constant noise: grinding machinery, humming air circulators, the ceaseless murmuring of too many families packed in too little space. But on Kalath, there was endless space to explore and endless silence to be lost in: even arguments were conducted quietly. Close your eyes, and you'd be away in your own world.

"You like the contrast?" Mom asked. I nodded. My new life was lovely, even though Dad was anxious and worried all the time, thinking the peace wouldn't last.

"Noticing contrasts is at the heart of what we do," Mom said. She had been studying the dead languages of Old Earth stored in our archives for inspiration. She explained that the sounds of a language do not form a continuous spectrum of variation, but are grouped by perception into discrete, contrasting units, called phonemes. There are an infinite number of ways that sounds can vary, but only certain differences are meaningful. Some languages care about tone, others don't. Some distinguish between aspirated and unaspirated plosives, others don't. Some assign significance to devoicing sonorants, others don't. Knowing which sound differences are meaningful, phonemic, is critical to learning to speak a language well.

The Kalathani speak with their hands, but based on analogy with human sign languages, Mom believed that there nevertheless must be equivalents to phonemes—cheremes—that map to meaningful contrasts in motion, position, location, shape, and light.

"You'll help me, Sarah," she said. "Your brain is still flexible, not yet frozen into the pathways of humanity's long history. You'll be able to learn to think like a Kalathani as you play with them, become their friend. We'll refine our alphabet until we discover the complete set of cheremes and add entries to our dictionary until we have the keys to unlock the Kalathani mind."

"Be careful. You might be disappointed by what you'll find there," Dad said. "All apex species want the same thing: to dominate those who are different, to survive."

"I would hope that we've long advanced beyond that," Mom said. "I'm certain that we and the Kalathani have much to teach each other."

Then she turned to me. "You will be the prism through which we see the beautiful colors of an alien society."

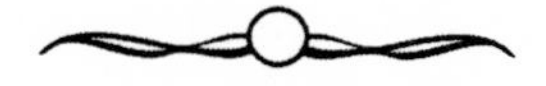

A rainbow hung in the western sky. The rain had been quick and the air smelled fresh and invigorating.

I was trying to teach and learn from Tunloji the words for the colors of the rainbow and not having much luck.

"Red," I said, pointing to the rainbow. And then I pointed to a pentagonal flower nearby, red as the clouds near the setting sun, red as the bleeding edge of the rainbow.

Tunloji gazed at the flower, and then made a sign, her fingers—today she was calm and contemplative, and so I thought of her as a girl again—tapping out a flowing pattern in the air. It looked like she was caressing the side of a large animal.

I tried to imitate her sign, pointing at the flower again. Tunloji looked at me and lowered her head in a gesture that I had come to interpret as the equivalent of a noncommittal shrug.

I pointed to the rainbow again, and then pointed to the grass around us. "Green," I said. The wet grass reminded me of the olives in the hydroponics bay on the *Rapa Nui*, reserved for special occasions.

Tunloji looked at the grass and made the same sign as before.

"No," I shook my head, frustration bubbling up. Were the Kalathani all color-blind? I had been trying to find out the words for colors for several days and had made no progress. Mom had consulted the biologists in the Concession about what they knew so far of Kalathani physiology. The decorative patterns in their clothing and buildings suggested that their color vision was similar to ours. It made no sense that I couldn't even get such a simple concept across.

Tunloji curved her neck and lowered her head. It was a sign that she was frustrated too. She beckoned me closer with her hands, and then folded her multi-jointed legs to squat on the ground.

She pointed at one blade of grass, making sure that I knew exactly which one, and made the same sign she'd made a hundred times already.

"Yes, I know," I said, impatiently. "Red, green, yellow—you have only one word for color, every color in the world." Half-heartedly, I repeated the sign.

Tunloji grabbed my hands. Her touch was cool and leathery, like the skin of a lizard. I gasped. It was the first time a Kalathani had ever touched me.

But Tunloji's touch was gentle, and I resisted the urge to scream. She guided my hands through the air, in a gentle repetition of her sign, tracing out a subtle waveform. Only when she was sure I had gotten the speed, position, movements right did she let go.

Then she pointed to a different blade of grass, and then made the same sign again.

Before I could repeat it, she grabbed my hands and guided me. As my hands moved through space, it again traced out a gentle waveform. But now that Tunloji was moving my hands, I could tell that there was a slight difference from before: some parts of the wave were more prominent, other parts less.

I looked at the two blades of grass again. There was a slight difference in the shade of green, but not in a way that I had ever thought could be captured by language.

I pointed at the rainbow again, and picking up a stick, drew a schematic of the rainbow in the sand, dividing it into seven bands. I pointed at each band and named the colors: "Red, orange, yellow, green, blue, indigo, violet."

Tunloji was utterly baffled. She looked between the rainbow, my diagram, and me. Then she began moving her hands slowly in a circle, pausing from time to time to make the sign she had been making all this time and pointing at various flowers, rocks, sun-lit clouds.

But now that I was attuned to it, I saw that the sign she made in each iteration was subtly different. Mom and I had never attributed significance to such small differences in the Kalathani signs, treating them as analogous to the inevitable range of variation in the pronunciation of a phoneme in a spoken word. But it finally dawned on me that she was naming the different shades of colors arranged in a wheel: a dark crimson (like that flower), a light indigo (like that leaf), a bright yellow (like that cloud), a shimmering purple (like that insect).

How could the Kalathani speak, when they had a million words for the colors of the rainbow alone? My head hurt with the notion. *Could the Kalathani not see colors as broad categories, but only infinite shades of difference, of variation?*

"The most interesting ways in which languages vary from each other aren't differences in vocabulary," Mom said. "To really understand the differences between languages, you must observe how they differ in what qualities of the world they *require* to be encoded."

Some languages, she explained, divided nouns into classes with classifiers. Thin and flat objects were different from round and compact objects, for example, and so you always had to assign everything you wished to talk about into such categories. Other languages had different verb forms for different tenses, aspects, moods, voices, persons, and so you always had to encode these elements into speech and couldn't leave them open to interpretation.

"The Kalathani language is directed towards encoding minute variations through context and comparison," Mom said. "It needs details and concrete references, but that's not the same as precision. To speak, the Kalathani require a level of specificity that probably makes abstract thinking quite difficult."

"This is just a difficult moment," Mom said, "a temporary misunderstanding."

I could see Dad biting back the impulse to tell Mom that he had predicted something like this would happen. Instead, he tried to reason with her gently. "People are afraid. They want safety. We all do. It is not your fault that the experiment isn't working."

We were huddled inside the house, and Dad was again clutching his gun tightly. He had demanded that all of us move back to the Concession, but Mom had stubbornly refused to leave.

"They *ate* them, Ellen."

Two of the colonists had died of age and had been buried at the edge of the Concession in a new cemetery. In the middle of the night the Kalathani had come and dug them out, cut up the bodies, and dined on them in the dawn light as the colonists watched in horror. Some of the Kalathani even offered to share with the colonists. A fight broke out. Guns were fired. One colonist and two Kalathani were severely injured, though no one was killed.

"I saw their formations and their ability to fight. They may not have our weapons, but they *are* fast, deadly, and organized. They know how to use their advantage in numbers. Jordan's leg was sliced off by three of them working in coordination."

They retreated. But soon came back carrying some of their own dead. They began to eat those too and offered bits to the colonists.

"They offered their own dead as though they were sharing the carcasses of animals, just food. I don't think they even distinguish between sentience and non-sentience. It was all meat. How can we ever hope to understand them? They're barbaric, without any respect for life, any semblance of morality."

"Perhaps they did it as a peace offering," Mom said, her voice trembling, uncertain. "They may be as confused about this as we are. We can't give up trying."

"I've always loved your idealism," Dad said. I saw that it pained him to speak in a way that hurt my mother, but he went on after a brief pause. "But sometimes we can't afford to be idealistic. Everyone at the Concession is already on edge. The next time a conflict occurs, it *will* cost lives. I can't stop you from risking your own life and the life of our child, but we have a responsibility not to risk the lives of all the other children."

The Council ultimately took Dad's suggestion and erect-ed a wall around the Concession, complete with watchtowers and mounts for guns.

The Kalathani watched as the wall went up, their fronds still and unmoving.

Tunloji pointed to the wall in the distance, and asked a question. I shrugged, not knowing how to explain.

After a month apart, we were playing together again. Mom had grown less hopeful about the prospect of understanding the Kalathani, but she thought I was making good progress with Tunloji.

I took out a loop of string and we sat down together, a small gap of space between us, where we watched our thoughts take different shapes.

This was a good game when there was nothing to say.

While nothing more was said diplomatically about the incident that led to the wall, the Council asked the scientists, my mother included, to continue to study the lives and habits of the Kalathani for signs of danger.

The Concession biologists had discovered that the Kalathani are asexual.

"Well, not exactly *asexual*," Mom added. "More like unisexual."

It had never been the way on the *Rapa Nui* to hide the facts of life from children. There was no room for it. "The biologists have been discreetly observing the Kalathani—"

"Trying to make alien sex tapes," Dad said, chuckling.

"—and they found that the Kalathani don't have a reproductive biology based on two or more sexes. The supposed sexual dimorphism we've seen is a bit of an illusion: in fact, Kalathani physical features just vary in gradations across a range, a spectrum. Each Kalathani is born asexually from one parent. But the child is not an exact clone of the parent. Adult Kalathani exchange bits of genetic material throughout life with each other. We don't understand the exact mechanism yet, but it probably involves a form of intimacy much like human matings."

"The men aren't men, and the women aren't women," Dad said. "It actually explains why they're so impossible to understand. There's no sexual competition among these people, no drive to achieve greatness."

"It's even more strange than that," Mom said. "The Kalathani apparently also exchange genes with other, non-sentient species, albeit in much smaller degrees. Indeed, the very notion of 'species' is ill-defined given their biology. It may explain to some extent the general trouble they have with boundary-drawing, which seems to permeate many subjects. Their kinship patterns, for example, are entwined and complex, and account for many different types and degrees of relatedness. The various languages and dialects we've investigated don't differ from each other in clear ways, but shade into each other."

"Sounds like even the notion that they're divided into various tribes and nations is questionable," Dad muttered, shaking his head. "How can we ever gain enough insight into their thinking to predict their moves?"

"It will require some definite shifts in our perspective to understand them," Mom conceded. "Even the practice of eating the dead is probably also related to genetic exchange in some way. Lacking a general capacity for abstraction, they may also lack the impulse towards transcendence and thus don't share our innate taboos."

But I was focused on just one thing: Tunloji was neither a boy nor a girl, neither a he nor a she. Tunloji wasn't an *it* either, because Tunloji was my friend.

My language and the flow of my thought required me to assign Tunloji to a category, but there was no category that fit.

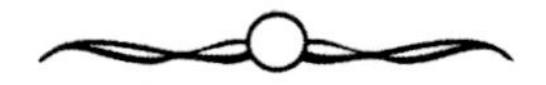

Over the years, Tunloji and I progressed through the full range of shades of friendship. At first, we were two hands apart, carefully cupping a space in-between. Then the hands came closer, until the fingers were almost touching, as if bound together by invisible strings, like two hands playing Cat's Cradle.

No matter how much Mom tweaked her alphabet of cheremes, it could not capture the infinite variety of the Kalathani language. She added numerical intensity indicators for such qualities as brightness, speed, degree of curvature. But it was an impossible task. Just as the Kalathani saw in infinite shades rather than distinct colors, their speech resisted any scale that could divide up the quality under observation into discrete steps.

Dad spent less and less time in our house in the Capital. Instead, he seemed to always be at the walled Concession. I missed his presence, the way the sound of his voice made me feel safe.

When he did show up at home, Mom and he often argued.

He was growing more and more concerned about the opacity of Kalathani intentions, as was the Council. But my attempts to explain what I had learned about the Kalathani to him ended in failures.

"Sarah, I don't know how to turn what you're telling me into a strategy to make us safe, to guarantee us a secure future," he would say, disappointed with the lack of progress and angry at himself.

One day, he told Mom that he was the proponent of a plan to have some of the Kalathani children live on the Concession and go to school there, so that they could be exposed to human culture.

At first Mom was pleased, thinking that Dad was looking for a way to tear down the wall. It sounded like the complement of what we were doing, another way to build bridges between two peoples. She spoke to the Kalathani leaders, with me and Tunloji acting as translators. Except for some holidays at the Concession, I spent all of my time in the Capital. And by now Tunloji and I were able to converse pretty well, and I was starting to dream and think in Kalathani signs.

The Kalathani agreed, and ten Kalathani children were sent to the Concession school.

Mom visited the school about a month later, and what she saw made her furious.

"It isn't a school," she said to Dad without preamble. "Yes, they're fed well and given plenty of entertainment with the computer, but they're kept virtually as prisoners. There's no effort to *teach* them anything, to *communicate*. What are you really doing?"

"They're insurance," Dad said, simply.

"Against what?"

Dad sighed. "Why do you think the Kalathani agreed to have us live here, in their Capital?"

"Because they're interested in learning about us as much as we are about them?"

Dad shook his head. "You are still talking as if these are the Noble Savages of your dreams. Give them some credit for thinking strategically! By keeping you, me, and Sarah here, they have three hostages that could be easily rounded up in the event of hostilities with the colony. Conversely, by allowing the Kalathani to keep us here, the colony is showing our host trust, promising that no hostilities will break out. That was why I finally had to agree to have you and Sarah live here: for the good of the colony. But this diplomatic equilibrium is only stable when there's balance: we need to have Kalathani hostages as well."

Mom's eyes grew narrower. "That's how you think about me and Sarah? We're just bargaining chips in some Great Game? You think of children as *hostages*?"

"I'm trying to keep us alive on a hostile planet," Dad said.

"Why do you insist that they're *hostile*? Why can't you just see them as neighbors, good hosts who have allowed us to share their planet?"

Dad's voice grew quiet and sorrowful. "I wish you were right and I were wrong, but the rules of evolution are constant throughout the universe. All intelligent species who came to dominate their planet must be equipped with a hostility to outsiders to be successful. Intelligence and aggression are two sides of the same coin. Those who insist that it can be otherwise only delude themselves."

"We'd be delusional to continue negotiating," Dad muttered. "They're planning something."

"They're different," Mom said. "*Alien*. But they can be reasoned with."

It had been ten years since the founding of the Concession. In the interim, the Kalathani only grew more incomprehensible and opaque to the settlers, and save for Dad's "school" and Mom and me, there was little interaction between the two worlds.

But now the colony needed more room, more space to expand, and the Council was forced to initiate new negotiations with the Kalathani, which had gone nowhere. As translator at the negotiations, I thought I knew what was wrong and tried to explain the problem to the Council. But they heard only what they expected to hear, and my words were ignored.

The rumors going around the Concession said that the Kalathani were alarmed by the growing human population. There were also angry whispers that despite all that we had done, despite the special school for the Kalathani children, the aliens had not shown much interest to learn from us, to become educated in our ideals.

Dad laughed bitterly. "This is a people who still cannot comprehend the concept of writing, whose language seems designed to be impossible to write. They live in a perpetual haze where their intentions are as inscrutable as fish darting through a murky sea. Reasoning with them is impossible."

Mom didn't say anything, which meant that she didn't and also did agree with Dad. Over the years, as she had failed to truly comprehend the Kalathani, she had become disillusioned about her earlier, more hopeful vision. But I did not think she shared my father's beliefs either.

Yet I wondered if such subtle distinctions mattered any more. Dad and the rest of the Council now talked as though everyone had to pick a side: either they were with them or they were against them.

I read about the history of the peoples of Old Earth in the ship's archives. There was a time when humans were divided into thousands of tribes and spoke thousands of languages, each with its own competing array of dialects and scripts and ways of classifying and seeing the world. But over time, the dialects in every language died out until only one remained. Then every language also died out except one, and every script died out except one—the one spoken and written by all of humanity.

"Why did this happen?" I asked Mom.

"It's a matter of progress," she said. Every language shaped the way the speaker thought about the world. And so languages were like genes, and their speakers like species, competing for survival in the world. The language that out-competed the others and survived must, by necessity, represent the one that was most enlightened, most fit for effective thinking and reasoning, conferring on its speakers the best chance at developing advanced technology and gathering wealth. This was the Sapir-Whorf-Mair Hypothesis, developed in ancient times by the great philosopher and general Mair, who synthesized the observations of previous thinkers and pushed them to their logical conclusion.

"Through exploration and colonization, languages competed, dominated, taught, and enlightened. We settled on the one best language, which gave the best shape to our thoughts.

Along the way we eliminated scripts and sounds and distinctions that were not as strong, not as good. This was how humanity became united. Even the people for whom our ship was named ceased eventually to speak their own language."

The story seemed obvious, even inevitable. The best language led to the best thoughts which led to the best weapons which led to victory and dominance.

Yet I could not fully believe it. I had learned in some measure to speak as a Kalthani, to think in their ways. In the Kalathani language, one must always think about shades of meaning. There's never a simple, definitive way of saying something. Everything is a matter of degrees, every quality subject to careful parsing and nuanced delineation. I could not embrace the notion that this way of seeing the world was doomed.

This was why the negotiations were failing. The Kalathani did not say no, and they did not say yes. They were asking questions, questions about why the humans were so reluctant to share their technology, why they were so insistent on building walls. But such subtle shades of meaning were lost in translation. The questions sounded like denials to the Council, like the prelude to war.

It is a language that resists abstractions and categories, Mom wrote. *It is not surprising then that the Kalathani never developed a full script, a system of writing. Besides a formal notation for mathematics and a specialized set of diagramming conventions for engineering / architecture, the Kalathani are functionally illiterate.*

"It is the way of the world," Dad said. "The Kalathani have been exposed to a different and superior culture. They can learn and adapt, or they will die, but either way there will be war."

Tunloji and I sat on the sloping grassy knoll as Tunloji learned the last few of the Two Hundred Variations from me.

As the string passed between us, we watched the Concession in the distance.

You like building walls, zie said.

That was as close as I could render zir words into English. In reality, instead of "you," what Tunloji said was more akin to "those who bear degrees of relatedness to you," and instead of "like," what Tunloji literally said was closer to "prefers more than the love of the hungry for food and less than the love of the lonely for company."

It was very tiring to have to strip away so much nuance, so much meaning from every utterance. The English translations, if I were to try to do the original justice, would be as awkward as the artificial pronouns I was forced to use to refer to Tunloji. I far preferred to think in Kalthani than English.

It makes them feel safe, I said, trying to keep the defensive tone out of my signs.

Don't you mean "us"*?*

Tunloji used the English word. The "s" sound was difficult for the Kalathani, but I understood zem.

Kalathani pronouns, like other signs, also held endless shades. English words like "we" (including or excluding the addressee), "you" (singular or plural), "they" (with the addressee being potentially included or excluded), and so on were just crude stops along a subtle spectrum of meaning. I had used a sign that excluded myself from the people being spoken of, the settlers of the Concession, but Tunloji had insisted on the human "us."

I flinched.

Always it is this way with them, Tunloji said. The way zie signed, I was on the verge of being included in "them" but it was still a shade short of "you." *Always they think of everything in terms of* "us" *and* "them."

I could not contradict zem. Just as I had learned to think like a Kalathani, zie had learned to think like a human.

There is talk of war among them, I said. I hesitated and almost shaded the sign into *us*, but did not.

Tunloji's fronds vibrated with anger. *You speak of peace, of learning, of being guests and helping each other. And yet you're also always thinking of war, of using your superior weapons. Always you have two sides, two faces, speak in two voices. You lack tsuko.*

The eagle clutching the arrows and the olive branch. The arguments between my parents.

The sign that my mother named *tsuko* is not a single sign but a family of signs, indicating degrees of authenticity. Tunloji had slapped zir chest hard, as hard as zie could.

But even in anger zie had been careful to phrase *you* in a way that left it open whether I belonged to it or not. I sat there, ashamed, the Cat's Cradle string forgotten in my lap.

There is also talk of war among them, Tunloji said after a while. I was surprised. Zie was not referring to the Concession, but the Capital behind us.

Why? I asked.

The children who have lived among your people have learned more than your father thinks, Tunloji said. *There is much talk of what your weapons can do, of the strength of your ships, and of the way you can see such a sharp line between you and not-you.*

Self and Other, yin and yang, male and female.

I despise their speech, Tunloji said. *It is not tsuko. They speak of mirages.*

Again, Tunloji had spoken of *tsuko* with such force that zir chest thumped as though zie had been punched.

I held zir hand, my fingers warm around zir leathery ones. After a moment, zie put zir arm around me. Tunloji and I had kept pace in our growth, and we were about the same height.

We embraced, not quite the way the Kalathani embrace, with legs and arms all entwining, and not quite the way humans embrace, with our heads on each other's shoulders. Instead, we wrapped our arms around each other and touched our foreheads together. Tunloji's fronds gently massaged my skull.

Then, before I knew what was happening, zie slipped an arm under my shirt, zir delicate fingers placed against the bare skin of my breasts and my heart pounding underneath.

I sucked in a breath. I had shown Tunloji the sex-ed videos from the *Rapa Nui*, and Tunloji had shown me how the Kalathani can be intimate as part of their process for exchanging genetic material, secrets that the Concession scientists had never seen.

Then I relaxed, and placed my fingers against zir lips. In a moment, zie opened zir mouth and took my trembling fingers inside, where they sought and explored the warm, delicate membranous folds.

Are you sure? Tunloji stopped and asked.

Yes. I spoke from inside zem, my fingers caressing and massaging the yielding, sensitive layers of a new world.

Zie closed zir eyes. To allow the organs of speech inside, to take in the words spoken by a lover—there's no more misunderstanding—trust, intimacy, *tsuko*.

And we moved together under the stars, long after it was dark, while the Concession and the Capital drifted further and further apart, and talk of war solidified, passing through the unnamed stages between dream and reality.

I was inside the Concession when the war began.

Dad had planned it that way. In his view, Mom and I were hostages, the only bits of leverage the Kalathani had.

He could not believe how easy it was to bring us into the Concession without the Kalathani objecting. All these years he had carefully planned for either Mom or me to remain inside the Capital while the other visited the Concession because he thought it was important to show the Kalathani how trusting we were.

It had been a wasted performance.

At the same time, more than twenty young Kalathani were inside the Concession, and the Council, under Dad's direction, captured them and brought them to the wall to show the

Kalathani that the colony meant business.

Unless the Kalathani agreed immediately to vacate an area about a million square kilometers around the Concession, the colonists would put the Kalathani children to death.

I tried to leave the Concession but Dad slapped me hard. "Do not forget who you are, Sarah. You are a member of the human race."

"Don't worry," Mom said, trying to comfort me. "This is only a negotiation tactic. We'd never really kill anyone." I listened to her and tried to judge how much *tsuko* was in her words.

It took hours before the Kalathani finally understood that the colony had declared war on them. Their response was to gather into a massive army marching towards the Concession walls.

At the sight of the massing Kalathani, the guards holding the Kalathani children panicked, and two of the children were killed, perhaps by accident, perhaps not.

"Stop!" Dad shouted at the Kalathani army, and I, standing next to him on the walls, had to translate. Projectors cast giant images of my moving hands in the air over the walls like fantasy creatures dancing in the fog. "Do not come any closer."

Thousands marching in close ranks, the army advanced silently towards the wall, coming closer and closer. The Kalathani were dressed in their strongest armor and held their most powerful weapons, but they were mere toys against the human defenses.

"It's no use," I said to Dad. "They—we—don't think this way." But he was not listening.

He pointed his gun at another Kalathani child, who looked back at him impassively.

"What is wrong with you people," he croaked. "Aren't you afraid to die?"

My father was closer to the truth than he realized. The people he so feared did not value life the same way he did.

I wanted to explain to him that the Kalathani do not see life and death as distinct states. It is not true that death is the worst fate of all, something to be avoided at all costs. There is a spectrum of stages in between life and death and also beyond: there is living free, living in fear, living with little to no *tsuko*, enslaved-and-surpassing-dead, dead-but-also-free, all the way to transcendence.

This was why, years ago, the Kalathani had tried to partake of the human dead, to explore fully the shaded region between the life and death of a new and strange people, to try to absorb the new into the existing by degrees. The people of this world had also offered to share their bodies with the colonists so that humans could learn to see past their fear of death.

"Stop it, damn you! Why won't you stop?" He stepped forward and shot the young Kalathani child near him and threw zem down the walls.

But the army did not stop or slow.

"We'll never stop," I told my father. His face was contorted into an expression of rage and fear that I no longer recognized. He looked like an alien.

"These people are barbaric," he said. "They'd rather watch their children die than give in to the inevitable, to concede defeat and accept the rule of a superior race. These people cannot be reasoned with." As he spoke, his voice grew more melancholy and also more determined.

He ordered more of the Kalathani hostages killed and thrown from the walls. Mom covered her eyes and left the wall.

The army continued to surge towards us.

Dad ordered the men to open fire against the Kalathani. There was no more hope for a negotiated peace. It was no longer triumph or defeat he sought.

"We have to wipe them out," he said. Gone from his voice was the sense of responsibility, the bass note of safety and security that I had always loved. I heard only fear and despair.

As the Kalathani near the front of the crowd died, more stepped in to fill their place.

It was an eerie scene and I shall never forget it. The Kalathani died silently, it not being their habit to vocalize in their final moments. The quiet hiss of the energy weapons was accompanied only by the thudding of Kalathani bodies falling to the ground. The Kalathani blowguns had no range to reach up the walls, and so they did not return fire at all.

Was it the fault of their language that they had no firearms and no energy weapons, but instead had to face us with only their bodies to shield each other?

The Sapir-Whorf-Mair Hypothesis was also a belief about blood, about violence and death. It was two-faced.

I had no idea what the Kalathani were planning either. Did they intend to simply march up and die until the piled up bodies of the dead allowed them to walk up the walls into the Concession?

And what then? Would they kill every human being they found? Would they believe it an act of mercy because they thought death was better than seeing the world only in separate categories, in clear lines that divided everything into pieces?

It was more horrible than any scene of slaughter I had seen in the ship's archives.

The day grew dark, and the Kalathani fingers moving in rhythm reminded me of the movement of stars in the void.

I did not want to pick a side. I was tired of sides.

The dancing light of the stars grew brighter as my head grew lighter.

I don't remember what happened next except a memory of myself jumping into a sea of stars, like a ship accelerating into a star field.

They say that Tunloji caught me as I floated down, but that is almost certainly a later embellishment. When I hear this, the speakers never infuse the signs with a degree of *tsuko* that tells me they believe they're reciting facts. In fact, they sign in the register of myth, of legend, of story and song.

What happened next? I would ask.

Your father, they would tell me, *he opened his mouth and the line between* "us" *and* "you" *disappeared.*

"You're the only one who ever understood them," Mom said. "I will spend the rest of my life to see if I can understand you."

I kissed her lightly on the cheek one last time.

"Why?" My father asked me, as the last of the colonists ascended into the *Rapa Nui* in shuttles, preparing for a new journey of generations across the stars in search of a new home. "Why do you wish to stay here?"

I wrapped my arm around Tunloji, and my father flinched. He refused to look Tunloji in the eye. For him, what Tunloji and I shared was an abomination that could not be borne.

Never mind that the Kalathani were allowing the colonists to leave without harassment. Never mind that the Kalathani had decided to not pursue revenge for the hundreds who had been slaughtered. My father was convinced that the Kalathani were without morality, without reason, because they refused to surrender as their children died.

"I should never have agreed to raise you among them," he muttered.

I was about to speak but Mom spoke first. "Do not be too harsh with him."

"He is a shell into which no understanding can penetrate," I said. "He is a fool."

"He also ordered the men to stop shooting when you jumped down the wall to be among the Kalathani. He gave up his responsibility to the colony, his soul, for you. He loves you more than you can understand."

I had no response to that. He saw my life as more valuable than that of a hundred thousand Kalathani. He would rather lose the war and put the colony at the mercy of the Kalathani than risk hurting me. For him there was a gulf that could not be crossed between "human" and "Kalathani," between "family" and "stranger," between "us" and "them." And upon that gulf he built his edifice of moral reasoning.

It was a way of thinking the Kalathani never understood, and I understood only vaguely.

"You're more them than us," Dad said.

You're right, I said. Then I pressed my fists against my heart. *Tsuko*. But I did it lightly. I wished more than anything in the world that he understood the subtlety of what I was saying and how I said it, that he could read how lightly I tried to tread, to hurt him as little as possible, to still recognize myself as his daughter.

I still loved him, in my fashion.

I unwind the string from around Ket's fingers. Then I form a new shape with the string, the Shape of Thought, a design of my own invention.

Shape of Thought turns into Rainbow turns into Handful of Stars turns into Twin Paths turns into the Two Hundred New Variations developed by bored Kalathani children trying to imagine the humans who once lived among them.

I look into Ket's eyes, asking zem with my gaze alone to take up this new shape, this fresh way forward.

One decision leads to another and some paths are opened while others are closed.

The Kalathani have been changed by the brief time the humans spent among them, as much as I have been transformed by my time among the Kalathani.

My mother was wrong, I now know. There is not and can never be only one language, one way of thinking. Already the colonists of the *Rapa Nui* speak differently from their ancestors who had stepped onto the ship. In the vast distance between the stars, phonemes drift and change, old distinctions are blurred and new distinctions born. The human race, scattered among the stars, again speak ten thousand languages, each shaped to and shaping a new way of thinking, a new way of seeing the world.

I can already see that the young Kalathani find it easier to see lines instead of shades, to see categories instead of spectra. The language is changing, becoming more staccato, less fluid, more amenable to distinctions. Perhaps someday they will see a rainbow of separate colors, and divide the world more distinctly into us and them.

Ket takes the string from me, zir fronds calm and zir body relaxed, joyful. I embrace the child more firmly, wind the string tightly around zir fingers, silencing zem and myself. The other children, thinking it a new game, embrace us in a tight knot.

I wish this moment, when there is no division but only variation, would last forever.

Under Falna's Mask

Alex Dally MacFarlane

See me! See me! Falna the fierce
with my son on my back, tenth child, battle-charm
—from the *Song of Falna*

Mar-teri broke her confinement to burn alsar for her dead sisters. Under thin moonlight she stepped out of the unmarried adults' caravan for the first time in two months—stones crunching under her feet, chives brushing against her bare ankles—carrying the bunch of alsar she was supposed to burn in her caravan. As if honoring them from afar could be enough.

The opening lines of Falna's song slipped into Mar-teri's head. Such a fierce song, when the woman wearing Falna's mask channeled generations of anger—how Mar-teri had longed to wear that mask! Now, walking as quietly as possible towards the ten burials, she hated it. Fighting the far-off people did nothing. They changed the sky and poisoned the land and none of the Tuvicen people could change that.

Ahead of her lay her sisters, with alsar-sweet feet.

Behind, her group lay in caravans and under blankets on the ground. They had stayed awake late into the night, keening, drinking fermented befil milk—and now they slept like stone markers, pointing to a place of grief.

None heard Mar-teri.

She stopped by the first body: Peto, who had married into

the group, wearing all of his wealth and a short wrap that hid the horrid jutting of his hips, the sunken flesh of his waist and thighs. But it couldn't hide his chest, his ribs like a line of sticks, his hollow face and the scant strands of long, dark hair remaining. It couldn't hide his skin, once such a deep brown, turned ghost-grey. Seeing this death up close, even in such weak light, made the fermented befil milk in Mar-teri's stomach shift unpleasantly. Peto looked weeks dead, preserved by the dry air, not days dead. And beside him, in a neat row, the other nine looked identical. Gold ungleaming in the night, bodies wasted and—Mar-teri's sisters, side-by-side, twinned even in death. "Nalna," Mar-teri whispered. "Mara." Their names would not be forgotten. Beside Mara lay her wife, Natia, pregnant with their first child. Beside Natia lay her second lover and the unborn child's birth-father, Civo. "Natia," she whispered. "Civo." And she named the child: "Nat-uvo." Under Natia's wrap, there would be a piece of gold placed between her lips for the child.

Shaking, Mar-teri crouched at her sisters' feet. The smell of alsar lingered from the night before, when everyone in the group had burned as much of the plant as they could gather, speeding the dead's journey away from this land. Mar-teri divided her small bundle of stems and minute white flowers into just two parts and dropped each at Nalna and Mara's feet. She clicked her fire-starter only once at each and the alsar caught. Thin smoke touched the tears on her face.

They were dead, they were gone, their illness unknown and untreatable by the group's medical unit. Mar-teri crouched at their feet, sobbing, saying their names. Her tears splashed on the alsar, leaving parts of it unburnt—but it was good smoke, nonetheless, for a long journey. Her sisters would do well. "Nalna, Mara, Natia, Civo, Nat-uvo..." She spoke the others' names too: "Tarici—" her father's new partner, still a stranger "—Elio, El-tuo, Peto, Teqi, Teq-tuo."

She cut bones from her sisters' toes, for remembrance.

Eventually the sky started to lighten, black to grey—and

orange, in the northeast, where the sky sickened—and she needed to return to her caravan.

When the sun came up, the dead would gleam gold, and how could the sky forget them then?

Mar-teri felt even sicker thinking that if the far-off people found this burial, they would probably strip the bodies of their wealth: easier mining than the ground.

She left her sisters—as her group would soon leave this part of the world, to join with another group and journey far to the south, to new, uninhabited lands. Forget Falna. Forget fighting. Mar-teri wanted nothing more to do with the far-off people.

These stones mark
your laugh, hanging in the air,
well-wrought as Narata's gold
and brighter,
brighter.

I do not know where your bones are.
—written by El-uvi on a marker stone for El-qaro, who was taken by the far-off people

New stones! New masks of wood and bones!
Sing fast like hooves,
Sing fast!
—sung by Mar-teri and Tala's joined group, after avenging the dead of Mar-teri's group

Viqa was a Tuvicen town. It grew and shrank throughout the year on the shores of Viqa Lake, at the base of the Elpeca Mountains. Only a few permanent structures sat alongside the lake: stone buildings for storage and shelter, if any Tuvicen needed them. Unadorned, they blended into the landscape, and when the town gathered it swallowed them like a stone wrapped in gold.

At the northwest side of the lake, pipelines drew water towards the far-off people's great farmlands. The Tuvicen avoided that shore.

There were so many groups.

Caravans of more than five—no, more than *ten* different colors clustered around the lake shore and along both sides of the river that ran down from the mountains to fill the lake. Mar-teri had never seen caravans of all those colors, never even heard of a dark orange caravan group or a black caravan group—never seen tents, either. Mountain groups.

Far across the grass in every direction except northwest, befil grazed, minded by sharp-eyed children. Mar-teri and Tala's group passed between their gazes.

They went around the lake, crossing the river on a stone bridge, and continued to the south shore. There, the group's children ran excitedly from caravan to caravan, unfastening the befil and leading them away to thicker grasses. Some of the adults carried lightness on them: the town meant trade, reuniting with siblings and children and friends, perhaps finding fun with other adults.

The orange sky was already faint on the northeastern horizon, half hidden by the mountains.

Mar-teri readied herself. In the privacy of her caravan she combed her hair and re-braided the parts of it she did not keep loose, tying slim gold bands to the braids' ends. She wore red trousers only, clean and bright. She wore every necklace she owned and many necklaces from her group, and she covered her wrists with thick, engraved bracelets. When she stepped down from her caravan, she felt the weight of her people's wealth on her body. *I will do this. I will speak for them well, to get what we need for our journey south.*

What she didn't know was what such a great number of groups gathering here meant.

Already people from her group worked at the shore, setting up the rarely used fishing nets and wading out to look for edible plants and crustaceans. Others prepared the felting and the weaving. One man collected clay for pot-making.

Those that Mar-teri walked past nodded at her with respect—all but two.

Less than a month had gone by since she had killed her father to take control of the group, to join it with Tala's and lead it to safety. Most had supported her—the orange sky and its sickness had demanded a drastic response. Any response! Her father had helped bury the ten dead and still hadn't believed in the threat they faced—had spat at Tala's feet when the two groups met. Mar-teri's well-placed spear had ensured the group's survival, but after such big changes, discomfort remained. Mar-teri suspected that she would be navigating it alongside the new land as they journeyed south.

First: ensuring they were fully prepared for that journey.

Together, Mar-teri and Tala set out for the nearest group.

Retracing their caravans' route around the lake, they first came to the circular, felted befil hair tents of a mountain group. Each tent's door was brightly painted—green and blue and yellow—and covered in words, so rich against the creamy-pale hue of the undyed felt. One tent, in the center of the group, was banded around with fabric in several shades of blue, like the sky.

The few befil grazing around the tents were long-haired, like all befil, but their hair looked thicker: thick enough to lose a person in, Mar-teri thought. The group had wrapped bright blue fabric around the befil's long, curling horns. A man stood by one, combing out its hair and collecting the thick, pale hanks, dropping them in a basket at his side.

"Their befil are adjusting to the warmer plains climate?" Mar-teri asked Tala, remembering a song.

"Yes." Tala led her between the tents. "This is Inaqa's group, unless their leadership has changed. I have only met with them once." They stopped by the blue-banded tent. One person sat outside, mending a sturdy undyed jacket. "I greet you," Tala said. "I am Tala, one leader of the green caravan group."

"I am Mar-teri, the second leader of the green caravan group."

"I am Nataga," she said, smiling—though her gaze lingered, curious, on Mar-teri, whose name was a child's. "I will take you inside to meet with Inaqa. She's resting at the moment, but I'm sure she'll be delighted to have guests." Nataga gathered up her work and went inside. The wind only gusted once before she opened the door to say, "Please do come in!"

The inside of the tent was dim and cool. Daylight slipped through an opening at one side of the slanted ceiling. Under it, Nataga crouched by a pot suspended over fire-bricks to stir milk and meat. It smelled of herbs that Mar-teri didn't recognize. Another person sat beside the pot, with wrists sheathed in gold.

"Inaqa," Tala said, sitting down beside her. They gripped wrists. "It's good to see you well."

"I must look better than I feel," Inaqa said, weary-voiced. Her loose-fitting tunic arced over a well-progressed pregnancy.

Tala laughed. "I'm glad that's all in my past."

"You must be! Seven." Inaqa shook her head. "I think I won't even have a second. I've been sick almost the whole time. At least *you* will be able to enjoy Nataga's cooking."

Nataga smiled across the pot.

Against the wall behind her, sheets and cushions made a high pile: evidence of the rest of Inaqa's family. Perhaps they too had recently arrived at Viqa and wanted to be outside, by the lake, between the lines of the distant horizon.

Mar-teri sat beside Tala, awkward as a blue thread in a red weave through this talk of pregnancy.

"And you are Mar-teri, a new second leader," Inaqa said, scrutinizing her after they gripped wrists.

"Yes. My group joined with Tala's shortly after I became a leader. Very shortly."

Inaqa laughed like a fox: short and harsh. "These are times of change, indeed."

"Many changes," Mar-teri said, wondering what Inaqa faced.

"You are newly arrived, then?" Inaqa asked.

"Yes, just after noon today."

"Well! Then you might not have heard that some hunters in my group discovered a small settlement being built by the far-off people in the mountains to the north of here. We are planning an attack on it to drive them away. We are still building our numbers and gathering information—we would be very glad to have your group join us."

In the silence that followed, Mar-teri glanced at Tala. Nothing in her expression or the way she sat indicated shock or curiosity or any emotion at all.

Nataga brought Mar-teri and Tala two big bowls of milk and meat and rice, steaming fragrantly. For politeness, Mar-teri ate several mouthfuls. It was an unfamiliar type of rice: long and black, chewy, more earthy than any other rice she had eaten. She liked it. She was not hungry.

"This is very good," Tala said. "Pepper? And esit?" Nataga nodded, her mouth full from a bowl of her own. Inaqa was not eating. "I thank you for your hospitality—and for your offer. We will consider it. What specifically is being planned?"

"Scouts from my group and Qaneri's are gathering information about the settlement," Inaqa said.

"The settlement is not under the orange sky, is it?" Tala asked urgently.

"No. We know that going under the orange sky kills. From experience." That last Inaqa said with bitterness.

"Ten of Mar-teri's people went under the orange sky. They all died. The medical unit couldn't diagnose their sickness, couldn't suggest a treatment."

Inaqa nodded. "I saw that news on the hub. Thank you for putting it there," she said to Mar-teri. "Two people of my group died a week before your ten. We were worried that our medical unit was outdated, even though it's less than ten years old and updates regularly."

"Ours is less than a year old," Mar-teri said. How helpless they had felt. How much gold it had cost, only to let ten of their people die!

Inaqa's lips twisted. "I suppose we should be wishing it was just a matter of updating our medical units."

They knew no more than their medical units about the cause of the sickness and the orange sky, just theories—useless as befil shit.

Unable to remember if she had put it on the hub, Mar-teri added, "There was an eleventh person, a child, who was taken by the far-off people under the orange sky, when she was still alive." The words tasted like sour milk in her mouth.

Inaqa and Nataga looked angry enough to throw spears.

"When the scouts give us the information about the settlement," Inaqa said, sharp-voiced, "we will decide how to attack. I'm sure your people will be glad of an opportunity to remove these far-off people from our lands."

Mar-teri nodded, not sure what to say. *We've already taken an opportunity to do that.* Just two weeks ago, they had found a small group of far-off people investigating the orange sky and killed them: vengeance for the ten buried near the orange sky and lost, stolen El-qaro. *Now they want to go south.* But anxiety lurched and gusted in her like hair in the wind—because she knew that while many people imagined their new lives and used the medical unit to access information about the topography and climate and fauna of the areas they might turn into their home, others quietly voiced frustration.

And now: a large attack. Something more meaningful than killing a handful of investigators and turning their equipment into glinting dust.

Or would it only be a chance to bury more people under the orange sky?

Tala turned the conversation onto other matters: the livelihood of Inaqa's people, the possibilities for trade, the children who might be suitable for exchanging. No decisions were reached. The nature of the attack on the far-off people's settlement would determine too much about the groups' futures, and Tala remained vague about her plans.

Burials stayed in Mar-teri's thoughts.

Eventually they left. They walked some distance from the blue-banded tent before Mar-teri asked, "What do you think about the attack?"

"We need to speak to Qaneri first. Do you know of sem?"

"No."

"Se is the great-grandchild of Falna and Tadi."

Mar-teri had heard of that group from her father's new partner, who had come from the other side of the mountains and met that group several times in se's childhood. The stories had mainly been of Falna and Tadi's grandchild, Faraqo, who had grown disillusioned by the failure of many attempts to drive away the far-off people—and had added frequently unsung lines to the end of Falna's song.

"Do you think it could work?" Mar-teri asked—wanting Tala to say *No.*

Tala sighed. "Impossible to say for certain. Unlikely." No. How could it work? There were so many far-off people. "Those grey caravans are Qaneri's," Tala said, gesturing ahead.

"They got them through the mountains?"

"There are one or two good routes, although it looks like se hasn't brought them all."

"Or they're a small group." There were seven caravans, as many as Mar-teri's group had owned before joining with Tala's group.

"No."

Tala set a quick pace to the grey caravans, which had two bands of stories around their exteriors. What stories would Falna and Tadi's descendants tell? Mar-teri hoped for the time to read—or hear—them later.

Qaneri was immediately recognizable from the amount of gold se wore: thick and bright as armor in a song.

"Tala!" Qaneri called out. "And who is this with you?"

"I am Mar-teri, the second leader of the green caravan group."

"Green now?"

"We have joined," Tala said, flat-voiced. "Tell me of this attack you wish to lead."

Qaneri's teeth flashed like bone knives as se spoke.

They learnt nothing more, but to hear Qaneri was important: to hear se's anger and ambition and hope, which put power in se's words.

Over bowls of milk and meat or skewers of fish or natari-sweet rice, they heard those words and wants reflected in people of other groups. How good it would be, to fight against the far-off people! To force them from these lands!

To be buried, Mar-teri thought, *under that sky.*

They walked back to their green caravans as the sun fell below the horizon, silent.

News travelled like the wind through Viqa: fast and strong. As Mar-teri walked along the star-bright dots of her group's fire-bricks, glances landed on her like spears. They knew. She crouched by Valiqa and Tema's fire-bricks, where fish grilled on long sticks.

"There will be an attack," Valiqa said, half-questioning.

"Yes."

"A lot of people want to be a part of it."

"El-uvi is ready to tear out throats now," Tema murmured, and Mar-teri wondered how much she—parent-less Tema, sibling-less Tema, who had burned too much alsar near the orange sky—shared the girl's longing for revenge.

She had grown up with Valiqa and Tema, who had been Til-qav and Teq-uvo before they married each other. She couldn't bear to imagine their deaths. Their wasted bodies—or bodies filled with burnt holes from the far-off people's energy weapons.

"What do you think?" Valiqa asked.

"I..." *I don't want it.* She imagined it: forcing the far-off people to leave their large settlement, putting an end to whatever activity was causing the orange sky—and would it recede? Would her group be able to return home? The longing hurt. Worse—stronger—was her doubt. Her memory of burials. "I want our safety. I want... I want everything Qaneri and the others want. But I'm not sure attacking the settlement will be the victory people want it to be."

They sat in an unhappy silence, waiting for the fish to finish cooking. *We were supposed to be safe,* Mar-teri thought, bitter as raw natari stems. When humans had come to this star system hundreds of years ago, settled some of the moons and terraformed this planet, the ancestors of the Tuvicen had left space craft and cities and come to the far side of the planet to make their own lives.

Safe until the far-off people needed this bit of the planet too.

Conversations hung in the air like clouds of midges. Soon they turned louder: into songs, into requests for drums and masks to be brought from the caravans.

The first full song, performed around a mound of fire-bricks, did not surprise Mar-teri.

It drew Mar-teri closer, to stand where the fire-bricks' light made her face glow. It always drew her.

They chose El-uvi as Falna. A bold statement: a person so young—and so focused on her hatred for the far-off people.

El-uvi bound the mask to her face: carved from the hefty shoulder blade of a befil, painted skin-brown and engraved with the lines of an older woman—the woman Falna had been by the end of her life—in bright yellow relief. Drums pounded a beat and El-uvi's gold-heavy braids swung as she danced, moving as if she fought unseeable people with her fists. Others gathered around her to sing the exclamations and the names of the dead.

El-uvi, in her high, fierce ten-year-old's voice, performed it well: Falna's grief at her birth-family's deaths, Falna's anger, revenge and triumph over the far-off people. The others shouted the names of the dead, unforgotten. El-uvi punched the air in front of her, like a spear-point entering flesh, and flung herself around the fire—and sang Falna's final lines loud enough that surely the satellites above their heads heard:

See me! Falna the fierce—

their weapons didn't kill us!

This power, this determination—what could stand in its way?

Mar-teri shivered, wanting that strength. Wanting it to be real: that with enough fighting, they could convince the far-off people to leave them alone.

In silence, the mask of Falna was put away and others were brought out. A dark mask splashed red like blood: a murdered man's song, mourning for the mine he had tried to defend. A mask left utterly bare of adornment, except for narrow gaps at the eyes and mouth: bone for a song of the long-ago-buried. A mask covered in blue fabric, the sky's blue, for the song of Tall Tihaqi, se who stood on the tallest mountain blowing out every wind that raced through the mountains and across the plains. But in that song, the dancer—Cani, a person as tall as Tihaqi, surely, as strong and full-lunged—improvised old lines into new ones, putting a promise into Tall Tihaqi's fabric-lipped mouth: that se would blow behind those who attacked the far-off people's settlement, lending them se's strength. No matter what songs were suggested, they turned back and back to the far-off people. The unending power of it blew over and into Mar-teri, as if she stood facing the wind with her mouth open. It filled her, it stung her.

She felt like fabric caught on a thorn: torn between her own hurt and anger and fear.

At one point, she murmured the final, un-sung lines of Falna's song. Their omission was an un-truth.

At another, she almost stepped forward to promise her presence in the attack.

And then there were three songs in a row about family. Not dead family, not bones. Masked and unmasked voices sang of life: generations of families in their caravans, living on the plains with no orange blemish in the sky, no far-off people wanting their land for tests, for farms, for factories, for the gold—and that echo of a line from Falna's song brought a sigh to Mar-teri's lips. The people of these families hunted, weaved, traded, carved poetry into the horns of their befil. They sat together—there were three sisters, part of a big family, so many generations and relations—and those three sisters sat under the stars, composing poetry together, mapping the constellations in verse—

There were three sister-dancers, arms linked—

Mar-teri slid away to hide her tears in the dark parts of the night.

At dawn, Mar-teri walked to the lake shore, to join the people already fishing: good, simple work to drive away the mess of her thoughts.

She saw tall, broad-backed Cani, apparently un-tired by the extent of the night's singing. She saw others, blinking away sleep as they waded out to collect baskets and set out nets. A white-backed crustacean was the baskets' main catch. The markings on its back looked like words. What would the stories of a crustacean be? Mar-teri helped remove the bigger ones from the baskets and bind their mud-brown pincers, ready for pots. The smaller ones were released.

And Mar-teri listened: to the slowness of conversation around her, to the few things said.

Cani was more direct. "Tell us, then," se said in the midst of nets and defiant pincer-clacks, "when is this attack? Will we be joining it?"

Heads turned.

Mar-teri straightened her back and said, in as level a voice as she could, "Tala and I are still discussing the attack."

"You'll let some other group's leader decide our actions?"

"We are one group now," she said, aware that people from Tala's original group worked with them—aware that several of her own group had murmured agreement with Cani's question. Others had not. Some had indicated their agreement with her instead. Too many opinions butted against each other, like female befil grazed too close, and she could not force an opinion on them all—not here, not without debate. Not without much more agreement. "There is a lot to consider."

"What, exactly?"

"Safety."

"You'll let those far-off people force us away from here? From our land?"

She opened her mouth—there were no words in it, nothing but burials and fear that the group would not go south.

"That land is nearly gone!" someone else—the surviving father of El-uvi—said. "Lost under that orange sky!"

"And that doesn't make you want to fight?" Cani shouted. "We thought we had no chance to strike back, nothing to do but run, but that's not true! Qaneri will lead us in an attack that will force the far-off people to leave this land alone."

"Might," Mar-teri said, as loud as Cani, though her stomach twisted like nets in a current.

No one in the thigh-deep water was working now. Nets and crustacean-filled baskets still in hand, they stood, listening: looking at Cani and Mar-teri with longing, surprise, anger.

"We don't know if it will change anything," Mar-teri added.

"It is a chance! Will you let that just drift by? Slink away with your neck lowered like a submissive equ?"

"We might all die!" she shouted.

Cani turned to others, saying to them, "We might not lose this. Imagine it! A chance to stay in our own lands!" Their excitement was palpable, thick as pollen on an early summer wind over grasslands. How quickly this had happened. It was like nets falling from her hands and swept away. To Mar-teri, Cani said, "What is there to discuss?"

"More than this." Mar-teri walked away, hating every step, hating herself for not finding the words to convince Cani—and the others, whose voices rose in conversation at her back. Deciding to join the attack?

Hating the far-off people, for bringing this to them.

The two story-backed crustaceans she gave to the people tending the morning's pots, where a rich broth would soon bubble. Beyond them was Tala's caravan. At its curtained entrance, she asked to talk with Tala, but when Tala granted permission she didn't enter—she stayed in the doorway, curtain held aside, her hand shaking on the fabric. "Maybe we should join the attack," she said, with the wind tangling the unbraided parts of her hair around the backs of her arms, "and then go south, then—after."

Tala regarded her with a face like a half-finished mask, painted but not carved: ungrooved with emotion. "If there are people from your original group who want to join the attackers, you must convince them otherwise."

"It isn't just the people from my group."

At that, Tala frowned. "What have you been hearing?"

Mar-teri recounted the conversation in the lake: how Cani's fervor spread, how people of Tala's group joined se's enthusiasm. "And did you hear the singing last night? How every other song was about fighting back or attacking or something that mentioned the far-off people and how we could chase them away. How El-uvi was given Falna's mask!"

"We won't rid this land of them," Tala said, firm as a mountain. "Anyone who believes otherwise is a fool."

"They say it's like we're just running away. Like an equ with its neck lowered."

"It *is* running away. *Surviving.*"

Mar-teri knew how Cani would see that statement: not as

difficult truth but as weakness. They were like a poorly set warp and the weft that would not weave into it, and she didn't know how to fix it, not now.

"I suspect there will be a meeting of all the leaders today," Tala said—adding, with distaste in her voice, "as well as other people, no doubt." People like Cani? "In the meantime, we must talk with our people."

"Yes." If any of them would still listen to her.

"We will do it together," Tala said. "Our group is one, after all."

But at the shore, Cani and several others were gone: holding their discussion elsewhere in Viqa.

The leaders gathered in a place where natari grew thick on the ground, scenting everyone's legs. They sat by several pots, passing around bowls of fermented befil milk and food and talking loudly.

Mar-teri was so much younger than the other leaders. Among white and grey-streaked braids and bearded chins, among people who wore age on their faces like fine tattoos, she stood out. Did they see her as a child or a woman?

She spoke out, not letting her age silence her.

A few welcomed her, pleased to see her father replaced. Others regarded her with open suspicion—a leader who had killed the past leader, her own father, to take control—or a disinterest as heavy as befil bones.

Conversation circled around the attack.

One important piece of business, with so many groups gathered, was the exchange of children: an important way to ensure each group's genetic diversity. Mar-teri, who had begun to broach the subject with the people of her original group, listened carefully. Of her people, she said, "There are two children already interested in moving groups. They have no preference for where they go, although one said he would love to see the mountains." And there was El-uvi, who had left her felting to tell Mar-teri that if going to a different group meant a surer chance to attack the far-off people, she wanted to move.

If only Mar-teri could swap all of the people in her group who wanted to fight—but what group would she have left?

As the shadows lengthened, the conversation left children and trade and news.

Qaneri set out a unit on the natari. It projected five images: a settlement of white mounds—nothing like Inaqa and Nataga's tents, not bright-doored or sashed with blue—and white devices and the far-off people, white-garbed, all within a white wall. The images were from higher ground. "These," Qaneri said, holding everyone's attention like a fishhook, "are the first images of the far-off people's settlement in the mountains, near the edge of the orange sky. With these, we can begin to plan our attack."

"You speak as if everyone has already decided that they will do this," Tala said, drum-loud.

"Has your group decided not to join the attack?" Qaneri asked.

"Has yours? My group is undecided: some want to attack, some do not. From what I have heard, all groups are similarly split."

"Those who do not wish to fight will wait in a safe location, as in any other attack."

They could do that, Mar-teri thought—but what then? Would Cani and the others come south after the attack? It seemed that south had been discarded: an old plan, Mar-teri's plan, not Cani's.

"And those who attack," Tala said, "they will kick dust into the far-off people's faces and hope that it will keep them away?" No one liked that. Anger leapt up around the pots, in glares and hisses and thumped earth, as if Tala and Mar-teri sat with teeth-bared foxes. "Do you really think that you can stop these people? Do you really think your deaths will mean anything?"

Even Mar-teri hissed. What words—

Qaneri's hand clenched, as if around a spear. "You spit on our deaths before they have even occurred!"

"I do not wish to see any of us dead! Not under that sky, and not fighting for no gain—for just a temporary revenge."

"Revenge." Qaneri spat. "Yes, it is that, but it is not the squabbling of two groups who cannot agree upon the boundaries of their routes. It's about keeping these people out of our land! Not all of us are prepared to give up on our land as easily as you are."

Mar-teri wanted to punch sem in the face—or drag sem out to the ten burials. Show sem what the far-off people had done. "Some of us," she said, fighting to keep insults away from her tongue, "do not have the luxury of choosing whether or not to hold onto our lands. Mine are almost all under the orange sky: lost lands. Dead. How nice it must be for you, to still have something to fight for."

"How readily you act as if we do not."

"I—"

"These are our lands. We will fight for them."

Shouts thundered like befil hooves. Mar-teri closed her eyes against it, silently repeating the last lines of Falna's song—a later addition by Faraqo, grandson of Falna, old and angry and tired.

See the far-off people's craft!

How they fly like chives re-growing.

How she wanted Falna's other lines to be truer, but all she could believe in was that final pair.

"If we do this," she heard someone say, loud above the consensus, "then they will know not to come back to this place!"

"Ha!" Tala said. "Qaneri, tell me, how many far-off people did Falna and Tadi and their children kill?"

"Over a hundred," Qaneri replied, "but individually or in small groups, never so many in one place."

A whole hundred! Mar-teri started to laugh, and suddenly

a lot of people were looking at her: more faces in the twilight gloom than just the leaders. "Do you realize how many of them there are? There are billions of people on Cai Nu." And though it was millions of kilometers away, a moon orbiting another world, it was not far enough. "*Billions.* And billions more in the cities here on Krak-vi. If this thing the far-off people are doing here is important to them—and it is, because why else would they remain in this area—then they will find a few hundred more scientists out of their billions and billions of people. And they will find a few hundred people to defend their new compound. And they will bring more weapons. And they will get rid of us, if they need to, and *we* will not re-grow like chives."

Several people winced, hearing those words. Others nodded. So not everyone agreed with Qaneri.

"We will not give up," someone said from beyond the firebricks' glow. Cani.

And shouts thundered again.

When they quietened, Qaneri said, "We will plan our attack carefully."

"We will convince them that this is the wrong place for their work," Cani said.

"We don't know why they are here!" Mar-teri said. "We don't know what it would take to get them to leave."

"We will attack," Cani went on, as if she had said nothing, "and then we will hide. The mountains are so big and we—" looking at Mar-teri, "—are so few. If they return, we will attack again."

Beside sem stood three others from their group. Determination gleamed like wealth.

Tala placed her bowl on the natari and pushed herself to her feet. "I think you are a group of fools," she said, her voice as flat as the western horizon, and she turned her back on them. No one spoke as she walked away. Several people followed: all of them people that Mar-teri hadn't known before this meeting.

Everyone remaining looked at Mar-teri, expectation clear on her their faces: she should leave too.

Mute, Mar-teri stood—and then realized there was something else she wanted to say, though the conversation had resumed around her. She said, loud enough to carry across the pots and voices, "I want to lead my people to life!"

But Cani shouted, "What if your people don't want that distant life? What if they want a life *here*?"

Without the moons' light, Mar-teri walked cautiously through the town, trying to navigate by the few amber dots of fire-bricks: an unreliable constellation. Tala and the ones who had followed her must have walked in a different direction. None of their voices carried clearly. Mar-teri tripped over pots left out to dry. She walked right into a befil, not even smelling it in time, and yelled her frustration into its long hair. In this blackness, she couldn't see her own feet, couldn't tell her direction except for the innate sense that guided her this way, this way—into more pots, rocks, sudden dips in the land. A cold wind made her shiver. Fists clenched, she kept walking.

Would Tema join the attack? Would Valiqa? Would they be buried like her sisters, side-by-side, not wasted away but bloodied, burned. Alsar-toed. Bones.

Tears stung Mar-teri's eyes. They wouldn't die. They wouldn't. They—

She hit something solid with her whole body. A tent. A door opened, painting light across the crumpled grass. "Is someone outside?" asked a familiar voice. Nataga.

"Um, I'm..." *Lost. Can you lend me a light so I can get back to my caravan?* The words wouldn't come out. Mar-teri didn't want to go back to her caravan—to what? A group that wanted mountains and attack, not her plans? A group that had once contained her family, small and flawed but *hers.*

Now there was no comfort there, only loneliness. Utter

solitude on her cushions.

Tears fell over her cheeks like rain in the mountain-stories.

Nataga stepped outside and let the door nearly close behind her, turning the night dark again. "Is there anything I can do to help you?"

Mar-teri managed to say, "I couldn't find my way back to my caravan. It's so dark."

"Would you like me to walk you there? I have a light."

"Yes."

Nataga ducked inside to fetch the light, which burned moons-white. In its light, Mar-teri saw that Nataga was dressed for sleep: bereft of wealth, her feet only in slippers, her hair unbound. The tight fastening of her hair in the day had made it look far shorter; it fell to her thighs, straighter than Mar-teri's, but just as thick and dark. It was beautiful. It looked like something a lover would see, and Mar-teri blushed, looking away, though clearly Nataga saw no need to bind it up outside her tent.

The ease of walking beside someone in clear light didn't still Mar-teri's fears.

Would everyone in her group go? Would she go south alone, utterly alone? Just her and a befil—and madness. Not another voice. Not another hand gripped in dance. No, she would join another group: offer her skills with hunting, cooking, singing.

Would every group go?

"Has your group decided what it's going to do?" she asked, in an imperfect, weak voice. "About the attack?"

"Some people want to go. Some people don't."

"Oh."

"Inaqa isn't sure what to do about it," Nataga added, weary-voiced.

One of Inaqa's siblings had represented her in the meeting—had walked away after Tala.

"My group wants to go. Well..." Cani and se's supporters. El-uvi. Tema? And there were others who had followed Mar-teri when the other option was her father's refusal to act, but now, given a chance to fight back, might no longer look south. "Everyone. Most of them. I... I lost all my family under that orange sky! All of it." Her father had barely counted as family. "I don't have any family left to die but I still don't want to go, I don't want people to die, I don't..."

She felt useless, blown about in the wind, like natari torn up from the ground and scattered across rocks kilometers apart.

At her side, Nataga walked: a presence as reassuring as a marker stone in the midst of the plains.

"I don't want to go," Nataga said. "I want the attack to succeed, but... I don't want to be a part of it."

Silence fell on them companionably. In it, Mar-teri dried her face and regained some of her steadiness.

"I suppose I'm selfish," Nataga finally said. "I don't want to die."

"I don't either."

I am not a fucking clump of natari. But nothing felt resolved: Mar-teri's thoughts tangled and hurt.

Soon they reached the place where Mar-teri's group had set up its caravans. Several people sat together, wrapped in blankets against the cold wind. Fire-bricks glowed between them. Mar-teri recognized Valiqa and Tema—and three others, including her cousin Lata, who had all come into her caravan not so many weeks ago to plan the union with Tala's group, the journey south.

Her caravan—and sleep, easy, conflictless sleep—were so close.

"I'm going to join them," she said to Nataga. "Thank you for helping me find my way back here. And for talking to me."

Nataga gripped her arm in parting. "I hope we have a chance to talk again."

Then Nataga strode away, a quickly receding glow amid the dark camp, and Mar-teri approached the small group. Fear tried to still her legs. She stopped where the fire-bricks illuminated some of her body and asked, "May I join you?"

"Of course!" Valiqa said.

"Would you like some milk?" Tema asked.

A small pot bubbled on some of the fire-bricks. Everyone had a bowl in their hands or laps, warm against the night. Mar-teri shivered.

"Sit here," Tema said. "You can share our blanket."

Under the thick felt, with a hot bowl between her hands, Mar-teri felt stronger: less alone, less adrift. One side of her body was pressed against Tema, who was warm like rocks in the sun, and her other knee touched Lata's.

When Lata asked, "Is the big meeting over?" she didn't entirely want to flee.

The bright glow across the lake plainly stated that some people still stood there.

"I left," she managed, then sipped her milk. No one spoke. She needed to. "I have been talking to Nataga," she said, relieved at the steadiness of her voice, "who is important in Inaqa's group, one of the mountain groups with those tents instead of caravans. She told me that their group is divided too, between those who want to join the attack and those who do not. They haven't decided what to do."

"You're still against the attack, then?" Valiqa asked.

Mar-teri looked down at her swirling, pale milk. "I am."

"This is our land," Lata said, hot-voiced, angry.

"I know."

Mar-teri suddenly felt so weary that she thought she could fall asleep if she leaned against Tema.

"I don't want to join the big attack," Tema said. "I want to live somewhere—anywhere, though I'd prefer here. It's beautiful here and it's ours. But if the far-off people are doing their work here, perhaps..." Sadness filled her voice. "Perhaps this means we cannot live here anymore."

"What do you want to do after the attack?" Mar-teri asked Lata.

Lata frowned. "I suppose it depends on what happens."

"I know that Cani wants to stay here afterwards, to hold onto the land. I want to go south." With what people? Tema and Valiqa—if she shared her wife's reluctance to join the attack—and Tala and a handful of others. Too small a group. Unviable.

"I'm not sure," Lata said. "I'll have to think about it. I think I'd rather stay with your part of the group, though."

The two men murmured agreement.

Oh.

"I'm not sure what will happen," Mar-teri said, when the silence started to fill with yawns. She was so tired too, unable to put all these thoughts together: the knowledge of so many different desires among her group and others.

Lata gazed into the fire-bricks as if answers might appear on them, like a medical unit's screen. Then she got up, shaking out her blanket, and wished everyone a good night. The men stood too and drifted away into the night.

It was only Mar-teri and Tema and Valiqa, huddled under their heavy blanket. Valiqa started turning off the fire-bricks. The night got colder. Mar-teri sipped the last of her milk and thought of her caravan, silent and empty. With such a cold wind blowing, almost everyone would sleep in their caravans, packed close together: surrounded by breath, life.

As they stood, Mar-teri said, "Would you like to sleep in my caravan tonight? There's so much space."

"I'd like that," Tema said.

"Yeah." Valiqa chuckled. "There's no snoring in your caravan either."

"Oh," Tema said before dissolving into laughter—and Mar-teri felt adrift again, without a family's nighttime antics to bring mirth in the morning. How Nalna had kicked in her sleep. How her little cousin, years ago given to another group, had sleep-talked about flighted birds made of fire.

"Come on," Valiqa said, and led them all by the meager light of a fire-brick—stumbling over pots, laughing—to Marteri's caravan, where they slept side-by-side like sisters.

Mar-teri woke with realization hanging around her like wealth: heavy and welcome.

A warm breeze greeted her at the caravan's entrance. There she stood and saw that the fishing was underway, the pots were already bubbling, the felting would soon resume for the day. People were talking.

By one of the pots, Tala argued loudly with Cani and three people from her original group. Mar-teri walked to them—feeling foolish for the night's fears when now she was barely nervous.

"Can I speak?" she said, when the shouting did not abate.

"I welcome it," Tala said.

"No doubt it will be as useless as what she said last night," one of Cani's allies said, not even looking at her.

Cani flicked a displeased look at him, saying, "Let her speak," though reluctance filled se's voice like milk in a bowl.

"What we are discussing is too important," Mar-teri said, "for anyone to be forced, to be obliged to follow their group and leaders. Cani and many others want to fight the far-off people. Tala and I and others want to go south. Our group will have to split along a new line—unless those who fight the far-off people want to come south afterwards. Then we need to wait. But I do not think many of those who want to fight the far-off people want to go south."

"No," Cani said. "We will remain here. It was agreed with the other groups last night."

Did Lata know of that now? Did everyone?

How quickly Cani had taken control of the group.

Tala turned to Mar-teri with anger like new tattoos on her face. "We are to let our people throw themselves at the far-off people and, if they survive, wait to die in these lands when the orange sky spreads, while we few with sense go south, so few that we might not survive. If I had wanted to take a small group south, I would not have bothered to join with yours."

"Yours *will* be a very small group," Cani murmured.

Their words bit into Mar-teri like spear points. She smiled. "Not too small, once we have talked to every group and offered to let anyone who wants to get far away from the far-off people join us. I know there are people reluctant to fight in some groups. Perhaps they share our fear that this attack won't be enough."

Cani nodded. "Then perhaps it will work."

"It will."

Tala's expression remained unpleasant.

"We also," Mar-teri said, "need to find out if any of the attackers from our group—and other groups—want to come south afterwards."

"They will stay here," Cani said, "as agreed."

"No," Mar-teri said. "We will let them do what they want. We will go some way south, I think, to a place we can wait for several months before beginning our long journey with a full group."

"People are fighting to keep these lands," Cani said, stone-hard.

"People are fighting—and not fighting—for many reasons." Mar-teri thought of saying more, of listing every reason she knew, but realized that that was enough.

"So you will steal from my group by offering the choice of attacking and going south?" Cani said.

Tala laughed. "As you are splitting from our group, I do not think it is your place to complain about those who would rather stay." To Mar-teri, she said, "You will need to talk to everyone in our group today, and begin talking to other groups. I want to make the first leg of our journey soon."

"I will."

"And I will look through the maps for a suitable stopping place," Tala said. "While we find additional people, we need to exchange some children, ensure excess fish are caught and dried for our stores, trade for some of Inaqa's medicinal herb harvest..."

So much work. The thought of it couldn't take the smile from Mar-teri's face.

With the other groups, the exchange of children was a good beginning: easy, from there, to lead to her sundering group's plan. The first conversations went well.

At Inaqa's group, she gained Nataga's help.

"I've spent most of my life moving between groups," Nataga explained, crouching outside the door to Inaqa's tent. Inside, Inaqa's wife—who was the second mother of Inaqa's baby, biologically and practically—helped Inaqa, along with several siblings. The baby had been born easily in the night. "I know a lot of people. Besides," she added, lowering her voice, "I'd like a break from the baby."

Nataga's presence helped smooth introductions and, before they entered each tent or caravan, she offered Mar-teri advice about the leader's likely reaction. At two groups they only spoke to the leader about the usual transfer of children, then went to other people to quietly make their offer.

The transfer of children was concluded by sunset. Some of the children in Mar-teri and Tala's group were already going with their families to Cani's new group, making the rest simple: El-uvi joined Qaneri's group and one other child went independently to a different group. Mar-teri and Tala's group gained twelve children, due in part to several groups with enough children that they did not need any in return.

The adults who wanted to join them, whether alone or with some or all of their families, arrived more slowly.

Some came immediately, bringing their family's befil and caravan—or tent. One mountain family, mostly relatives of Nataga, were too frightened by the far-off people's settlement in the mountains to stay. They brought another pair from their group. Some promised to join Mar-teri and Tala's group when it departed, but said that they needed to discuss with their families and the rest of their groups what they could bring. "If you can bring befil," Mar-teri always told them, "that will be most useful. We'll need a big herd. And supplies of dry food, if possible." Others came in pairs with only one or two possessions and asked Mar-teri to join the group, offering their skills with hunting or weaving or finding medicinal plants or singing. One person came alone. Mar-teri welcomed them all. After five days, Tala said that their group might be big enough when they departed.

"Which will be soon," Tala added.

"We need to wait a bit longer. People are still coming."

"Two more days."

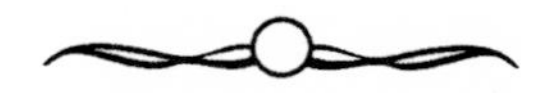

See the bones in her hair!
How they sing out the names of the dead!
—from the *Song of Falna*

With the main business between all of the groups at Viqa complete—the attack's date decided, its strategy nearly planned—someone suggested a befil race, and the departure of Mar-teri and Tala's group was delayed by another day.

"Soon," Mar-teri reassured Tala. "Once everyone's hangovers have passed."

Tala snorted. "At least it will give our patched-together group a chance to get drunk together. A few songs, a few sore heads, and we'll all be friends."

"Then we'll paint the new caravans green and be on our way!"

"If it is that easy *after* we leave, I will eat a bowl of hair."

Separately, they went among their group, talking and watching and hoping—at least, Mar-teri hoped, imitating Tala, who hopefully knew from some experience—that this would help to ease the joining of so many people.

Mar-teri wondered when the anxiety that matted in her

stomach like felt would stop. *Never,* she guessed.

When she saw Nataga among her relatives, watching the preparations for the race, she joined her.

Though El-uvi would leave the group soon, the girl announced her intention to race one of its finest befil—and recruited several of the new children to help her prepare it. They braided its long fur, strung bells along its sides, painted its horns green and selected the finest fabrics to go on its back. Arguments raged: each child pointed to another's work, insisting that it was the best. One of the new boys pointed to another boy's fabric, which was lost under the continuous embroidery—geometric patterns as bold as the mountains against the sky—and shouted that nothing beat that.

"He has a point," Mar-teri murmured.

Nataga chuckled. "It's beautiful work, isn't it? We trade with his birth-group often. Those patterns are passed down within families—hopefully, if he has children, he will pass the patterns to them."

"Our patterns were our routes. We covered our cushions and befil-fabrics with them." Children would grow up only knowing those routes from threads. Mar-teri smiled as El-uvi and the others agreed on the mountain boy's fabric and spread it over the befil's back. The children cheered at the sight of it. Surely none would be finer! Then, of course, everyone wanted to see El-uvi practice riding—and join her, two or three or four on the befil's back—and the air filled with excited screams.

"There will be new patterns," Nataga said, subdued. "And, I hope, the old ones will be usable again, one day."

"Maybe." For now, they lay under plainer or meaningless designs in Mar-teri's caravan. It hurt to look at them.

"How far do you think you'll go?"

"Tala and I haven't decided yet. We need to see the land for ourselves, look for a good place, fertile, well-watered. A place we can be self-sufficient. But far. We both want to go far."

Nataga nodded. "What are you going to do about medical supplies? Come back when they run out?"

"Some people will have to, if we need something the medical unit can't manufacture or if there's a bad illness or a complicated surgery's needed."

Nataga laughed as one of the boys—her nephew—stood on the befil's back, both hands out in the air. His long braids flicked out behind him like the befil's tail. "I'm thinking of joining your group," she said, "if I would be welcome? The only question is: I haven't yet decided if I want to have the surgery to remove my penis. The hormones make such a difference, but I might still want the surgery. Will that be possible?"

Shock stiffened Mar-teri's tongue: the surprise of Nataga's request and the pleasure of it. She had enjoyed talking to Nataga. Now she did not need to lose that friendship—now it could be built like a marker stone. "Of course you would be welcome," she said. "Definitely. And we would definitely be able to give you that surgery, wherever we are—our surgeon, Valiqa's mother, is staying with us, and she's excellent—and our medical unit will manufacture the hormones."

"Thank you." Nataga smiled into the wind, which still brought the distant shouts of the children.

"Won't Inaqa miss you?" Mar-teri said, hesitant, not wanting to step into private business.

"I'll see her again. We're both far too young for that not to be the case. And so many of my family are going south, and it's been too long since I've lived with them. Come on, I want to show you something."

The bright befil and most of the children were dots on the horizon.

Nataga led Mar-teri to her family's tent—where someone had already woven a small strip of lichen-dyed fabric and tied it to the door-post, its loose ends swaying in the wind like hair—and past it, towards an older befil, a female with its racing days behind it.

Nataga and Mar-teri waved at Nataga's grandmother as they walked by the tent. The old woman looked up from her work of sorting equ feathers and smiled back. Beside her, cushion covers waited for their contents.

"Look," Nataga said. "The horns."

At a distance they looked darker, grey rather than creamy-pale. No. *Patterned.*

Black-filled lines covered the horn, so old it curved twice. The befil placidly let Mar-teri examine it. The lines denoted mountains: rows and rows of them circled the horn, mountains above mountains, from the arm-thick base to the tapering tip. "There's no horizon," Mar-teri murmured, running her finger from peak to peak to peak. Scattered among them were details: befil, people, tents, plants. Not even at the top was there sky, though shallowly scraped clouds hugged some mountain-sides. Tall Tihaqi blew from an un-pictured mountain. The six-winged mirnu birds, which nested only on the tallest peak, were not here.

"There isn't, really," Nataga said. "In the mountains, you're always surrounded: peaks and slopes and trees—and clouds, always getting in the way. There's no line that neatly marks land from sky. And you can climb up and up and there are more mountains on the other side."

She spoke with her eyes narrowed, as if against the mountains' sleet.

"You don't look like you could live anywhere else," Mar-teri said.

"Oh," Nataga said, smiling, "I always have the mountains with me. I've left them plenty of times before." She patted the befil on the hard, short-haired place between its horns. At Mar-teri's guess, it had at least another five years of life left in it. "And where this group is going, the land will not be flat like this."

"True."

Mar-teri glanced at Nataga's cheeks. There were the circles for betrothal, as on Mar-teri's cheeks, and the lines for marriage, but no more. No lines for important times, no circles for separation and re-marriage. Mar-teri had already heard the explanation from one of Nataga's relatives: a marriage that lasted only one year, then living unwed from group to group.

At least Mar-teri would not be the only unwed adult.

She knew that in these last remaining days at Viqa she should have been looking for a partner among the young or separated people of the other groups. Tala had said it, outright. Valiqa had suggested it. As a leader she technically didn't need to—and there had been too much to think of that. It would be strange to remain Mar-teri for months or years: to be an adult with a child's name. Or could she change it without marrying?

Nataga's situation was rarer, stranger: a young person without a marriage for over five years, unsafe if their group sundered. Such a life occurred rarely in stories and songs.

"We'll be an interesting group," Mar-teri said, stroking the befil's mountainous horn.

"Yes. The songs are going to be like no one else's—"

A drumbeat stopped their words. The race would soon begin. Mar-teri and Nataga hurried to the place by the lake's shore where forty-three gleaming, garish, glorious befil gathered, their riders equally bright.

Of course there would be new songs, unique green caravan songs: a collaboration between the new lands and the people. Mar-teri wanted to hear them already.

The quickening drumbeat tied her to the present. The riders paraded their befil and everyone judged their appearance. El-uvi's got many favorable remarks—as did another from Mar-teri's group, its long hair braided and clattering with fish bones. Then, at the drums' silence, the riders readied their befil. Then, with a shaking of the ground like an earthquake, they raced: away to a distant turning point, then back. Silence hung over the group by the lake, watching the receding dots and the cloud of dust, waiting to see who would return first.

It happened quickly. Mar-teri shouted to see the bone-strung befil and El-uvi's befil both near the front. They came third and fifth, but the beauty of El-uvi's befil earned her one of the winning positions. Mar-teri and Qaneri both congratulated her, promising bowls of meat and fermented milk as soon as the pots were heated.

"She will bring strength to your group," Mar-teri said to Qaneri, still awkward around sem.

"We are glad to welcome her."

They could have parted then, but—as El-uvi encouraged several children to get on the befil with her for a victory race—Mar-teri added, "Fight well. I hope you rid this land of the far-off people."

"As do I."

They shared a brief smile.

The pots did not take long to heat. Mar-teri ate and drank with the disparate people of her group, hoping that it was not just the alcohol that made her imagine good knots forming between them all. Stories were sung. Masks were brought out: all so varied, the masks of many groups. Some songs needed to be taught to some people. Even if they did not know all the words, they cheered and cried together.

In the midst of the evening, Mar-teri went to Cani's group, where one of the women performed Falna's song and Cani took the role of Tadi, striking first.

They didn't sing the final lines.

"What have you come here to say?" Cani said, afterwards, in front of the whole group.

"I offer you bones from the feet of my sisters," Mar-teri said, holding out a piece of blue fabric that contained four of the bones, "to wear in your hair when you attack the far-off people's settlement. May they lend you strength."

Cani took the bones, quiet—and everyone was silent as se received this gift.

"I thank you," se said finally.

"I want there to be no anger between us," Mar-teri said. "My anger is for the far-off people."

"And mine."

Someone brought string. Mar-teri and Cani together tied the bones into Cani's hair. "May Nalna and Mara go with you," Mar-teri said, wet-eyed as they fastened the final bone: a toe, still faintly scented with alsar.

Her sisters' other feet-bones she would tie into her hair as her group rode south.

The hangovers did not last long. The new members of the green caravan group painted their caravans, helped by the others. Readiness coursed in them like blood.

In her empty caravan, Mar-teri heated the tattooing metal. Names circled like foxes around a burial, vying for ownership. Anaqa: the first name she had wanted, at just four years old, after meeting a so-named woman whose dancing strength she admired. Niva: a woman of childhood stories, who had mated with a flighted bird to produce the equ. Bold Niva, who had wooed her winged love with her sprinting speed and perfect pitch. Qena: the name she had considered during the end of her confinement, because it was like the word 'sky'.

Fara: one that had occurred to her just the night before. The sun's name. Whatever new land she led her group to, it would be under that sun. A strong name, because the sun never stopped burning. An arrogant name.

The metal was tattoo-hot. Mar-teri opened the jar of black ink.

With a steady hand, she drew the first line: a bold vertical line, alongside her other tattoos on her left cheek.

There, in the place between her old name and her new name, she said, "My name is Fara."

She drew the second line, on her right cheek.

When she had tidied away the metal and ink and brazier, she stepped outside. Tala waited for her.

"Who are you?"

"Fara."

Amusement twisted Tala's lips, but she kept to the usual words. "Welcome, Fara. May you bear your name well."

Especially that one, Fara thought. "I plan to."

With the sun resting on all of them like hot, bright wealth, the green caravan group departed.

It would take two weeks to reach the temporary stopping place that Tala had chosen: a good valley, tucked into the edge of the mountains, well suited for awaiting the rest of their group.

Fara rode the befil that pulled her caravan. A wind born far to the south coaxed songs from the gold on the ends of her braids and scraped her sisters' newly fastened toe bones against her cheeks. She looked back, sometimes, at the orange sky—at the lands she might never see again. She looked at Tala and Valiqa and Tema and Nataga and the new children, who rode with a bit of the race still in them. She looked forward.

She sang the songs of journeying, loud and clear—and approaching happy.

As the days passed, she imagined two masks that she would make when she had access to wood again: masks for a new song, one sad, one joyful, both skin-dark, marked with the contours of their new lands.

Mimesis

Martha Wells

Jade spotted Sand as he circled down from the forest canopy, a grasseater clutched in his talons. She said, "Finally." It would be nice to eat before dark, so they could clear the offal away from the camp without attracting the night scavengers.

It was Balm who said, "I don't see Fair."

Jade frowned, scanning the canopy again. They were standing in the deep grass of the platform they had chosen to camp on, and it was late afternoon in the suspended forest and getting difficult to hunt by sight. The open canyons under the heavy canopies of the immense mountain-trees were filled with green shadow. The breeze stirred jungles of foliage that grew on the platforms formed and supported by the immense intertwined tree branches. Raksuran eyes were designed to track movement, and between flocks of colorful birds, treelings, flying frogs and lizards and the myriad of other life, the whole forest was moving. But after a heartbeat's concentration, Jade could see there was no one else flying anywhere near Sand.

She turned to Balm, lowering her voice so the other warriors wouldn't hear. "Why did I think it was a good idea to send them off together?"

"I thought it was a good idea, too." Balm shrugged her spines helplessly. "I just can't think why at the moment."

Jade growled in her throat and waited for Sand to land.

She should have known something was wrong. Sand and Fair had been gone too long; Aura, Serene, and Balm had already had time to put together a lean-to for shelter on the platform where they had decided to camp. Now Serene and Aura sat by the fire pit in their soft-skinned groundling forms, watching Sand's solo approach with sour expressions. Aura muttered, "Male warriors shouldn't be allowed out of the court until they're old enough to know better."

Serene laughed. "When is that, exactly?"

Balm caught Jade's expression, then said to the other two warriors, "That's not helpful."

Serene and Aura subsided. Balm was Jade's clutchmate and they had been born within moments of each other; it gave her an authority over the other warriors, though Balm occasionally had to demonstrate her fighting ability to prove it.

Jade tried to keep her spines from bristling. If Fair and Sand had gotten into a fight, at least it had happened on the way back from their trading visit.

Fair was a warrior of Pearl's faction and Jade had brought him along because he was young and seemed less hard-headed than the usual run of male warriors who attached themselves to the reigning queen. She had wanted to give him a chance to spend time with warriors of her own faction. As sister queen, Jade had a soul-deep bond with every member of the court, though at her young age she didn't always feel it. It wasn't necessarily her duty to try to make the warriors all get along whether they liked it or not, but the Court of Indigo Cloud had become increasingly divided for the past few turns. Fighting off the Fell and moving to the new colony had forced them all to pull together for a while, and she wanted to encourage that to continue by making the warriors of the different factions interact more. It had seemed a good idea at the time. It still seemed a good idea.

Sand cupped his wings at the last moment, dropped the grasseater to the platform with a thud, and landed nearby. He folded his wings, shook his spines out, and looked around as if surprised everyone was staring pointedly at him. He said, "I got a nice fat grasseater."

Aura, before Jade could, said, "Where's Fair?"

Sand looked around again, his spines starting to flatten in dismay. "He's not here?"

Jade hissed. "No, you can see he's not here. Did you—" *Lose him somewhere and just fail to notice until now?* she started to say, but managed to hold it in. Acid sarcasm was Pearl's habit. Jade didn't think it was a good way to deal with the warriors, no matter how tempting it was at times. "—split up?"

"Yes. I mean, we didn't have a fight." Sand was genuinely upset, which did help calm Jade's urge to slap him senseless. "We saw a few different platforms with grasseaters, but all the herds were too small for both of us to hunt. Fair said he was going after the hoppers."

Jade saw the others' expressions turning from annoyance to real worry, and felt her own spines start to bristle. They had all assumed that Sand and Fair had had an argument and Fair had stopped somewhere to sulk and tend his wounds. Sand added, "It was just hoppers. Small ones, even, hardly bigger than us. That's not dangerous."

Balm glanced at Jade. "Maybe he missed a strike and got hurt."

Jade knew Balm was just saying it to calm Sand. And there was no point in overreacting until they found a body. Jade said, "Sand, show Balm and me where you saw him last."

Serene and Aura came to their feet and shifted to their winged forms, their scales in shades of green. As Aeriat Raksura, they all had retractable claws on hands and feet, long tails with a spade-shape on the end, and manes of spines and frills down their backs. Both were a half-head or so shorter than Jade; she found herself wishing she had brought along some of the older female warriors, who tended to be almost as large as young queens and vicious fighters. Serene said, "Shouldn't we all go?"

"No, stay here and wait." Jade stared them down, until

she got reluctant nods from both. Though it warmed her a little to know that they were so willing to go after Fair. Their court might be plagued by factions and infighting, but at least no one wanted to see anybody eaten. "I'll send Sand if we need you."

Jade turned and leapt off the platform, snapped her wings out and flapped for altitude. Balm and Sand followed her. Jade kept her pace slow, so Sand could pull ahead of her and lead the way.

She found herself trying to remember who Fair's clutch-mates were. *Oh, damn, I think one of them is Blossom.* Infertile warriors came from the clutches of queens and consorts, like Balm, or from the clutches of the wingless Arbora. Jade was sure Fair had come from the same clutch as the Arbora Blossom, who was a teacher and particularly well-liked by the court. When Jade clutched, she meant for Blossom to be one of those who would raise her fledglings.

Trying to put aside the vision of telling Blossom her mouthy but affectionate clutch-brother had been eaten by something horrible, Jade concentrated on her flying.

Sand led them between the multi-layered platforms of two towering mountain-trees, all supporting small forests of spirals and fern trees and other varieties. None of it was good territory for hunting grasseater herds. The Reaches and the suspended forest might be the ancestral home of the Raksura, but the Indigo Cloud court had only recently returned here. There were too many dangers here that they didn't know about yet.

They passed the heavily forested platforms and came out into a more open area that had formed around a larger mountain-tree. Its canopy was so heavy and extended so far, it had kept any other mountain-trees from forming around it. Falls of water gushed from several knotholes, falling down the hundreds of paces toward the dark of the forest floor. Mountain-trees drew so much water up through their roots, most of them had to expel the excess. In a Raksuran colony tree, the water would be used for drinking, bathing, irrigation.

Jade spotted the platform that held the scattered remnants of Sand's grasseater herd. They were big brown-furred creatures, obviously recently agitated by his hunting run. Most had taken cover in the sparse trees towards the far end of the platform. Some had started to cross one of the bridges formed by a larger branch, heading for another grassy platform that curved further around the mountain-tree's enormous trunk.

"Fair went this way!" Sand called, and slipped sideways and down, toward the lower platforms on the opposite side of the tree.

Most of the platforms to this side were smaller and overflowing with a thick jungle growth that might have hidden anything. It was bound to be unexpectedly deep; young male warriors could be feckless, but Jade couldn't imagine Fair thinking it was a good idea to land there. Then she spotted a lower platform, extending further out from the tree. It had formed atop the stump of a long dead mountain-tree, probably killed by the stronger roots of the larger one. The platform was covered with grass and trees, and its surface was rolling with small hills formed by the underlying branches of its parent tree and what must be the uneven surface of the dying stump below. "That one?" she called to Sand. There was no sign of hoppers now, but the platform had several branch-bridges dropping away to other platforms, so the herd might have fled.

"Maybe," Sand said. "I didn't see which one he was heading for."

Jade heard an annoyed hiss from Balm and had to squelch her own anger. *Little idiot warriors. If only Arbora could fly, we wouldn't have these problems,* she thought. *Find Fair first, then punish them both later.* She just hoped Fair was alive to be punished.

Jade gestured for Sand and Balm to stay back and surged ahead. She reached the platform, passed over, and then turned back to circle above it. There was high grass on the hills and a few stagnant ponds in the low spots between them, but much of the terrain was concealed by the feathery canopies of fern trees. In the open areas, she could see disturbed trails through the grass. It did look like a small herd of hoppers had dashed across the open area of the platform, heading toward the cover of the trees. But she didn't see any sign of Fair.

That wasn't good. If Fair had missed a strike and hurt his wing, or knocked himself out, he might have involuntarily shifted back to his groundling form. In that form, warriors had soft skin, and no wings, spines or claws; he would be vulnerable to a far larger number of predators.

She slowed, coming in over the platform, then cupped her wings and dropped to a landing atop one of the hills. The ground under her claws was soft, grass coming up past her knees. From here she could see under the fern trees, where the trails of flattened grass led. The birdsong and hum of insects was fainter, as if there had been a recent disturbance. She couldn't hear any treelings. She turned, eyes narrowed, looking for movement, a flattened spot in the grass that might be a body, anything. Then she hissed in dismay, waved an arm to signal Balm, and bounded down the hill and toward the trees.

The grass trails led under the round canopies of fern down to a hollow where a dark hole gaped in the dirt and grass of the platform. As she reached it she could see the disturbed dirt, the rips in the grass and underlying moss. Jagged parallel lines, clearly the marks of Raksuran claws, began a few feet from the opening and disappeared over the side. Cautiously, Jade stepped to the powdery dirt at the edge and crouched.

It led into the ground at an angle, a dark tunnel extending down toward the dead stump of the mountain-tree below the platform. She took a deep breath, tasting the air, and caught the rank odor of predator mixed with a trace of dead grasseater, and just a hint of Raksura.

The air stirred as Balm and Sand landed behind her. Sand made a noise of pure dismay. Balm moved to Jade's side and hissed under her breath. Jade said, "I'm going after him." She wasn't quite aware of having made the decision until she said the words. But once she had, it seemed obvious. There was nothing else she could do.

"No." Balm stared at her. "Jade—I should go."

Jade shook her head. Sending anyone else down there, let alone her clutchmate, was so out of the question it hadn't even occurred to her. "Wait here with Sand."

"Let me come with you, at least!"

Jade thought it was bad enough she was risking herself, she didn't want to risk her clutchmate too. "No, stay here."

Balm growled, real fear under it. "You can't do this."

Jade grabbed Balm's collar flange and pulled her close. She put all her authority as queen into the words: "Stay. Here." It wasn't just for Fair's sake, or the sake of Blossom and Fair's other clutchmates and friends, and it wasn't for dread of Pearl's reaction when she heard the only warrior Jade had lost was one of hers. *I don't want to be the kind of queen who leaves warriors to die.* Courts didn't follow queens who couldn't protect their own, and Indigo Cloud had enough trouble without losing faith in its sister queen.

Balm bared her teeth, but after a moment dropped her spines and muttered. "All right." Jade released her and Balm stepped back, but said, "If I come home without you, Moon will kill me."

Jade didn't want to think about her consort's reaction. Moon was a survivor; whatever happened, he could handle it. He was Jade's first consort, and first consort over the court; if she died, his place was assured and he wouldn't have to accept another queen unless he wanted to. Though the idea of another queen taking her place with him made her disemboweling claws itch. She just said, "I intend to come back with you."

Jade turned away from them and leapt down into the tunnel.

She moved cautiously, her mouth open to test the scents, her feet silent on the soft dirt. The light didn't last past the first twenty paces and then she was moving though pure darkness.

She couldn't hear anything except the distant sounds of the birds and insects, and those faded as she went further down.

The predator scent was strong enough for her to tell it was nothing she had ever encountered before. *Oh good, something new,* she thought wryly. The one thing they had discovered about the suspended forest was that it was never dull. But it was confusing that it was mixed in with other predators' scents. She could still catch hints of Raksura in the still air, and at least it wasn't dead Raksura.

The dark began to weigh on her. Stepping into the tunnel had been easy; continuing to follow it grew harder with each step. *Some sort of lesson in that.* It would be nice to live long enough to discuss it with Balm.

Of course, the lesson might be that instead of the court losing one warrior it was about to lose a warrior and a sister queen, just because Jade didn't want to look like a coward. And maybe a predator's burrow wasn't a good place for an inner debate about responsibility and leadership.

Then her eyes found faint light ahead. It revealed the tunnel walls of dirt and rotten wood streaked with white mold, hung with webs of dead roots. As she drew closer the light was murky, but more distinct. She looked up to see the tunnel roof was riddled with cracks and fissures, leading to tiny holes that let in dim daylight; she must be all the way down into the mountain-tree stump.

Then the tunnel widened and twisted down, and Jade heard something ahead. A slight rustle, air movement, maybe. *Or maybe not.* She eased forward, climbed down the twisted passage. The light grew measurably brighter, and she could hear distant birdsong again. It was the murky grey-green light of the lower part of the forest, below most of the platforms.

Then abruptly the wall to her right ended and she found herself looking out into a large open space.

She was at the top of the stump of the dead mountain-tree, and much of it had been rotted away by rain and wood-eating beetle swarms. The soft craggy wood left behind was permeated with holes, festooned with drapes of moss, with odd bulbous shapes of mold clinging to every crack and crevice. White tendrils of vine had grown all through it, winding throughout the space. They were strung across the hollowed-out arch of the top of the chamber like a web. Jade started to step forward, then she froze for a heartbeat, biting back a hiss.

Fair hung limply from a web-like net of the tendrils, suspended from the upper part of the web. He was in his groundling form, curled into a huddle, one bronze-skinned arm dangling down, his head tucked against his shoulder. He was unconscious, not dead, his breath making the tiny copper beads on his armband tremble.

Jade hissed, relief mixing with a strong sense of vindication. She had been right to come down here, she could still save Fair. *Save him from what, is the question,* Jade thought, and carefully stepped forward. There were more openings on the far side of the chamber, leading down and away into the rest of the stump, though it was hard to tell if they were rotted holes or tunnels. But the predator had to be down there and she needed to get Fair and escape before it returned.

She picked her way through the chamber, careful not to touch the web of tendrils. The wood was brittle under her feet, and she could feel a myriad of tiny snaps and cracks as her weight came down on it. Her bones were light in her winged form, being mostly hollow, so hopefully she didn't weigh enough to fall through. Fissures in the delicate surface were large enough for her to see big white mushrooms feeding on the wood and mold lower down.

As she drew closer to Fair, she spotted more of the vine nets strung from the web above, many containing shriveled corpses. Most were large furry predators with wide fanged mouths and curving claws almost as big as Jade's. They were very like the predators that preyed on hoppers and other grasseaters on the platforms closer to the Indigo Cloud colony. Hanging next to Fair was a web holding a creature that was still intact, but it was curled up too and all she could tell about it was that it had slick dark green skin and a large knobby skull.

She passed its net and reached Fair. He was dangling about four paces above her head and she crouched to leap. A wordless cry stopped her in mid-lunge.

It wasn't Fair, it was a groundling, hanging in another tendril web-net twenty paces or so across the chamber. And it was staring at her with big, startled blue eyes.

Jade stared back, surprised she hadn't noticed it before. It was smaller than Fair's groundling form and had pale, almost luminescent skin, with dark blue hair or fur in a fuzz on its head and down its back. Its eyes were wide and round, nose flat and protected by an extra flap of skin, and mouth small. It wore a belt and a wrap woven of dark leaves around its narrow hips. She couldn't make a guess if it was male or female; its legs were folded under and tucked into the bottom of the net, hiding any genitalia. Its hands were large and clawless, the knuckles big and gnarled where it gripped the tendril net.

Jade had never seen a groundling like it before, but in the Reaches that didn't mean much. The Kek lived around the roots of colony trees, and there must be other civilized species occupying similar niches in the lower parts of the forest. But this groundling didn't seem to have ever seen anything like her before, despite the fact that Raksura had been native to the Reaches since time began.

Jade realized she must look like another predator, especially if Fair had shifted involuntarily when knocked unconscious and this groundling had never seen his winged form. She could shift, but queens didn't have the same groundling form as warriors. She would be without her wings and some of her spines, but not without her claws, scales, or any of the other things most soft-skinned species found intimidating. And she weighed more in her other form, and might just go right through the weakened wood beneath her feet. So she lifted her hands, palms out, claws retracted, in a gesture she hoped the groundling would recognize.

It blinked, as if it couldn't believe what it saw, and its eyes widened with an emotion that might have been hope. Jade sighed. Obviously, she would have to rescue it too. It would be pointlessly cruel to leave it here. She would free Fair first, then it.

She reached for Fair, but the groundling cried out again, waving at her frantically.

Jade stopped, baffled. The groundling twisted around and pointed urgently down. A tuber from one of the tendrils trapping it was attached to its pale skin. He pointed up and she traced the tuber up through the web, into the mass at the top of the chamber. A growl building in her throat, she looked to Fair, and spotted the pale shape of another tuber across his back, disappearing under his arm where it must be attached to his body. "It's feeding on you?" she said aloud, the words coming out in a low growl. Obviously, if she removed the tubers, the predator would know instantly.

She thought of going back to get Balm and Sand to help her, but her spines twitched at the thought of leaving. The thing was *eating* them while she stood here. She didn't know how long they had left. Keeping her voice low, she said, "This is going to be tricky."

The groundling stared worriedly at her. It said something in Kedaic that was so distorted, it took her a moment to realize the words had been, "I hope you understand, whatever you are."

Jade had spoken in the Raksuran language. She said in Kedaic, "Can you understand me?"

"Yes!" It twitched in surprise. "You speak—I didn't think—I mean—" It wiped its face wearily. "Forgive me, I have been trapped here with no hope and still half-think I am imagining you."

"You're not. How big is this thing?"

It waved one big hand in a helpless gesture. "Very big. Its body is down there, I think." It pointed back toward the openings on the far side of the chamber, and shuddered. "I only saw its limbs."

"Lovely." No, much as it pained her, she was going to have to go back up and get Balm. To make this work, they would have to free Fair and the groundling at the same time, and then flee. Two could do that better than one. "I'll have to go and get help. It won't take long."

She thought the groundling would protest, but it only nodded and said, "Yes, please, bring others! Hurry!"

As Jade turned, the green creature in the other net stirred and lifted its knobby head. Its face was wide and flat, eyes and nose and mouth just slits. Then its eyes opened wide and blinked at her in amazement. It gasped out words in a deep voice, in a language she didn't understand. So it wasn't dead, and it wasn't an animal. "I'll free you too," Jade said. "Just wait—"

It waved its webbed hands at her frantically, staring past her in terror, and spoke more urgently. She didn't understand any of the words it said, except for one. *Raksura. It said Raksura, it knows what I am*. It had a feeding tube attached to its chest, this one with a large sucker on the end, and the green skin around it was bruised dark and swelling with blood.

Jade realized three things simultaneously. It was odd that the other groundling had never seen Raksura before, when this creature clearly had. It was odd that the other groundling's feeding tube hadn't bruised its skin, when that skin appeared so pale and delicate. It was especially odd that the two trapped prey had been speaking so loudly and it hadn't brought the predator down on them.

She turned, meeting the groundling's blue eyes again. Was there something wrong with the expression in them, were they not quite focused on her? She said, "Before I go, show me your legs."

It stared at her for a moment more, then its mouth opened in a rictus and it lunged out of the net. By that point it wasn't a surprise to see that the whole lower part of its body was made up of the white tendrils.

Jade didn't wait to see what it would do. There were plenty of predators that had body parts that mimicked groundling forms in order to draw prey in, and obviously, this thing was one of them. The Raksuran ability to shift to a groundling-like form had originally been just that, a way to move unnoticed among groundling species and kill them. Some predators could even modify the appearance of their lures, adapting to whatever prey they were after.

Jade leapt for the web, flipped and hung by her foot-claws. She slashed open Fair's net prison and yanked the feeding tube free. She caught Fair before he could tumble out and tucked him under her arm.

The tendril predator took a swipe at her, wielding its decoy groundling body like a club. Jade let go with her feet and slammed into the net holding the green creature, the real groundling. She slashed through the tendrils and the feeding tube, and with a desperate cry, the green groundling lurched toward her and wrapped its arms around her neck. It was heavy, and Jade thought, *Good.* As the tendrils closed around her, she dropped to the brittle wood below, then bounced back up and flipped to push off from a projection of wood above. She shifted to her heavier Arbora body, then flung herself at the nearest fissure in the floor as hard as she could.

The rotted wood gave way with a crack and she smashed through. They fell through open air into the dark canyon of the main part of the stump. The whole space was covered with mushrooms, some of which were bigger than Jade. The real groundling shrieked as she shifted back to her winged form; she thought it might have cut its arms on her spines.

She snapped her wings out and flapped frantically to stay aloft, heading toward a hole in the far side of the stump. The groundling, looking back over her shoulder, keened an urgent warning. Jade flipped sideways as tendrils reached for her, slashed them with her foot claws, and dove down and away.

More tendrils pushed through the hole above, the decoy dangling from them and jerking around like a horrible toy. It shouted, "Don't go, you have to stay and rescue me! Bring more help, bring more help!"

The groundling in her arms whimpered and shuddered. Jade was running out of room to fly. She came around again, making for the opening. Tendrils snatched at her legs.

In the next heartbeat, Balm and Sand shot through the opening and passed Jade, snarling and slashing at the tendrils. The predator drew back in confusion, and Jade shouted, "Go, go now!" They all three dove for the way out.

Jade flew out into the slightly lighter dimness of the lower part of the forest, just after Balm and Sand. The platforms above cut off much of the dim green daylight that fell through the canopy, and the air was heavy with moisture and all the muddy scents of the ground far below, but it had never felt better to Jade. They spiraled down to the branch of a twisted mountain-tree sapling a good distance from the stump and landed.

"Are you all right?" Balm demanded.

Breathing hard, Jade handed her Fair's still-unconscious body. He didn't look well but he was breathing. "Yes. You heard this one screaming?" She patted the green groundling reassuringly. It let go of her shoulders and stumbled away a few steps to sit down heavily. It was bleeding sluggishly from the wound where the feeding tube had been, as was Fair.

Balm felt Fair's throat to make sure he was breathing, then handed him to Sand. "It echoed right up through that tunnel. We heard something crack and fall, and we thought you were coming out somewhere underneath the platform."

"I'm glad you did." Jade shook her spines out. The skin under her scales still itched with the feel of those tendrils. "Get Fair back to camp. I need to find out where to take this one." She gestured to the green groundling, who had propped itself up on its hands, still reeling.

Balm nodded, and gripped Jade's shoulder. She couldn't say anything for a moment, then muttered, "Next time, take me with you." Then she backed away and jumped off the branch. Sand followed with Fair, and the two flew back up toward the light.

Jade turned to the groundling, who was watching her worriedly. She said, "Now for the hard part. I have to figure out a way to talk to you."

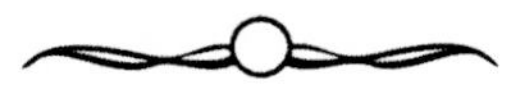

After ascertaining that they had no language in common, not even the few words of Kek that Jade knew, she resorted to gestures and pantomime, and the green groundling tried scratching out symbols and drawings on the bark. Once it finally understood what she was asking, and she understood its answer, she was able to fly it down to the forest floor. On a lake a short distance away, almost impossible to see in the twilight dimness, she found a small island with complex structures made of hardened mud, and a large group of similar groundlings who were ecstatic to have their friend back. Jade deposited her relieved groundling, waved, and took off immediately. She was worried about Fair.

Darkness had fallen by the time she arrived back at their camp. The others had built a small fire to heat water, and Fair lay in the shelter, with Serene, Aura, and Sand sitting with him.

Balm was at the fire pit, and stood as Jade landed. She said, "I made tea."

Jade shifted to Arbora and shook her spines out. She wanted a bath, to scrub the memory of the predator off her scales, but that would have to wait until they returned to the colony. "Good."

She sat beside the fire pit with Balm and asked, "How is Fair?"

"He woke up for a bit and talked." Balm poured a cup of tea from the small kettle and handed it to Jade. "We cleaned the wound and put a poultice on it. And I'm glad the mentors insist on sending healing simples with us, because it looked terrible."

"We'll leave before dawn," Jade said, and sipped the tea. They needed to get Fair back to the colony as soon as possible. The tea took the memory of the acrid scents of the rotting stump out of her throat. She said, "I almost did something very stupid," and told Balm about the predator's decoy. "I think it must prey on other predators. I saw a lot of those things that go after grasseaters down there. Fair and the other groundling must have gotten close to it thinking it was an injured groundling." Dying while fighting off a predator was one thing, dying because she had almost fallen for a trick was another. "The damn thing even spoke to me."

Balm grimaced in disgust. "You should have let me come with you." Then she waved that away. "I'm sorry, I don't mean it like that, I'm not criticizing your decision."

"I know." Balm was criticizing her decision, but that's what clutchmates were for. Jade felt the whole encounter with the predator could definitely have gone better, but they were all alive at the end, including one helpful green groundling, and that was enough. Though when Pearl heard what happened, the reigning queen was sure to have some pithy words about it. "To make up for it, I'll let you tell Pearl."

Balm looked horrified, and Jade smiled and sipped her tea.

Velocity's Ghost

Kelly Jennings

I hate planets. Filthy, heavy, smelly, and this one was leaking.

"It's rain," Rida said. "It's not a leak, it's part of their exchange."

"It's snow." Tai lurked just up corridor, close enough that I could hear him both hard and via the uplink. "Rain is the wet one."

"This is wet," Rida objected.

"Can we focus?" I demanded. "Rida?"

Braced on the rim of the rock pool by the bistro hatch, Rida flashed me a capture of his desk screen, with the vid of our target unshifted. "She's still talking, boss."

I grunted. On the bulkhead across the corridor from me, a glitchy slap-up ran over and over, sputtering and sticking at the same bit each time: *Con Pirians vor liberda U—Con Pirians vor liberda U—Con Pirians vor liberda U—*

Ever since I'd come out to the Drift, every tank and bistro I went into, the same story: Pirians would sweep into Republic space any minute, overthrow the Combines, free the oppressed. Coming first Topwatch, Year Never.

"Here we are," Rida said, and then corrected: "Ah, trade on the way, boss."

Down by Rida, the bistro hatch creaked open. Saddeka Thorne exited, all smiles, the slick with her. I watched Rida fall in behind them. Just as they reached my corridor, he touched the patch to the slick's neck.

The drug hit fast. Rida had another patch ready, but Saddeka danced out of his range. Lots more muscle than her sister, she also reacted better than I'd expected. No panic, keeping her balance, keeping both Rida and me in her range of vision. I spread my hands at her, widening my eyes as if in surrender, and from the far end of the corridor Tai took her with a single shot.

We prefer patches. Even gas-fired makes some noise. But guns work too.

When I was sure she was down, I pulled out restraints. Rida dragged the collateral damage off to stow him and I jerked Saddeka over to wrap her arms behind her body, just as the overhead collapsed.

Well, that's what I thought. Before I hit deck, though, I knew what it had to be: the shitting bird.

I rolled as I fell. Caught deck with my shoulders, rolled again. Huge, powerful, it was all wings and claws. Its beak tore at my thumb. Against my will—no, that's not right—bypassing my will entirely, a yell ripped from me.

Tai hit it, got a grip on its throat, his other fist around its legs. I shut myself up. It did not let go. "Break its neck," I snarled.

"It's a mechanical," Rida said, doing something I couldn't see. "Metal under muscle, is it? Let go, Tai."

Tai started to protest.

"Let go!"

He did. A jolt went through the bird and (since it was connected to me) through me—like touching an ungrounded cable. I nearly pissed myself. When I could see again, the bird was limp, its beak lax. Tai worked it loose from me gingerly.

I sat up. The gash was deep in my thumb. I wrapped my fist around it. Rida knelt, holding the zap, looking half-pleased, half-guilty. "Is it dead?" I asked.

He shook his head. "Just resetting."

I rubbed flakes of rain from my face and climbed to my feet, somewhat unsteady, I'll admit. "Stow it with the damage," I said. "Let's get."

On Free Trade planets, it's never an issue crossing customs, no matter if you are hauling an unconscious bit in restraints, and not this time either. As Rida and Tai loaded her onto our launch, the deckhands working other slips didn't even look up. Of course, half of them were contract labor. Probably they'd gotten hauled through cargo like that themselves, maybe more than once. *Con Pirians vor liberda Unido.* Any minute here.

Once on the *Calvin*, I sealed up behind us, linked to the ship via the launch's grid—sweet relief, to be back in our system—and set about breaking planet. Good to go on both fuel and feed, Tai had seen to that before we went out. Flight control had cleared our exit. Opening a link, I said, "Trade secure?"

"In the bin, boss," Rida said cheerily.

"Ready for break."

Which was when the bird smacked into the hull.

I didn't know what it was at first—prybar? Slap-up IED? A bullet, even, it was a planet, after all. Free Traders will do anything. I jumped, and linked to the exterior. Didn't see anything at first. The contract labor were far out of range.

Scowling, I tightened my fist around the makeshift bandage Tai had knotted on my thumb. Blood had soaked through it. No flags showed on the board, so if it had been a bullet or whatever, no serious damage. As I started to shut the feeds, a sweep of darkness caught my eye. My fist tightened further. The dark swirled: the bird. It flew in a tight circle and dove at the launch. Another hard thud.

I heard myself make a sound, a grunt halfway between pity and contempt. Then I shut the feeds and went on breaking planet.

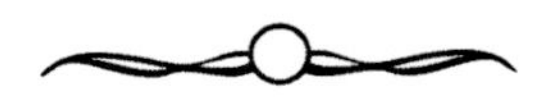

As soon as we were up in the ship and had made it through the first jump, I hit the pit. The dagan was waiting in its locker, as always. It came awake as the hatch scrolled wide, its black eyes focusing. Its muscles, slender and hard under the flex-skin, worked and tensed. Stepping from the locker, it touched its palms together, bowing to me just faintly. As far as the dagan was concerned, it outranked me by quite some measure.

First string, warming moves. The dagan wasn't talking. Usually it wouldn't shut up, since it considered that I had a spiritual gap in my psyche. According to the Pirian who had sold me the program, spiritual assessment was a feature, Indaiyi being only one part self-defense training and about six parts enlightenment training.

Thanks to the flex-skin, the dagan could be anything, within the limits of its frame – the metal chassis, the muscle over that chassis. The Pirian had told me it would take on the features that it thought I needed: show me the face I needed to see. This sort of ooga-booga gets down my neck, but I hadn't argued. All I was in the market for was something to give me a workout and teach me self-defense, and a robot dagan would do that fine, I thought, especially one cut down to half price, which it had been.

Anyway, apparently the face I most often needed to see—according to my cut-rate dagan—was an androgynous acerbic little shit who knocked me around and made caustic comments. Spiritual advice of sorts, I guess.

When we moved to second string, defense moves, I said, driven itchy by the silence, "I've taken another Core job."

I knew this would tick it. The dagan hated it when I worked for the Core.

Catching my shoulder, it slammed me into the bulkhead, its forearm locking across my throat. Dark eyes stared into mine.

I smacked the mat, surrendering. As it pushed off, releasing me, I hooked its right knee with my heel, reaching for its left forearm. Except it caught my wrist as I reached, sliding under my arm and hooking the back of my neck with its other hand. I knew enough to roll at this point—that or go face-first into the mat. It added torque as it threw me, slamming me down. I continued my roll up to balance—or tried to reach balance—but got landed on, hard, and slapped to the mat again. The dagan pushed a tanto to my throat.

I went limp, the way you did in the pit to show surrender. Its knee was on my spine; one fist kept my wrist torqued, the other jamming the tanto against my windpipe.

"What's the first rule?"

"Get out of the way," I said. It had taught me that long ago.

"Why didn't you get out of the way, Captain?"

I started to speak, and shut up. The dagan never called me Captain.

It pushed harder. "Tell me why you left the Core."

I tensed. The dagan reacted as though this were resistance, leaning harder on my wrist. Any attacker in Indaiyi would react that way. I would have too. My tension said I meant to fight, so the dagan defended against it. I forced my muscles to relax, fought my breathing steady.

In my ear, the dagan said, "You left. You ran all this way. Yet you still suck for the Combines."

"Get off," I snapped.

To my surprise, this worked. The grip on my wrist went limp. I kicked out and down, shoving to get torque—

And nothing. The dagan lay loose on the mat, its eyes empty. It was already beginning to morph back to its neutral state, the bland, featureless poppet I had bought. If it was powerless for long enough—twenty hours or so—it would completely reset, I knew. I knelt beside it, gulping air, vaguely troubled, wondering why it had shut down. Then I took the steel and ivory tanto from its limp fist, moved the silky hair aside, and pushed the reset button under its ear.

Nothing.

Muttering a curse, I tucked the weapon back in its sheath, got to my feet, and hoisted the dagan to my shoulder to haul it back to its locker. We were only at a fifth gee, pushing toward jump. It wasn't heavy.

Tai was in the galley, as fresh-scrubbed as I was, though I suspected a different cause. He and Rida had been steady-bunked for some time. Wearing a blue undershirt and dark grey thermal leggings, he was pulling dishes from the sterilizer, stretching to secure them in the overhead locker, a chore that showed off his lean frame nicely. His inky hair, which he usually wore in a braid, was loose down his back. I kept my hair cropped short, as almost everyone who lived in space did, but both Tai and Rida had refused, so far, to cut theirs. Another contract thing, apparently.

"Coffee?" I slid into the booth, reaching with my uplink for the grid. We were halfway through midwatch, still some hours from the next jump. I ran the system. Only flag close to critical was a filter in exchange. Taking Rida onto the manifest was the best move we'd ever made. Tai had ever made. Whichever.

Tai tossed me a bulb—his coffee, heavy on milk and sweet. Since the alternative was mixing my own, I sucked it down without complaint. "Rida knows about this filter," I mentioned, just to be sure.

"He's watching it," Tai said. He brought his own coffee over to the booth. "We don't have a spare, but he says he can keep it running until we make port."

"Why don't we have a spare?" I said mildly.

"That is the spare." Tai paused. "It's that stock we got from Hell in a Bucket."

Which Tai had hinted at the time hadn't been such a great bargain. You deal with Free Trade merchants, half the time you end up with crap biscuits.

"It's not a critical filter," Tai added. He was watching me from under his eyelids. He'd been contract labor all his life and it still scared him, I knew, to talk back.

"Good thing we have Rida onboard," I said. Tai relaxed a little, smiling faintly. I had already noticed that any mention of Rida made him happier. Six or ten stations back, in the middle of the previous job, Tai had come dragging Rida onto the launch, an underfed, apprehensive kid, big-eyed and edgy. *He's just what we need,* Tai had claimed. *A Tech contract, can run any sort of code and he's great with tools.*

I had kept myself from the obvious joke, mainly because Rida had been so terrified, and so young—well under nineteen, if I had to guess, which was the legal age on Dresden. Out here at the Drift, hah, if you could work your own trouser buttons, you were legal.

"Will his contract holder sell him?" I had asked, and Rida and Tai had exchanged a guilty glance. I'd groaned. "Tai."

He'd begun arguing desperately, telling me some scrambled panicked tale of Rida's holder, what he'd done and would do, why we had to help Rida jump his contract, how it was absolutely worth it—

Which it had been, I admitted. And probably I would have done it even if it hadn't been. Even though I knew this was a stupid way to deal with the contract labor issue, lifting contracts out of forced labor one fugitive at a time.

"How's the trade?" I asked Tai now.

"Awake. But on a hunger strike."

I grunted, linking the brig feeds. "How far to the Core?"

"Thirty jumps now."

I had another suck of coffee. "I think she'll start eating before we get there."

"Your neck is bleeding," Tai said.

I twitched and put my fingers to my throat. A thin smear showed on my fingers. "The dagan."

"The dagan cut you?"

"Object lesson."

Tai kept frowning. I didn't blame him. It seemed unlikely to me, and I had been there. "You don't want to talk to her?"

he asked. "Find out why she won't eat?"

"The dagan shut off mid-run. Get Rida to run a check on the program." I finished my coffee and started for the hatch.

When I bought the *Calvin* from a rich boy in over his head, the notion was I'd be a Drift merchant, a job of work it developed I had very little ability for. The rich boy felt deeply cheated when I wouldn't be his woman even after he sold me the *Susan Calvin* (he'd called her the *Annie Bonny*) so cheap; I felt deeply cheated when I found out how much debt the *Calvin* carried.

After it became clear that I had no talent for dealing cargo, I built the brig in the hold. It's nothing but a cage, metal grids bolted together, a mechanical rather than an e-lock on its door, no desk, no board, and absolutely no access.

So I was surprised, dropping into the hold, to hear music. A quick haunting rhythm, clear vocals in a strange language. The cage lay in dusk. Within it, Saddeka Thorne lay untethered, wearing only a linen singlet. Her short hair, as light as her sister's, floated around her skull.

That she was loose was the first surprise. Every runaway I had dragged back to the Core, and that would be eleven counting this one, hated low-gee. None had dressed so skimpy, either—they all kept their Combine belongings wrapped tight to their bodies, jackets, trousers, fancy shoes; they had clung to their gear, terrified of the dark around them.

Her sister, who had traveled out to the Drift to hire me when I refused to travel into the Core to be hired, had been your standard Combine item: remixed bones carved down narrow as wire, heavily-regulated, hyper-thin body. Most upper-shelf Core women look like this. I don't, but Dresden, where I came up, is not quite the Core—we're outer-Core, eleven jumps out—and also my mother was opposed to remixing children. The claims that it was done for health reasons, she said, were obvious nonsense, when so little of the genetic work had to do with health and so much of it had to do with standards of beauty. And though my mother was killed when my sister and I were very young, my father did not have us modified.

Saddeka was unmodified as well: she had normal body fat and muscles, and she lacked the fine-grained skin universal to upgrades, as well as the enhanced pheromones meant to make people like and trust her—or at least, if she had these last, they weren't working on me. She could have been Free Trade, or even contract labor, if not for her attitude, which was pure Core.

And she was not singing. That music did not come from her.

The bird.

"The corvão is a teaching toy," the sister had told me—Nur Thorne, heir to Rexel-Thorne, one of the top Combines out of the Core. "Simple academic skills, basic socialization." She smiled, lowering jeweled lashes. Flirting with me. Though her geek must have done research, must have told her I was set to het. "Saddeka always did have… problems."

"She's nearly your age. She still has this toy?"

"The corvão seemed just to make her worse. My parents tried taking it away when she was twelve. She threatened to fail her prelims on purpose." Nur shook her head winsomely, inviting me to share her outrage. "She could have done it, too. She always was clever. Just—no sense!" Widening those sapphire eyes.

"You're the heir?"

"I wasn't then."

"And she's the spare?"

"The corvão need not return with her. In fact, we would prefer it does not."

I sat back in my chair. "Are you hiring me to bring back your runaway spare or to take her toy away?"

Nur's expression set. "My family loves Saddeka very much. We need her to come home so that she can get the help she needs." Her jeweled lashes lowered. "Or, if that's not possible," she said, and shut her lips together.

She didn't go on, but she didn't have to. In the station bistro, I sat shifting my bowl of tea on the table, thinking how much I would like to get up and walk away from this job. I found myself remembering, among those Free Trade pirates, the garden in our enclave at Dresden. The fig trees, the pear trees, the pecan trees I would climb to hide out from my bodyguards with my own Pirian toy—nothing nearly so elaborate as this corvão, just a Pirian handheld filled with games and stories, music, datafiles I never found the end of, and Little Bee, the interactive who always helped me find what I was looking for.

I shook my head. As much as I wanted to tell Rexel-Thorne and its heir to go help themselves, the *Calvin* was short on fuel and needed parts, plus we had a payment due. We always had a payment due. "Half up front," I told her. "Half when we deliver."

She paid me a fifth up front. Filthy Combine rats.

The singing stopped. Saddeka swirled, her eyes darting through the shadows. I used my grip on the stanchion to swing further into the hold.

"Hah," she said, spotting me. "How's your thumb?"

I dropped to the deck in front of her cage. The hold was dark, but I have feeds everywhere, and I had been running them since I'd heard the music. And I saw nothing. If the bird was here, it was well hidden. "How did your parrot get on my ship?"

She raised her chin, her eyes pale as water. "He is a corvão. Not a parrot. Or you may call him Robin. That's his name."

Her voice was low, musical, compelling. I wrapped my

fists around slats of her cage. "Oh, he has a name?"

"Of course he has a name. Don't you?"

I smiled. "Velocity Wrachant, Miss Thorne. Captain Wrachant, in this case. Welcome to the *Susan Calvin*."

She frowned. "Who hired you? My brother?"

"I see you haven't kept up," I said, with false cheer. "Your brother is dead. Peacefully, in his sleep," I added. "The way all Core heirs go."

Her eyes widened. "Bao." She reached for the cage slats, and then dropped her hand.

I had been where she was. I knew what she was feeling, that combination of shock and fear. Oh, grief, too, certainly. Bao Thorne had been her brother. But the sorrow was drowned, I knew, under all the crashing terror.

My sister was the spare. My father, who had watched two older cousins die ahead of him, who lost my mother (who had held her own Board seat), had taught me from the time I could toddle through our guarded enclave, among our army of Security, daily lessons in political theory, in self-defense, in packing code, in trusting no one. When I was sixteen, I used my knowledge and skill to hop a freighter for the Drift. I imagine no one was more surprised than he was. Not much later, living my hot life among the Free Trade merchants, I heard about my sister, the spare. Killed by terrorists. I heard about my father, also dead. I heard about my cousin, who now held the Taveri seat.

That old story.

"Your sister," I told Saddeka Thorne, "is paying me an enormous amount to either get you back to the Core or to make sure you aren't anywhere else ever again."

She stared at me.

I strolled around the cage, my gaze interior, running every feed in the hold again. Of course, the bird didn't have to be actually in the hold, no more than I had to be here to see this space. I widened my search to feeds throughout the ship.

Saddeka's fists gripped the grid of the cage. "You can't

take me back there."

I gave her a sidelong glance, running the schematic Nur Thorne had linked me for the corvão. If it had latched onto the exterior of the launch—I shook my head. It was organic muscle and flesh over metal frame. It couldn't survive the burn through the atmosphere. Or get through the hull.

"You're from the Core," Saddeka said. "You know why I ran."

"I get paid whether I bring you back alive or dead." I gave the flat strap of the iron cage between us a tap. "Keep it in mind."

Jumping up for a stanchion, I swung back toward the hatch.

The wail of the alarm kicked me awake. I couldn't get balance, couldn't get linked. I grabbed for anchor and found the dagan kneeling by my pod. "What?" I said.

He bowed.

I looked around. "You can't be here. This isn't the pit."

"Then obviously I am not," he said in Pirian, a fine language for irony.

I reached again for a link to the ship's grid, again couldn't get it.

"What alarm is that?" he asked.

I started to answer, and didn't. I couldn't link, but he was right: why did I need to? Every idiot knew the alarms.

He vanished. Bracing one foot on the hatch anchor, I began unshipping the e-release. It broke quickly, as it was made to. I still couldn't access atmosphere or pressure, but the alarm squalled faster.

Not to mention, I wouldn't be having hallucinations unless something was seriously off in the counts.

I slithered out. The ship was dark and still. Engines down. No rush of air from the vents. Cold, too, though that was probably my imagination. Couldn't cool off this fast. Kicking toward command, I nearly collided with Tai. "Rida?" I asked.

"Com, I guess," he said. "Can you link?"

I hurtled through the hatch to upper deck. Sure enough, Rida was in Com, jacked, two separate desks clamped before him. He spat a curse when I tried to talk to him. The boards were lit with all the links we couldn't access. I spun in midair, trying to read everything at once. Tai muttered; but I was reassured. Not so bad. Pressure too high, nitrogen off, but other than that—

The dagan folded his arms. "That mix has a name on our side of the Drift."

So I had heard: Sweet Death. Kills entire ships, but everyone dies happy. I smiled. It seemed like a good joke at the time.

My sister peered around the dagan's shoulder. "Tally won't die?"

"Such concern," the dagan said.

"Oh, don't sound surprised," I said. "Some of us Combine rats have hearts."

Behind me, Tai spoke warily: "Velocity?"

He was nervous. Well, he would be, his captain talking to ghosts. I turned to focus on Rida: his skinny shoulders tense, his lower lip caught between his teeth. "Getting anywhere?" I asked.

He shook his head, not answering, just wanting me to shut up.

Beyond him, the dagan lifted my sister up onto the console. She swung her heels, the skinny child she had been (we had been) at our Qualification, except instead of wearing our presentation gown, deep blue velvet that had itched madly, she was dressed like a Pirian—knit thermal leggings, short curls floating loose. While I watched, transfixed, a black moth like those that sometimes escaped from the exchange back on Dresden fluttered around her. I blinked. She let it rest on her forearm.

"Vel?" Tai said.

I blinked again. She was gone, and the dagan. The moth, much bigger, moved slowly, as through thick and sticky air.

"Velocity!" Tai was almost shouting.

I dropped through the open hatch.

Saddeka was braced in one corner of the cage. I gripped anchor. "What are you doing?" I demanded. "If we die, do you think you escape? Do you think I'm stupid enough to give that cage a virtual lock?"

She lifted her head. "We'll die here in this cage before we'll go back to die in that one."

I stared at her, taken aback, I'll admit. "What?"

"You would not be a slave. But you think we will?"

I laughed in a snarl. "Heir to Rexel-Thorne Combine. Interesting definition of slave."

Her chin raised further. "Chains of silver are chains all the same."

"Tai was mining actual silver when I bought him! And guess who held his contract?"

Her pale eyes gazed at me.

I moved closer to the cage. "And what's this we?" I demanded, flinging my gaze around the hold. "Is that bird in your pocket?"

"Rexel-Thorne?" Saddeka asked.

I wheeled on her. "What?"

"Us? Our Combine? We held your lieutenant?"

The alarm stopped. I stood, gulping air.

Saddeka came to wind her long fingers through the cage. "You understand why I had to leave. It wasn't that I was afraid. It was that. How could I live like that? Eating the blood of slaves?"

I shouted at her, "Where's the fucking bird?"

She gazed back, her pale eyes calm.

"You downloaded him," I said.

She shrugged, fractionally.

"Shit," I muttered. It should not have been possible—our shieldwalls were excellent; Rida had built them. But, as Rida himself had told me, there is always someone better. And also, frankly, I hadn't expected her to have an in-skull uplink. They're not only proscribed at the Core, but most Combine members are terrified of them, believing all manner of rumors about how easy uplinks are to infiltrate. Except—obviously—Saddeka was not your typical Core bit.

Which I should have kept in mind.

I moved away from the cage, closing my fists. "We're taking you to Harvest," I told her. "You crash this ship, my crew takes the escape pods, leaves you to die."

Saddeka Thorne stared at me through the iron slats of the cage.

Lights and air came back as I neared the com. In the com, Rida was still jacked. Tai, gripping an anchor, was chewing his lip. Before I could speak, Rida said: "Ain't a thing I did. Whatever that is, that corvão, it codes circles around me."

I locked my fist behind my neck. My headache was worse.

Rida slid his finger along his desk screen, sorting files. "Playing with us," he muttered. "Soon as you got down there, it dropped the barriers. Let me in to reset everything."

I grimaced. "You've got control now."

"Long as it lets me have it."

"I still can't link," I mentioned.

"Right, wait." He leaned to the other desk and slid over another file, punched two or three drops. Something popped in my head, and my uplink was back.

"Gah," I said, dizzy with relief.

"Only as long as it lets us," Rida warned again.

I shook my head. "A shieldwall."

"We *had* a shieldwall."

"A better one."

My link went down. The ship went dark. "Boss," Rida said, into the silence.

I swore viciously. "All right," I yelled. The lights came back up. So did my link. Rida and Tai watched me, keeping still. "I'm in my hive," I said.

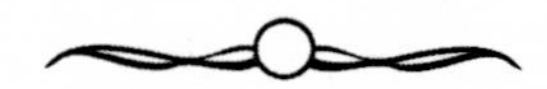

Not precisely to my surprise, the escape pods were dead. We skated across system. I brooded, thinking what to do. I wasn't going through jump in the grip of this bird. I knew that.

Spacing them was an option. The brig is in the hold for a number of reasons: that some trade might infiltrate was among those reasons. If I had to, I could send Tai EVA, pop the e-latches on the loading bay, vent the air in that entire section.

I mulled over this solution half the watch. Then I went to the pit.

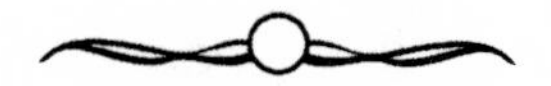

The dagan bowed. I braced myself in the hatch. "I know it's you."

Its dark gaze held, steady as Saddeka's. Then it knelt.

"Leaving Rexel-Thorne," I said, gripping the beveled rim of the hatch, "why? What did you think you'd accomplish, selling off-market drugs to thieves in the Drift?"

Kneeling, the dagan studied me. I should have knelt too, of course. In Indaiyi, kneeling indicates a readiness to work together. *Let's listen to one another*, it says. *Let's learn together.* Each Indaiyi session starts with kneeling, greeting one another, bowing. Very friendly. And not how I felt now. I stayed in the hatchway, on my feet.

"Better to stay and subvert from the inside, Taveri?" it said.

I squeezed the hatch frame harder. The bird had recognized me—or Saddeka had. "I was an idiot to run," I said.

The dagan went motionless: not as humans do, but as programs do, when they glitch and freeze a fraction of a second. I realized I had taken the corvão by surprise.

It recovered. "Guilt is a trap. An infiltrate program, meant to compel you to act in someone else's interests, rather than in your own."

My own interests. I snorted. "Alone, I'm nothing. Others are all I am."

A longer glitch this time.

"If I had inherited the seat at Taveri—what can I accomplish, alone in the Drift? Trouble-shoot for Free Trade? Mend labor disputes? Or what you said, suck for the Core?"

The dagan—the corvão—knelt bright-eyed. It was loving this, I realized. Programmed as an educational tool, this was its element.

"You believe you would accomplish more holding a seat on the Taveri Board," it said. "This is your argument. That Saddeka should return, and take the Rexel-Thorne seat. Then she would have the power to reform the system?"

"As opposed to the power she would have selling drugs to Drift miners?"

"You think that if you had stayed, you could have made a difference."

I shook my head.

"You know that is not how changes are made. At least," the corvão added, "you did know it. Why else leave?"

I let the rim go, dropped into the pit. My heart banged hot blood through me. I saw Tai in that filthy dock on Sarat. Bruises on his face.

The corvão did not retreat. Why would it? Ghosts don't bleed. "You don't change the demon by becoming the demon."

"You don't change it by running away." The words leapt from me.

"That's the only way you do change it."

I bared my teeth and flung myself at it.

It slid aside easily. I slammed into the side of the pit, rebounded, spun by the reflex the real dagan had taught me, and stabilized, tense.

My sister unfolded like a flower, rising to stand in the hatch.

"No," I said, and said it louder, "No!"

"Tallis," she said, her eyes merry.

I clenched my fist.

"You don't have to be afraid anymore," she said, holding her hand toward me. "Really. You did the right thing."

"I'll come down there and wring your chicken neck," I said, strangled. "You think I'm messing, you try me."

My sister smiled. "You aren't superstitious, Captain. Surely? One mask or another, what difference?"

I shook my head. I couldn't look away from her. All our lives, she had been the good child, the brave soldier, the one our father loved.

It shifted, sister to light to bird, its wings spread wide. I grimaced. Only a bird for an instant, though. Then it was me, in my ship gear: grimy leggings, ratty leather ship shirt, scar on my chin, the nose that looked so sweet on my sister looking very beaky now; her jeweled eyes squinty and mean on me. I blinked, and my doppelgänger grinned.

"Better?"

"You can't just be the bird?"

It knelt. "That's not what I am any more than this is."

I shifted my weight, hunting balance. "What are you, then?"

It crooked an eyebrow. My eyebrow. Like looking in a flawed mirror. "I thought you had deduced it, Tallis. My research showed you clever."

It waited, peaceful as the dagan. In my mind, sudden clarity tumbled. "You're an infiltrate program," I said, staring across the pit. "A Pirian infiltrate."

"Not the only one," it agreed.

I felt like I'd swallowed a glitch.

It sighed: my sigh, my intonations. "Look," it said, exactly as I would have said it, explaining issues to Tai or Rida. "How to win a Revolution? Really? With bombs? Terrorism? Shooting people?"

I could not speak.

"You don't open minds by breaking heads."

"You win it with toys?" The word came out feeble, only half-voiced.

It shrugged. "The infiltrates are not our only path."

I kept staring.

"If we persuade enough top talent of the Republic to come out to the Drift and join us, if we weaken them sufficiently…" it gazed at me from my own bony face.

I shook my head again. "No one persuaded me to leave."

It paused, just as I would pause when I was spinning the odds. Then it said, "Are you sure?"

We left Saddeka and her shitting bird on Resto, a useless planet twenty-eight jumps from the Core. She claimed she could find her way from there, and whether she could or not I was beyond caring. I kicked the *Calvin* back toward the Drift.

Tai bunked up with me after we made jump. I didn't ask him to, but I was glad he had. We had some push, scooting toward the next jump, so the sex was good. (Zee sex is possible, but takes more effort than I am usually willing to put into the enterprise.) After, we cuddled in the hive. I like how Tai smells, especially after sex. But this time I couldn't help being aware of his scars, those on his back, the ones still marking his wrists. The mines at Sarat were not held by Rexel-Thorne. I wish.

"When you found out who I was," I asked, "that I had been the Taveri heir, were you angry?"

Half-asleep, he turned his head. After a moment, he said, "I knew who you were."

I'll admit this surprised me. "What do you mean? Do you mean—always? On the docks, you mean, before you talked to me? You knew then?"

"Everyone did." He watched me from slitted eyes. "Vel. Did you think we wouldn't?"

It was a bit before I knew what I was feeling: queasiness.

He rolled to his elbow. "Taveri Combine heir comes to our planet, you think we don't know that? Pit miners? Shit, Velocity. It's all we talked about."

I ran my fingers over the mat cover between us. "I wasn't the heir then. Not anymore."

He snorted. I lay down, touched his chest, knit with healthy muscle. He still flinched when I touched him, every time, though he had been so long off Sarat. If I had left him on those docks, he would be dead by now. Sometimes I wondered if he thought about that.

He cupped my face. "Did you think I ran away from that mine on a whim?"

I smiled. "No," I said, though in fact I always had.

He smiled back, not fooled, and leaned to kiss my mouth. "Fucking Combine rats," he told me fondly. "We'll get you educated yet."

Exit, Interrupted

C. W. Johnson

The Door wasn't so much heavy as *reluctant to move*, as if they were carrying it, one at each end, through molasses. "Why is it like this?" Saiyul asked as she leaned into the resistant thing.

Ashil shrugged the best he could with his hands full. "How should I know?"

A bead of perspiration slid down Saiyul's face, right into the scar on her cheek. It had healed, mostly, but it itched where her oxygen mask rubbed against it.

"*You* work in the factory," Saiyul whispered, then said loudly, "Good morning, Teacher Thufeli!"

Teacher Thufeli passed them in the alley. "Good morning, Saiyul! And what have you stolen now?"

"We're helping old Watil," Saiyul said. They had wrapped the Door in a dirty cotton sheet, but that wasn't fooling anyone. "Clearing his late cousin's flat."

Thufeli shook his head and walked on. Saiyul felt bad lying to him; the teacher was kind and though she could not pay even the tiny fees he charged, he had still tried to teach her to read.

"Slower," Ashil pleaded. "My lungs hurt."

The next block was full of abandoned buildings; the gaps where airlocks should have been made them look like a row of rotten teeth. Saiyul led them into one, where they lowered the Door to the earthen floor, and flicked on a sallow portable lamp.

"Now what?" Ashil asked. The question made Saiyul's

heart race with anger, but it was really her remembering the fence's contemptuous tone. "What good," the fence had said, "is a Door if you don't know where it leads?" When they left, the fence had added, "You should know, Kawada's boys are looking for you."

Saiyul yanked off the cotton sheet. The Door itself had flexible, metallicized plastic stretched over the frame. The blunt muzzle of the oxygen mask made Saiyul's crinkled reflection look like the dog demons in vidnovelas.

"Your father," she said, "could he tell where—"

Ashil interrupted. "If he knew what we'd done, he'd beat me." When Saiyul laughed, Ashil scowled. "I only did this for you."

She turned away from him, her face stinging with warmth, and faced the Door. You wouldn't guess it could take you light years away, away from this planet, away from thugs with knives.

"If I can't get money to pay off Kawada," she said, rubbing her scar, "maybe we can use this Door to go offworld."

He lifted his head. "My father needs me."

"He needs you to give him money. He..." She paused and put her hands on her hips. "No matter what you do, he'll end up dying in an alley. Come with me," she said.

When Ashil didn't respond, her stomach squirmed, and she turned to face the Door. "Do you know how to, uh, open it?"

Ashil shrugged. "We pull the cover off first, I think. Are you sure about this?"

But Saiyul was already peeling back the metallicized plastic. In the frame, there was—well, it was hard to look at. *Hard to see.* A bruised nonexistence, darker than the night sky, and duller. She tentatively stretched out her hand.

"Don't touch it," Ashil said, and Saiyul curled her fingers back. "You know the hot piss, the foam they dump into the pits?"

Saiyul nodded. Nasty stuff, it burned the ground, everything, even the air so it scarred lungs.

Ashil scratched his head. "This is the opposite. It's freezing, so cold it also burns. You've seen my father's hands." Ashil knelt and felt around the frame. "There's some kind of, uh, refrigerator, or pump. And a switch... Here."

"That opens it?"

Ashil shrugged. "My father says Doors are temperamental. Sometimes they won't open. Or they open and nothing goes through. He said why but I didn't understand."

Saiyul stepped closer and swallowed. "Let's try."

"Now? You're going?" His tone made it clear he was not going and would not.

"Kawada said he'd start taking fingers. And the only person I have to say goodbye to is you."

They faced each other for a long moment, embraced awkwardly, then faced the Door. Ashil pressed the switch then hopped back.

At first nothing happened. Then the darkness inside the Door changed. Saiyul couldn't have said how, but it hurt to look at it, as if a bright light filled the room, even though it was still dark. She put an arm over her eyes, and all she saw was darkness, and her eyes still shouted she was staring at the sun.

"Go through!" Ashil shouted. "If you're going to."

Her first step toward the door was hesitant, and then fear seized her, that the Door might close before she got through, and she knew Doors worked only once and never again. She ducked down, hurled herself at the Door—

—and collided with someone else, coming out of the Door.

Saiyul blinked. She could look at the Door again. The frame was empty, the frozen nothingness gone, all that was left was the carbon-fiber backing covered in tiny etched lines like wormtrails.

And curled up on the earth floor, gasping, was a boy.

Ashil recovered faster. He knelt down, tore off his oxygen mask, and cupped it to the boy's face. The boy greedily sucked at the oxygen.

The boy was thin and delicate, with girlish features, a few years younger than Saiyul and Ashil, with dark circles under his eyes, a bruise on his forehead, and bare feet pale like the underbelly of a fish from the market. His clothes were dirty, but they were rich people's clothes.

Ashil took a few breaths out of his oxygen mask and passed it back to the boy.

"What's your name?" he asked. "Where do you come from?"

"Gaa—" the boy stuttered. "Gaa… Gaa—"

"Gatil? Gamil? That your name?" Ashil asked.

But he just kept repeating the syllable.

Ashil finally asked Saiyul, "Don't you have a spare oxygen mask?"

"Uh—"

"You were going to sell oxygen from a cart. How can you not have a spare mask?"

"That's why I borrowed money from Kawada," Saiyul muttered. But she rooted around the room until she found one. It was filthy, but it worked, and she also found a nearly full canister.

"We have a high carbon dioxide content," Ashil said to the boy, loudly, the way one did to offworld tourists. "And low oxygen. If you're not in a sealed room, you'll always need a mask and a canister."

"Gaa—"

"Do you think he hit his head?" Saiyul asked. "We could just leave him at the charity clinic."

But Ashil shook his head.

The boy was quiet and compliant as Ashil's father, old Baapashil, looked into each eye and then turned the boy's head first one way, then another. Gamil—Ashil insisted that was the boy's name—could say individual words now, like "water." He sipped from a dirty cup.

"Will your father beat you now, or wait until tonight?" Saiyul whispered to Ashil as they stood in a corner of the cramped flat.

"Shh."

After a while Baapashil clucked his tongue and turned to Ashil and Saiyul. His dark face was wrinkled as a walnut, and his eyes had the perpetual red and his breath the stinking sulfur smell of the *jhaant*-addict.

"What happened to him?" Ashil asked.

Baapashil sighed. "I think the more important question is, why did you—"

Ashil interrupted, "I'm truly sorry, Father. I am ashamed. I only thought—"

"You did not think!" Baapashil roared, so that Saiyul shrank back. You wouldn't have thought such a stick-figure of a man could roar like that.

But then Baapashil closed his mouth and gestured to Saiyul. With trepidation she stepped closer. For a moment she thought he was going to hit her, even though in all the years he had never raised a hand to her.

Instead the tip of his outstretched hand hovered over the scar on her cheek.

"It was foolish," he said at last. "What I don't understand is why you opened an out Door?"

Saiyul looked at Ashil. He shrugged.

"When you make a Door," Baapashil said, "a pair of Doors, there is an in Door and an out Door. You can only go one way." Seeing the puzzled looks, his face twisted into a crinkled smile. "Ah. When you stole a Door—stole a Door from your employer, Ashil, who puts bread on our table—you took one from the lower rack in the warehouse. Am I right? The *in* Doors, they are on the upper rack."

Ashil said quietly to Saiyul, "I didn't know."

"To be a thief is shameful," said Baapashil, "but to be an incompetent thief—

"Water," Gamil said, holding out the empty cup. "Thank. Thank."

"Is he hurt?" Ashil asked.

Baapashil spoke quietly and thoughtfully. "If, as you claim, he came through a Door," and he paused, "then this young master may be suffering from 'quantum censorship.'"

Saiyul wrinkled her nose. "What's that?"

Baapashil sighed and leaned back. "It's complicated, and I am tired. Old and tired, and I need my medicine."

Ashil opened his mouth to protest, but Saiyul slipped past him, and opened the drawer where she knew Baapashil kept his *jhaant*. She brought a patch to him and held it out, cupped in both hands.

Baapashil's mouth slackened a bit at the sight. "O, is this paradise?" he said, his mouth twisted up, "where a beautiful young woman brings me bliss?"

Saiyul's face burned. She knew she was not beautiful, and the old man's words stung.

Baapashil peeled off the backing and slapped the patch on the inside of his arm, scarred from the countless patches before it. He stretched himself out onto the tattered divan and closed his eyes.

Gamil looked at the old man. "Ss. Sleep," he said.

"Why?" Ashil asked angrily of Saiyul.

"You were going to argue with him. And—" She gestured emptily at Gamil.

"Huh," Gamil said. "Huh. Hungry."

Ashil squatted down next to Gamil. "You're hungry?" He brushed a lock of stray hair out of Gamil's eyes, then turned to Saiyul. "Can you get some food?" When Saiyul put her hands on her hips, he added, "I'm late for my shift already."

Saiyul refrained from saying *If only Baapashil had held onto his job at the factory*, but instead rolled her eyes and held out a hand. Ashil dropped in a couple of small coins.

It was creeping up on midmorning and the alley was streaming with people. At the baker's she found herself standing behind Teacher Thufeli.

"No students this morning?" she asked.

He shook his head, his oxygen mask waggling. "The factories cut wages again. I reduced my fees, but everyone says, 'I'm so sorry, but my son, my daughter, they have to work or we won't eat, we will get kicked out into the street.'" He sighed and scratched his ribs. "I didn't think to get rich, but even with the little I've saved, I don't have enough to go home."

Saiyul saw the sprinkle of grey in Thufeli's black hair. When he had arrived ten years earlier—one of her earliest memories was of him handing her, a child shivering on the street, a piece of bread—he had been a young man.

"Your home, is it beautiful?" she asked. "Not like here?"

"This world has its attractions. It's not all slums and ugly factories. The hoinist temple here, it's one of the oldest, and its gate of refuge is the most spectacular for a hundred light years around. To say nothing of the local hoinist festivals."

Saiyul didn't care about any stupid festivals, except that it was easier to get food then. "Where you come from, do you need an oxygen mask?"

But Thufeli was looking past Saiyul. "Kawada's boys," he said quietly. "Turning this way."

She edged past Thufeli, then hopped up and over the counter, pushing past the protesting baker. A moment later she slammed through the back door into another alley. By the time she reached the main boulevard, she thought she had lost them.

A crowd was marching down the boulevard, holding up banners—they were either for or against the hoinists, or maybe for or against the factories, and Saiyul didn't really care much which. She stood impatiently on tiptoes, hoping to cross over and slip into one of her hidey-holes.

But from behind her she saw a commotion pushing through the crowd. Saiyul squeezed in with the marchers and mimed chanting their slogans.

They marched towards the glowering factories across a dead and pitted landscape. A sudden gust blew acrid stench, making people hack and cough, and Saiyul's eyes watered. A crew of men were pouring toxic hot foam into a pit, sending up crackling sparks. Saiyul had heard the hot foam could be used to grease ships for their journeys between stars. She'd also heard that Kawada used it to dissolve bodies he didn't want found.

As the march circled the factories, Saiyul broke away. Her lungs began to hurt, from running and from the poisoned air, but if Kawada's boys caught her she'd lose a finger, or more. She kept running, until she lost sight of her pursuers in the shimmering orange haze.

The next morning she crept back to Ashil's flat and rapped on the airlock. At first it didn't open, but when she knocked all the more insistently, the lock finally opened.

"I thought you might be Kawada, come back," Ashil said.

Saiyul's heart squeezed in her chest. "He came here?"

"Everyone knows we're friends. Fortunately," Ashil said, glancing back over his shoulder to the cot where his father lay twitching, "baapa had finished dreaming, and thought to hide Gamil. Can you imagine what Kawada would do if he got his hands on Gamil? He'd be off to a pretty-boy brothel in no time." He sat down by Gamil and put an arm about him. "And I checked Gamil's pockets—no residency permit, no ID, nothing at all." He sighed, stood up, and strapped on an oxygen mask. "You'll have to stay here with Gamil. Baapa's dreaming, and I can't miss another shift."

"It was because I ran into Kawada's boys," Saiyul said. "They chased me. When I lost them, they must have come here."

"Well, don't open the airlock for anyone," Ashil said, "in case they come back," then cycled out.

Saiyul sat down across from Gamil, who gave her a vacant, happy look. "Ashhh," the boy said. "Ashil."

"Yes, Ashil. He'll take care of you. He takes care of his father. He takes care of me, when I let him, though sometimes we—" She stopped and bit her lip. "I guess he likes to take care of lost people. And so you'll be his favorite."

"Favorite?" Gamil said. Saiyul nodded. The boy's eyes flicked in the direction of Baapashil. "Bb. Bah."

"Yes. Do you have a baapa? An aama? Or have you lost them? It's really not so bad. I get along fine." But as she stared down into her own lap, she kept circling back to two thoughts. *All I have is Ashil*, was one thought. Kawada was the other. Kawada and his boys and his knife.

She stood up. "We need to get you back to your baapa and aama. They must miss you terribly. And," she said, fingering the fine cloth of his dirty kurta, "if they have money, they might even be offering a reward."

Saiyul rummaged around the flat, until she found a spare oxygen mask. She put it over Gamil's face, took his hand, and led him out the airlock.

She took him to teacher Thufeli.

As Thufeli poured out three small cups of tea and set a tiny plate of sugared olives on the table, Saiyul said, "I think he's suffering from quantum censorship. That's why he talks funny."

Thufeli gave her a sharp look. And then he smiled. "So. You think that?"

Saiyul hadn't known who else to go to. Dolo, the neighborhood constable, would pocket any reward and laugh at Saiyul. The charity clinic would hand Gamil to some faceless magistrate, and again Saiyul wouldn't get any reward. Teacher Thufeli was mostly honest, but also kind. She figured him the best bet to at least share any reward. He also came from offworld, and so might know someone to contact.

She nodded. But Thufeli kept staring at her, the look that said *I know you're lying*, and she let her head sag.

"I don't know what that means," she said quietly.

So he explained. He was a teacher, he liked to explain things.

Air is full of atoms and molecules ("I know," she protested, "I know about oxygen and all that."), but even if you took out the atoms and molecules, the nothingness left behind, the vacuum, would still not be empty. It boils with a gas of half-real, half-imaginary quantum particles, winking in and out of existence, like djinn in a vidnovela.

But one can heat up the vacuum, which allows starships to travel fast, faster than the light from distant stars, using a Kaz-i-meer pump, and one can also freeze the vacuum. Freeze space and time itself.

"Cold foam," Saiyul said. Thufeli liked you to say things once in a while, to prove you were listening.

"Cold quantum foam," he corrected. "Frozen quantum foam."

"With hot foam, hot *quantum* foam, made as waste. I remember now Baapashil telling me that. Why don't they sell it to starships?"

"It's not good enough quality," he said. "So they dump it into the waste pits, fouling the air and the ground. I don't know how anyone..." He shivered, then continued.

In the factory, where Ashil worked and Baapashil used to work, a volume of vacuum, a moment in space and time was frozen, and then split in two. And that forms two halves of a Door.

When a Door is opened, and the frozen chunk of quantum foam is allowed to warm up, for a few moments both halves think they are still in the same place, the same time.

"Do you see?" Thufeli asked. "The same time. The same place. And you can travel between the two halves of a Door in an instant, without getting into a ship.

"Of course, you have to make the two halves of a Door. Ships take the Doors made in our factories to distant stars, to make life easier for people to travel between stars."

"For tourists," Saiyul said, disdainfully. "Rich people."

"Yes, and others. But there is a problem. It's possible for

one end of a Door to open before the other. Imagine you came out a Door before you went in?"

Saiyul frowned. "Is that possible?"

Thufeli smiled. "It shouldn't be, but if both ends of a Door are on distant planets, how can you be sure?

"This is why sometimes, a Door fails. It doesn't let anyone through, because it could lead to what is called a 'paradox.' Luckily, that only happens about a quarter of the time. Many smart people have tried to understand this.

"Sometimes, instead of keeping you from going through, some piece of knowledge or memory doesn't go through. Something that would create the paradox. They call this 'quantum censorship.'"

Thufeli folded his hands and contemplated Gamil. He said quietly, "Eventually, most people regain their memories, when the danger of paradox is over. But this looks like an unusually strong case. I've never seen or heard of any like this."

"I think he comes from a rich family," Saiyul said. "I mean, doesn't that face look like wealth? And he was wearing very fine clothes when he came through. Dirty, but very expensive."

The teacher examined the rags Gamil wore now. "What, these?"

"I didn't want to attract any attention—like Kawada's." Then she lowered her head, and her voice. "That's what I told Ashil. On the way here I sold his clothes. I need the money, to get out of here before Kawada gets to me."

Thufeli gave a soft laugh. "And that's why you stole the Door."

"I was thinking," and Saiyul's heart sped up, this was the tricky part: what if she offended Teacher Thufeli? "thinking that someone might be looking for him. His family. And them being rich, there must be a reward."

"You know this?"

She blew out a breath. "Of course I don't *know*. I'm just an alley girl. I can barely read. But, you," and she swallowed before continuing, "you're a respected teacher, an offworlder. You know lots of people and you can ask questions. I'll split the reward with you."

"Reward," Gamil said. "With you."

"See?" she said. "He thinks there's one."

"I don't know," Thufeli said, sipping his tea.

Saiyul felt despair choke her, as if it was filling her throat and lungs. She was slipping down into the darkness, drowning. With shoulders slumped she unfolded her legs. "Come on," she said to Gamil.

"Wait," said Thufeli. He stood up and walked to the sealed window that overlooked the alley, where he leaned against the frame, thinking. Then he turned to Saiyul. "I'll ask around."

Relief rose inside Saiyul, a bubble of pure oxygen.

The teacher put a gentle hand under Gamil's chin. "Better leave the boy with me. Then I can prove it's really him. Come back tomorrow—no, the day after tomorrow is better."

To Gamil Saiyul said, "You'll be safe here. Safer than at Ashil's. He means well, but..."

Thufeli asked, "Do you need money for food? Oxygen?" And he dug in his pocket for a couple of coins, adding, "And watch out for Kawada's boys."

Not wanting to face Ashil, Saiyul spent both nights curled up on the earthen floor of her abandoned room hidey-hole, shivering next to the useless, empty frame of the Door. She hardly slept, wondering what Teacher Thufeli had found out about Gamil. When the second morning finally came, she imagined the boy already in a soft, comfortable bed with all the oxygen he needed.

The light just past dawn was grim and grainy, as if filtered through dirty glass. She climbed the stairs to Thufeli's flat and buzzed the airlock. When he let her in, he was still in his nightshirt and rubbing his unshaven face.

"And?" she asked.

"Not even waiting for a cup of tea?" Thufeli asked. He yawned and produced out a large handful of plastic bills.

Saiyul's eyes widened. "So there *was* a reward!" She looked up at Thufeli. "Did you learn what happened? A kidnapping? Or did he just run away—"

He closed his eyes. "It was suggested that I not ask many questions. When these things happen, well, unofficially..." And opening his eyes again, he handed the bills to Saiyul.

She stared at the money. "I thought you were saving up for a trip home."

Teacher Thufeli smiled and dipped his head. "I think I can afford that now." Then his face took on a serious look. "But you should leave right away. I heard Kawada is furious you have eluded him. He won't just maim you if he finds you. He boasts he'll kill you."

Saiyul swallowed. "I'll just say goodbye to Ashil."

He put a hand on her upper arm. "I wouldn't even do that. I know he was your friend, and Baapashil... But Kawada'll look for you there. Let me make your goodbyes for you."

She ran down the stairs, pausing to check up and down the alley before darting into the stream of weaving figures.

It took nearly until midday to find the forger, sipping a cup of kaffi at the fence's. The fence smirked but said nothing. After Saiyul handed over her bills, with only enough left to refill her oxygen canister a day or two, the forger produced a travel permit.

The sun was at its highest in the sky, a red and angry eye, and the light and heat came down in thick waves, like honey, as Saiyul stood in line to cross over to the next zone. She kept her head tucked down while surreptiously scanning for Kawada and his boys. She didn't see them, but with an electric shock she spotted Baapashil crouching against the wall, his hand out begging.

Feeling her face flush, Saiyul turned her head away and hoped he hadn't noticed her. So intent was she on becoming invisible that she herself failed to see the constable, Dolo, until it was too late.

Dolo planted herself next to Saiyul, feet apart. It was a joke of the gods that Dolo, broad as a wrestler, had a beautiful face, and her savagely shorn hair and her gruff manner and day-laborer's tongue did nothing to hide it. With deliberate theater the constable unhooked the sparkpain from her belt. "Papers," she demanded.

Saiyul felt her stomach upend itself as she handed over her documents. She didn't have much money left with which to bribe the constable. Dolo returned Saiyul's residency permit but closely examined the travel permit.

"This," Dolo said at last, "is the worst forgery I've seen in my life."

Saiyul would have run away, but Dolo was pressed up against her. "You say that to every one," she managed to say. "To get better bribes."

Dolo laughed, the kind of laugh a bit of scrap iron might make. "You insult me by presenting such a bad forgery." Saiyul could smell her breath: beer, and a bit of ginger. "You went behind my back," Dolo said. "You know how that makes me look?"

The constable flicked on the sparkpain, which began to tremble and hum. People backed away.

"I'm a poor, humble constable," Dolo continued. "And it's hard to live on my meager salary. All I ask for is a little respect. A few modest donations."

"I've always paid—"

Dolo jammed the sparkpain into Saiyul's stomach, and she doubled over as agony exploded inside her and radiated through all her limbs.

"You went behind my back! You sold that boy, that beautiful boy to Thufeli, and he sold him to Kawada. And Kawada, well, you know Kawada. He thinks he's not afraid of me. Doesn't mind if I beat up a few of his boys to keep in shape. I won't see the tiniest coin from him."

"Thufeli...?" Saiyul gasped, and the stab of the realization was almost as bad as the sparkpain. Almost.

Dolo swung the sparkpain around and brushed it against the top of Saiyul's head. Lightning shot through her brain; it felt as if she had been thrown into the sun. She tried to scream but her lungs were paralyzed. She crashed to her knees, tasting blood in her mouth and smelling burnt hair.

"Did you really think," said Dolo, pushing her face close to Saiyul's, "I wouldn't find out? That you could slip away?"

The constable withdrew her face, and last thing Saiyul saw was the blunt, angry tip of the sparkpain.

Then red oblivion gobbled her up.

She became aware of a cool pressure on her forehead, a small island of relief in a vast, restless ocean of pain. Saiyul tried to lie as still as possible, even as crackles of discomfort coursed up and down her limbs.

"Are you awake?" It was Ashil's voice, and she recognized the musty odor of Ashil's flat, overlaid with the sharp tang of ozone from an airlock. Ashil came and stood over her. "It's been two days."

"What? Happened?" she asked, though it came out as a groan.

"Dolo kept hitting you with the sparkpain. My father, he saw it, he stood between you and—" His voice broke.

"Did he bring me here?" Saiyul whispered. Ashil shook his head. With an effort that caused her to gasp, she raised her head and glanced around the flat. "Where's Baapashil?"

Ashil turned away. "At the charity clinic," he said, choking on the words, "I had to make a choice. They had only one bed free, and they said you'd live, no question, but baapa..."

Saiyul closed her eyes and turned her head away. A cold fist gripped her heart.

She heard the sounds of Ashil fiddling with the teakettle.

At length he came and sat down by her. "Why did Dolo beat you?"

Instead of answering, Saiyul forced herself to sit up. Her body screamed in agony, as if hot needles had been jammed into every muscle, but she stiffly limped over to the small mirror on the wall. Her face had dark bruises on it, bruises that reminded her of the frozen emptiness in the Door.

At last she managed to croak, "Thufeli..."

"Thufeli? He's gone," Ashil said. "I heard he bought a ticket home. He told people he had gotten money from family, but there's a rumor—" He stopped. Saiyul turned around and saw he had screwed his eyes tight, but tears were leaking out from under his lids. "With baapa in the charity hospital it hardly seems to matter, but I can't help asking. What happened to Gamil? I thought he had run away, again, but last night I saw him with this tourist, you know, the kind of tourist who likes boys, the kind of tourist who goes to Kawada and—" He opened his eyes and his mouth and clenched his fists. "*What happened with Gamil?*"

She couldn't look at him. Her gut was turning over. "Baapashil," she said, and it hurt her to say it, not the pain in her transient, treacherous flesh, but the shame splitting her soul deep down, "your father, is a better person than I am."

The next afternoon Ashil spotted Gamil in tow of an old, fancy off-worlder woman climbing the steps to the hoinist temple. "Probably to make an offering," Ashil said. "She had a cage carrying a couple of dwarf goats from the market."

"How did Gamil look?" Saiyul asked softly.

"One of Kawada's boys was close by, what do you think?" Gamil had an oxygen mask, Ashil added, but it fed out of the woman's canister, making it impossible for him to run away.

Saiyul sighed. She had seen this before. Runaways. Boys and girls left without family. Kawada would beat them, force them into sex with customers until they were too terrified to resist, and then sell them on to a trafficker. The only reason Saiyul hadn't been snatched up was she was too ugly. That, and Baapashil had always given her a place to stay.

Saiyul wouldn't let this happen to Gamil.

Ashil insisted on helping. "The brothers only let me visit baapa for an hour a day." He grabbed Saiyul's hand. "Please. I need to do something. The waiting just gnaws at my stomach. The charity doctor, he said he'll lose an eye. At least. He hasn't woken up. The charity doctor doesn't know if he will."

At sunset they waited outside the hoinist gate of refuge. On the black marble a vast mouth was carved, swallowing up an entire galaxy of people.

Out of the satiny dusk came a silver-haired woman in fine clothes. Saiyul thought the shadows didn't hide the sour look on her face. The fancy woman trotted towards a waiting air-car, with Gamil leashed by an oxygen tube, and Kawada's boy just a few steps behind.

Ashil staggered in front of them, a barrel hoisted on his back, as any honest laborer might carry. Right before Kawada's boy he dropped the barrel. Hot quantum foam, scooped up from one of the waste pits, sluiced out, sending up cloud of toxic steam.

Kawada's boy yelped and started to swear at Ashil. The fancy woman threw up her hands and cried out. Just then Saiyul slipped in, cut with a knife the tubing that led to Gamil's oxygen mask, and grabbed his hand.

"Come with me!" she said.

But he stood like a tree, rooted to the spot by fear. Saiyul knew he'd be like that, so she just gripped his hand hard and pulled. She was tough and strong, and though he was a little taller, he was thin and birdlike.

A moment later they were racing through the cool air of the alley. Saiyul handed Gamil an extra oxygen mask and canister. "Put this on," she said, panting. "But don't stop!"

As the last light of dusk fled the sky they met up with Ashil, whose right hand was tucked under his left arm. When Saiyul looked quizzically, Ashil said, "I got splashed. Let's go."

Saiyul turned to Gamil. "The factory'll be empty now."

The boy shivered. "He'll hurt me," he said, his words as musical and plaintive as birdsong. "He said he'll hurt me."

Ashil said quickly, "Do you remember where you come from? Your mother or father?" He shook his head. "Why you came through the Door? Do you remember anything?" Gamil just trembled, his arms wrapped around himself.

With Saiyul on one side and Ashil on the other, they guided Gamil down the main boulevard. The air became noxious, and Gamil began a racking cough. "Watch your feet," Ashil whispered. "Don't step in a waste pit." The night sky above was freckled with bright stars, and against it the hulking mass of the factory looked like the silhouette of a sleeping monster.

They stopped just short of the fence around the factory and crouched down. Just beyond the fence the lone light of the night watchman moved erratically along the ground, like the wanderings of a moth. Gamil coughed, and for a moment the watchman halted. All three of them held their breath. A few moments later the watchman moved on.

They ran to the fence. With his left hand, Ashil clumsily took out a stolen key chip. When he pressed it against the lock, however, nothing happened.

"Try again," Saiyul whispered.

"It won't work," Ashil said. "After we stole the last Door, they must have changed the chip codes."

"Can we climb over?" Saiyul said, stepping back to gauge the fence.

"A room," Gamil said suddenly. "I remember a room. It was blue."

"Not now," Saiyul said.

"But I was happy there. I remember being happy."

Saiyul shushed him again, but from behind them in the dark came shouts, among them a shrill, nasal, gut-wrenching voice: "Move it, you stupid dogs. And spread out. I tell you, they'll come here."

Kawada.

Saiyul's heart froze, as cold as the vacuum frozen in a Door.

Gamil must have recognized the voice, too, for he tore away from her grasp and crouched on the ground, hiding. "Try again," Saiyul said to Ashil.

"It won't—" he began.

Gamil stood up, a stone in his hands so heavy he could barely lift it. He heaved it against the lock. Saiyul's heart was pounding wildly, and she grabbed the stone from Gamil with both hands, elbowed him aside, and bashed the lock again, hard.

It buckled and sparked, and as alarms began to wail like a thousand million funeral mourners all crying out incoherently, the gate swung open.

Saiyul dropped the stone, narrowly missing her foot, and grabbed both Gamil and Ashil by their clothes. "Go!" she cried.

They ran to the warehouse. All the lights were coming on, leaving no shadow in which to hide. The cool night air, threaded with toxic fumes, burned Saiyul's lungs and eyes, and tears streamed down her cheek. "Oh, *hurry*!" she urged Gamil and Ashil.

Inside the warehouse, Ashil cried, "Top rack," and Saiyul impatiently replied, "I know!" Ashil couldn't climb with his hurt arm, so Saiyul monkeyed her way up, dropped a Door to the floor, then jumped after it. Ashil was already tearing off the metallicized plastic over, and pressed the switch. Saiyul slid between Ashil and Gamil and grabbed their hands, so that no matter what happened, they wouldn't be parted.

But nothing happened.

"Did it break when it fell?" Saiyul said, her stomach curling.

"I told you, Doors sometimes don't open. Something wrong would happen..."

"A paradox, Thufeli called it. Does that mean none will open?"

"I remember a door," Gamil said. "A blue door." Both of them looked at him. He lowered his head and said, "Not this kind of Door..."

Before they could ask any more questions, the door into the warehouse—an ordinary door on hinges, of metal and extruded hydrocarbon chains—swung open, and there stood Kawada. He was a smallish man, and looked like a piece of weather-eaten leather; but his face, pale like old milk, was full of rage. He yanked a knife from his belt and ran at them.

Saiyul turned and shimmied up the rack of Doors again, her lungs burning and her arms aching. Sweat pooled on her forehead and chest.

"Come down, girl, or I'll slice up your friends!"

Saiyul glanced down, saw Kawada had the knife to Ashil's throat, and was gripping Gamil's arm tightly with his other hand.

She pulled herself up to the second rack of Doors. Kawada roared, "You're dead either way, but if you don't want your friends to die too—!" as she grabbed a fistful of metallicized plastic and ripped it off. It floated to the floor, like a downy feather from a chick.

"I'll cut the throat of the *jhaant*-addict's son's first!" Kawada shouted, and she heard Ashil cry out in pain. She turned her head again and saw the knife pressing at Ashil's throat.

Saiyul stretched a few centimeters higher and slapped the switch for the Door.

She just wanted out of there, away from all this misery, away from the horror of this life. As the Door began to glow, her vision was swallowed up; at the same time her ears were filled as Kawada shouted obscenities, and Ashil called her name, and Gamil began to wail like a siren. Her arms aching, Saiyul grabbed the frame of the Door, and with the last of her strength she tried to pull herself through the Door and away.

She had more strength than she thought; she yanked the Door so hard it jerked off its mooring, bounced off her scalp, and tumbled over her head.

It fell to the floor, face down.

All was silence.

She was still clinging to the rack, panting, when the night watchman and Dolo burst into the warehouse floor. Dolo yelled something, but Saiyul didn't listen. She climbed down, exhausted, stumbled over to the Door, and flipped it over.

Under it she found Kawada's knife. But he, Ashil, and Gamil were gone.

Years and years later, Saiyul was pushing her cart when two well-dressed men came up to her. "Oxygen refilled?" she asked.

"Understand you shelter children," the taller of the two men said, in an off-world dialect.

She nodded. "Any child in need. Runaways, orphans. Children of *jhaant*-addicts. Children escaping the hoinists. If you wish to give donations—"

The shorter man showed her an image. A pale wisp of a boy with delicate, almost girlish features.

"Does this child have a name?" Saiyul asked, her heart beating fast.

"Jora. Enili pin Jora."

"Jora," Saiyul repeated softly.

"There is reward," the tall man added.

Saiyul said nothing.

"Have been told," the short one said, "how fiercely you defend children. Do not suspect us." He paused. "Family is wealthy. Gang took Jora for ransom. Militia tracked and ambushed gang. They found no Jora, but unregistered in Door had been opened."

"Door manufactured here," the tall one said.

Saiyul looked up from the image to the men. "The factory has been shuttered for six years," she said, and the men nodded.

"With Doors," said the short man, "never know. We look for out Door. But record of location has been lost. For months we have searched warehouses, transport manifests, everything."

"We ask about stored Doors, but everyone denies knowledge," said the tall man. "Please. Family is desperate."

Saiyul stared at the image for a long time. "After all this time, can you still hope to find good news?"

The men glanced at each other. "Hope is oxygen to family. To give up hope would be to give up breathing."

Saiyul nodded. She felt her throat constrict, but managed to say, "My own best friend—I was an orphan, and he was like a brother, or more—disappeared one night. Oh, it must have been ten years, no, twelve. I never saw or heard from him again."

She tapped the image with a finger. "How long...?"

"Eight months. Eight months ago."

So Baapashil had been right all along. After she brought him home from the charity hospital and nursed him back to health, he had hid his grief by speculating about Gamil. "He hasn't gone through the in Door yet, I'll wager," he said. "Somewhere out there on a distant planet, he hasn't gone through... His memories might not catch up until then. Could be years. When he does, he'll help Ashil come home, I'm sure." But as time passed, *jhaant*'s seductive despair wracked Baapashil's mind. Eventually he sought refuge in the hoinists and took the final pilgrimage, leaving Saiyul orphaned once more.

The men handed Saiyul a contact code. "Would I want to know if he were lost forever," she asked aloud, nestling the contact code in her palm as if it were a small bird, "or would I want to cling to my hope, keep breathing that oxygen?"

Tears rolled down her cheek. Both men bowed, and she was touched by the respect they showed. Saiyul told them, "I'll need a little time, but before you leave," and she had trouble speaking for the lump in her throat, "I promise I'll bring you what news I can."

And swallowing her grief she pushed the cart past the men and down the alley, singing out “Oxygen! Oxygen!” to her customers.

Dagger and Mask

Cat Rambo

If you had asked Eduw if he loved Grania, he would have been indignant. Naturally he did. He loved all his targets.

Not at first. He was put off. That scar that marred her face, it hurt to look at. It wasn't an uncommon condition, despite what the meddies said. Some people rejected plas-flesh. It didn't take, didn't renew lost skin, didn't rebuild damaged features. For some it even seemed to make things worse.

So with Grania. And she hadn't chosen to go the route most people did, some other form of concealment, like veils or cloaking devices. Instead, she'd tattooed borders around the ruined skin, studded it with crystals embedded in the roughened flesh, taking the grotesque damage and turning it into something inhuman and beautiful, ruin and design mingled until you couldn't tell what was accidental, what purposeful. Her right eye looked out from that artifact as though pressed against a peephole in order to see the world.

It made you wonder what she was trying to say by not covering it up. What she was trying to tell you about herself by not concealing it. What it meant that she didn't try to hide it.

But that was it, that was all she was saying, Eduw realized later. That she didn't hide anything. It would have been wasted energy to her.

He came on board at Epsilon-5. Grania didn't hire him. She had a ship of over five hundred members to oversee. So he'd talked to the first officer, who made a perfunctory check of his forged documents, but was more interested in quizzing him to make sure he knew what a Volant engine was. Twenty or so new crew members came aboard the *Chalice* at that station, replacing the attrition of six long cycles wandering along the Kehrli border.

Maybe they'd sent a monitor along with him, maybe not. Usually they didn't with long-established assassins, ones who had proven themselves before.

It didn't take him long to get used to life aboard her ship. Decent food, good working conditions, a happy crew for a change. But he didn't glimpse its captain until over a week in.

A netgrom failed and he was the only one who knew what to do. None of the others even thought it could go. They stood there wide-eyed amid the acrid yellow steam, watching it roil around them until he pushed the chief engineer out of the way and patched the Leicht collar, just in time.

Everyone knew they would have been goners without that and he got a lot more attention from the crew at large than he'd hoped for. But it did what he'd wanted. He met Grania when she came to thank him.

Her eyes were grey. Not grey as in a lack of color, but a grey that held them all, just below the surface, like a bruised opal.

She said, "Eduw, right? You've earned yourself a bonus, next time we dock."

She reached out and they shook hands. He tried not to look at the scar at first. But why would you have it if you minded people seeing it? So he did look, stared at the red frilled edge where it began, at the pebbly, silvery surface and the facets gleaming on her cheek, at the way it tugged her eye down and the corner of her mouth upward.

That was when she first really noticed him, he could tell. Before then he'd just been a work item to tick off— "Thank crewmember who saved the ship" —but now he was a person and she looked back in a way that made him uneasy, as though she were seeing straight through his skin, down to the depths of his soul, finding out that he'd sabotaged the net-grom in the first place, trying to create this moment.

But she couldn't have, because she just smiled at him. He ducked his chin, triggered the pheromones he'd prepared. Couldn't do that anywhere but in the close confines of a ship, with the fans in this section disabled for his repairs while the netgrom was being dismantled.

Sometimes he surprised himself with how well he planned. He dared a glance up into those cool grey eyes, wondering what thoughts lurked behind them like scaly predators below the water's surface.

He expected the call before it came, confirming another fragment of his plan had clicked into place. Captain's prerog-ative, ordering someone to her cabin for mutual recreation. Rarely against someone's will, but that had been known to happen on some ships. Not this one, though. He'd already noted how carefully it was run. When he'd come on board, they'd promised him a share in the profit, once the two-trip probation was over. A munificent offer. No wonder the *Chalice* was hotly sought after as employment. He'd even had to dis-pose of some of his competition beforehand.

He'd hoped for this. Beyond the pheromones ready to dose her again, he had the right chemicals ready to go in his system in case they were needed, in case he had trouble performing. In case he was put off by that scar, the way it slid across her cheekbone, glinting in the light.

To his surprise there was no problem with his performance at all. Odd for him, who'd eschewed so many pleasant things as part of his determination to succeed. He wasn't celibate, not that, but he'd never played at love and romance the way some did. Sex was a transaction, an exchange of certain intangible or tangible things, like touch and attention and sometimes money and sometimes power.

Lying in her bed, he wondered if this would give him power, that he'd been here. He thought not. She surely knew better than that, knew that it was a way to make a crew dissatisfied. He thought that if anything she'd be harder on him as a result.

He rolled over and touched the scar with his fingertips as she slept. The grey eyes opened, watching him. Was it the scar or amusement that gave her the look of a smile?

He had always thought that what he felt for the people he was sent to kill was love. Wasn't that what love was, attention so close it could kill you? He helped them find their destiny. He helped them before the people that had sent him could send someone, something worse. He spared them pain.

Grania made him falter in his convictions. That was new. That was unexpected. And because of that, he toyed with it, savoring the strange sensation of *caring*. Caring what she thought, caring what she did.

He'd allow himself that, he thought, but only for a little while. He had been sent to kill her, after all. That was his mission. He hadn't known why then, but now that he had been aboard the *Chalice* for a while, he had suspicions. The merchants and political consortiums that dealt with trade between solar systems weren't interested in letting crewmembers have expectations of a share in the cargo and its profits, getting ideas above their class. She refused to pay pirate tolls and border bribes. It let her undercut merchants who wanted to keep the money where it was, in the hands where it had rested so long.

Long shifts working, the occasional pleasurable hour in her cabin. He thought he wasn't the only one, but she was discreet and careful.

Sometimes he stared at her closed face, wondering: what was he to her? Convenience? Indulgence?

Something else?

When he'd first seen the ship, looking out the shuttle window on his way with the other new crew, he'd thought it looked like a great silvery bird, its wings caught half-rising, half-falling. Cannons bristled along it but they were small and light, other than the three great lasers that rode the command center, which might have been the bird's head seen from a particular angle.

A shiny ship, which he didn't understand then, not until he saw how clean it was inside, until he realized that the crew kept it that way, kept it ready, put in extra hours to do so simply because they loved the ship. Some crewmembers had lived almost all their lives aboard, had come in as teens. It made him wonder how old Grania was.

It was against human nature, such a ship. She must have come from one of the deprived planets, to have such a revolutionary, anti-social streak, to create an order on her ship that was so unprecedented. But when he asked, the planet she named was small and ordinary. Hardly the sort of furnace in which she should have been forged.

Maybe it was just the experience of having been born there, on an actual planet. He'd been birthed on a crèche station himself, readied to go into labor like everyone else. Someone had seen his scores and pulled him out of the general pool destined for the factory worlds. Instead he'd been trained as a weapon, a dagger to be used.

She'd chosen to become what she was. Had he ever been asked if that was what he wanted? He didn't remember it, but surely they must have made sure that he consented to his role.

He said to Grania in bed, "Aren't you worried, going against the flow like this? The Powers That Be don't like the lower classes getting ideas in their heads and you're the one putting those concepts there, reawakening old and obsolete ideas. Making people think they might have a right to profit. It's not fair to lead them on like that."

She propped her chin on his chest, considering his face. "How do I lead them on?"

"You make promises that no one ever lives up to."

"I will."

It was true. He'd spoken to the other crew who'd been there longer. The share wasn't a false lure, and even more intriguingly, it worked. The invested crew spoke differently of the ship, used a tone he'd never heard before. He found himself cheered by it. He thought about giving up his mission, staying there with her. She'd tire of him soon enough, but here was a place that he might, intriguingly, call home in a way he'd never known any other place.

The thoughts stayed with him, a daydream he could escape into, a garment he could wrap around his mind and relax into. It snuck up on him, began to seem more and more plausible, more and more possible.

At least, until he returned to his bunk after a shift and saw what lay across his pillow.

Anyone else might have mistaken it for a strand of white thread, barely a half meter long, fallen in an odd, knotted pattern. But to someone who could read it, it was a message. There was a monitor aboard, watching him.

Irritating, that someone had thought he might falter or fail. Even more irritating that they had been right.

Maybe Grania had done the same thing he had. Maybe the air here held chemicals to convince him. To make everyone on board gullible. To force her crew members to buy into an impossible dream. Because it was impossible. Human nature wasn't compatible with her ideas. It was meaner, smaller than she thought.

He had to kill her or he'd be killed. And that was a waste—they only had to succeed once. Eventually they'd win. They had the money, the resources. She had a ship and idealism. She couldn't succeed, couldn't change the way the universe worked.

He picked up the thread and knotted it around his wrist. Acknowledgement that the message had been read, would be heeded. He found himself watching the others who had come aboard when he did, but there was no guarantee the monitor was among them. They could have been placed earlier, when Grania first came to someone's notice.

The monitor might be the one who'd decided to enlist him, even.

He didn't like the feeling of being watched. It made him twitchy, made his skin crawl. Made him look over his shoulder while pretending he wasn't. Another mask to put on, and one the watching monitor would see through effortlessly.

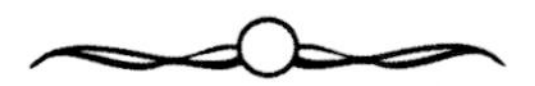

Pirates plagued the Gussoff run, but the *Chalice* was ready for them. He knew what to do when the attack alarm shrilled. They all did, they'd drilled and practiced. He climbed into one of the tiny fliers, more suit than ship, smelling the reek of plastic and hyperfuel, feeling the controls clamp along his arms and legs, and launched himself into space like the others.

A hundred tiny ships, a swarm of them, shot at the pirate vessel coming at them hard and fast, its lasers swiveling, trying to pick them off. But they were too small, too fast. Individually, they could do nothing, but together they were a force to be reckoned with, strafing the other ship, carving gouges in its sides as they rocketed past. He swooped and glided, moving almost faster than he could react, frantically monitoring the controls.

Someone flashed past, headed straight for the attacking ship. He expected to see the impact—had they miscalculated? Was their suit not working? But they veered away at the last minute, leaving a trail of damage along the ship's hull like a silver scar, taking out two turrets. The pirate had its revenge, though. As the suit pulled away, another laser flashed, clipped them, sent them spiraling in a pinwheel of limbs.

He barely managed to change course to intercept the tumbling form, caught them in his arms as he'd been taught, a hard jolt that would leave them both bruised.

Saw the grey eyes through the faceplate searching his. Through the thick glass, the scar gleamed like mercury on her skin, dotted with color.

He'd known she might be out there. Knew they all risked themselves for the ship. But he'd thought that was a sham, that she'd stay back, her presence only a token. That there would be some small things in which she'd prove hypocritical.

Wrong again.

He remembered the feel of the thread around his wrist, remembered how it bit as it had tightened. When he returned to his bunk, another thread lay there. Scarlet now.

If he didn't kill her soon, he would be killed.

He lay down on his bunk, thinking, winding the thread back and forth through his fingers, feeling it drag against calluses, calluses he'd acquired working here on this ship. He'd never had calluses like that before except from weapons practice, working to shape himself. Not working to make a home.

What if he told her how he had been sent? What if he asked her aid and promised her he would be her weapon now? He could return to those who had sent him, return and do what needed to be done to save her.

And if he did that, could she change things? Could she rally others, bring a corrupt system toppling down? No more crèche planets shipping labor off to where it was needed. All those babies like himself could grow up and *choose*. Could choose where they wanted to go, what they wanted to do.

The thought terrified and exhilarated him. He could remove his mask. He could be himself, no longer someone who changed themselves to fit from role to role. What would that be like? He wondered who he would become, if he allowed himself. With her encouragement, he could be someone different.

Dangerous. He'd tell her there was a monitor. They'd have to act carefully, lure them out. With her help, though, he could do that. Perhaps.

His stomach churned as he thought, as he tried to pick from the whirl of possibilities. At least if he died that way, he would have tried. Did that matter? It seemed as though it should, but often things were not as they seemed.

She must feel some loyalty to him. Some tie. He'd dosed her with the pheromones every chance he got, touched her arm to rouse oxytocin, used every trick he could. But she was so reserved, kept herself so well hidden. Was the scar a mask, something you'd look at rather than seeing deeper? By now he loved it, could have drawn its outlines, could have told you how many of each color of gem spangled in a complicated constellation across the ruined skin.

Would she listen? Any other captain would kill a spy on their ship, would do so instantly in case of triplecross, do it before the spy might have a chance to get a coded message squeal out. Before any damage could be done.

He'd drawn the string so tightly around his fingers that it was cutting into the skin. The pain made him sit up. He swung his legs off the bunk. He'd talk to her. That was the only choice.

But standing outside her cabin door, he heard voices. Had she brought someone else to her bed? The thought brought an unexpected tightness to his chest. He cursed his weakness. There was no reason to give his mission this kind of mind. He must kill her and escape, must get off this ship that had so deranged him.

The door slid open and the first officer exited, barely sparing him a glance. Not sex, then. His muscles loosened, then tightened again as he told himself that he couldn't give way to false sentimentality, mustn't buy into a future that couldn't exist, that was entirely imaginary. That could never be realized.

His preferred weapon lay inside his own body, a sliver of poisoned steel that could slide through skin and into another's brain or heart. It was ready now. He could feel it lying along his forearm as she beckoned him in.

"You've saved my life twice now," she told him. Her hand cupped his cheek. He closed his eyes, swallowing. Now would be the time to speak, the time to reveal himself.

But the moment was past. She was drawing him to the bed.

It was a different moment now. The steel throbbed deep under the surface and he could feel muscles flexing, ready to act.

Strike fast. Strike now, before regret overtook him and made him slow. Strike before the grey eyes opened and saw what he was doing.

The steel slid out...

And the eyes, open and regarding him, were cool and calm and strong. Before he could step forward, something clamped down along his spine. He was unable to move, falling forward on the cool metal of the floor. His eyes, unable to close, watched as she removed the filters from her nose, watched as she came nearer. His throat constricted as he tried to ask how and why and when she'd known, but the world shrank to her unreadable expression, to her hand, then the circle of the gun's muzzle, as she fired and then he was gone.

She'd suspected what he'd try when he came on board, Grania thought as she pressed the call button. She'd known when the netgrom failed. He hadn't been the first, he wouldn't be the last. Sometimes they waited long enough that her hopes roused, that she thought they might come over to her. That was when she tested them with the thread.

She was sorry for this. A little, at least. She'd had hopes for Eduw. Now she'd have to try again, try tricks of touch and trust-building, hoping that eventually an assassin would waver, switch his or her allegiance, become the dagger she'd use against the forces opposing her.

If you had asked Grania if she had loved Eduw, she would have been indignant. She did. Certainly she did.

But not enough to stay her hand.

Ouroboros

Christine Lucas

The dead philosopher came out of his cavern only when both the moons of Mars were below the horizon. Or so the legend claimed.

Under a clear sky over the Martian wilderness, Kallie focused her hearing and sought the faintest sound that might confirm his existence. Nothing. The nanobots lining her auditory nerves redoubled their efforts. Still nothing. Yet. She turned her attention towards the base at northeast, under the shadow of Olympus Mons. No alarms, no sirens, no one on her trail. They hadn't noticed her absence. Yet. But they would, and they'd unleash the Enforcer.

She broke into a light jog. The nanobots set into gear, repairing, fueling, sustaining her system, while she put as much distance as possible between herself and the base. A few clicks later, just over Ulysses Fossae, the wind picked up, and Kallie turned southeast under the cover of the sandstorm. She didn't stop to catch her breath until she found herself under clear skies again. Panting inside her environmental suit, with her thin brown hair plastered on her sweaty forehead under her cowl and over her goggles, she leaned against a rust-colored boulder. Her respirator vibrated softly over the lower part of her face, filtering out the red sands.

They had built her well—too well, but not for Mars. Not for the desert. For the ocean. This desperate run could kill her. Well. She'd be dead anyway in a week from now, ten days tops. But she couldn't die without knowing what her makers wouldn't—or couldn't—answer.

He had to know. Of all the creatures on all the planets, *he* had to.

She straightened up and marched on. Southeast, to the caves on the flanks of the Arsia Mons volcano, where shuttles went missing, strange whispers lingered at the edge of the radio frequencies and lights danced over the caldera at dusk. Southeast, towards the dawn over Tharsis Montes. Her nanobots urged her on, perched at the edge of her consciousness, echoing tales hidden deep into the folds of her brain, reminiscing never-taken roads on brittle ground, amidst the laurel and the olive, strips of rocky land between the ever-stretching blue of sea and sky—*Sikinos, Seriphos, Crete, Santorini*. The scent of wild oregano and thyme filled her nostrils and she halted light-headed, her heart racing.

She could *not* know such things. Was she hallucinating? Had her oxygen levels dropped? She checked the readings on her scanner. Arterial blood oxygen at 98.4 percent. No. It wasn't that.

Perhaps she was just mad. Perhaps the nanobots her makers had given her had dug into her brain too hungrily, too deeply, rewiring synapses and short-circuiting neurons. New—false?—memories resurfaced in dreams and waking; the voices of her foremothers crowded around her, their forms flickered in her peripheral vision within shadows and corners. Perhaps—

The shuffling of feet on sand.

Kallie held her breath and listened. Something stirred down southeast, under the shadow of Arsia Mons; something slouched out of a hole in the ground, inch by inch, bone on sand, metal on stone, grunting and moaning and cursing. From the north, over the volcanic deposits of Alba Mons, came the humming of the algae farms, slowly but steadily enriching the thin Martian atmosphere with oxygen. At the east, in the wilderness of the Eos Chasma, the terraforming plant buzzed and grunted, struggling against the whims of a stubborn planet that just wouldn't be tamed. Nothing from northwest. They hadn't caught her trail—yet.

Kallie ran.

At the feet of a low hill close to the volcano, she heard her doom at northwest. The station's outer doors opened, and heavy boots stomped on red pebbles. The Enforcer had been dispatched to bring the wayward daughter home.

Between hurried strides, she dared a glance up, seeking the homeworld she had never walked on. Phobos and Deimos were below the horizon, but Earth was not. Strip-mined, overpopulated, famished Earth. Was it still blue from orbit, as in the old images? Could the dead forests, the polluted oceans and the desperate, hungry mankind be seen from space? Over the last century, raw materials had become a rare commodity, unlike genetic material—unlike *flesh*. These days, Earth Central wouldn't waste probes of titanium and steel to explore the icy oceans of Europa or the craters of Ganymede. They'd send Kallie and her kin.

They were cheap. Expendable. And no one would miss them.

Her fists clenched. *No*. Not yet. Not like this. Not without knowing.

She strode on. Almost there—then something changed beneath her soles that made her nanobots purr. A barrier—no, a *border*, the point where two opposite forces met, each one struggling to claim Mars as its own.

The dead philosopher loitered outside the mouth of a low-roofed cavern, basking in the low humming of an unfamiliar force. It lurked beneath the surface, ancient and complex and aloof, murmuring in sync with her bots. A weird magnetic rock? The wreckage of some alien spacecraft, or even a base of a long-extinct species, stranded there from the planet's youth? *That* was not a threat, the bots assured her, welcoming the presence beneath like long lost kin. *H*e, however, *could* be.

Vourkolakas, cried her bots, with the voice of black-clad crones, spitting thrice on the ground. *Katahanas*, old goatherds hissed under their grey moustaches, making the sign of the cross. *His kind cannot cross water*, sailors warned her, flashing images of shrouded corpses brought to rest on dry, desolate isles away from shore. Priests with ascetic faces mumbled exorcisms; priests of many a time and many a place, clad in black and gold and white, robes and chitons, all reciting prayers against evil. All but one: the lone priestess with her grey hair loose on her shoulders, chewing on laurel leaves, her eyes wild and unfocused.

Listen, she slurred. *Listen, Daughter, and heed not our last warning to the king: the talking water is not silenced, the blessed laurel has not wilted. They come in new, strange shapes and voices now. But they never perished.*

Kallie blinked the vision away, biting back her frustration. Why wouldn't they let her focus? Why wouldn't they let her *think*, when she had to deal with… that? She had studied as much material as she could find on the undead creatures of the old Earth: zombies, ghouls, vampires, along with efficient methods of termination, in case that one proved to be hostile. Kallie measured him from bald head to bare, scrawny feet half-buried in the loose soil. Countless descriptions of this particular specimen were whispered amidst the Martian dwellers, and none of them matched the truth. He wasn't seven feet tall, nor was he a dwarf of an alien species. He didn't charge her to devour her brains, neither did he dart back into the cave, howling curses and obscenities. Sitting cross-legged at the mouth of the cavern, he didn't even glance up at her, only uttered three words.

"Got any smokes?"

Kallie shook her head, confused. Smokes? *Tobacco*? Hadn't those been banned decades ago? She blinked. He didn't sound like a philosopher, but what did she know? Nor did he look like any death-defying creature she had read about. Bits of metal glinted under desiccated strips of flesh, dried sinew and parched skin. His eyes glowed red in the twilight. *Dead* eyes, she realized, from the way he held up his head, turning his ears instead—what was left of them, brownish flaps of dead skin—towards her.

"Bah! I have no breath anyway—not anymore. But bad habits die harder than flesh." He raised his chin as if sniffing the air.

Kallie cleared her throat. "I thought you were…"

"What? A prophet? A messiah?" He snorted. "I'm not even dead, although that would have to depend on your definition of death, I guess. Yes, *yes*, missy, I know the stories they tell about me. If I know one thing, it's this: they all grew in the telling." He spat on the ground, only no spit came out of his long-desiccated throat. His fingers traced circles on the dirt. When he spoke again, his voice was low—weary. "I'm a blind poet, a lost relic no holy books will ever mention, tied on the mast of that—" he pointed a blackened thumb over his shoulder, at the mouth of the cavern— "of that *thing* down there, whatever that is."

Her nanobots acknowledged his gesture and concurred. *A friend*, they purred, *sleeping in the deep. Dreaming. Waiting. The Apple. The Ankh. The Rose. The Hourglass. Everything and Nothing*.

"B-but…"

"Do you have a name, missy?"

"It's Kallie," she lied. Her makers had labelled her *K 95667*, but her nanobots had dove deep into the inactive parts of her brain and resurfaced with the voices of wrinkled crones in black kerchiefs mending nets and spinning threads. They'd resurfaced bearing names she'd never heard of but felt oddly familiar, like fragments of dreams forgotten at dawn. *Kalliste, Kallinike, Kalypso, Kallipatera. Remember our names. Remember your foremothers when you tread amidst the stars*.

"So, Kallie." An inhuman grin of parched, thin lips. "Here's the truth—or, at least, *my* version of the truth. I died long before you crawled out of your incubator." He tossed a red pebble away and his wrist joint creaked, bone on metal. "But before that, I had money. I had power. So I wanted to live forever, and power and money can buy a lot of things. I bribed and bullied my way into the science labs, and I got first-generation nanobots, still untested at the time, and implants that enhanced the faulty flesh with titanium and steel."

"And?"

His hand balled to a fist, oxidized metal and burned rubber jutting out of his knuckles. "That accursed Martian shuttle crashed north of here. I should have known better than to trust anything other than Terran ships. I crawled here, to this… *purgatory*, screaming while my flesh withered, my wires melted, my circuits fried. That thing in there showed me mercy and kept my batteries charged and my bots going, as long as I remained close." Another sigh. "Sheer dumb luck, if you ask me. Heavens know I don't deserve divine intervention." He patted the dirt beside him. "Please, sit. It won't be long now, until the sum of my parts crumbles down and returns to the dust. It's been decades since anyone came this way. None of them stayed."

I won't stay long either, she thought, and measured the distance to the mouth of the cavern, the dead guy—or whatever he was—and the foot of the hill. Then Kallie sat at the edge of a flattened rock a few feet away, her back straight, her shoulders rigid. She could outrun him, if she had to. He was just a blind, dying man.

Not a philosopher. Not a prophet.

Her shoulders slumped. Had she made a mistake coming here? Had she— "Hey! Don't do that!"

He had moved with unexpected agility and pinched her thigh over the suit—not hard enough to bruise, but enough to threaten. Kallie had almost jumped up to start running, when her bots purred comfort down her spine. *Please, sit and listen.*

He raised his arms with a whirr of gears. "No offence meant, Kallie. Just wanted to see how they make you these days. My ear bots still have their good days, and occasionally I hear news and reports—even music. Oh, how do I miss music! That thing sometimes sings to me, but it made my skin crawl—when I still had skin." He turned his blind eyes towards her. "Long ago, I heard about your kind. What is it called? The New Human project?"

The New Drone project, her nanobots spat.

"That's right," she said—to both him and her bots.

"Hmm." He shook his head. "In my days, such enhancements were only for the powerful and the rich. I never thought that mankind would devolve to *that*." He lowered his head. "They're coming for you, little slave girl. The shepherds are coming for their little lost lamb."

"I know," she said, her voice quiet. The steady rhythm of the Enforcer's boots matched her heartbeat now, every step closer to her capture—to her death. That one she could never outrun.

"So, where are they sending you?"

"Europa."

"The oceans under the ice?"

"Yes."

"Why you? Why there?"

"I—I do not know."

"Of course you do."

Her fists clenched. She—no, *he* was wasting minutes she couldn't afford. "No, I don't." A sharp inhale. "Look, I—"

"Shush. What do you think led you here?" He chuckled. "Your slavers have no idea what they've created, have they? Those extraordinary little things that enhance your hearing. Have you not learned to listen yet?"

"Listen to what?"

"To what lies betwixt and between."

Kallie opened her mouth, anger stinging the tip of her tongue, when the alien presence distended and throbbed and swarmed her bots. Waves crashed against resurfacing memories and took on the form of her forefathers back to the world's making. Sailors, navigators, sea-captains lining up behind her for countless centuries, salt on their hardened skin, eyes on horizon's trail, following the Trident and facing the

Mermaid—*tell her he lives and conquers, tell her, tell her, lest she unleashes the storm*. Barefoot children, scrawny goats, the soil brittle and the sun merciless. A desperate, famished people now selling parts of their bodies—blood, sperm, eggs—no, more than that, much *much* more: memories, legacies, past and future—to feed their *real* children on this Earth that was no longer blue.

Forgive me, daughter, cried her progenitor in silence, when the needle entered her body to harvest her eggs—cheap raw materials for mankind's mules and drones. The sharp pain shoved Kallie out of the vision and pushed the air out of her lungs, leaving her breathless and bereft.

Damned faulty filters. They could not keep the sand from making her eyes mist. *Damn*.

They had chosen her for this; for her seafaring ancestors, to sail onward, forward, outward in new, uncharted seas. No, not to sail; her journey would not be on the helm against the weather under alien skies; she would sludge through the mud of the ocean's bottom, in a heavy suit, in pressure and temperatures no normal human could survive, where vision was secondary but hearing was vital. No nereids laughed and danced with the dolphins in those waters, no shape-shifting deities sunned their crotches on sandy beaches, no Mermaid prowled the deep mourning the death of her brother the king. Kallie had no kinship to any lifeforms she'd might encounter there. Only darkness and silence awaited her—silence and death.

Willing away any tear that dared to surface, Kallie managed a whisper, keeping her gaze on the ground. "Please. I need to know."

"To know what, child?"

"What is death?"

He *had* to know. He had to.

A chuckle.

So, he didn't.

"Even if I could tell you, no complete answer could fit into the few moments you have left." A sigh. "Does death scare you?"

Her head snapped up. "No." The word rolled off her tongue before her mind had the time to process the thought, and its truth caught her unawares. No, death did not scare her. Everyone—everything—would eventually die. Unlike normal humans, Kallie had the luxury to know when, where, and, most of all, why. It was a small consolation, to know her purpose. Most humans spent a lifetime without ever knowing. Of course, she wasn't a human. Not really. She was less than that. Her shoulders slumped even more.

Purpose. Life. Neither one of her choosing.

The icy depths of Europa's oceans.

When she spoke again, her voice was barely a whisper, as truths often are. "Silence scares me more."

"Ah, but they've built your auditory bots well, child, to let *that* scare you. Too well. The fools, they had never expected to encounter what lurks in the silence between breaths, between heartbeats, between synapses."

"And that is?"

"Don't you already know?"

She opened her mouth to reply, but instead held her breath. There it was, at the edge of breath and pulse and blink and *everything*, caught between one moment and the next. Echoes. Voices. Memories. The collective wisdom of an entire species yearning to leave their mark on the cosmos. The ripples across the sea of stars of an ever-changing universe, matter into energy into matter, never-ending cycles that her finite mind could never fully grasp.

But no death. Not really. And never silence.

This time she allowed the tears to mist her goggles, wishing she could taste the salt, to taste the seas of her homeland she'd never seen, the wide stretch of—

"Unit *K 95667.*" The Enforcer's dry command, coming from the foot of the hill, made her back rigid. "You have been reported absent without leave and you are now ordered to return to base."

Kallie bit her lower lip, drawing blood.

"Unit *K 95667*? Do you acknowledge?"

"Yes!"

"You will follow me back to base, or I'll drag you there." The threat came with a flat, neutral voice that didn't lessen its impact.

Kallie pulled herself up, and under the blind stare of the not-quite-dead-yet not-philosopher she marched downhill, hands balled at her sides. His presence weighed heavy upon her shoulders, the burden of a choice that hung loose. With every step, her nanobots whined, until their protests waxed to a wail that drilled through the soil to the presence beneath. In return, it hummed and whispered words in strange tongues and, for a moment, Kallie wished they'd all shut up and let her *think*.

The Enforcer stood straight, tall, bulky, engineered for strength, whereas Kallie had been made for endurance. Male or female, she couldn't tell; they were all made sterile anyway, the true mules of mankind. Hard eyes through the goggles, hard body under the suit, hard skin to withstand the Martian wilderness, should the need arise, clean-shaven head—

The mark of a slave, scoffed her nanobots. *Not like* you.

Were they now speaking for the presence? Was there ever really a presence, or was it all an elaborate hallucination springing out of some malfunctioning fold of her brain?

"Move," said the Enforcer, impatience now lining her voice.

Hmm. *Her* voice. The nanobots had decided it was female. Not that it changed anything. Kallie would have to follow regardless. Enforcers were incapable of mercy, or leniency, of anything but obedience.

No, her bots protested. *Speak the names of your foremothers. Recite the deeds of your forefathers. Call upon the Trident and the Mermaid. Tell her, remember, tell her he lives and conquers, lest she unleashes the storm.*

Kallie's gut clenched. No. Even if she believed for a moment that it would change something—anything, she couldn't speak aloud any of these things she didn't even understand.

Her throat would close on the names, her tongue would lay limp in her mouth, her mind vacant of their meaning and their resonance.

But *they* could.

She stopped three steps away from the Enforcer, her heartbeat counting her days and numbering her months. So be it. This was the one final choice no white-coat maker or thick-skinned Enforcer would take from her.

On the first step forward, she pulled off her gloves and goggles. On the second step, she pulled down her respirator.

"Are you insane? You'll die," spat the Enforcer.

"So I die." On the third step, Kallie reached out and pulled down the Enforcer's own respirator. "Go forth and multiply," she whispered to her bots. Then she grabbed the stunned Enforcer's face between her palms and pressed her mouth on hers.

Fingertips on hardened skin, teeth against teeth, lips pressed on lips, and nanobots swarming forward, crossing over with joyful cries. *Listen, listen, listen*, they chanted, *listen to the breeze against the pebbles, to the slow tides of the planet's core, to the storms on Jupiter, to the colliding asteroids.* The Enforcer squirmed and tried to break free, but Kallie's hands and nanobots had hooked her well, murmuring in sync with the universe.

She held on to the kiss, lamenting the first—and last—moment of intimacy she'd ever know in her adult life. Her makers had denied her reproduction, foolish little godlings, deluded in their assumption that they understood any one of the many forms of Creation. They didn't. Nor did Kallie, but when the Enforcer pulled back from the kiss, she met her gaze with eyes glistening in one moment of understanding.

It ended with a slap.

Kallie's face burned and she rubbed her cheek under the sudden, stunned silence of her nanobots. The Enforcer's face twisted in a grimace of painful disgust, facial muscles never used before twitching under her skin.

"You are malfunctioning," she said, her voice no longer flat but rumbling with distant thunder. She pulled her own respirator back on, grabbed Kallie's wrist in a bone-crushing grip and pushed the respirator back over Kallie's mouth and nose. "Come. You need to be reprogrammed."

Without another word, she turned and marched on, away from the dead man outside the cavern, away from the alien presence, dragging Kallie behind her. Kallie struggled to keep up, her gut numb, her mind empty, her voices silenced.

Was that what death felt like?

When they crossed the point where the two forces met, Kallie's step faltered. *Alone*. Her knees went weak. She stumbled and fell, and still the Enforcer dragged her on over the rough, rocky soil. It took her captor several steps to realize that her prisoner wasn't actually walking. She stopped, never letting go of her wrist, and measured Kallie from head to toe.

"Are you injured?"

"No." *Not yet*.

"Then get up."

"No." Somewhere inside her mind, a lone nanobot chuckled at her insolence. Kallie let out a long sigh. She was not alone.

The Enforcer rolled her eyes. "I *will* drag you, if it comes to that. But you will sustain too much damage to be cost-efficient to repair. You will be disassembled."

Kallie shrugged. More nanobots chuckled. *Ask her name*.

The Enforcer pulled her wrist. "Get up."

"Tell me your name, first."

The grip loosened for a moment. Not enough for Kallie to break free, but enough to *know*.

"My *name*?" Her brows arched. "I am Unit *A 5789*. Whatever that may mean to you."

Kallie shook her head. "I didn't ask for your serial number. I asked for your *name*."

"Your cognitive functions are compromised. We don't have names."

"I do."

Kalliste, Kallinike, Kalypso, Kallipatera. We know. We remember.

The Enforcer let go of her hand.

Of course you don't have a name, thick-skinned, thick-headed brute, hissed the nanobots, and the Enforcer flinched. She too could hear them now. *Names have power. Why do you think you were not given one? So you wouldn't have choice. So you wouldn't have self.*

So you wouldn't have spirit.

The Enforcer rubbed at her temples, at her ears, her face distorted. "Who? Wha—?"

So march on, ignorant drone. The nanobots' hiss grew to low rumble and then to a roar. *Run back to your masters. Run back and lick their bloody hands, lick their boots and wait for your next orders. You're nothing but a gelding, like the gelded warriors of so many centuries ago. Stolen children, their bodies mutilated, their minds knowing only their masters' purpose. So march on,* gelding. *Live and die without knowing your name, your place and your true purpose.*

"Stop it!" Breathing hard and fast, she reached down, grabbed Kallie's wrist again and pulled her on her feet. "Stop it!"

The nanobots stopped, their silence more intimidating than their roar.

Kallie did not resist. She waited until the Enforcer's breathing slowed, until her eyes refocused.

"Your ailment must be infectious," the Enforcer said, her voice lower now—*uncertain*. "There were reports regarding a new virus attacking last generation nanobots, but they said it had been contained." A sigh. "Apparently not. We will both have to be terminated now. Come." Holding her head high, she spun around and marched on towards the base, her grip on Kallie relentless.

Kallie followed, numb at the absence of her bots' comforting chit-chat. All she could hear now was a low hum, as though they had gone into hiding once their true nature had been revealed. Was that all they'd been? Just a software virus? False visions of the past? False promises? False memories?

False self?

Doubt clenched her chest like the straps they'd use to immobilize her on the stainless steel slab before they started her vivisection. They'd take her apart to see what had gone wrong, how to prevent it from happening again, how to—

The Enforcer stopped abruptly and Kallie, caught unawares, crashed onto her rigid body. Slowly, the clean-shaven head turned to stare at her in silent wonder. When she spoke, her voice faltered.

"They… they call me—"

"They call you what?"

"They…" After a moment that lingered on, she shook her head before resuming her march, her grip tighter now. "I will *not* listen to hallucinations!"

Ten steps later, their march came to another sudden stop. This time, the Enforcer turned around, releasing Kallie's wrist. It was Kallie's turn to reach out with both hands and take the Enforcer's gloved hand into hers.

"They have given you a name."

She nodded.

"Speak your name then," Kallie whispered.

"Aleksan—Alexa—" She gulped, her neck muscles visibly straining. She coughed, as though her engineered body choked up on her audacity to take a name.

"Alex?"

"Sounds like it." She tilted her head sideways, as if listening, then glanced around. "Was this wilderland ever underwater, I wonder? A river? An ocean? I think… I think I hear the sea." She pulled her respirator down. "I can smell it, too."

A shy smile lit up her face when Kallie pulled down her own respirator. This time, the kiss was softer, a brush of lips against lips, acceptance instead of conquest, with the lingering taste of *goodbye*. When the Enforc—no, when *Alex* pulled back, with her eyes wide and her pupils dilated, Kallie thought she caught a glimpse of the Eternal.

My doing. My creation. My sin and salvation. Sister. Disciple. Daughter.

The King and the Mermaid reborn as one.

Tell her to live and conquer, whispered the bots into her ear.

Kallie smiled, and reached out for a final brush of her knuckles against her kinswoman's rough cheeks.

She already knows, she whispered back.

Without one word, Alex pulled her respirator back on and turned around. She marched on into the wilderness toward Terra Sirenium, her strides less assured but easier, to seek her own meaning, her own purpose in a universe now full of sound.

Kallie stood and watched until her form vanished in the distance. Then she stood some more until her legs hurt, until her freezing skin reminded her of her discarded gloves and goggles, until her airways ached for breath. She pulled her respirator back on and turned around, where her own purpose awaited.

When she crossed the border again, when the alien presence welcomed her back into her sphere of influence, her nanobots shivered. She had to stop lest she fell, her breath catching and her eyes blurring.

So *that* was what lay beneath the surface.

Creation.

Humans were not the first to try and terraform Mars.

As she pulled herself together and made her way back to the cavern, she listened to the alien whispers, a crude translation from her bots. A species accustomed to a dry climate, dwellers of pyramids and builders of obelisks, along the banks of ever-flowing rivers. She listened to fragments of reports, of accounts of events she didn't fully understand, of some undetermined malfunction or disaster that collapsed the surface and buried the device underground. There it lay for countless empty centuries, still struggling to change the surface, still true to its builders' programming to change the dead soil to something more.

In the stretch of eons it had also changed itself.

Panting and light-headed, Kallie reached the end of her

journey. He waited by the mouth of the cavern, and she followed him inside.

One step inside, and the darkness burst with sounds. The drafts of air amongst the red rocks. The whispers of the meteorite fragments embedded under her feet. The incessant buzzing of the drones in her blood dancing in new patterns and sequences. Molecules and ions, transformation and transmutation, elements and particles and amino acids and proteins. The tireless nanobots building, disposing, transferring and relocating the sum of her parts, chirping and chattering in their own tongue, singing tunes from long-lost eras and futures yet unformed.

Two steps inside, and the presence of the alien terraforming device engulfed her. She could see it now: the markings on the bleached-white surface, alphabets and syllabaries, letters and numbers and runes, Alpha and Omega, AIEN and NYN, and the serpent devouring its tail. Its influence reached far above and below, higher than Olympus Mons, deeper than the planet's core, cutting through all possible dimensions, a protruding shard of the universe's backbone.

Three steps inside, and the galaxies murmured and gossiped in her ear. *Perhaps it's now a god*, whispered a far-off nebula to her newborn stars to put them to sleep. *Why would any god care about that useless cluster of rocks and its pests*, scoffed its last words a white dwarf on the event horizon of a throbbing singularity. And the universe yawned with the bored indifference of the immortal and stretched in circles and spirals.

Ever-swirling, ever-moving circles.

And circles have no ends.

Kallie comes out of her cavern and sits on the mouth of the cave when both the moons of Mars descend below the horizon—Phobos and Deimos, Fear and Dread. She doesn't *have* to, but she likes the allegory.

The remnants of her predecessor remain on the ground by the alien device where he fell so many nights ago, when he reached out and his fingertips connected with hers. In a moment of brilliant, effortless fluidity, all that he was—memories, thoughts, dreams, knowledge, spirit and soul—crossed over to her, carried upon the backs of his tired nanobots. As his empty husk hit the ground, so did his bots inside her. Having fulfilled their purpose, they were disassembled and reassembled by her own, to create the next generation.

Many lifetimes ago, when her nanobots were still cutting-edge technology, she heard her daughter's footsteps on the Martian surface and the echoes of her conquest. Until she did not. Her makers did not send anyone else to bring her back; they'd been busy containing the aftermath of their own hubris. For many years, the ripples of her presence in the universe still reached her: gatherings, congregations, revolt— *change.*

Never-ending change.

She has stopped tracking such changes now. She's tired. Her bots merged her environmental suit with her flesh, to replace dried skin and ropy sinew. But even this now suffers from the prolonged exposure to the Martian elements. Her mortal coil has reached its limits. She yearns to move on. There have been visitors over the years, all of them human, seeking truths and answers and prophecies. None of them stayed. Now the stars have changed, and her circle remains incomplete.

Not yet. Not yet, she chants into the night, her prayer and comfort every time she hears footsteps approaching. Like now.

Will this one stay?

The footsteps reach the foot of the hill, and her night vision kicks in—what's left of it. Not a human, but one of her own kind.

Well. It's time for *that* type of change. *Again.*

Perhaps this time humans will listen. Perhaps they'll learn.

They build their mules and geldings shorter now, and greener, their eyes further apart. No longer a predator's eyes, but of prey's. What has mankind encountered out there? For a fleeting moment, she regrets not having monitored the radio frequencies more closely. It matters little now. She has finally come full circle.

At the edge of her consciousness an endless shore stretches on. Under skies brewing heavy weather awaits a ship with black sails, with a three-headed dog on its figurehead. Different waters, different sails, but familiar faces crowding the decks. Not all of them are human, but all of them are kin. The Ferryman beckons, one skeletal hand on the tiller, the other palm up, requesting the fare. And her weary nanobots line Kallie's fingertips, ready for their final journey, each of them a miniscule coin for her passage.

Her guest stands in her presence shy, controlled. Obedience has been imprinted in those too, but in the end, he speaks.

"Are you the dead philosopher of Arsia Mons?"

For the first time in countless years, Kallie smiles, and pats the dirt beside her.

"Come, sit with me, and listen."

Cathedral

Jack McDevitt

Matt Sunderland gazed at the Earth, which was just edging out from behind the Moon. From the L2 platform, Luna, of course, dominated the sky, a vast grey globe half in sunlight, half in shadow, six times larger than it would have appeared from his Long Island home. Usually, it completely blocked the gauzy blue and white Earth. On the bulkhead to his left, the *Mars or Bust* flag still hung, its corners fastened by magnets.

Mars or Bust.

Well, everybody knew how that was going. Sorry, guys, but the funding's drying up. Looks as if we're going to have to put it off for a couple of years. The way we'd put off the solar collector that was going to beam energy back to ground stations. And the way we'd put off Moonbase. To somebody's credit, NASA had broken through and gotten the L2 station, the ideal place to launch whatever kind of space mission you wanted. Anything at all you wanted to do, any place you wanted to go, this would be where you started.

He could hear Judy back in the workout area, grunting and stretching, trying to keep herself in decent condition. They were the only two left on the platform now. He shook his head, and his eyes slid shut. He used to love using the main scope, training it on nebulae and clusters and sometimes places like Neptune which, for a short time, had almost seemed within reach. But the magic had gone away as it became increasingly apparent that no human being would ever actually touch any of them. When he'd first come to the L2 station, to Earthport, it had been heralded as a kind of bus terminal for traffic headed in all directions. It was hard to believe that had been only a year ago.

The radio beeped. Incoming from the *Cernan*. He pressed the key. "Earthport here," he said. "Go ahead, *Cernan*."

A familiar voice responded: "Earthport, I'm on my way." It was *Laura*. "How are you, Matt?"

He leaned over the mike. "Laura, is that really *you*?"

"Far as I can tell."

He wasn't sure what to say next. "When did they start sending ops managers out to do retrievals?"

"About the same time ops managers starting going over their bosses' heads."

"Again?"

"I guess so."

Matt had loved her since the first time he'd seen her, lying sprawled in center field after running into a fence, but holding the ball aloft in her gloved hand. But he'd long since given up. "What happened?" he asked.

"One of the cable news shows started running stories that we were on board with the defunding. That it was okay to shut down you guys. Dr. Prevost went on Worldwide and denied the story, but he looked so weak that it just made things worse. You know how Prevost is. Doesn't want to offend the politicians. I complained to Louie. He told me to keep out of it. But I got myself invited onto *Brick Collier* and I guess I said a little too much."

"So they demoted you?"

"I guess Louie thought this would be an appropriate way to send a message. Send me out to turn off the lights."

Matt stared at the mike. "I'm sorry to hear it."

"I'm sorry about a lot of things. We have a chance to get some serious results here and we're walking away from it." He listened to her breathe. "You guys packed and ready to go?"

"Yeah. I guess so."

"Very good, Matt. See you Friday." Three days.

He leaned over the mike, savoring her voice, as smoky as her dark grey eyes. He'd always pretty much had his way with women. But his charm, whatever that might have been, had been insufficient with Laura. He'd had only a few weeks with her. And one glorious weekend. The weekend of his life. Now she was coming to take him home from the only assignment he'd ever really cared about. At the moment, she was in every sense of the phrase, far away.

"By the way," she said, "I'm alone. There were supposed to be a couple of us on this one, but I guess they wanted to give me time to think about what I'd done."

"Well, okay," he said in a level voice that was supposed to come across as detached. "We'll have a party when you get here." She liked parties. She liked living, and being with other people, and watching the sun rise.

Laura had red hair and a bewitching smile. If she had a problem, it was that she'd never learned to hide her feelings. You looked at her and you knew immediately what she was thinking. He would not have described her as beautiful. At least not when he first met her. But his impression had changed as he worked with her, and got to know her. During those first few weeks she'd grown increasingly hard to resist. She was animated and funny and smart and she took over his life. But he'd made the colossal error of letting her see too soon how he felt. Damn, that had been dumb.

"I'm sorry, Matt," she'd told him on that last night. "But we're going to have to break it off." They'd been out celebrating her thirty-second birthday, and she'd grown increasingly quiet during the evening. Then they'd gotten back to her apartment, and they stood just inside the doorway, the door not quite shut, and she'd turned on him. "Can't do it anymore."

"Why?" he'd asked. It had come as a complete surprise.

"Because my life is here, on the space coast. With NASA." Her eyes had grown teary. "Matt, I want to walk on another world. I want to go to Mars, if that's ever possible. It's what I've always wanted. It's the only thing I've ever really cared about."

And he hadn't known how to respond. Hadn't understood what she was trying to say. "What has that to do with *us*? You could ride off to *Pluto*, if you like. I'd be cheering."

"It would never happen if I were a mother."

"Well, okay. Whatever—I mean, we haven't talked about kids. Or anything like that."

"I don't do things halfway, Matt." She'd looked at him, brushed his cheek with her lips, and virtually pushed him out the door. "I'm sorry it has to end like this. Truth is, I'm sorry it has to end at all. But there's no other way." It was the last thing she'd said.

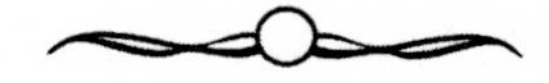

He looked down at the mike. It still hurt.

"You know, Matt," she said, "this is the first time I've been out here alone." She hesitated, about to say something more, and he could guess what it might have been, something along the line of her being uneasy lost in all this solitude. But she pulled back. He understood the feeling. And he knew her well enough to be aware that she didn't like admitting any kind of weakness.

He'd learned that at their first meeting, which had been at a ballpark rather than at work. She'd been playing center field for the NASA women's softball team. Matt had allowed a couple of the guys to talk him into attending the game because they claimed it was a good way to meet attractive 'babes.' He hadn't really noticed Laura until she crashed into the center-field fence tracking down a line drive late in the game. She'd bounced off the wooden planks and crumpled onto the grass.

Matt had served as an EMT in the past, and he'd wasted no time running out to her. Her only response when he arrived was to hold up the glove to show him she still had the ball. Her eyes were closed.

"Can you hear me?" he'd asked.

"Of course," she'd said.

The stated purpose of Matt's current assignment was to help determine what effects long-term zero gravity would have on the human body. There'd been some slight deterioration in bones and muscles, both his and Judy's, but nothing that suggested a Martian voyage would not be possible. When the results had first come in, Matt got the impression that some of the people back home were disappointed. As if they were looking for a reason to call everything off. "I just never thought," he continued, "it would end like this."

"Nor did I," said Laura.

He could visualize her, seated on the bridge, looking at the same quiescent Moon. And he wondered how she'd reacted when she'd been assigned to come out to the platform to pick *him* up.

Laura had launched from the International Space Station, which had become obsolete with the construction of the platform. Out here, vehicles could come and go without having to deal with gravity. Now, very likely, the window was closing and the space age was, finally, over.

"We need a cathedral," she said.

He didn't think he'd heard right. "Say again, Laura?"

"A *cathedral.* Matt, we went to the Moon because one night in 1957 the country looked up and saw Sputnik passing overhead. The civil rights movement got its start because one woman refused to go sit in the back of a bus."

"What's that have to do with a cathedral?"

"If you're going to get somewhere, you have to have a symbol, something that stands for what you're all about. You're lost in the Middle Ages, going nowhere, with nothing to live for, but when they build the cathedral at Chartres, you find out what matters in life. What really counts. It's what NASA needs right now." She was suddenly there with him, in the operations center, drinking coffee, her eyes looking past him somewhere, sending the message that there were far more important things in the world than any personal relationship between them.

"Well, maybe. You have any ideas?"

"Sure. Maybe the Chinese will do it for us."

"How do you mean?"

"Think how we'd react if they started setting up a base on the Moon. Or, even better, if we could spot an alien vehicle out around Saturn. Lord, *that* would produce some results."

"You read too much science fiction, Laura."

"Yeah. Maybe. I don't want to see everything go under." Her voice caught. It was the first time he'd sensed that level of emotion in her. "Maybe we could fake something?"

There wasn't much left to do on the platform. The project seal, which had been imprinted on one of the bulkheads, a rocket crossing through a set of Saturnian rings, seemed especially sad as he and Judy sat quietly in the operations area, talking about what they would do when they got home. Their careers with NASA were pointless now. Judy Parker had been the pilot when Matt came to the platform. "It's time," she said, "to go back and find something else to do with my life. Maybe even start a family."

"You serious?"

"Sure." She'd flown jets in one of the endless Middle East wars. But she was one of the gentlest people Matt had ever known. It was hard to imagine her in the cockpit of a fighter. She was an African-American, cool, calm, impossible to rattle. When they'd blown an engine on the ride to L2, she'd told him to relax, had put on a pressure suit and pushed out through the airlock. Then she came back, shrugged, threw some switches, and the problem had gone away. But the decision to shut down the L2 had gotten to her. "I've given most of my adult life to NASA," she'd told him when the announcement had come in. "I'm done. I'm tired of politicians who can find money to throw into one war after another, but can't fix the highways or hire teachers. And certainly can't get themselves together for something that requires a little bit of imagination."

She stared at Matt. "You know," she said, "I suspect if, several thousand years from now, somebody goes back to the Moon—" Her eyes brightened and her voice caught. "—If they go back to the Moon, they might be surprised when they see footprints." She cleared her throat. Stiffened. "Well, we'll see what happens."

Matt was more optimistic. "Eventually, we'll make it. We'll put a colony on Mars and keep going. It might not be you or me. But somebody will head out of town."

"I'll believe it when I see it," she said. She was an attractive woman. She wore her hair short, and she had an easy smile. But there was something in her manner that always reminded you who was in charge.

"Judy, are you going to stay with the Agency?"

"The Agency's leaving me, Matt," she said. "I don't know them any more."

The radio beeped. Matt picked up and heard a male voice: "Earthport, this is Houston. We have reports of an incoming asteroid. Data is being fed to your computer. It's not very big. Coming in from behind the Moon. Out in your area. It's why we didn't pick it up earlier."

"They think it's our fault," said Judy, smiling.

Matt held up a hand while he tried to listen. "We just got word half an hour ago," Houston continued. "It's probably not a problem, but we do not have a good angle. Please get us a reading."

"Houston, you guys sent the scientists home last month. What precisely do you want? Vector and velocity?"

"That would be helpful, yes."

Snotnose. "I'll get back to you." He sat down at the control board, grumbled, and turned dials.

"Need help?" asked Judy.

"No, I've got it." Display lines appeared on the monitor. Auxiliary screens lit up. "Okay," he said. "Here's the data coming in from Houston." He relayed it into the direction finder and studied the results. "They're right. They can't see it from the ground."

"That's good, isn't it?" said Judy. "If the Moon blocks it off, it can't get anywhere near Earth, right?"

"The Moon doesn't stay in one place," said Matt.

"Oh. Yes. Good point."

Stars moved steadily across the main display. A blinker appeared. Matt tapped the screen with his index finger. "There it is."

"How big is it?"

The rock was shaped like a chicken leg, bulbous at one end, relatively narrow at the other. It was turning slowly, tumbling, moving in the general direction of the Moon. "Looks about fifty meters across at its widest point. Maybe two hundred meters long."

"That's not exactly small."

"Nope."

"Got a velocity?"

"Hold on." He waited for the numbers to steady up. "Looks like about twenty klicks per second."

More lights appeared and began blinking. Matt pushed one of the pads with his index finger. "And we have a vector."

"Is it going to hit the Moon?" said Judy.

He brought up images representing the asteroid and the Moon. A red line extended out from the asteroid. It moved toward the lunar rim. And narrowly missed it.

"No," said Matt. He zoomed out, bringing the Earth into the picture. The line continued toward the planet. And again skipped past the edge.

"Not by much," Judy said. "But I guess they can stop worrying."

Matt went back to the mike. "Houston, this is Earthport."

"Go ahead, Earthport." A different voice this time. One of the comm ops.

"We've forwarded the data. You guys can relax."

"Thanks. Glad to hear it."

"Let us know if you need anything else. Earthport out."

"You know what would be *really* nice?" said Judy. "If that thing was headed directly for New York, and we had a ship to go out there and hit it with a laser cannon. Like the *Enterprise.*"

Judy was back in the washroom while Matt sat quietly watching the *Cernan.* Its course was bringing it around the side of the Moon. "Laura," he said, "I have you onscreen."

"Roger that. I see you too."

A long pause, while he tried to think of something else to say. "It'll be good to get back to the Cape."

"I'm sure it will. You've been out here how long? Eight months?"

"A year." He stared at the blinker. "I hate to leave, but it'll be good to get some fresh air again."

"I guess so." Another long pause. "Well, I'm looking forward to seeing you again, Matt."

"You, too," he said. "Still playing ball?"

"When I get the chance. But I'm not hitting much. I think the coach is hoping I'll run into another fence."

Matt felt as if his mind had emptied. "Well," he said, "I better get back to work."

"Okay. *Cernan* out."

He took a deep breath. When he was in contact with her, it was as if he was back in high school.

When the Earth moved out from behind the Moon, allowing direct transmissions to the L2 platform, Houston routinely beamed a bundled TV signal. It tended to be a collection of films, current news shows, and whatever else might be of interest. Judy and Matt hadn't seen anything for several weeks, so they scanned the latest package with interest. It included several late night comedians. AMC was running an old John Wayne marathon. Sports Center was talking about the new fan movement that had resulted from continuing escalation of ticket prices. Millions of the baseball faithful had signed a pledge to boycott games and cancel TV service during the coming major league season. Nobody, though, believed they would actually abide by it.

California was considering a law that would legalize group marriage. Chester Winslow was throwing his hat in the ring for the GOP nomination. Another candidate, William Forrest, was attacking the current administration for defunding NASA. And CNN announced breaking news: Margo Everett, the enormously popular singing sensation, had been arrested on a DUI.

While the onscreen experts were discussing the impact of the Everett arrest, the crawler reported that an asteroid had been sighted, and that it would pass close to Earth.

They went to financial news. Then, when they came back to the newsroom, the story had been elevated: The host, Clive Thomas, introduced Professor Edward Albright, from the American Museum of Natural History. "What can you tell us about this asteroid, Professor?" said Thomas. "Is it a threat?"

Albright was young, probably still in his twenties. He looked worried. "We know," he said, "the asteroid's present course will bring it very close to us. It'll pass through the southern sky Friday at about 5:00 a.m. In fact, we should be able to see it. But, to get to the important part, it *will* miss us. If it stays on its present course."

"Good." Thomas smiled, but then his face clouded. "I think. What do you mean '*If it stays on its present* course'?"

Albright tried a lighthearted laugh, but he wasn't good at it. "It's simple enough, Clive. The asteroid will also pass very close to the Moon. That's going to have an effect. And we're not sure yet how that might change things."

"An effect on the direction it goes, you mean?"

"Yes. The Moon's gravity will bend its vector somewhat. In our direction."

"So you're saying it *might* hit us?"

"I'm saying *probably not*. But at this point we can't be sure."

"Okay, Professor. If it *does* come in on us, how much damage will it do?"

"It's two hundred meters long. Judging by its reflection, it looks like nickel-iron. Unfortunately."

"Why *unfortunately*?"

"Nickel-iron is heavier, more massive, than rock."

"Okay. It keeps getting worse, doesn't it?"

"We'll probably be okay. I really wouldn't begin to worry yet."

"So how big an impact would it have, Professor? I mean, how big is two hundred meters?"

"About two football fields."

"That doesn't sound good. So, how big an impact?"

Albright took a deep breath. "Clive, have you ever been out to the Barringer Crater in Arizona?"

"You mean Meteor Crater?"

"Yes."

"Yes. I've been there." An image of the crater appeared onscreen.

"The object that hit out there would have been about the same size and density as this thing that's coming in now."

"My God, Professor. Do you have any idea *where* it would

hit? If it *does* hit?"

"We don't, Clive. And look, I don't want to start a panic. The thing will probably just pass across the sky. Let's hope so."

"When will we know for certain?"

"After it gets past the Moon."

They went to commercial. A smarmy lawyer came on, and started explaining how he would stand up for any viewer who got injured in an accident. In the middle of it, the radio beeped. It was Laura. "Matt," she said, "I'm being diverted."

"To the Moon?" It wasn't really a question.

"Yes. They're timing it so I can get a good look at this thing during its passage. They're calling it 2024-MY. Anyhow, I wanted to let you know I'll be a little bit late picking you guys up."

"I guess so. So you're going to get a close-up? What's the point of that?"

"You haven't heard from them yet?"

"Not since the first time."

"Okay. They're trying to figure out whether there's a problem. Whether this thing is going to get pulled off course enough to cause a collision. To do that—"

The radio beeped again. Another call. "Hang on, Laura. I think we're about to hear from them. I'll get back to you." He switched over.

"This is Houston." The lawyer went away and was replaced by pictures of asteroids. "We're trying to get a handle on where the asteroid will go after it interacts with the Moon. We're sending Laura to track the passage. We want you to coordinate with her so we can watch this thing from both angles. That should provide us with enough data to figure out where it's going."

Matt looked over at Judy. "You know how to do that?"

"Sure," she said.

"Okay, Houston. When's all this going to start?"

"In about eighteen hours. We want you to lock onto the asteroid and follow it all the way in until it passes the Moon."

Scopes were mounted fore and aft on the *Cernan*. Matt watched the Moon slide slowly into the center of his auxiliary screen as Laura turned and headed directly toward it. "I'm going into orbit," she said. "If we have it right, the asteroid will come directly over the top of the Moon. Around the side from your perspective. I'll get close to it on the back side my second time around. The plan is that as it makes its closest approach to the Moon, I'll leave orbit and assume a parallel course. I'll be in front of it when we start, but it'll catch up and pass me pretty quickly. I should be able to get a good read on it, though."

He was uncomfortable. "I wish I was there with you."

"I'm fine. Don't worry."

Judy opened her mike. "There's a lesson to be learned from this, Laura," she said. "I hope the PR guys at NASA take advantage of it. There's no reason we should have to be concerned about incoming rocks." She took a deep breath. "Idiot politicians."

Laura laughed. He remembered the last time he'd seen her, at an award ceremony for the people who'd designed the L2 platform. She'd been seated toward the front, caught up in the celebration, lovelier than ever, pretending not to see him. And then she'd surprised him by tracking him down outside to congratulate him on getting assigned to the station. Then she'd been gone again.

"You know," she said, "it almost makes me wish the thing *would* hit. A desert somewhere, maybe, where it wouldn't do any harm."

"I'm not sure there's any place on the planet where it wouldn't do some serious damage," Matt said.

And Judy picked it up: "Six to ten megatons. If nothing else, that would throw a lot of dust into the atmosphere. We'd be in for a cold summer."

"I know. That's why I said *almost.*"

Another hesitation. Judy glanced at him. "I'll be glad," he said, "when this is over."

"Me, too." Laura's voice was soft. But very far away. "You guys were right about the laser cannons."

"I know," said Matt.

"Maybe I could throw something at it."

Matt tried to think of a witty response. What could she throw at the rock that would get a laugh? A shoe, maybe?

"The only reason I joined NASA," said Laura, "was that I hoped one day I'd get a chance to go to Mars. My folks always thought I was deranged."

"We all are, Laura. You have to be to come out here. But hell, we haven't even made it to the Moon."

"Matt, you're well out *past* the Moon."

"But I've never set foot on it. Despite all the talk the last few years we've done almost nothing."

"We built Earthport."

"It's not the same thing. Earthport is supposed to be a *gateway,* a first step to serious space exploration. But what happened? We changed administrations and a new president comes in, looks at the budget and shakes his head. Cost-cutting always starts with us."

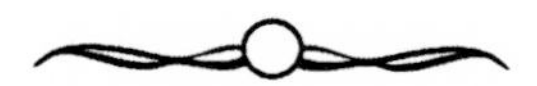

When Matt arrived back in the operations area next morning, Judy was talking with Laura. "Just don't get too close," she said.

Laura's voice was electric: "Don't worry, babe. That is a very big rock."

"Maybe you'll get a promotion out of this, Laura."

"Maybe I'll get invited to the *Jerry McComber Show.*"

"Why on earth would you want to do that?"

"Are you serious? That guy's really a hunk."

Judy's lips tightened slightly. Then: "Oh, hi, Matt."

"Good morning, Matt," Laura said. "Finally got up, I see."

"Hi, ladies. How's the flight coming?"

"Laura's getting close to the Moon."

The lunar surface, still on view through the *Cernan's* scopes, had still been relatively smooth last night. Now it was all craters and ridges and broken rock. "You still on schedule, Laura?" he asked.

"As far as I can tell."

"Can you see the asteroid?"

"Not right now. The Moon's in the way. Houston tells me it's beginning to accelerate."

"Lunar gravity."

"Yes."

"Okay. If you need anything, let us know. And—"

"Yes, Matt?"

"I still think we'll get to Mars."

"It would be nice."

"When we do, could I persuade you to have dinner with me?"

"You think we could find a good pizza place there?"

"If that's what it takes, sure."

"Maybe," he said, "we'll get a break. If the asteroid were to go close enough to scare the devil out of everybody, maybe they'd realize they need us."

"Maybe," said Judy. "I think they'd be rattled for two days, and then they'd forget. By the way, can I offer an observation?"

"Sure."

"I can't imagine you're ever going to be able to get Laura into that Martian pizza place. But, from the way she sounds, I'd say you have a pretty good shot at Rusty's." Rusty's Seafood was a popular spot down at the harbor.

The radio beeped. "This is Houston. Laura won't have enough fuel left to pick you guys up when this is over, so we're going to bring her home after she completes the asteroid survey. We'll be sending somebody else out for you. They haven't told me yet who it'll be. But the pickup will be a couple of days late. Sorry."

Damn. "Roger that, Houston."

"By the way, we've gotten a better read on the asteroid. If the Moon weren't in the way, it would pass well outside the upper atmosphere over the Atlantic, and keep going. The experts think now that the lunar passage won't affect it much. The consensus is that we'll probably be okay. Maybe get a light show, but nothing more."

Nobody had ever affected him the way she had. Looking back now, he realized that she'd been sending signals all along: *we do not have a future*. And finally, after they'd come home from celebrating her birthday and were standing in front of her apartment, she'd pulled aside and told him. That had been two years ago and he still couldn't get her out of his mind. Maybe there was a chance, but he didn't want to get his hopes up. If he got another opportunity, he'd play it more cautiously. Not let himself look too eager. Maybe she'd see what she'd let get away.

Laura had begun as someone to fill in during a slow period in his life, and had become, in just that handful of evenings, *unforgettable*. He didn't understand how that could have happened. Maybe it was because he'd worked with her, knew her, had spent time with her, and all that had come into play. She was not simply a stranger he'd picked up in a bar, but a woman he'd thought of as a friend who'd turned out to be so much more.

And she shared his passion for walking on another world. "My life won't be complete," she'd told him once, "if I don't get to do that." And she'd realized how that sounded and they'd both laughed.

"As long," he'd replied, "as you don't leave a large hole in the ground."

The way he had—

The news channels couldn't let go of the story. Scientists and politicians were showing up and warning everyone to look out. The usual political experts were discussing the effect an impact might have on the presidential race. It would, according to the common wisdom, very likely hand the election to the challenger. They all admitted no one knew whether the asteroid, after its brush with the Moon, would simply continue on its way, or whether, as one commentator was saying, it would blast into the Atlantic and generate tidal waves that would spell disaster around the world. If it hit, the least we could expect, they were saying, was another round of climate change which would dwarf everything that had gone before. There'd be widespread famine, clouds of dust would block off sunlight possibly for years, forests would burst into flames.

Churches had begun holding special services. Homeowners were storing supplies and filling containers with fresh water. FEMA announced it was going on standby. The White House issued a statement that there was no reason to worry, which probably scared the general public as much as anything. William Forrest, whom Matt thought of as generally deranged, told a town meeting in Oregon that, if he were elected, "this sort of thing won't happen again. I guarantee it." Will MacReady, on the *700 Club*, announced that the asteroid was at the very least a warning that we all needed to pray harder.

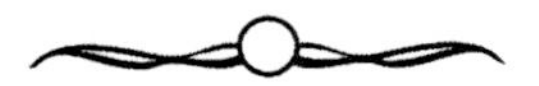

"We're picking up the *Cernan* again," said Judy.

She need not have said anything. Matt had been watching the time, and the monitors, which would acquire any signal from Laura. And, virtually to the second that Laura had a clear line to the platform, she was back. "Hi, guys," Laura said. And they were looking through the *Cernan's* aft telescope at a slice of lunar landscape. "It's getting close."

Judy nodded. "We've been watching it."

"Seventy-four minutes, looks like."

"That's how we read it, Laura." Judy looked over at him. Did he want to say something?

While he tried to come up with something, Laura took it: "I've been listening to the reaction at home. They sound as if they're all hiding under their beds."

Judy was still watching him. "Maybe a good scare is what they need," she said.

"I hope this doesn't become a problem, Judy."

He thought he picked up a note of frustration. "Nothing's changed, has it, Laura?" he asked.

"No. Just one thing. I don't know whether you've been informed or not. They're calling me back home when this is over. I think they want me to go on TV. The official story will be," she laughed, "that we scared the thing off."

"You'll look great."

"I've always wanted to be a hero. Actually, I won't have enough fuel to make it out to the platform."

"We know. They told us."

Her forward scope provided a view of the Earth rising over the lunar horizon. "I'd never seen that before," said Laura.

Matt smiled. Yeah. Wish we could watch it together. "Okay, Laura," he said. "Be careful. Let us know if we can help."

"Roger that. See you back home."

Judy's eyes glittered and she pretended to be concentrating on her notebook. But she was smiling. "Are you seeing her, Matt?" she asked, finally.

"No," he said. He was about to say something more but he wasn't sure what so he shut up.

Judy let her disappointment show. "She'd be a good catch."

He shrugged. "The Cape's loaded with attractive women."

Judy looked over at the control panel. "I think the mike's still on."

The comment startled him. He glanced down at it, trying to look casual. "Best way to win a woman's heart," he said, "is to pretend to forget to turn off the mike and then let her know she has competition."

Laura got to the front side of the Moon, out of sight on her second orbit. The auxiliary display had gone blank again.

They were watching the *Clive Thomas Show* again. Another scientist was seated with the host. An elderly guy with a fringe of white hair lining his skull and thick bifocals. "We can't really get a decent look at the asteroid now, Clive," he was saying. "It's behind the Moon, so the only place that can see it is the L2 platform. And they don't really have the kind of telescope we need for this."

"And we can't use any ground-based telescopes?"

"No, the key player in making the determination about this thing will be the *Cernan.* If it gets a good read as the asteroid passes the Moon, we'll know very quickly exactly what we're facing."

"But you're optimistic, Dr. Capers?"

"Let's say I'm hopeful."

"When will *we* be able to see it? Earthbound telescopes?"

"In another hour so. It'll come around the side of the Moon."

"If it's bad news, will you be able to determine exactly where it'll hit?"

"Oh, yes. Once we get the readouts from the L2 Platform

and the *Cernan*, especially the *Cernan,* we should be able to put it right together. But I don't think it's very likely there's anything to worry about."

"How long will it take to get here?"

"Clive, it's been picking up speed on its approach to the Moon. It'll add some more velocity when it gets inside the Earth's gravity field. We estimate when it passes us it'll be moving at about twenty-three kilometers per second."

"So how many hours?"

"Four and a half. More or less."

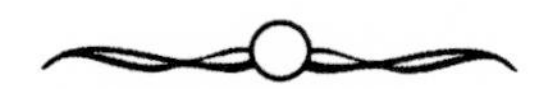

Matt's assignment was to handle the telescope, to keep it trained on the asteroid. He'd also oversee data collection and relay to the *Cernan*. Judy would try to interpret what they were getting, deliver a verdict, and send the results to Houston.

They were watching the asteroid through the *Cernan's* aft telescope. It was battered and scarred, a grey cold object, now more club than chicken-leg, tumbling end over end, slowly closing on the Moon.

Laura's voice came over the speaker: "Adjusting orbit. Have to pick up some velocity."

"You're going to make the rendezvous okay, right?" asked Judy. "Before it gets past?"

Matt had seen her once with a guy he didn't know. He'd been on the beach when they'd come out of the surf. And he'd overheard a nearby male say *Hell, look at that. How'd you like to do that one, Walt?*

He replayed the scene in his mind, as vivid now as it had been when it happened. He had no recollection what the guy she was with had looked like. But he took some satisfaction in the knowledge *he* hadn't been able to hold onto her either.

Then Laura's voice: "Looks good, guys."

It was coming right up her tailpipe. "Laura," said Matt, "aren't you out of position?"

"Negative. I'm right where I should be."

"You're too low."

"I'll be at two thousand meters during passage."

"For God's sake, Laura, that's lower than the rock. You're supposed to stay above it."

"How about you let *me* steer this thing, Matt? I can get a better look at it from where I am."

Judy shook her head. Mouthed her next words: "Let it be."

"Roger that," he said.

Judy was studying her display. "It's coming in lower than they predicted."

He knew that the higher it was as it crossed the lunar surface, the less likely it would impact Earth. "That's not good news," he said. "How low?"

"Looks like about forty-five hundred meters."

"You hear that, Laura?" he said.

"I heard it."

"Okay. Stay out of its way."

Silence poured out of the mike.

He took a deep breath. "Laura, are you in direct contact with Houston?"

"Negative."

"Okay. Pass everything to us. When we have a result we'll send it to them."

"That's what I'm doing."

The asteroid was growing larger, still tumbling slowly, a lopsided dancer coming out of the stars. Matt could pick out a couple of craters and a broken ridge line.

"Leaving orbit," said Laura. "Moving onto parallel course."

Below, the moonscape rippled past.

Matt couldn't help holding his breath.

Laura was accelerating, but the target was still coming up fast. In a minute or two it would sail past, above and off to her port side.

Judy stared at the monitors. "I don't like the altitude numbers. I think they're still within a safe range, but she's too close."

Laura again: "What do you think? Is it going to clear?"

"Hold on, Laura," said Matt. "We're working on it. Stay out of the way."

"Where's my laser cannon?"

"Laura," he said, "would you please—?"

"I'm not kidding, Matt. The numbers don't look so good."

"What do you mean?"

"What do you *think* I mean?"

"Laura—"

"There's a decent chance that thing's going to impact."

"It *isn't*."

"We don't know that."

Judy broke in: "Laura, we can be pretty sure it will make a clean pass."

"*Pretty sure* isn't good enough. This thing goes down, it'll be a killer."

"Laura—"

"Running out of time to make a call, Matt—"

"Don't do anything—"

"—If it gets past me—"

A chill ran through him. "Damn it, there's no way we can be certain, but it is *very* unlikely there will be a problem."

The lunar surface began to drop away and the asteroid filled the screen. "Back off," said Judy. "Laura, you're only 500 meters away from the damned thing."

"I can't be sure, guys—"

"What are you doing, Laura?" demanded Judy. "Back off, damn it."

Everything froze. Matt stared at the asteroid, at the crevices and craters and ridge lines and the bleak cold rock. All slowly turning. And growing. "Laura," he said. "Get the hell away from it. What are you *doing*?"

"No choice," Laura said. "I just don't know—"

"Laura." Judy all but strangled the mike. "It's still too high. It's not going to hit anything. Get away from it."

"Laura," he said, "answer up. Do you hear us?"

"Damn the torpedoes," Laura said. "Oh, I forgot. I don't have any torpedoes."

They were both screaming at her when the display went blank. "What happened?" said Matt. "What the hell did she do?"

Judy was staring at the screen. "I think she crashed the goddamn thing."

Matt went to full mag, seized the monitor, and shook it. "Come on, damn you."

It stayed blank.

"She's gone," said Judy.

"No no no." Matt banged his fist on the chair arm. "No! *Please, God, no.*"

For a long time no one spoke. Matt trained the telescope on the asteroid and they watched as it continued on its way. And there was the *Cernan,* crumpled, falling away.

Air moved through the vents. Judy was silent for a long time. Then: "It's changed course. Not much. But a little."

"Laura." Matt called out her name. "Laura, are you there? Please—"

Judy put her hand on his arm. "Matt."

He was having a hard time breathing. "Is it going to miss?"

She extended the asteroid vector line toward the blue globe representing Earth. It came close but passed well outside the atmosphere. "Yes. Not by much. But it *will* miss."

"Judy, did *she* do that? Push it aside?"

A second vector line appeared, paralleling the first. It was slightly closer to the globe, but still a miss. "No," she said. "This is where it *would* have gone. Whatever she did, it made no significant difference."

The radio beeped. Transmission from Houston. They ignored it. "She had no way to know whether it would hit or not," said Matt.

"That's not true." Judy took a deep breath. "She had the same information we did. Except she had it a few seconds earlier. She *had* to know it would miss. She panicked. Or she just got too close—"

Matt shook his head, fighting back tears. "I can't see her panicking. She said something about once it got past—"

Judy's eyes darkened. "She intended all along to ram the thing if she had to."

"Not if she *had* to," said Matt. "I think she made up her mind to do it no matter what."

"That can't be right. Remember? She said how we were running out of time to make a call."

"Judy, that was for the media. She knew everything she said would show up on *Clive Thomas*. That comment was for the voters."

"I don't get it," said Judy.

Matt stared at the asteroid. He hated the thing with a venom unlike any emotion he'd felt in his life. "Have we relayed any of this to Houston yet?"

"No. Why?"

"We might have to make some adjustments." He took a deep breath. "Nobody except us knows the rock would have missed regardless of what she did."

"What are you saying?" demanded Judy.

He closed his eyes and watched Laura charging across the outfield. "She's handed us a cathedral."

About the Contributors

Athena Andreadis (editor)

Athena Andreadis was born in Hellás and lured to the US at age 18 by a full scholarship to Harvard, then MIT. She does basic research in molecular neurobiology, focusing on mechanisms of mental retardation and dementia. She's an avid reader in four languages across genres and the author of *To Seek Out New Life: The Biology of Star Trek*. She also writes speculative fiction and non-fiction on a wide swath of topics and cherishes all the time she gets to spend with her partner, Peter Cassidy. Her work can be found in *Harvard Review, Belles Lettres, Strange Horizons*, *Crossed Genres*, *Stone Telling, Cabinet des Fées, Bull Spec, Science in My Fiction, SF Signal*, *The Apex Blog, World SF, SFF Portal, H+ Magazine*, *io9, The Huffington Post*, and her own site, Starship Reckless, www.starshipreckless.com.

Aliette de Bodard

Aliette de Bodard lives in Paris, in a flat with more computers than warm bodies and two Lovecraftian plants in the process of taking over the living room. In her spare time, she writes speculative fiction: her short stories have appeared in *Interzone*, *Clarkesworld* and the *Year's Best Science Fiction*, and her Aztec noir series, *Obsidian and Blood*, is published by Angry Robot. She has won the British Science Fiction Association Award, and has been a finalist for the Hugo, Nebula and Campbell Award for Best New Writer.

Visit www.aliettedebodard.com for more information.

Terry Boren

Terry Boren is an expert in surviving winter. Her science fiction has appeared in the anthologies *The Northern Review, Universe 3, Tierra,* and others, and in the magazine *Interzone.* A native New Mexican transplanted to Alaska, she lives with her family outside of Fairbanks where she cooks, gardens, gathers blueberries, and teaches at the University of Alaska. She makes the best chile in Fairbanks and has the medals to prove it.

Kay Holt (co-editor)

Kay T. Holt grows wild near Boston with the family, pets, and houseplants of her dreams. She loves science and art, and uses both in her everyday life.

For *Crossed Genres Publication*s, Kay is co-founder and editor. In addition to *Crossed Genres Magazine*, she edited *Salsa Nocturn*a by Daniel José Older, *Broken Slate* by Kelly Jennings, and *A Festival of Skeletons* by RJ Astruc. Kay also co-edited the *Fat Girl in a Strange Land* anthology with Bart R. Leib.

Kay is a core contributor to *Wired.com's GeekMom* blog and *Science in My Fiction*. Her fiction has appeared in *M-Brane SF, Rigor Amortis, Beauty Has Her Way, Full Throttle Space Tramps,* and the *Subversion* anthology.

Find her online at subvertthespace.com/kayholt and twitter.com/sandykidd.

Alexander Jablokov

Alexander Jablokov (pronounced 'Ya—') is the author of *Brain Thief*, which will be out in paperback this October. Previous books are *Carve The Sky* (Morrow/Avonova, 1991), *A Deeper Sea* (Morrow/Avonova, 1992), *Nimbus* (Morrow, 1993), *River of Dust* (Avon, 1996), *Deepdrive* (Avon Eos, 1998). His stories have appeared in the Fifth, Seventh, Eighth, Ninth, and Twenty-Eighth *Year's Best Science Fiction* (ed. Gardner Dozois); and in *Asimov's, Amazing*, *The Magazine of Fantasy & Science Fiction*, and *Aboriginal SF*. *The Breath of Suspension*, a collection of his short fiction, was published by Arkham House in 1994 and was a *New York Times* Notable Book of the Year.

He lives in Cambridge, Massachusetts, with his wife, Mary, his son, Simon, and his daughter, Faith.

Kelly Jennings

Raised in New Orleans, Kelly Jennings currently lives in northwest Arkansas, where she is a member and co-founder of the Boston Mountain Writers Group. She has published fiction with *Strange Horizons*, *Crossed Genres*, and *The Future Fire*, among others. Her first novel, *Broken Slate*, was released in 2011 by Crossed Genres Press. For more about her and her work, see her website at http://delagar.blogspot.com/.

C. W. Johnson

C. W. Johnson is a professor of physics at a California university too modest to be named. His scientific papers have appeared in *Physical Review Letters*, *Physical Review C*, *Nature*, and elsewhere, while his fiction has appeared in *Asimov's Science Fiction*, *Analog*, *Interzone*, *Realms of Fantasy*, and elsewhere. He is currently working on a massive computer program to calculate the quantum wavefunction of atomic nuclei, and a novel.

Sue Lange

Sue Lange's novel, *Tritcheon Hash*, was rereleased as an ebook in 2011 and was included in Kirkus' *Best of* list for that year. Her novella, *We, Robots*, was included in *io9*'s "Thirteen books that will change the way you look at robots." Her short stories have been published in such venues as *Nature (Futures)* and *Apex Digest of Science Fiction and Horror*. She is a founding member of Book View Café. Her Singularity Watch blog is updated irregularly and can be found at www.suelange.wordpress.com. She lives in Pennsylvania with her SO, a dog, four sinks, and a bidet.

Ken Liu

Ken Liu (http://kenliu.name) is an author and translator of speculative fiction, as well as a lawyer and programmer. His fiction has appeared in *The Magazine of Fantasy & Science Fiction*, *Asimov's*, *Analog*, *Clarkesworld*, *Lightspeed*, and *Strange Horizons*, among other places. He has won a Nebula, a Hugo, and a Science Fiction & Fantasy Translation Award, and been nominated for the Sturgeon, the Locus, and the World Fantasy Awards. He lives with his family near Boston, Massachusetts.

Christine Lucas

When her Feline Overlords permit it, Christine Lucas scribbles tales of historical fiction in all its subgenres. It comes as no surprise that most of her stories feature cats. Born and raised in Greece, now a retired Air Force Officer, she has had her work appear in several online and print magazines, including *Daily Science Fiction, Triangulation: Morning After, Cabinet des Fées,* and *Andromeda Spaceways Inflight Magazine*. Her short story "Dominion" (also known as "The Book of Genesis According to Cats") appears in Ellen Datlow's anthology *Tails of Wonder and Imagination* from Night Shade Books. She is currently working on her first novel.

Visit her at: www.christinlucas.com.

Alex Dally MacFarlane

Alex Dally MacFarlane (www.alexdallymacfarlane.com) lives in London, where she is pursuing a MA in Ancient History. When not researching ancient cities and warrior women, she writes stories, found in *Clarkesworld Magazine, Strange Horizons, Beneath Ceaseless Skies, Shimmer* and *The Mammoth Book of Steampunk.* A handbound limited edition of her story "Two Coins" was published by Papaveria Press. She is the editor of *Aliens: Recent Encounters* (Prime Books).

"Unwritten in Green", another story of the Tuvicen people, can be read in *Futuredaze: An Anthology of YA Science Fiction*, edited Hannah Strom-Martin and Erin Underwood. Two poems about Falna and Tadi, "Sung Around Alsar-Scented Fires" and "Tadi", appear in *Stone Telling* and *Strange Horizons* respectively.

Jack McDevitt

Jack McDevitt has been a naval officer, an English teacher, a customs officer, a taxi driver, and a management trainer for the US Customs Service.

His first novel, *The Hercules Text,* was one of the celebrated Ace Specials series. It won the Philip K. Dick Special Award. McDevitt has produced seventeen additional novels since then, ten of which have qualified for the final Nebula ballot. *Seeker* won the award in 2007. In 2004, *Omega* received the John W. Campbell Memorial Award for best SF novel.

Recent books include *Firebird* and *Echo*, both from Ace,

and *Going Interstellar*, a Baen anthology on which he served as co-editor. *The Cassandra Project*, a collaboration with Mike Resnick, has just been released. McDevitt claims it will reveal the truth behind the Watergate break-in.

His other interests include chess, classical history, the sciences, and baseball.

He is married to the former Maureen McAdams, and resides in Brunswick, Georgia, where, assisted by the requisite German shepherd and four cats, he keeps a weather eye on hurricanes.

Cat Rambo

Cat Rambo lives, writes, and reads a lot in the Pacific Northwest, beside the shores of eagle-haunted Lake Sammammish. Her second solo collection, *Near + Far*, appeared in 2012 from Hydra House Books. Her 100-plus published short stories have appeared such places as *Asimov's*, *Weird Tales*, and *Clarkesworld*, as well as numerous anthologies. She is the former editor of *Fantasy Magazine*, makes a mean Welsh rarebit, and usually has pink hair. In answer to the usual question, it is her real name. Find links to more of her fiction at www.kitty-wumpus.net.

Melissa Scott

Melissa Scott is from Little Rock, Arkansas, and studied history at Harvard College and Brandeis University, where she earned her PhD in the Comparative History program with a dissertation titled "Victory of the Ancients: Tactics, Technology, and the Use of Classical Precedent." She is the author of more than twenty science fiction and fantasy novels, most with queer themes and characters, and has won Lambda Literary Awards for *Trouble and Her Friends, Shadow Man,* and

Point of Dreams, the last written with her late partner, Lisa A. Barnett. She has also won a Spectrum Award for *Shadow Man* and again in 2010 for the short story "The Rocky Side of the Sky" (*Periphery*, Lethe Press) as well as the John W. Campbell Award for Best New Writer. Her most recent novel, *Lost Things*, written with Jo Graham, is now available from Crossroad Press.

She can be found on LiveJournal at mescott.livejournal.com.

Nisi Shawl

Nisi Shawl's story collection *Filter House* won the 2009 James Tiptree, Jr. Award; it was praised by Ursula K. Le Guin as "superbly written" and by Samuel R. Delany as "amazing." The collection and the original novella first appearing within it, "Good Boy," were nominated for 2009 World Fantasy Awards. With Cynthia Ward, Shawl co-authored *Writing the Other: A Practical Approach*, which helps authors create believable characters whose race, gender, or other demographics differ from their own.

Recently her stories have appeared at *Strange Horizons* and *Crossed Genres*. She has also been published in *The Year's Best Fantasy and Horror*, the groundbreaking *Dark Matter* anthologies, and *So Long Been Dreaming*, home to the story "Deep End," for which "In Colors Everywhere" is a sequel. Shawl reviews books for *The Seattle Times* and *Ms. Magazine*, and edits reviews for *The Cascadia Subduction Zone*, a literary quarterly from Aqueduct Press. In 2011 she was WisCon 35's Guest of Honor. She is a founding member of the Carl Brandon Society and serves on the Board of Directors of the Clarion West Writers Workshop.

Shawl is active on Twitter and Facebook. She promises to update her website, www.nisishawl.com, soon. She likes to relax by pretending she lives in other people's houses.

Vandana Singh

Vandana Singh was born and raised in India and currently lives near Boston, where she teaches physics at a state university. Her short stories have been published in numerous venues, such as *Strange Horizons*, *Lightspeed*, and various anthologies including *Clockwork Phoenix* and *Other Worlds Than These*. She is a winner of the Carl Brandon Parallax award (for *Distances*, a novella published by Aqueduct Press) and many of her stories have been reprinted in *Year's Best* anthologies. Some of her work is collected in *The Woman Who Thought She Was a Planet and Other Stories* (Zubaan Books, New Delhi).

For more about her, please see her website at http://users.rcn.com/singhvan.

Joan Slonczewski

Joan Slonczewski is the first author since Fred Pohl to win a second John Campbell award (for *The Highest Frontier*, and previously *A Door into Ocean*). *The Highest Frontier* (Tor Books, 2011) depicts a Cuban-American woman going to college in a space habitat powered by solar bacteria and threatened by cyanide-producing aliens. Frontera College is run by a male couple, while on Earth a lesbian is running for president. *A Door into Ocean* (Tor Books, 1986) creates a world covered entirely by ocean, inhabited by an all-female race of purple people who use genetic engineering to defend their unique ecosystem. In *Brain Plague* (Tor Books, 2000; Arc Manor, 2009), intelligent alien microbes invade our brains. The secret of these unique addictive microbes was discovered by a human-gorilla woman scientist in *The Children Star* (Tor Books, 1998; Arc Manor, 2009). Slonczewski and her students investigate bacteria in extreme environments at Kenyon College, where she teaches the course "Biology in Science Fiction."

Eleni Tsami (cover artist)

Eleni Tsami (http://www.planewalk.net) is from Athens, Greece. She studied linguistics at the University of Athens and art at AKTO. She started painting in the early 2000s with a love for fantasy and science fiction. Her work has been featured in book covers (Night Shade Books, Hieroglyphic Press), *Digital Artist* magazine, and various online galleries. When she's not working and not otherwise plugged into the internet, she likes to read, play games, and hike.

Martha Wells

Martha Wells was born in 1964 in Fort Worth, Texas, and graduated from Texas A&M University with a BA in Anthropology. She is the author of fourteen SF/F novels, including *The Element of Fire*, *City of Bones*, *Wheel of the Infinite*, *The Wizard Hunters*, and the Nebula-nominated *The Death of the Necromancer*. Her most recent novels are *The Cloud Roads* (March 2011), *The Serpent Sea* (January 2012), and *The Siren Depths* (December 2012) published by Night Shade Books. She has a YA fantasy, *Emilie and the Hollow World*, due out in April of 2013 from Strange Chemistry Books, and a second YA fantasy and a *Star Wars* novel due out in 2014. She has had short stories in *Black Gate*, *Lone Star Stories*, *Realms of Fantasy*, and the anthologies *Elemental* and *Tales of the Emerald Serpent*, and essays in the nonfiction anthologies *Farscape Forever*, *Mapping the World of Harry Potter,* and *Chicks Unravel Time*. She also has two *Stargate Atlantis* media tie-in novels *Reliquary* and *Entanglement*. Her books have been published in seven languages, including French, Spanish, German, Russian, and Dutch.